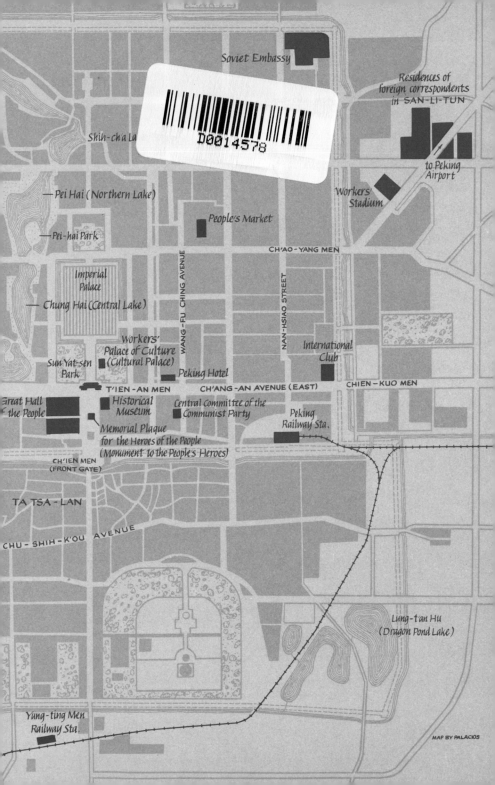

Soviet Embassy

Residences of
foreign correspondents
in SAN-LI-TUN

to Peking
Airport

Shih-ch'a La

Workers'
Stadium

Pei Hai (Northern Lake)

People's Market

Pei-hai Park

CH'AO-YANG MEN

Imperial
Palace

Chung Hai (Central Lake)

International
Club

Workers'
Palace of Culture
(Cultural Palace)

CHIEN-KUO MEN

Sun Yat-sen
Park

Peking Hotel

T'IEN-AN MEN

CH'ANG-AN AVENUE (EAST)

Great Hall
of the People

Historical
Museum

Central Committee of the
Communist Party

Peking
Railway Sta.

Memorial Plaque
for the Heroes of the People
(Monument to the People's Heroes)

CH'IEN MEN
(FRONT GATE)

TA TSA-LAN

CHU-SHIH-K'OU AVENUE

Lung-t'an Hu
(Dragon Pond Lake)

WANG-FU CHING AVENUE

NAN-HSIAO STREET

Yüng-ting Men
Railway Sta.

MAP BY PALACIOS

The Coldest Winter in Peking

The Coldest Winter in Peking

A NOVEL FROM INSIDE CHINA

HSIA CHIH-YEN

Translated from the Chinese by
Liang-lao Dee

DOUBLEDAY & COMPANY, INC., GARDEN CITY, NEW YORK
1978

ISBN 0-385-13402-9
Library of Congress Catalog Card Number 77–26522

Author's Preface

     I still find it difficult to believe that I have actually written this novel. Some years ago, around 1960, I was living in Peking. One day I stood in front of a deserted construction site and looked at the steel framework that had already begun to rust and the cement foundation already soiled with bird droppings. The building had originally been intended for a large steel factory, but it no longer had the sound of gongs and drums to accompany the workmen laboring through the night under bright electric lights. In the midst of large machines and chunks of metal scattered on the ground, somebody had planted a garden, and young corn was growing, stretching out its green leaves.

     Right then, I deeply regretted that I had not studied literature. I was filled with a desire to record everything I had seen and had witnessed, so that none of it might perish into oblivion. I wanted to preserve the historical evidence.

In the People's Republic of China today, no one can write anything. One can only observe and reflect. After I left China, I did not find many opportunities to write. There were the demands of earning a livelihood. Time is indifferent; it passes by, whether one is fulfilled or not.

In 1975, I organized a study group with a few friends, all of whom shared a love for the great writer Lu Hsün. I was inspired by the dedication of my friends, and, gradually, I plunged myself into the spirit of Lu Hsün's writings. Late into the night, I reflected on my experiences, evaluated my abilities, and asked whether I could describe the China I knew as realistically as Lu Hsün had. I wondered if I could muster up his unshakable courage.

Then the T'ien-an Men Incident of April 5, 1976, broke out. That outbreak affected me deeply. Trembling with anger and with tears in my eyes, I wrote the chapter "Young Tiger." It is Young Tiger and his friends, Ch'i Yen, and the young people who work at the core Command Headquarters in Ta Tsa-lan whom I love most. They are the best representatives of present-day China. They have endured the greatest suffering and yet see no future. But they are in the majority, and the future of China belongs to them.

The characters in *The Coldest Winter in Peking* are, of course, my own creations. However, there is no fiction behind the sufferings and the oppressions described here. That part is real, without exaggeration or distortion. Many of the incidents depicted I have personally experienced or witnessed; others have been related to me by individuals who left China recently. While this novel may seem, at first, to be a political fantasy that seems to predict inevitable events still to occur, I hope the reader will also read it as a realistic portrait of what has happened in China and is still happening.

The manuscript was finished in August 1976, but the T'angshan earthquake made it necessary for me to rewrite it. In addition, the death of Mao Tse-tung in September required still another rewriting. In October, the news of the attempted coup by the "Gang of Four" spread throughout China, but I learned of it only after the Japanese translation of my manuscript had been completed and the book was in the process of being printed. I had no chance to rewrite it a third time. Thus, what started out as a political novel set in the future quickly became, by virtue of a sudden turn of events, a contemporary novel. This book should give the reader an idea of how the Chinese have been oppressed and how devastating will be the consequences when the ultimate rebellion finally erupts.

The difficulty I encountered while writing this novel far exceeded my expectations. From time to time, I even wondered if someone were testing my spirit, to see if it would crack under political, economic, and psychological pressure. Particularly after the first installment of the book was published in the November 1976 issue of *Bungei Shunju,* political pressures were brought to bear on me with the weight of Mount Everest. But a writer who loves his country must be courageous. Still, my mother is over seventy years of age, and my relatives are still living in China, so I have no other choice but to adopt a nom de plume in order to protect them from political harassment. I believe that anyone who is aware of the political realities in China will understand my dilemma well enough. It is impossible for me to remove this pressure singlehandedly. It is now apparent to me that I shall lose everything I have, despite all my precautions. But the experience of writing this novel made me understand why China has not produced, *for almost thirty years*, a realistic novel that describes honestly the life of her people.

I believe the saying that "the eyes of the people see everything and see it truly." My hope is that my readers will understand how precious democracy and justice are. Their understanding will be encouragement for all the Young Tigers in China and for all of his struggling friends who survive underground. What they need now is sunshine and air, warmth and encouragement, democracy, and freedom. Young Tiger and his friends are hurt just now, but the victory will be theirs one day.

This novel of blood and tears has many defects in its structure. I am too painfully aware of its immature and sometimes clumsy technique. However, being a Chinese who cannot write in any other language, I must rely on the help of editors and translators and I am deeply indebted to them.

Hsia Chih-yen

January 1, 1977
Tokyo, Japan

Translator's Introduction

In the modern struggle for freedom—by individuals, by nations, by "third worlds"—nothing is more inspiring than the dauntless expressions of the individual imagination against oppressive regimes. Novels written in prison on toilet paper, books buried in the ground, manuscripts circulated furtively to trusted readers—now familiarly known, fittingly enough, by the Russian term *samizdat*—all these attest to the unquenchable thirst for freedom in the human soul. For years, the voice of dissent was eagerly awaited from the Soviet Union, and it was not until Boris Pasternak, in 1958, and Solzhenitsyn and Voznesensky in the early sixties, that the individual Russian sensibility found its international audience. This literature of dissent may not teach us much about the inner workings of the Soviet Union, but we are better acquainted with individual

Russians: Brodsky, Mandelstam, Sakharov, Sinyavsky are only a few of the writers who have given the West a *particular* vision of Russia. The exchange of specifics for generalities, of personal expressions for official statements, of "you" for "they," signals the beginning of true "worldliness," the end of provinciality.

The Coldest Winter in Peking—more than all the visits by Richard Nixon, more than all the tours by visitors seeing approximately the same score or two of Chinese, seeing the same pre-programmed, well-trodden ways—is a glimpse into the heart of the People's Republic of China.

Unlike countless accounts of China, since first "discovered" by Marco Polo, *The Coldest Winter* admits its subjectivity and its commitment: the story that Hsia Chih-yen tells is true, not necessarily in the sense of verifiable fact (though it may be that in part), but in Ionesco's sense of "emotional truths." I hope its truths have not been compromised by my translation.

Modern Chinese narrative, unlike its traditional fiction, is always grounded in reality; it seldom aspires to fantasy. Political fiction in particular has been actively developed ever since its introduction in China at the turn of the century. Liang Ch'ich'ao, perhaps the first modern journalist in China, wrote an unfinished novel entitled *The Future of China*, in which two characters engage in a heated debate on two alternative forms of government: republicanism and constitutional monarchy. Other reform-minded journalist-*littérateurs* wrote popular novels attacking the corruption of late Ch'ing officialdom and society. Not long after, revolutionaries exploited fiction as a means to rally adherents to their cause. All of these works had a clear purpose: to educate the people and to change Chinese society and to reform if not overthrow the government in power.

The Coldest Winter in Peking is only the most recent—though perhaps the most startling—attempt at Chinese political fiction. It is clearly based on firsthand knowledge, and many of the incidents related are, with slight modifications, modeled on actual events. Whatever its value as a portrait of a historical period, it is intended as a serious "version of events" from someone who has experienced them. However, what is truly remarkable about *The Coldest Winter* are the portions that could *not* have been true when Hsia Chih-yen wrote it; the book was written months before the actual downfall of the "Gang of Four" in October 1976. That event occurred even as the Japanese translation was being prepared for publication by *Bungei Shunju*. Indeed, there is an uncanny sense of the prophetic about the book. As I was working on the translation, the insurrections, plots and counterplots detailed in the final chapters of the book bordered on the improbable: they seemed to be fictional *Götterdämmerungen* with no basis in reality. Yet, in a dispatch issued by the Hsinhua News Agency from Peking, it was reported that "the day after the death of Mao Tse-tung six million rounds of ammunition were issued to the Shanghai Militia as part of a plot to seize power." The official Chinese press agency went on to relate "how close the city came to civil war in the twenty-seven days last fall between Mao's death and the arrest of four radical leaders, including his wife, Chiang Ch'ing" (New York *Times*, May 17, 1977). Not all portions of the work are, of course, anticipations; the author has indicated that adjustments were made to take into account the death of Chairman Mao on September 9, 1976. But the bulk of the book was already nearing completion through the summer and autumn of 1976. No doubt, events in the People's Republic of China will overtake these words in the time it takes for the translation to see print. The up-down-up-down-up career of Teng Hsiao-p'ing over the last decade is symptomatic of the seesaw character of contemporary Chinese history.

The author has taken great pains to adopt an objective stance in the book by depicting the various conflicts from different ideological points of view. But his sympathies clearly lie with Chou En-lai, and he is bitter about Mao Tse-tung and disillusioned with his legacy. Still, it would be unfortunate—

and totally unwarranted—if what Hsia Chih-yen has written were to be used for uncritical propaganda against the People's Republic of China. He is, like most Chinese, a dedicated patriot, and he has written this book out of a deep-seated sense of commitment and love for his country. It is the experience of his compatriots that he has described: their triumphs as well as their failures; their joys as well as their agonies. In the realm of human truths, there is no partisanship. Where abrogations of human rights are concerned, culprits may be found in both extremes of left and right. In the distortions of extreme ideologies, the vision of the people is, invariably, lost. It is this vision that Hsia Chih-yen tries to restore.

In letters to me, the author confesses that he has never read much in Western literature, though he has had some exposure to Soviet fiction and film. The novel he has written derives unmistakably from traditional Chinese narrative, with its highly episodic structure, its scenic approach to plot development, its pluralistic treatment of character. In this, it resembles the classics of Chinese fiction, *The Romance of the Three Kingdoms* and *Water Margin*, both of which are, incidentally, fictionalizations of historical figures and historical events. From *The Romance of the Three Kingdoms* comes the nickname of Shao Yung-ts'un, the wily strategist of the People's Army* group in the novel. Shao Yung-ts'un is called "Chuko Liang," in reference to a figure from the late Han, early Three Kingdoms period (third century A.D.), famous as a necromancer, a superlative strategist, a loyal minister to the Kingdom of Shu. His exploits—memorably described in *The Romance of the Three Kingdoms* as well as in the official dynastic histories—show a character combining the resourcefulness of an Odysseus, the magical skills of a Merlin, and the intellectual elegance of a Richelieu.

What may be fortuitous is the similarity of narrative tech-

* The reader must be sure to distinguish the "People's Army," which is an underground group, and the "People's Liberation Army," which is the national standing army—the largest in the world.

nique with such panoramic novels as John Dos Passos' *U.S.A.*, or André Malraux's *Les Conquérants*. There is a deliberate attempt to preserve the "fragmentariness," the disjointedness, the sheer confusion of political plots—in both narrative and non-narrative senses. Modern audiences, trained in a generation of movie-viewing, will recognize this technique as montage, either temporal or spatial: the juxtaposition of seemingly unrelated events and scenes to create meaning. While this technique may cause confusion for the reader, it would be wrong for an editor to "sort out" the plot threads, for it is precisely the interwoven texture of everyday political reality that Hsia Chih-yen wants to describe, a kaleidoscope of events in a critical five-day period. Single threads on a spool may be tidier; but it is the complex, multicolored tapestries that engage the attention. No doubt individual passages and scenes are sometimes weak in construction; the author seems aware of that. But he is not committed to a literary exercise to be performed flawlessly. He has already explained why a "non-literary" person, trained as an engineer, should attempt a work so ambitious. Modest as Hsia Chih-yen is about his literary accomplishments, one would be misled if one assumed that there was no literary value here. Thomas Hardy and Andrei Voznesensky started out as architects; Chekhov was a doctor: it is not always the literary specialists who create literature. Let the book speak for itself and for the author.

That is easier said than done—particularly in translation. Much of what dominates the human landscape in the People's Republic of China—from the "big-character posters" to the poems in *Chinese Literature,* published by the Foreign Languages Press in Peking—is political ideology. The passionate, often long-winded harangues and diatribes will not always be easy to read—except for political scientists, who seem to have a taste for such rhetoric. No compromise has been made in the translation, however. I have tried to preserve the drift of these statements; the political terminology, however harsh to the literate ear, has been scrupulously preserved. The "cadres," "struggle meetings," "Marxism-Leninisms" may have less ideological, more commonplace meanings; but it is ideology that is familiar in the People's Republic of China. To tamper with this aspect of diction would be to distort the reality that is being presented.

Personal names and place names constitute a special problem. One of the main characters is referred to, literally, as "Little Tiger." In English, this strikes my ear as a little cute, slightly Kiplingesque. I opted for "Young Tiger." Other names, particularly on the fictional characters, have similar ironic or generic allusions: I have tried to retain the meanings in parentheses at the first mention in the hopes that the reader of the translation will have some notion of the overtones. Place names would appear to pose no problems; but the disheveled history of transliteration systems of Chinese presents inevitable anomalies. I have used the Wade-Giles system throughout (which is why I spell "Chiang Ch'ing," not "Chiang Ching," and "Teng Hsiao-p'ing," not "Teng Hsiao-ping"), but in those cases where geographical names have been conventionalized in the Chinese postal system by a previous transliteration system, the long-familiar version has been retained: hence Soochow (not Suchou), Hankow (not Han-k'ou), Peking (not Pei-ching), Tsing-hua University (and not Ch'ing-hua University). Incidentally, place names also perform an important though subtle function in the setting of the book. There is a quiet but devastating irony in the fact that the riots and demonstrations (in fact as well as in fiction) should take place in T'ien-an Men Square ("The Square of Heavenly Peace") and along Ch'ang-an Avenue ("The Avenue of Eternal Peace").

Some key terms deserve special attention because they are well-nigh untranslatable, despite their familiarity. The binome compound rendered as "contradiction" is one such example. In the original, the word, *mao-tun*, means "spear-shield." The concept derives from a pre-Han text entitled the *Han-fei-tzu*, in which a merchant (the original used-car dealer) boasts of two items he has for sale: one is a spear that will not fail to pierce any object, and the other is a shield that will not be penetrated by any object. It is clear that both statements cannot be true, and hence the term acquired the sense of "contradiction." But the English word misses some very important connotations of the original term: first is the notion of opposition or confrontation implicit in the spear-shield image; the second is the martial overtones in the references to instruments of war, which the logical word "contradiction" fails to convey; the third—and probably the most important—is its use by Mao as the key term to render his own conception of the Marxist dialectic: the push-pull of history, the thrust and counterthrust of social struggle, and the "antagonistic" and "non-antagonistic" confrontations between classes with all their complications and implications. What is unsettling for the Western student of contemporary Communist politics and literature is that when the term *mao-tun* is used, it may refer to any one or more of these meanings. A graphic instance of the loss of meaning in the translation of *mao-tun* by "contradiction" would be to consider the case of the eminent leftist writer who punned on the term when he chose a nom de plume and styled himself "Mao Tun": who would call himself "Contradiction"?

As a bibliographic note, it should be mentioned that the Japanese translation† leaves out some scenes that were in the original manuscript or that were added; in particular, the episodes describing Washington's strategy sessions in Chapter 14 and the scolding of the Japanese reporters in Chapter 18 are left out in the Japanese. Furthermore, the Japanese editors rearranged the chapter divisions into five chapters, with a prologue and an epilogue. At the request of the author, I have restored the original twenty-chapter format, with prologue and epilogue, though the author's Afterword now appears as a Foreword.

† Although the work has appeared, in a Japanese translation (in serial and book form), it has not been published in the original Chinese (though at least seven translations *into* Chinese from the Japanese have appeared in Taiwan).

It would be a disservice to author and reader to extend this introduction much further. Where confusions arise, I have tried to provide partial remedy in a section at the back. There the reader will find a complete Cast of Characters and charts on the political and military organizations in the People's Republic of China.

Liang-lao Dee

December 13, 1977

The Coldest Winter in Peking

PROLOGUE

Saturday, February 9
5 p.m. Peking Standard Time
Lunar Calendar: 12th month, 25th day

The primeval sun passed from one azure-splitting layer of dark cloud to another, dipping in and out. Its silken rays darted over thousands of miles, swallowed up by the ridges of the ten-thousand-foot Yen Mountains. It left behind a deep purple evenglow that cast an eerie light on peak after peak, now ablaze with purple sage fire. At the horizon to the southeast, darkness encroached on the twilight, its line extending over the great North China plain.

On the western outskirts of Peking, on the asphalt road running toward Hsiang-shan, four black limousines sped along. Not far beyond the enclosure of the old, gray-tiled Temple of the Reclining Buddha on the right, in the midst of a thick grove of pines on the left, the barren, paved road wound its way toward the southwest. After thirty minutes, the cars bolted out of the grove and came to a gradual stop in front of an iron sentry gate.

In the glare of the headlights, clearly visible from the road, behind the gate, stood a concrete structure resembling a fire station. A guardhouse faced the road, flanked by several high wooden doors which were tightly shut. The back half of the building formed a turret-shaped lookout tower, four stories high, an imposing and sinister sentinel in the middle of the plain.

A great searchlight atop the tower flashed on, casting a strong beam of light toward the sentry post and beyond, revealing a corridor of some fifty or sixty meters. On both sides ran Y-shaped cement posts, strewn with barbed wire and shimmering with white porcelain insulators, like a giant yellow python, snaking its way into the distant mountain range.

The leather-belted sentry of the Central Garrison Division hung up the phone, carefully checked the number of people in each car, and raised the gate to let them pass. The four cars moved slowly through a series of zigzag curves designed to reduce their speed, swung around a promontory with a pillbox on top, and then hurried down a straight road, heading west. A dark, secluded canyon appeared, after which the cars passed through one more sentry check and descended into a basin extending to the south.

In the middle of this sizable area was a small lake. The road leading from the south entrance to the lake bisected the lower sector; on the left were four complexes, with row upon row of two-story dwellings. In the middle were four or five large mess halls. At the foot of the mountain, there were several tree-lined basketball courts, their basket posts bent toward each other as if paying mutual respects.

Along the right side of the road were rows of one-story tiled houses, with long corridors in the middle of these buildings connecting scores of office alcoves. Light from the rooms shone through the windows, an indication that a night shift was busy collecting, sending, analyzing, and organizing materials and reports coming in from all parts of the country.

From a steel chimney pipe almost as high as the rim of the surrounding hills, wisps of white smoke, churned out by the turboelectric generator on the ground, rose to the base of a radio tower perched high on the right flank of the hillside.

The four cars continued along the slope of the hill down to the edge of the lake. Then, following the road by the east bank, they stopped in front of a guesthouse. From each car emerged ten or more people, who walked briskly along the lake toward the north.

From the northern edge of the small lake to the foot of the hills there was a large stretch of open lawn, surrounded by thickets of pine on three sides. In the center of the lawn sat a complex of four interconnected buildings, raised more than a meter off the ground, on a platform foundation of granite and masonry.

On the platform, two well-built military types, wrapped in army coats, were waiting. The older of the two was beetle-browed Wang Tung-hsing ("Prosperous-east" Wang), formerly Vice-Chief of the Public Security Department, now Superintendent of the Secretariat Office of the Party's Central Committee, as well as Commander of the Central Garrison Division. Slightly behind him stood Mao Yüan-hsin ("New-distance" Mao), thirtyish and dark-complexioned, who had been Political Commissar of the Shenyang Military Region.

At the head of the arriving entourage, clutching a black attaché case tightly in his arms, was Chang Ch'un-ch'iao ("Spring-bridge" Chang), Standing Member of the Politburo and Vice-Premier. When he saw who was waiting on the platform, he hurried to the steps, and going up to Wang Tung-hsing, he asked in a low voice:

"What has happened? How is Madame Chairman's health?"

There was no answer, unless it was Wang Tung-hsing's furrowed brow, his gaze fixed on the distant mountains. When the rest of the group arrived, he saluted abruptly, turned, and walked inside, with Chang Ch'un-ch'iao scurrying after.

Wang Hung-wen ("Cultural" Wang) and the others did not wait to greet Mao Yüan-hsin, but one by one went through the door into the large chamber at the entrance.

It was a spacious hall, divided into three main areas. On the thick, whitewashed walls were large wood casement windows. On the back wall hung a huge photograph of the landscape at Lu Mountain. Along the wall were several red leather armchairs, and in the middle, a long table covered with a clean white tablecloth, able to seat twenty or more. In a blue-and-white porcelain vase, a handful of plum blossoms flared out, giving the room a certain serene elegance, an air of freshness. A steel fireplace blazed brightly, heating the entire room.

Ma T'ien-shui ("Heavenly-water" Ma) one of the new arrivals, Vice-Chairman of the Shanghai Revolutionary Committee, as well as Political Commissar of the Shanghai Military Region, had felt the cold edge of the northwest wind as he stepped out of his car, and sensed the chill penetrating deep into his back and spine. Only after entering the room did his flesh dispel its numbness, his limbs loosen, and he was able to notice the oppressive silence.

◈ ◈ ◈

That morning Ma T'ien-shui had been presiding over an important meeting of the Party members of the Lung-hua industrial district in Shanghai. The conference had been attended by the chief officer and secretary of each of the revolutionary committees in every factory in the district, as well as by those who headed labor, youth, and the People's Militia groups. There had been only one item on the agenda: how to solve the increasingly grave problem of laxity and lagging productivity among the workers.

Each factory had described its situation, but when it came to actual solutions to the problem, everyone had suggested temporary or superficial proposals.

Ma T'ien-shui had looked out over the assembly, hoping that a sound plan would emerge from the collective discussion, but as the meeting dragged on toward two o'clock in the afternoon, there had been no definitive solutions in sight.

Of course, restoring the old rules and regulations would probably work best, but who would advocate such a step? Since the campaign to criticize the capitalist route was taken by Teng Hsiao-p'ing, there was no one now who would dare propose such a restoration. To adopt a system of higher wages for greater productivity, or bonuses for production over quotas, would be tantamount to following Liu Shao-ch'i's revisionist policy of stimulating the material economy, and that would not do. There was nothing left but to find a way out of the problem through ideological rectification. Political campaigns had followed one after another for ten years. When the toughest thread is pulled taut over a long period of time, it too will snap.

Shortly after the shock of the national mourning period during "Black September," when the population had been recovering from the death of Chairman Mao, production had taken a turn for the better. But as the sense of grief had abated in the face of pressing realities, the old problems had surfaced, and this time they were more serious.

Ma T'ien-shui had wondered why the various factions assembled in the conference room could not join together with one mind. Each one had risen to the challenge many times in the past, and each had vowed to do his utmost to carry out the directives bequeathed to the nation by Chairman Mao. But this day-to-day backbiting, this constant bickering, was there no way to get rid of it?

What was obvious was that, within the Party itself and within the workers' organizations, the power of the "capitalist-roaders," although still incipient, had been growing in strength every day. There had been a reactionary stance that submitted to the less admirable instincts in society. It would suddenly burst forth, in some crisis or other; it was certain to break out

5

and lure away revolutionary elements loyal to Chairman Mao's policies. For the moment, one could only depend on the ideologically stable People's Militia.

The urban People's Militia were chosen from the younger Party members, the Youth Group members, as well as the most active young people whose political commitment and ideological stance were exemplary; they formed a united disciplined rank and file in each factory. They had been trained to know that their first duty was to identify those parts of the factory operation that could be improved, and to subject them to open review and exposure.

In the beginning, these measures were effective, but as time went on, the objectives and duties of the People's Militia organizations were confused with those of the Party, of the Youth Group, and of the workers' unions. Tensions and hostilities had been created, and inevitably, factions emerged. Leadership had not been able to form a unified line and the masses naturally had pursued their own way, manifesting an independent, almost indifferent spirit. Workers had been slow to report for duty, but quick to leave; others had become "uncontrollable," neglecting their work altogether. Production slowed to a standstill, and there had been no guarantee of either quality or quantity of goods produced. All these problems had been set clearly before those present, but no solutions had been forthcoming.

Ma T'ien-shui had been worried. When the three leaders who had managed things in the city of Shanghai, Chang Ch'un-ch'iao, Yao Wen-yüan, and Wang Hung-wen, had been sent for by the Central Committee, they had summoned him just before leaving and had spoken to him in confidence.

"When the three of us leave, we take with us some important cadres. You will no doubt have more than your share of difficulties, but you must stand firm. Are you strong enough?" Chang Ch'un-ch'iao had looked directly into Ma T'ien-shui's eyes.

"With your help in the Central Committee I should be

strong enough. If anything comes up, I will let you know by phone and secure your good advice and counsel."

"No, no, that will not do. We will have more than enough to handle in the Central Committee. You will have to settle your problems on your own. Moreover, you must stand ready to lend a hand when we need your help with our work at the Central Committee."

"I assure you I will do everything I possibly can. Anyone who relies on the masses should be able to overcome difficulties."

"But one should organize the masses, lead the masses, not rely on them. If you do not provide leadership, then someone will usurp your authority. Comrade Ma T'ien-shui, the Shanghai district has been a staging ground for revolution; it remains the most important of the few revolutionary bases that survive. Now that we are going to Peking to initiate a nationwide 'struggle,' you must do this job well. On this point, make no mistake."

Everyone had been deep in thought when Secretary Yang Hsiao-pang rushed into the room, and handed Ma T'ien-shui a dispatch. The message had been from Wang Hung-wen, the man who had built up the militia forces and organized a new peasants' militia in the Shanghai area. In a hurried hand, the message had read:

"Emergency! Come immediately to Chiang-wan Airport. Hung-wen."

◈ ◈ ◈

Forty minutes later, at the military airport at Chiang-wan an Ilyushin jet passenger plane touched down, and just as it came to a stop at the end of the runway, a jeep rushed up and parked near the cabin door. After the boarding ladder had been secured, Wang Hung-wen, Ma T'ien-shui, and four key staff members went inside the cabin and joined Chang Ch'un-ch'iao, who had arrived earlier by plane from Hankow.

The Deputy Chief of the Central Garrison Division, Hsu

I-ming, on instructions from Madame Mao, had taken this special flight to bring the group to Peking. There had been situations before when special planes had been dispatched for urgent meetings, but never with Hsu I-ming to take personal charge, and with such an obvious emphasis on secrecy.

The plane had not landed at the busy Nan-yüan Military Airport in Peking, but at a small, narrow landing area, used as a military mail-drop and as a practice airstrip, situated west of the I-ho Garden (the former Summer Palace of the Empress Dowager Tz'u-hsi).

Four cars had rushed over. Ma T'ien-shui, excited by the attention, had climbed into the back seat of one of the cars which then proceeded immediately toward the center of town. Ma T'ien-shui had thought that they would go immediately toward Chung-nan-hai Park (where the government headquarters are housed), but the cars had turned suddenly, just after they reached White Rock Bridge. This had made Ma T'ien-shui somewhat uneasy.

The cars had entered a narrow gorge where they had undergone the strictest security checks; only then was Ma sure that they were entering the private enclave of the Special Headquarters of the Chinese Communist Party. For several years, he had heard of this place, constructed as a shelter against any possible attack by modern weaponry. But those who spoke of it had never been there, and those who had visited never said a word about it. Who would have thought he would now actually be there? His presence reflected the faith of the Party and of its leadership in him.

Ma T'ien-shui expected that Madame Mao would personally preside over this meeting; unfortunately, he had been rushed too much, and had left his memoranda on his desk. Should Madame Mao ask for a report on the current Shanghai situation, for instance, his account would suffer from his not having any notes with him.

❖ ❖ ❖

At the doorway, Wang Tung-hsing signaled Mao Yüan-hsin with a nod of the head, whereupon Mao addressed Chang and Wang with a smile:

"Madame Mao is waiting. We had better go in. The rest of you, comrades, will please wait here."

The new arrivals followed Wang Tung-hsing through a hallway, into a middle room in the back.

Ma T'ien-shui pulled out a chair and was about to sit down in front of the long table when Chang Ch'un-ch'iao suddenly reappeared. Across the table, he said: "You had better report on the situation in Shanghai to Madame. Come with me."

The middle room was an ordinary home-style living room, with the cotton coverlet on the rattan lounge at the armrests so worn that the red sheen of the wood underneath was beginning to shine through. Four bamboo chairs around a small round table were clearly the local handiwork of the Chairman's home province. In the middle of the wine-red wood table was an inlaid segment with a black marble pattern, and on the table sat a marble ash-tray along with an unopened tin of Panda brand cigarettes.

Madame Mao was in deep mourning over the deceased Chairman, and the room was arranged exactly as it had been when he had lived in it. It was rumored that when the Chairman was alive, doctors on several occasions told him to cut out smoking. But the Chairman had insisted: "Not to eat hot peppers, not to smoke cigarettes, not to carry on the revolution, these three prohibitions I cannot abide." It appeared the story had been true.

But Madame Mao was not in this room.

Chang Ch'un-ch'iao led the way through the living quarters, and they entered a study on the right, piled up on all sides with layers of string-bound Chinese texts on bookshelves. In the middle of the room, on a redwood reading desk, a large book was spread out, a scenario from traditional Chinese drama, *The Tale of the White Snake*. It appeared that, aside from the countless burdens of her official position as the Chairman's wife, Madame Mao still managed to study the classic Chinese theater.

On the table were scattered many books as well as thick sheaves of notes. An inkslab was nearby, at its edge an elaborately detailed figure of a water buffalo with curved horns. Sticking out at all angles from a bamboo pen box tooled with flower motifs were five or six writing brushes, topped with white copper caps. There was no telephone on the desk, only a desk lamp with a bentwood base made of pine with an orange-red lampshade.

Madame Mao was not in the study either.

Behind a leather desk chair, there was a massive wooden door. When Chang Ch'un-ch'iao pressed a button on the wall, the door slid open and disclosed a large elevator.

Following Chang Ch'un-ch'iao, with the door closing automatically behind them, the party descended quickly and silently.

Ma T'ien-shui stepped back a little, looked up, and saw a name plate which read: "Built by the Shanghai Elevator Works." He smiled with ironic pride; that firm was established with foreign capital, and had developed ten- and twenty-fold since the Liberation. The faces of many of the old comrades at the elevator works came back to him; no doubt he would recognize them if he were to go back. If only he could tell them that the fruits of their labor were being used in the Special Headquarters.

The elevator came to a stop, and as the doors opened, gusts of humid air hit Ma's face. Emerging, one could see dim corridors with walls of pale yellow tiles, and with lamps set among the tiles every ten meters or so.

After walking twenty meters or more a large room was reached, in which were two battery-operated carts. Seated in the first cart, along with three others, was Wang Tung-hsing. Ma T'ien-shui followed Chang Ch'un-ch'iao into the second cart, which started up noiselessly to follow the first cart.

The passageway was long, passing several "crossroads" where one could see other intersecting tunnels, like the design of a giant spider's web.

The vastness of the structure overwhelmed Ma T'ien-shui.

◈ ◈ ◈

When Chairman Mao had issued his three directives on tunnel construction in 1973, the district of Shanghai had also ordered mobilization of the masses toward this effort. At that time, Ma had come to Peking for a "defense-alert" meeting called by the Central Committee. During this session, he had visited subway projects as well as underground constructions beneath the Ch'ien-men ("Front Gate") with the happy-faced Vice-Chairman Wu Teh ("Virtuous" Wu) of the Peking Revolutionary Committee as his guide.

These two projects had been part of Peking's air defense network, but they had differed in character and design. Vice-Chairman Wu had made a special effort to explain the function of each to Ma.

In the first phase, the subway project had extended a main trunk from the Peking Railway Station to the western suburb of the Shih-ching Mountains for a distance of some twenty kilometers. The second phase had seen a route extended due east from Peking to the center of T'ung-hsien, a distance also of twenty kilometers.

According to available data, a fifty-megaton hydrogen bomb had a devastation range of a circle fifteen kilometers in diameter. In the event of a nuclear attack on the capital, the population could very quickly be transported to areas of relative safety through the two escape routes.

The second route joined up with another underground railway that ran near the Cheng-yang Gate, just behind the expanse of T'ien-an Men Square, and passed the Great Hall of the People, the Chung-nan-hai and the Pei-hai parks, around the Ministry of National Defense, and came out of Te-shang

Gate, past Hai-tien, ending at the I-ho Garden. This route was called the northwest route, and although it was almost ready, it had not yet been made available for public use.

At the time Vice-Chairman Wu had been involved in a campaign to expose the traitorous crimes of the Vice-Chairman of the Party, Lin Piao. In order to save his own skin, Lin had hoped to provide himself with a quick getaway, so he had ordered a spur built off the northwest route from the Pei-hai Park station, a leg almost two kilometers long, which led directly to a spot below the bedroom in his own house. When they had been constructing that segment, they had discovered that Lin Piao's newly heated swimming pool was in the way, so the construction had been changed in order to build a new swimming pool in another location, causing the destruction of many residences, not to mention the squandering of the people's money.

The entire network of underground subways was built by the Special Engineering Corps, using the most modern technology. The workmanship was excellent.

At the beginning of the Cultural Revolution, construction had been affected, to be sure, by the strife between the workers and the Red Guards. By the time the People's Liberation Army and the Workers Propaganda Units had taken over in the schools, progress had been steady. After the Ninth Plenary Session of the Party Congress (1969), trial runs had begun on the main trunk of the line, and by the Tenth Plenary Session (1973), parts of the whole network had been working.

According to the original plans, this underground network had constituted a civil defense system which, in times of emergency, could evacuate a million or so residents of Peking at one time from the center of the city in the event of nuclear attack. Each segment of the route had a large shelter that could accommodate several thousand occupants, each stocked with medical supplies and communications equipment. Foodstuffs and drinking water were packed in survival bins, and there were ventilation ducts for filtering out noxious fumes and for guarding against radiation. Within forty-eight hours, the entire population of Peking could be evacuated.

Another project, a community construction effort, Ma T'ien-shui had seen just as it was getting started.

The construction site was located on the road leading from the Ch'ien-men, connecting with the Pearl Market area, a section called the Grand Palisade. On both sides, the houses and stores had been vacated: and digging began from the rooms right on down, with men and women, young and old, all vying to outdo each other in their efforts.

Ma T'ien-shui had gone down into one of the excavated chambers for an inspection, and found long sections of tunnel-way dug out of the earth fifteen meters belowground, bolstered up all around by wooden supports. Under the glare of the lights, several thousand workers had been efficiently taking the excavated dirt and stone and transporting them to ground level. All of this had left Ma T'ien-shui nodding his head in admiration.

Back in Shanghai, he had immediately tried to implement similar projects, but because the ground level in Shanghai was so low that water seeped in at a depth of two meters, pumps had to be sent for in a hurry. The masses, however, had risen to the occasion, and people had worked arduously and courageously night and day, with no thought of resting, as they had dug tunnels even underneath their own homes. Unfortunately, the digging had affected the foundations of the houses. When a series of cave-ins had occurred, there had been no recourse but to turn the community project over to the Special Engineering Corps.

Later, however, when there had not been enough cement dikes to hold back the water, the large chambers undergound had become rancid pools after a period of heavy rain. Shortly after, the people were mobilizing for the Chemical Industry Project at Chin-shan, and the tunneling activities had lost their momentum.

13

Ma T'ien-shui saw now that his grasp of the projects had been insufficient and that he had not exercised firm enough control over the work. When he went back, he must definitely do something about it.

◈ ◈ ◈

The carriers sped into a large chamber, and stopped just in front of a big iron door to the right.

Several guards opened the door; and the group followed Wang Tung-hsing into a brightly lit conference room of sizable dimensions. Three people were seated, apparently discussing a voluminous document. Ma T'ien-shui recognized Comrades Hua Kuo-feng, the Premier; Central Committee member Yao Wen-yüan; and Hsieh Ching-yi, Secretary of the Peking Revolutionary Committee.

In a moment, from an adjoining room, Madame Mao entered, dressed in a plain dark blue Mao jacket. Trailing behind were her two daughters and her two nieces.

It had been more than a year since Ma T'ien-shui had seen the much-admired Madame Mao. At a glance, he was shocked at her haggard look. Perhaps the burdens of official duty had been too much for her!

Madame Mao forced a laugh, and spoke in a delightful Peking accent, but in tones both somber and dark.

"Everyone has come from a very long way, and you are all no doubt very tired. Please sit down and relax."

Seeing her standing, the group did not move, but stood quietly awaiting their cue.

Madame Mao sighed deeply and said in a melancholy tone: "The revisionist capitalist contingent in the Party is mobilizing for action. They have made contacts with several die-hard groups in the military and are secretly planning a counter-revolutionary coup at the Lunar New Year (February). Luckily, Comrade Wang Tung-hsing found out about it. We must, at all costs, not allow the Chairman's blueprint for revolution to be changed; we must resolutely crush them into the ground!"

⧈ ONE

Sunday, February 10
9 a.m. Peking Standard Time
Lunar Calendar: 12th month, 26th day

Chia Hsiang-ying, Head of the Sixth Section, Central Garrison Division, stood in the arrival area of Hsi-chiao (Westfield) Airport. He thrust his hands into his pockets and stared at the passenger jet slanting upward and disappearing into the southeast dawn. Then he turned slowly and walked toward the control tower.

His eyes felt hot and dry, the result of a night on duty without sleep. The north wind blew in his face, and he was cold and exhausted. As he flipped up the collar of his army coat, he thought of hot Russian black tea. How delightful it would be, if only he could have a sip of that tea now.

◈ ◈ ◈

It was seventeen or eighteen years ago, when he had been a student at the Leningrad Institute of Telecommunications.

15

One weekend in winter, he had gone with his fellow students to the house of a professor to celebrate a birthday. The festivities lasted throughout the night, with much singing and dancing. Afterward, hand in hand, enveloped by the thin night fog, he and the other students had walked by the flickering light of the street lamps through the stone-paved streets toward the banks of the Neva River, still singing all the way. Shadows of the pointed cupolas were outlined against the sky. The old city was fast asleep, blanketed by the mist, and aside from the young people, the streets were empty.

Chia Hsiang-ying was captivated by the exotic quality of the city. The mist from the frozen river hovered over the stone embankment, and he had thought of the cold winter nights along the banks of the Sungari River in his native Harbin, of swimming off T'ai-yang Island, and of what had happened to him since his graduation from high school.

Every year, China selected a group of university graduates with outstanding academic records who were in good health and who came from families with reliable backgrounds to study in the Soviet Union. The policy was later changed to include high school graduates, so they could study Russian for one year before they went to the university. In this way, a wider pool of qualified students was developed, and as a result, more pre-university students with high qualifications were sent to Russia for training.

Chia Hsiang-ying had been only a mediocre student in high school, but because his family background was good (his father was a major general, a commandant in the artillery, and on good terms with both city and provincial Party committees in Harbin) and Chia was an only son, his father had managed to send him to Russia.

Nearly a thousand young men and women went to Russia each year to enroll in the universities to study either electrical engineering or military technology. Chia had chosen electronics and had been assigned to Leningrad, where there were four other Chinese students. Each was placed in a different dormitory so that he could live and study together only with the Russian students. On Saturday afternoons, however, some three hundred students convened at the Chinese consulate, where they were divided into small groups to study political thought and to catch up on developments at home. Chia's life had been on an even keel then, and he had felt fulfilled.

As dawn broke, the party had begun to disperse. The girl, Natasha, who had been leaning gently against Chia's arm, said softly, "Let's go to my place for a cup of real Russian black tea."

She lived on Pushkin Avenue, in the second story of an elegant, imposing building. In the large living room a fire blazed in an oversize fireplace, making the room cozy and warm. Chia knew, from the pictures on the wall, that Natasha's father was an officer in active service, and also a major general in the artillery. Thinking of his own father, serving in the same capacity and at the same rank, he smiled.

No one else was there. She said that her father was occupied in the south, and her mother, as well as her sisters and brothers, had gone there to stay with him.

Chia slouched comfortably in the big sofa in front of the fireplace, petting a large white cat. Patiently, he waited for the black tea, which seemed a long time coming. The high windows were covered with thick drapery, the room was dim, with only the soft light from a floor lamp at one corner of the room and the glimmer from the fireplace. All of this made him drowsy, and he closed his eyes and fell asleep.

The sound of rustling silk awakened him, and through blurry eyes he saw a white form standing in front of him. His hand went out fumbling to accept the cup of tea, which was scalding hot. Startled, he opened his eyes wide to stare at Natasha.

She wore a white silk robe, sashed around her waist, with a low neckline revealing her creamy white bosom. The straw-blond hair was in braids, framing her full, oval face, and her green eyes seemed to ask, "How do I look?"

"Please have some tea while I treat myself to a steam bath. I understand Chinese do not like steam baths. Is that true?" she said. Exposing a long, rounded thigh from the front of her robe, she began to warm her legs in front of the fire.

Chia stared at her slender instep and the gentle curve of her feet as she turned up her toes. He broke into a broad smile, and asked, "How would you know?"

"Show me!" With that, she twisted his nose, knowing that should he fail to catch and kiss her then, in the Russian fashion, he would be deemed a coward.

Chia had been in Leningrad for three years. Although many white Russians lived in his native Harbin, their lives ran in different spheres from his. He now understood something of the spirit of Soviet youth, and their passionate nature. In these three years he had become more and more attracted and had finally quietly fallen in love with this poised and attractive young woman, who seemed at times more cunning than a fox. But because there were rules against fraternizing with foreigners, especially foreigners of the opposite sex, he had cautiously held back.

At this moment, though, he would be thought less of a man if he did not grab and kiss her. Chia seized the moment and in one bound reached out for Natasha, but she slipped away nimbly and he managed only to pull off her sash. She screamed, and clutching her half-opened robe, dodged by him to escape into the bathroom. Flinging her bathrobe in Chia's face, she left him standing at the door, completely flustered.

Chia, taunted, followed her into the bathroom. Natasha had turned off the lights, and near the right wall, the red-hot pebbles made a sizzling noise as the water dripped down on them, filling the room with a white mist. So much heat enveloped his body that he felt as though his lungs would burst.

"Where is that little imp hiding?"

His damp clothes weighed on him like a suit of armor. Chia pulled them off and threw them out the door. He could hear Natasha snickering as he groped toward her and found her naked, lying on a wooden platform raised a few feet above the ground. Leaning close, he looked into her feline eyes, as she extended her arms and pulled his head down, to let him kiss her on her half-opened lips.

Their love was kept secret. At the Institute, they were distant, but whenever there was a holiday or vacation, they met in a small cabin near a lake in the countryside, which her father used as a hunting lodge.

Chia could not understand why an intelligent and beautiful Russian girl would love an Oriental. At first, Natasha would not tell him, but later, she admitted that she had been competing with a girl named Tanya, the head of the Communist Youth Group that had responsibility for Chia's academic progress. Tanya might have had the best academic record, but it was Natasha who now had Chia.

This explanation did not entirely flatter Chia, but he was pleased with their relationship. It gave him the confidence to mix freely with his fellow Russian students, and with the few students from East Europe he met.

The consulate gave each student fifty rubles a month for pocket money. For those who did not drink, this was more than enough to live on. Chia's father often asked the Chinese delegations to Leningrad to bring him clothing, household items, and cash, and he frequently carried two or three thousand rubles in his pocket. Moreover, with his big-hearted manner, and his tall, sturdy physique, Chia hit it off well with the Russian students. He was always included in their drunken sprees, and some even seemed to think there was Russian ancestry in his blood.

Natasha would say to him often, "After you graduate, you may as well stay on here in the Soviet Union. My father can arrange it for you."

Chia would reply that he wanted to go back home, and that she should come to his country.

Two years went by quickly, and his studies were coming to an end. Chia wrote to his father to ask him to arrange a marriage so that he and Natasha could return to China together. Unexpectedly his mother replied, advising him not to make his liaison public but to wait until after he returned home and had a chance to confer with his father.

So Chia returned to China, and was assigned to a military work detail in Wuhan. Having joined the ranks as a lieutenant in charge of technical services, he was prohibited in that post from any exchange of correspondence abroad.

Responsible for the maintenance and repair of telecommunications, Chia had a Soviet engineer working with him as an adviser. Since Chia had just returned from the Soviet Union, the two had much in common and through this channel, he was able to write to Natasha. He let her know that his father insisted on their waiting a year and that he was obliged to maintain the secret. His father had hinted that there might be changes in foreign policy, and he could not refuse.

Half a year later, Sino-Soviet relations were broken off. All Soviet advisers were called back, and his line of communication with Natasha was severed. Nationwide criticism of Soviet revisionism followed, and those who had studied in Russia had changed, in the public eye, from destiny's darlings to the devil's disciples. Chia was now contaminated by the virus of Soviet influence. Every aspect of his life was criticized. If he applied tonic to his hair, or if he pressed his military uniform, it was proof that he cared only for the luxuries of life. If he did the opposite, it was taken as a manifestation of listless, revisionist decadence. Any student returning from the Soviet Union was damned.

"Maybe," Chia thought with resentment, "it is because the others never had a chance to go."

Two years passed. Relationships with his colleagues and superiors were not good, and any attempt to advance his career was frustrated. Chia asked for a two-week leave, ostensibly to see his father, who was going to Peking for medical treatment. Actually, he intended to ask his father to pull a few strings and arrange to have him transferred to another city.

In Peking, his father introduced him to Commissar Hsiao, of

the Peking Military Command, who was convalescing in the same hospital. Chia came to know his daughter, Hsiao Mei-lien, a third-year student at the Peking Conservatory of Music, who also visited her father every day.

They were married a year later, with the consent of both parents. Through the good offices of his father-in-law, Chia was transferred to the Party's Advanced Institute in Peking, for further study. Assigned to a post in the distinguished Special Headquarters he shortly became a section head. Normally, he lived in a single room in the dormitory of the Headquarters, but on extended leaves stayed with his wife's family in Peking. Mei-lien taught at the August 1st Elementary School, and they all lived in her father's big, comfortable house in the western part of the city.

Then came the Cultural Revolution. Chia Hsiang-ying's father was "transferred downward" to work in a study group; his father-in-law also lost his job and had to undergo "ideological self-rectification." Chia was greatly pressured by this turn of events. As a result, he changed his given name from Hsiang-ying ("Toward Heroism") to Hsiang-tung ("Toward the East" or "Toward Mao Tse-tung") to reflect his deep loyalty to the Chairman. At this same difficult time, something else happened which was to affect his life even more.

Before the Cultural Revolution, if he was returning from home to Special Headquarters, his father-in-law had a requisitioned jeep to take him to the gate of the compound, where another jeep waited to take him to the hub of the Headquarters. Whenever he went on leave, on the instructions of Deputy Chief Ho of the Secretariat Office, a special jeep was sent to take him to his home in the city.

After his father and father-in-law suffered their setbacks, Deputy Chief Ho changed his attitude toward Chia, and no longer gave him preferential treatment. He told him he could accompany those with the rank of section head as far as the bus stop in Red Flag Village. From there, Chia would have to catch a bus to the zoo, and then take a trackless trolley home.

One hot day, in the early evening, he descended from the

bus and joined the crowd streaming from the zoo to the trackless trolley stop. As he was about to cross the street, he saw Natasha's familiar face, her green eyes fixed on him. A small gray sedan screeched to a halt beside them, and Natasha opened the door and crawled in, leaving the door open.

"Hurry up and get in. I want to talk with you." Chia had not heard Russian in a long time.

Chia quickly stepped in and sat down beside her, closing the door. The small car darted away, and on reaching White Rock Bridge, it turned right onto West Summer Palace Road, hurrying straight toward Hai-ting. Chia collected himself and noticed a girl of Mongolian stock was sitting in the driver's seat. She turned to Natasha and spoke with a perfect Moscow accent, "My, how lucky you are. You are in Peking no more than one week, and you bump into an old friend. I really envy you."

Chia glanced at Natasha. She sat quietly, with her head lowered. There was an alluring fragrance about her. Although she had put on a little weight, she looked as lovely as ever. What amazed him was that she wore on her wedding ring finger the green jade ring he had given her on the eve of his departure, over fifteen years ago. She raised her head and took off his military cap. "Oh, you have a few gray hair at the edges," she said gently.

Pangs of regret welled up in Chia. What could he say? His own marriage had been a disappointment from the beginning. Mei-lien had been an only child, the daughter of working parents who doted on her but who had not had the time to raise her properly. Growing up willful and self-indulgent, she liked to live well and to wear beautiful things, but she never had helped with the household chores. Why should she? There had always been a nursemaid, a cook, a chauffeur, and four house guards, all paid for by the people. After giving birth to their one child, she imagined herself chronically ill and had been a patient in every large hospital in Peking, and had consulted almost every doctor.

Chia eventually saw through her, and now no longer

worried or paid much attention to her complaints. Left to herself, she ran around shopping in her jeep, but when Chia came home, he would find her in bed, disheveled and ailing. Although she ached for his love, her strategies missed their mark. Chia almost forgot what her smile looked like. If it were not for an occasional meeting with friends, or an evening's outing, he would never leave the Headquarters to go home, where his marriage brought him no joy—only quarrels and recriminations.

At last the car drove into a courtyard surrounded by high walls, and into the garage to park.

The girl at the wheel turned and said, with a knowing smile, "Of course, you will not be able to attend tonight's party, but I have to go. Take care of supper tonight and have a good time." And with this, she left the car.

Natasha followed her out of the car saying sweetly, "Please, come in for a little while, won't you?"

"Do you have good Russian black tea?"

Hearing him just as she was going through the door, she turned and said, "Only if there is youth and love."

They fell into an embrace in the corridor. Warm air coursed through the hallway and beads of sweat seeped through their clothes. Natasha finally pulled away and said, "Shall we have our bath together?"

Hours later, lying in bed, Chia told her everything about himself, but about his work he said nothing. She was silent for a long time, then said, "I obviously cannot become your wife, but I can be your mistress."

"We can never manage that."

"It will not be so difficult. I am a member of the staff in the Peking branch of the Tass News Agency. I will stay here for two years, at the least. Father arranged this position for me through connections, because I wanted so much to see you."

"But how can we arrange to meet from now on?"

"This is my girl friend's home. She works in the Mongolian Embassy and knows all about us, and we can meet here."

"Do you really believe I can come here by taxi in my military uniform? The Chinese Security Department would find out in no time, and you know what would happen then."

Natasha flung aside the towel she had covered herself with and stepped naked out of the bed. She took out a map of Peking, a pen, and a piece of paper from the side table. After scribbling down a telephone number, she said, "Here, whenever you can come, call this number. Don't say anything, except to specify the time. I will ask a friend to pick you up at this spot." She pointed to the Ch'ing-hua Park bus stop. "If you do not wish to be seen getting into the car, then it will go past you two hundred meters and stop to wait for you."

"She really is a clever fox," he thought.

But Chia had underestimated her. The third time he came to the room it was not the beautiful, warm Natasha waiting for him, but a stranger, a middle-aged Russian man, who stood up and introduced himself.

He was a staff member in charge of protocol and security at the Soviet Embassy, whose name was Shlovsky. He was a good friend of Natasha's father, and very concerned about her future. "She has kept from me her affair with you, which is not right. I was informed, and when I spoke to her she told me everything. After our talk I decided to meet you."

"We have nothing to talk about," Chia said.

"Do not say that. First, let me make my position clear. As far as I am personally concerned, I have decided to help Natasha and you. You can go on as you have; in fact, I can secure a resident's permit for you, and find you a job, should you want to go to the Soviet Union."

"That does not concern me just now."

"But one day you will need to think about it, Comrade Chia! Of course, the promise I have just made will require some commitment from you. You will have to do a few favors for us."

"Sorry, there is absolutely nothing I can do for you," Chia answered firmly.

"Look, we know exactly where you work and what you do. Do not think for a moment we want you to steal documents or assassinate anyone; that sort of thing is only for the movies and for cheap fiction. We want only to be notified when anything extraordinary happens. All you have to do is pick up a phone and say a few words. It is a simple job."

"What do you mean by 'anything extraordinary'?"

"For example, a decision to launch a military invasion of Taiwan, or a declaration of war by China against another country, a coup in a major military sector, or the death of the Chairman —that sort of thing."

"What if I refuse?"

"If you refuse now, or you choose not to notify us immediately about events such as those we just mentioned, Natasha will be sent back to Russia immediately, where she will be treated as a mental case the rest of her life. As for you—ah, well!—there are many labor camps run by the Chinese Security Department. But that will be your country's affair. We have no control over what could finally happen to you, but we can supply the required evidence. Think it over carefully."

Chia was in a blind rage, but forced himself to think out the situation before him. He glared at the man, but gradually his look dissolved into a lifeless daze. His lips began to tremble, and he lowered his head in submission.

◈ ◈ ◈

Night duty was tiring and in his heart Chia Hsiang-tung cursed those who had instituted the policy of co-operative effort of "officers and soldiers together." A few years earlier, as the lieutenant in charge of technical services and as section head, he sat at his desk and processed work orders and repair projections, going over reports submitted to him by various units. But now, because of the policy of "alternating duties in three shifts," he had to lend a hand to repair the communications installations, which was a considerable comedown for a technical expert.

Assorted electronic and electrical parts were spread out on the table in front of him. He had been working on outdated Soviet transmitters, which had broken down several days before. Actually, all he needed to do was replace a few vacuum tubes and some parts, but he had done nothing. The vacuum tubes were no longer available from the Supply Section and had not arrived from Central Supplies. Although he knew these parts were available from the Telecommunications Section of the Hsi-chiao Airport, he had been on night duty for the last ten days, and he did not think it worthwhile to lose any sleep to get the parts during the daytime office hours. Also, if the equipment was not fixed, he could stay by himself in the workroom, locking the door and stealing a catnap whenever he liked, or listening with earphones to broadcasts from abroad. All of this gave him the feeling of illusory freedom and leisure. On the other hand, if he did finish the repair job, there would be no reason for him not to report for duty to the Communications Room. Twelve machines may not break down too often, but still, maintaining them was a full-time job.

Chia washed his hands before going off duty, and went into the mess hall. Little Wang, head of the Communications Section, bolted through the door.

"Section Head Chia! The division commander has just gone into the Communications Room and is looking for you."

Chia was startled, but he quickly put on his military cap, hooked up his collar, and strode into the Communications Room.

Division Commander Wang Tung-hsing was inspecting the work of the operators, and Deputy Chief Ho of the Secretariat Office stood timidly behind him. As Chia entered the room, Commander Wang turned around and fixed him with his gaze.

"Where have you been?"

"Sir! I have been repairing Number 4 Unit."

"Have you fixed it?"

"Not yet."

"You will have to work harder. In the next few days we must maintain full operational efficiency in the telecommunications system. Do I make myself clear?"

"Yes, sir! I will see to it."

"Here are some instructions that must be sent out right away. Take care of it."

Division Commander Wang handed Chia Hsiang-tung a piece of folded white paper, then began to chat with Deputy Chief Ho about the crucial factors in improving security in Special Headquarters.

Chia opened the paper and read the message; on the top were code specifications for transmission; on the bottom, the following instructions:

"Initiate action immediately according to Directive Number 3—Hsing."

Chia shoved aside the operator of the unit and sat down in his place. This was their most powerful telecommunications unit, capable of reaching as far as Tibet. With a practiced hand, he adjusted the dials to the proper frequency. Strange, these specifications seemed very familiar, perhaps because they read like an absurd Russian phrase.

He had come across something like this before, and remembered that after his father-in-law had been reinstalled in his new post, he had been transferred to the Inner Mongolia Military Region as Political Commissar. Once, when he had returned to Peking to attend a meeting, he brought with him some documents, and Chia had come across them. There was a chart with the particular code specifications for each division in the Inner Mongolia Military Region. Chia had looked at them with special interest, because the documents related to what he was doing. There was no question about it. The frequency before him now referred to the Armored Division.

Something must have happened. Why would Commander Wang of the Central Garrison Division be giving orders to the Armored Division in Inner Mongolia? This order should have come from the Joint Chiefs of Staff and routed through the Peking Military Command, down to the Inner Mongolia Command.

Chia adjusted the frequency and turned on the transmitter. The other side responded immediately, and the coded message was transmitted.

Division Commander Wang was pleased. He took back the piece of paper he had given Chia and repeated his order:

"Make sure that all communication systems are fully operational. This is an order." With that, he strode from the room.

Chia returned to the repair room, much relieved. He slumped into a chair and lit a cigarette. With the smoke he exhaled, he blew out the orange flame of the match.

What was Directive Number 3? Why was Division Commander Wang communicating directly with the troops under Inner Mongolia Command? Why was his message not written out on the usual forms, and why was it not being processed through regular channels so that it would appear in the communications log?

Questions crowded in on him, and possible answers ran through his mind.

Is the Armored Division being given the order to attack the Soviet Union? Are the tanks being deployed to Huhehot to lay siege to it? To what secret area are the tanks being sent? Are they being sent against Peking?

Chia decided on a dangerous move. Not long ago he had discovered that the Chairman's personal doctor and his medical attendants had all left their underground chambers in the northern zone of the Special Headquarters. Although they had not, on the surface, done anything unusual, Chia's sixth sense told him something was developing. Shortly thereafter, there was a commotion at the Headquarters, with "Red Flag" sedans coming and going throughout the day.

Soon Chia uncovered top-secret information of the death of the Chairman. Several months earlier, he had planted a listening device inside the telephone in a meeting room of the underground chambers. The device connected with the intercom system in the headquarters room. Only he knew where the connection led. Ordinary headphones would not pick up the signal on the line because a special amplifier had to be used.

Natasha had given him all these gadgets, and explained their workings in detail. Chia remembered being surprised at her technical expertise, a far cry from his image of her when they were students together.

Although he had the precious news of the Chairman's death, Chia Hsiang-tung could not notify Shlovsky right away. All leaves had been canceled, and no one was allowed to step off the compound. But as soon as the orders were rescinded, he left for home and on the way stopped off to use a phone in a neighborhood store to communicate the news to Shlovsky. He was still three hours ahead of the official announcement.

Shlovsky commended him for his actions. Afterward, when he met Natasha, she brought him a passbook and a card, which she asked Chia to sign.

"With this passbook, you can draw unlimited funds from the bank. In the Soviet Union there are only ten astronauts who enjoy this privilege. Now you have it as well. What an honor!"

Of course, this privilege was good only in the Soviet Union.

◇ ◇ ◇

With his amplifier connected, Chia heard every word that was being said in the underground meeting room. A matter of extreme urgency was being discussed. Ah! This news should be given to Shlovsky immediately, but what pretext could he use to leave?

There were some vacuum tubes before him on the worktable and these provided him with an idea. Chia Hsiang-tung jumped up and walked into Deputy Chief Ho's office.

"Sir!" Chia stood at attention at the door.

"What is the matter?" the plump deputy chief asked, raising his head.

"Number 4 Unit needs some vacuum tubes replaced. There

are none at the moment in Central Supplies. Our own Supply Section ran out of them long ago. The directives just given by the division commander may be difficult to carry out if we do not replace them immediately.

"Can Central Supplies be of any help?"

"I have been told that there are a few used vacuum tubes at Hsi-chiao Airport, but I will have to go there myself to get them."

"Well then, go right away. Wait! I want you to do something else. In ten minutes there will be a few dignitaries leaving for the airport. Take a squad of security guards as escort, and after you see them off, you can attend to your own business."

Deputy Chief Ho signed an exit permit and gave it to Chia.

With the permit in hand, Chia went to the Weapons Section and requisitioned a handgun, a .45 caliber automatic made in East Germany, which he hung from the belt at his hip.

❖　❖　❖

Chia watched the passenger jet carrying Wang Hung-wen, Ma T'ien-shui, and the other dignitaries disappear into the horizon. He then walked slowly back to the control tower. At the door he ordered the security guards and the "Red Flag" sedans back to the compound, but kept a jeep for his own use. He pushed open the gate and walked into a building which appeared to be empty.

It was Sunday, early morning, and there were only two staff members on duty at the Telecommunications Section. They had just arrived and were absorbed in reading an internal circular and an information bulletin that was intended only for the eyes of higher cadres and their superiors. They nodded at Chia and went back to their reading.

Outside, there was a roar as engines were tested, and the sound of metal parts being hammered together. Chia walked over to the empty desk of the section head and slid into the chair by the telephone, making sure that his body blocked the view from the others. He picked up the receiver, chatted a bit with friends in Central Supplies, and then, with his other hand pressing the disconnect button, carefully dialed a secret number.

The phone rang a few times, but no one answered. Was it because it was Sunday and no one was around? Or was it too early and no one had reported for work yet? Chia Hsiang-tung cursed to himself, and peered to the left and to the right. His palms were sweaty.

There was a click at the other end of the receiver. Someone had picked up the phone. As usual, there was no response.

"There is a letter from home," Chia whispered.

"How is everyone at home?" It was the same voice he had spoken to before, a man's voice, with a Peking accent.

"Third brother is ill with cancer. He must go into the hospital on the lunar New Year."

"How bad is he?"

"The doctors conducted their examination, and major surgery is prescribed."

"Which parts are to be amputated?"

"Six out of ten toes are to be removed, and two more are in jeopardy."

"How about the heart?"

"The heart is vulnerable. And the lungs and the liver are affected."

"Have they decided the exact time for the operation?"

"Tomorrow afternoon."

The conversation was over. Chia pressed the disconnect button.

▧ TWO

Sunday, February 10   9:30 a.m.

     The Peking City Planning Commission was established at the beginning of China's first Five-Year Plan. It was not until 1957 that the task of drafting the reconstruction blueprint was completed. With the Great Leap Forward and the tenth anniversary of the People's Republic, they began to implement it. Peking became a vast construction site. Workers tore down most of the inner and outer city walls that impeded traffic, thirty thousand families were relocated, and with astonishing speed, ten major building projects were completed. Before the eyes of visiting heads of state from the fraternity of Socialist countries, on October 1, 1959, Peking emerged transformed and radiant, with renewed splendor.

     With over eight hundred years of history, including reconstructions during the Ming and Ch'ing dynasties, the ancient capital had become the symbol of imperial rule, reflecting un-rivaled majesty and power. The feudal system of government dominated China for nearly two thousand years, but her complacency had been shattered in the last century by a series of military encounters with imperialist countries grown strong from technological development. These countries established military and consular quarters right in the shadow of the Forbidden City, and these quarters became a stain on the myth of imperial supremacy.

The history of humiliation was erased forever with the founding of the new China. All foreign legations were removed to a region east of Peking, and China adopted the foreign policy of "leaning on one side," cultivating only the Soviet Union, who was the Socialist superpower.

As a result, the Soviet Ambassador to China had presented numerous demands concerning the construction of their new Embassy. He insisted that it be set apart from the legation quarters of other nations, that their territory be vastly larger than that of any other country, that the blueprints for the Embassy should be supplied by the Soviet Union, and that they were also to dictate the style of the surrounding area, which they wanted to turn into a Russian garden.

A location site was finally selected in the northeastern corner of the Inner City, inside the Tung-chih Men ("The Eastern Gate"), making it the only foreign embassy within the city limits. It covered a huge area, and the residents there had to be relocated. This became a major undertaking. The residents occupying the sectors needed most urgently by the Soviet legation were the first to be evicted. Several hundred families who had lived in the same place for decades had to vacate the premises, and the massive construction began. A Russian-style palace soon towered majestically over a stretch of low-lying, rundown tenements, and a new thoroughfare was constructed, linking the big street by the Eastern Gate to the Soviet Embassy. It was renamed "Power and Glory in the East" Road, and the dilapidated walls on both sides of it were repaired and whitewashed. Every time a Russian sedan drove through, the passengers would think, "We must ask the Chinese to speed up their work, so that these tenements can be removed."

The masses who lived in the area hoped they would not have to leave their mud-walled houses in which they had lived for generations, and be moved far away to the new squalid and crowded chicken coops awaiting them. They had no recourse for their complaints and had no power to resist. They could only wait silently for the ultimate disposition of their fates.

Unexpectedly an angel of mercy appeared. Just as the second stage of construction had begun on the garden and the residents were about to be moved, orders came down from the highest echelons to stop construction. Only three families were relocated, and their homes, which faced the street, were not razed but were immediately reoccupied. Curiously, two or three single men lived in each of these households. What was unheard of, though, was that telephone lines, forbidden in private residences, were installed in each of the homes.

The majestic palace remained surrounded on three sides by shabby houses. The only through road to the Embassy was guarded by the Security Police of the nation's capital, and it was also under the constant surveillance of plainclothesmen. These plainclothesmen interrogated any Chinese resident they saw walking on this street, and if there was anything suspicious, they immediately invited the person into one of the three houses. Covered jeeps from the Security Department would arrive after a short time to remove the individuals to another location.

The palace was four stories high, built in the shape of a box, and in the center was a dome of two stories with marble columns on all sides and white walls inlaid with colored tiles. It looked resplendent, reminiscent of a fortress from the time of Catherine the Great. Among the hundreds living inside the Embassy, there were at least a score or more who were the direct heirs of Catherine's eastern expansion policy, and who were now carrying out her original plans. These modern campaigners were fully trained, their understanding of the China scene more thorough than that of their own country, and they were equipped with the most up-to-date scientific technology. Still, their melancholy betrayed their feeling of imprisonment in this desolate outpost which they had created.

Hierarchies are clearly demarcated in the Soviet Union. In its Embassy in Peking the situation was no different. General staff members lived on the third floor, the fourth was reserved for top-echelon cadres and for important offices, and only with special permission were the lower echelons ever admitted into these privileged precincts.

❖ ❖ ❖

In a comfortable bedroom at the east corner of the third floor, Vishinsky, the Deputy Section Chief of the Soviet Trade Commission to China, was stretched out asleep on his bed.

The night before he had attended a party in the home of an East German diplomat, where he had drunk a little too much. Under the pretext of being completely drunk, he had made advances to Comrade Alyoshenko, Telecommunications Consultant to the Tass News Agency, more familiarly known among her friends as Natasha.

Natasha had been totally unresponsive and would have none of him. Left to himself at the sidelines, continuing to guzzle vodka, he watched her as she gyrated in the newest dances imported from the West.

He had thought to himself, "Don't put on such airs! One day you will find yourself crawling to me."

Vishinsky was just over forty, a man who, from years of overindulgence in food and drink, now looked like a five-foot-nine football. He had a bald head and a bulbous nose: it had been no surprise that his much younger wife preferred the company of the movie-making crowd. She had finally divorced him three years ago, choosing to become the mistress of a famous movie director.

Vishinsky was totally unqualified in matters of trade and

commerce; he had only a superficial knowledge of his job, but in the matter of gathering special political intelligence in the Far East, his experience went back twenty years.

Because his father had been an administrative officer in the East Manchuria Railway, he had always lived in the Far East. As a child, he had learned to speak Chinese fluently, and after the Second World War he had lived in Harbin and Dairen for several years with his father. Along with his excellent command of Chinese, he had distinguished himself in college. Before he graduated he was picked by the National Security Committee to be a special agent.

His cover had changed frequently during the past twenty years. Using his diplomatic status, he lived for several years in Cambodia and Laos; he went to Mongolia as a journalist; he joined a travel group that went to Japan as tourists (on the trip to Japan, impressed by the success of the Japanese in adapting an ancient Eastern civilization to modern industrialization, he applied for a visa to study there for two years): soon after, he went to Hong Kong and Singapore as a seaman. Then, perhaps because his superiors considered him primed and ready, he came to Peking as a deputy chief of a section.

His superior, Section Chief Shlovsky, had not been compiling a good record of late. His recent ventures had all seemed to fail miserably. Fortunately for Shlovsky, he had been the recipient of the distinguished Dzerzhinsky Medal,* and on that record, he had been able to maintain his position with a staff of over ten under him, including Natasha and Vishinsky.

Vishinsky was assigned to monitor special intelligence reports sent in over the phone, along with two others fluent in Chinese, and they manned the phones around the clock in three shifts. The canny and seasoned Shlovsky took the precau-

* Commemorating Felix Dzerzhinsky, head of the "Cheka" (Extraordinary Commission), which was established by the Bolsheviks shortly after the 1917 Revolution to combat sabotage and counterrevolution; generally believed to be the forerunner of the KGB (the Soviet Secret Police). The medal was awarded to Soviet security agents for outstanding meritorious service—TRANSLATOR.

tion of never revealing the identity of his informants, but tucked this information away in a secret file in the office by his fourth-floor bedroom. He designated each informant by a code number. From Number 5 to Number 13, each informant used a different code, so that whenever the telephone rang, Vishinsky had to consult the code book before he answered. Shlovsky trained them rigorously, and this Vishinsky found annoying. Luckily, Vishinsky had the authority to arrange shifts, and he always set his own schedule to start at four o'clock in the morning. This allowed him to sleep undisturbed until noon.

The telephone had not rung once during the night shift for the year or so he had been in Peking. He hardly expected that, on this cold Sunday morning, after a night of carousing, the special telephone would ring like an alarm. Had he been dreaming? No, it really was ringing. Vishinsky stepped barefoot from his bed, and without bothering to put on any clothes, was about to pick up the receiver. But years of training prompted him to turn on the tape recorder, switch on the "record" mechanism, and open the code book. He took a deep breath and then slowly lifted the receiver.

Vishinsky waited for two or three minutes after the line was disconnected at the other end. Only then did he feel it safe to hang up. He wanted to rush out immediately, to report this startling news to his superiors. But he remembered drinking the night before, and sleeping until past nine o'clock in the morning. He realized that to rush out, even with pajamas on, was not the thing to do. He washed his face, threw on some clothes, and took the tape recording and the impedance readouts up to the fourth floor. He rushed up to Shlovsky's door and pounded on it.

The door opened a few inches. Shlovsky peered through at him, disgruntled. Vishinsky collected himself, cleared his throat, and said with due formality, "Number Six called in at nine thirty-five."

The door now swung wide open. Shlovsky snatched the tape, his face tense and excited, and ran into the office next door, forgetting to close the door to his bedroom. Vishinsky saw Natasha on the double bed between the windows. She covered herself with the sheets and sat up.

"Please close the door."

Vishinsky pretended to misunderstand. He stepped inside and closed the door behind him, smiling and thinking, "So you are not, after all, quality merchandise."

Natasha gave him a cold smile, turned finally to a seductive grin. Thrusting aside the sheets, she stepped naked out of the bed. She tiptoed to the sofa and reached for the discarded undergarments and clothes she had worn the night before. As she entered the bathroom, she turned around and smiled suggestively before slamming the door behind her.

Vishinsky stood dazed, his lust aroused. "This devil Natasha. Why is she tormenting me?" Then he remembered the telephone call. "Shlovsky must be reporting to his superiors, taking all the credit for himself." He opened the office door and stepped inside, where in addition to Shlovsky he found the first secretary and the Party chief. Shlovsky was at the machine console, adjusting the controls.

Natasha often had Chia memorize various code expressions, and she had instructed him carefully on how to modulate the tone of his voice and to regulate his pauses in order to convey his predicament and his frame of mind during a transmission. In addition, she had taught him tactics for evasions and routes of escape, in case of emergency. Finally, she had told him that when he reported anything important he must call a different number exactly one hour later. This was required to verify the authenticity of his report, and so he could be warned of any danger that would dictate immediate escape.

The tapes of Chia in his earlier rehearsals of the various codes were now taken from the files and played through the dual-trace oscilloscope. The tape of the telephone conversation was also played and the readings were superimposed on the graphic display so that the authenticity of the speaker could be verified by identical voice-prints.

As this was beginning, Natasha walked in, radiant and fresh. Vishinsky glared at her, but as if she had not seen him earlier she asked, "Do you have a headache today? Last night, I saw you drinking like a fish. I was afraid you would be laid up for several days, at least."

The voice-prints were checked through twice. Shlovsky announced with authority, "It is Number 6 all right. He has reported to us in complete safety and security. His intelligence has been transmitted in exact conformity with prescribed procedures."

After a moment of silence, he addressed the group with a dramatic flourish. "The conflict within the Chinese Communist Party that we have been expecting for so long will erupt tomorrow. Comrades, the hour of our great mission to transform the East is now at hand. From now on, each and every one of us will have his hands full."

"We owe this invaluable piece of intelligence to the efforts of our dear comrade, Lieutenant Natasha. I congratulate her on a mission well done." With that, he took out a bottle of wine to prepare a toast.

The first secretary took out a key, and together with another key from the Party chief, he opened the door to the vault in the adjoining room. He turned the combination on the cast-iron safe and removed a cache of documents. From it he selected a sealed yellow envelope, which contained working instructions issued in advance from Moscow precisely for this eventuality.

But they could not open the envelope yet. The second phone call must be received. Everyone had been so eager that the last check procedure was almost overlooked. Vishinsky rose from the sofa with his glass upraised. Natasha noticed that he had been sitting on the decibel tape read-out, which monitored impedance levels during conversations and recorded fluctuations that would betray a wiretap.

Shlovsky absent-mindedly picked up the read-out. He himself had checked this phone thoroughly on a number of occasions, arranging calls from various locations at different times, and he had no reason to suspect that the unit was being tapped. He gave the tape a quick look. Then his complexion changed, the wineglass fell from his hand, and raising the tape for a closer look, he mumbled, "But this is impossible. This is impossible."

The machine had been built at a research facility in Moscow. If it was infallible, he had to admit that he had slipped up. For the read-out indicated clearly the presence of an eavesdropper.

Number Six was finished. Perhaps an escape route should be arranged for him, according to predetermined plans. Personally, Shlovsky hated Number Six because this wretch shared his woman. But even if he were to be arrested, and even if he divulged all he knew, Shlovsky might conceivably be allowed to stay in China. Chia did not know Shlovsky's real name, nor his identity. Natasha was another matter: she would have to leave Peking. To lose such an attractive member of his staff, particularly with the affair that had been developing between them, was really a shame. Maybe he should help Chia escape after all.

He considered these alternatives quickly and spoke to the dazed group before him:

"From the read-out it is clear that someone was listening in on the conversation. Naturally, Number Six is finished. If the second telephone call comes in according to standard procedures, we have to warn him and arrange for him to leave the country.

"Now, the problem is whether 'our friends' understand the secret code we are using. Before China announces publicly what they have learned, we must get in touch with Moscow."

Natasha's face turned pale. What she had hoped for had happened, but it still took her off guard.

Shlovsky opened the sealed cache and removed the folder labeled "Number Six." He picked up a black marker and, with a sense of regret, marked it with a cross. Natasha opened the folder and found an enlarged photograph of Chia, the one he had used when he had applied for entry as a student into the Soviet Union. His handsome face and his high-bridged nose were so familiar, his eyes shining as they had twenty years ago, his square jaw showing determination and courage, and the curve of his lips, the lips she had kissed so many times. She could not forget him, nor give him up.

◇ ◇ ◇

Natasha had been born in Leningrad, during the time of the German siege. When she was barely three months old, her mother died. A brave pilot had rescued her, tucked away in his skiing jacket, breaking out of the encircling enemy force in a small airplane. At that time her father was fighting on the Ukrainian front, so she was sent to an orphanage in the Far East. It was to be ten years before she joined her father again.

Mother Wang had been her favorite among those who took care of the children at the orphanage. Natasha often lay in her arms, listening to her tell Chinese fairy tales. These childhood memories impressed her deeply, and she gradually came to love the mysteries and beauties of China. Finally her father brought her back to Leningrad, where he had remarried the year before. Her stepmother was not friendly toward her, especially after she had given birth to a boy and a girl of her own.

It was a difficult situation to handle, and her father's work kept him busy. He made up for his neglect by buying her the best and the most expensive things. In time, these gifts made Natasha greedy and unscrupulous. And all of these traits were factors in her love for Chia.

Chia was tall and strong. His father was a major general in the artillery, and he had good prospects for a secure and comfortable future. She had wanted to leave her family permanently, so it was for reasons of self-interest as well that she had fallen in love with him. The unexpected setbacks between her country and his had shattered her hopes. Filled with disappointment, she had started working at Novosibirsk, in Siberia.

A newly developed city, it offered not only a higher income but also the advanced scientific research installations that attracted distinguished, high-salaried scientists. Who knows, she might chance to meet one. And, in time, she did.

What she did not know was that the man she married was also involved in anti-Party and anti-government activities. A few years later, he was discovered by the authorities and relieved of his post. Without a job, and without an official residence permit, the two of them could not live in Moscow: they had to take up residence in a remote suburb. Every day, as if possessed, her husband engaged in his underground activities, holding meetings and distributing political pamphlets. Natasha was forced to look for work in order that they might have something to live on.

At this critical juncture, she received a visit from a friend of her father's who worked in a security organization, a visit that was to change her life completely. As a result, she publicly criticized her husband's anti-Party and anti-government activities, and offered incriminating evidence against him. Consequently, the National Security Agency was able to break open a number of subversive groups, and many activists (including her husband, whom she had divorced) were packed off to mental institutions.

She took a rest for three months on the Black Sea, during which time she was trained in intelligence work. From there, she was assigned to Peking on a diplomatic passport, her mission being to re-establish contact with her old flame, Chia Hsiang-tung.

She fell in love again with her first flame. Their brief rendezvous every three or four weeks only deepened her sense of loneliness. She wanted to contrive some kind of situation whereby Chia could engage in work so that, once exposed, he would be sent back with her to the Soviet Union. His contributions would then qualify him for favored treatment by the Soviet government, and in this way, she could again enjoy comfort and security and have him to herself forever.

But month after month had passed by and nothing had happened. Shlovsky held nothing against Chia, for he had been, from the very beginning, a long-term "plant." With Natasha, however, he began to have petty grievances.

Every time Natasha and Chia met, the Embassy covered for them, to safeguard their security. But on more than one occasion, Shlovsky said to Natasha, "Number 6 is already hooked. Do you still need to give him bait?"

Natasha really was not much occupied with her intelligence duties. The Embassy's powerful special radio station was used only in emergencies, and since there were only occasional test broadcasts it was not likely to fall into disrepair. As an electronics specialist, she had a lot of time on her hands and spent much of her time at the International Club, sunbathing by the swimming pool, attracting a circle of old-time bachelor journalists and tradesmen who lived in Peking. Shlovsky would have jumped at the opportunity to pump information out of these admirers, but since Natasha knew neither English nor Japanese, he had to let them enjoy her gratuitously.

Shlovsky also appreciated Natasha's physical beauty, but, as her superior, he could not bring himself to tell her. If she refused his advances, he would find her difficult to manage. Besides, he had a wife, and though she lived in Moscow, there might still be complications if he were to pursue Natasha. He had to be content with veiled suggestions.

Natasha gave the situation considerable thought, and, one evening, she appeared at Shlovsky's fourth-floor bedroom door, dressed only in her nightgown.

◇ ◇ ◇

The time for the second call was approaching. Shlovsky and Vishinsky had consulted each other and had concluded that the third alternative, flight, was the most promising for Chia. The group waited anxiously.

It was ten thirty-five, there was not a sound in the room, and the telephone did not ring. Five minutes, six minutes, seven minutes, ten minutes passed. The hour was up. Chia must have been apprehended.

Shlovsky stood up, and was about to open the sealed envelope when the telephone rang loudly. Everyone was startled to attention.

Shlovsky quickly turned on the tape recorder and pointed to Vishinsky, who picked up the receiver with unsteady hands. After a moment of silence, Chia's voice could be heard through the speaker on the table.

"Yesterday morning, I caught a cold. Today I have the flu."

"Have you been to see the doctor? Taken anything for it?" Vishinsky asked, trying to sound calm.

"I have taken something and the doctor gave me a shot."

"You had better take a rest for three days. Otherwise, you will not recover."

"Oh. What? Yes, I know. I will take it easy for three days." With a click, Chia hung up.

Natasha broke into tears, and ran from the room. Vishinsky was about to hang up the receiver, but Shlovsky snatched it from him and listened, holding his breath.

The room was quiet again. After four minutes or so, there was a "click" heard over the earphone and the needle on the monitor jumped, indicating that the conversation had been overheard by "friends."

Shlovsky hung up the receiver, took a deep breath, and said: "Okay. The campaign begins now."

◇ ◇ ◇

The special communications satellite with the hammer-and-sickle insignia was circling the globe every three hours and nineteen minutes, at an altitude of 200 kilometers, moving from south to north.

According to the calculations of the desk computers the satellite would pass over North China at 10:57 A.M. Shlovsky took the encoded message from the computer and fed the punch cards into the input loop of the telecommunications system.

In the basement control room, the transmitter for the telecommunications system had been set into motion. The dish-shaped antenna hidden in the dome on top of the Embassy building fanned out and adjusted its direction to the signal sent out every twelve seconds from the satellite.

The time was almost at hand. Natasha, who was now on duty again, stared at the dials and the signal lights of the automatic tracking system, and expertly pushed the various control buttons.

Everyone was intent as the indicators on the videoscreen began to move. Their eyes suddenly jumped to the center of the screen, where a small green signal light flashed on. Natasha pressed the transmission control button. The mechanism was set into motion, and the memory disc began to revolve at an incredible speed. The entire message was sent out in no more than three seconds.

The telecommunications satellite continued to circle the earth. In ten minutes it reached the area over Po-li in eastern Siberia. The satellite checked the input signal against preset specifications, and the message just registered and stored on its memory discs was relayed to the station on the ground. When the transmission concluded, the memory discs were cleared, and the message erased.

◆ ◆ ◆

At the same time as the coded message was being sent out from the dish-shaped antenna installed on the roof of the Soviet Embassy in Peking, another communications satellite, moving at the same speed, but in the opposite direction, named "Auditor" and bearing the stars-and-stripes insignia, received and recorded the same message from the same location. Forty minutes later, this other satellite passed over Alaska, and the entire message was sent to the communications base in the Arctic. Fifteen minutes after this, the decoded message, now translated into English, was placed on the big desk in a large room on the top floor of the CIA Building in Langley, Virginia. The message read:

"According to reports from a high-ranking source in the Special Headquarters of the Chinese Communist Party, issued at 9:35 A.M. on February 10, government and military officials are preparing to launch a coup on the lunar New Year (February 15). However, the Cultural Revolution faction, already forewarned, is planning a countercoup which they are to unleash on February 11. Please advise on further action. Awaiting instructions."

▨ THREE

Sunday, February 10　　1 p.m.

The winter this year was much colder than last. Early February had seen heavy snow, and the Peking residents felt as though they had been buried under layers of glacial ice. A fierce northwest wind blew constantly back and forth, provoking swirling maelstroms from the snowdrifts and turning them into ice crystals. The city byways were deserted, and the children were cooped up indoors.

The noonday sun filtered through the crystalline mist in the upper reaches of the sky, and not a single wisp of warm air penetrated the screen of cold. It was quiet in the housing compound at the eastern end of the city. Only the white smoke rising from the chimneys that stuck out of paper windows betrayed any trace of life as it blew in thin wisps over the heads of Chinese cabbage sitting on the window sills.

The door latch on the heavy front gate was dark and rough from disuse, for nowadays the two wings of the gate were always open. On its faded black lacquer surface was pasted a piece of red paper, and a couplet was written on it:

Socialist society is earth's paradise;
Multitudes all praise the red sunrise.

The red of the paper had paled into a dull brown, the lower part was coming unglued and flapped in the wind swirling in the courtyard.

The wind abated a little, and the murmur of voices could be heard through the windows at the southern end of the west wing of the compound. The west wing was originally a row of five rooms, with one door in the middle. But after five families had moved in, the Housing Bureau of Eastern Peking sent workmen to block up the single entranceway with cinderblock. In each room, they converted a window into a lattice door lined with paper, which was used as a separate entryway for each household.

Bits of charcoal were piled up by the base of the gray stone wall, at the southernmost corner of the compound, under the window. But at the corner of the wall facing south, there was a pile of little pamphlets without covers. Old firebricks weighed them down.

Suddenly a door burst open. A slender youth with large eyes, about seventeen or eighteen years old, bolted from the house into the courtyard, carrying in his arms some bedding wrapped tightly with hempen rope. Following him was another tall young man of twenty-five or twenty-six. His complexion was ruddy and his eyes glinted underneath thick eyebrows. Wearing a worn cotton-lined coat, and carrying a bulging knapsack, he walked calmly down the steps.

"Ta-yung. Be careful on the road."

The speaker was an old woman, who was the last to emerge from the house. She wore a black, old-style cotton jacket which had been carefully patched, a pair of gray pants, and black cotton shoes. In her face, lined at the eyes, was a hint of abundant kindness, and anxiety.

Hsiao Ta-yung, the older man, grinned. He donned his cotton cap and pulled up the collar of his overcoat. As he buttoned up, he turned and reassured the woman, who was standing beside the door:

"Mother Ch'i, do not worry. The day after tomorrow I will see Young Swallow."

The wind ruffled her short white hair. She smiled, but there were tears on her cheeks.

"It is cold outside. You had better go in." Hsiao looked at the knapsack he was holding, then turned toward the youth and asked, "Is that too heavy for you?"

"I have carried things weighing over a hundred pounds. This is nothing." To prove his strength, he swung the bedding on his back, but not without effort. The veins in his forehead bulged from the strain.

"Young Tiger, you do not have to come with me to the train station! See me to the end of the street. That will be good enough!"

"If I am going to see you off, it will be all the way to the station. Brother Ta-yung, please do not ruin it for me, let me do my part."

"Okay," Ta-yung said with a smile. Turning now to Mother Ch'i, "Mother Ch'i, I must go now. Young Tiger will take care of you this lunar New Year. Do not worry about anything. Go in now, please!"

Ta-yung swung the knapsack onto his back, gave Mother Ch'i a confident smile, and walked through the courtyard and out of the gate. Young Tiger followed him, walking out of the side street onto a large thoroughfare. Ahead stood the Pavilion of the Four Eastern Plaques. Ta-yung looked at the trackless trolleys passing by, jammed with people inside, and said to Young Tiger:

"With all this stuff, we will never get inside the trolleys. It is not far. Let's walk." Young Tiger's gaunt face flushed and Ta-yung said, "Let's change. You carry this." He took the bedding from Young Tiger's back.

The bedding was not too bulky, but it was very heavy. It held a change of clothing, a wool blanket as well as a wool vest, some undergarments, and several cotton-cloth shoes that Mother Ch'i had made for Young Swallow. In addition, there were dates, dried apples, and dried apricots, all of them Young Swallow's favorites.

◇ ◇ ◇

Young Swallow had been in Inner Mongolia for five years, on assignment with the Production Corps.

Ta-yung could still recall vividly the meeting at graduation from high school when the assignments to Production Corps were announced. The first deputation announced was to Inner Mongolia, and on that list, the first name was that of Young Swallow. But when the Workers Propaganda Unit representative read through the entire list, Ta-yung's name had not even been mentioned. For a split second his heart sank, and his chest felt tight. He thought to himself: "I am going to be separated from her. What will I do?"

He tried very hard to find Young Swallow in the crowd, to search out those big, clear eyes that he saw even in his dreams. But where had she burrowed herself?

Suddenly, she appeared at the head of a group of students whose names had just been read in front of the Workers Propaganda Unit representative, and as they raised their right hands, she shouted out with a clear, resounding voice, "We will resolutely answer the Chairman's call, to travel to the frontiers of our country and to develop agriculture there, and at the same time to protect our motherland from enemy invasion. We solemnly swear: no hardship will daunt us; no sacrifice will prove too great; we will forever fight for the cause of Chairman Mao!"

Young Swallow smiled at the crowd amid the rousing applause of the faculty, students, and honored guests. It was a

50

smile of pride and of joy, showing her even teeth and her dimpled cheeks.

Ta-yung and Young Swallow not only had superior academic records, they had also been the leading political activists. In the fourth year of high school, the resident Workers Propaganda Unit had chosen Ta-yung as the company leader of the class. He passed over to Young Swallow his previous responsibilities as platoon leader.

Working with her in the common struggle, studying with her at school, Ta-yung came to know this strong-willed, competitive girl, and he fell deeply in love.

But seventeen-year-old Ta-yung was in no position to confess his love to fifteen-year-old Young Swallow. Society forbade love affairs among young students and Ta-yung could not break the rule. He kept his love locked in his heart; the only indiscretion he permitted himself was a brief glance when no one was looking, and, on occasion, lending a helping hand.

Before long Young Swallow sensed his feelings. She was impressed by Ta-yung and by his dedication and hardheadedness. Her responsiveness could be conveyed only within the bounds of friendship, and could not be developed further. But she was a young girl who had grown up in a large city, and she discovered that Ta-yung still had something of the provinces in him. There were traits in his character she found incompatible; he was not spontaneous enough for her; they did not share similar tastes in literature, art, or sports; and his way of looking at things struck her as being too plodding.

Because their families lived close to each other, during periods of political activity they often formed "communication links." Ta-yung had occasion to visit her home, and after a while got to know her parents and her brother Young Tiger. In time, her mother, in particular, grew very fond of him.

Time passed quickly. New educational policies were instituted, and the three years of junior high school were combined with the three years of high school, to form a single five-year high school sequence, reducing the total period of study by one year. In the last semester of the fifth year, all classes came to a halt; students devoted all their time to matters concerning work assignments after graduation.

The highest goal among the youth was to be selected for the ranks of the People's Liberation Army, which would not only bring honor to themselves, but would also confer the enviable status of "military family" on their relatives, thus raising their political prestige. Moreover, they could acquire technical training in the PLA, good pay, as well as excellent prospects of being admitted to the university upon discharge. But this opportunity for young intellectuals was difficult to achieve. Of the more than ninety students in the graduating class the year before, only three had been selected, and they were all the offspring of high-ranking families.

The next best assignment was a job in the city, as apprentice workers in a factory, salesclerks in the government shopping outlets, sanitation workers in the streets, attendants in the restaurants, barbershops, or public baths. These jobs were already filled by previous graduates and there was not a vacancy to be had. In addition, there were so many young graduates who had worked a long time in the countryside who were desperately trying to get back to the city, that the chances of advancing along this route were very slim.

Most of the graduates were assigned to agricultural work details in the countryside, an assignment that took three forms: *hsia-fang:* "transfers downward"; *lo-hu:* "residential relocation"; and *nung-k'en:* "homesteading."

Hsia-fang was an assignment to the farm villages and the mountain regions for a period of two years or more. Whenever the need arose in the cities for laborers to work in newly built factories, a group of young workers with demonstrated political commitment would be transferred back. Sixty per cent of the graduates worked under this arrangement. By now ten million youths had been sent to the mountains and the rural areas, and the majority of them had been waiting four or five years to get back. This not only created a serious employment problem for the country, it also stirred up unrest.

Lo-hu referred to the transfer of residences to the agricultural communes, which meant a person was sent to the countryside for the rest of his life. These relocated youths were, for the most part, offspring of the "Five Black Elements" (landlords, rich peasants, counterrevolutionaries, criminal elements, and rightists), young people who had misbehaved in the Cultural Revolution or whose relatives had.

The third form, *nung-k'en*, was the most arduous and the most honorable. It involved joining the Production Corps to develop virgin soil in the outlying frontier regions.

Since 1950, on the southern, western, and northern borders, the policy of military colonization, traceable back to the Han dynasty, had been implemented in order to bolster national defense and to strengthen the people. Twenty-six Production Corps spread out into Heilungkiang (Amur), Chi-lin (Kirin), Inner Mongolia, Yunnan, Kweichow, Tibet, Ch'ing-hai (Kokonor), and Sinkiang (Chinese Turkestan). These Production Corps were under the direct command of the regional military authorities. Families were admitted to the Production Corps, but in general the military system was used so that, with a gun in one hand and a spade in the other, they were all incorporated into half-military, half-agricultural collectives. Since 1964, nearly three million young intellectuals had joined these celebrated ranks.

Ta-yung and Young Swallow were both leaders in school and so they submitted their application to work in the frontier regions. Ta-yung had been born in the countryside and therefore was only too willing to take on agricultural work and, at the same time, defend his country. Still, he nourished a thin thread of hope that he could be assigned to the same location as Young Swallow.

But reality and wish fulfillment are worlds apart, and Ta-yung was assigned to the Technical School of the Central Supply Section of the Military Command in Peking. This assignment not only surprised Ta-yung, it startled his classmates as well.

"This is not what I had hoped for! I do not want to stay in Peking," Ta-yung thought, as he sat listening to the scattered, sardonic clapping, and the murmurs of the assembly.

After all the assignments had been made, Hsiao Ta-yung bumped into Young Swallow. She looked indifferent. There was no trace of her previous affection for him.

"There are many classmates spreading strange rumors that you used family connections to get a position in Peking to study technology."

"No such thing," Ta-yung protested. "I volunteered for relocation in Inner Mongolia."

"In any case, it is not my affair. Why should it matter to me?"

"Do not talk that way. With all my heart, I would like to be with you always." Ta-yung was flustered, and he had betrayed his feelings. Both Ta-yung and Young Swallow flushed with embarrassment.

Ta-yung looked at Young Swallow. She lowered her head, her fingers twirling the tips of her long braids. She raised her head and said with a glow in her eyes: "We cannot talk about such things now. Let's have a competition, each in our different assignments, and see who can do the best."

The day his classmates left Peking to join the Inner Mongolia Corps, Ta-yung went to the railroad station to see them off. The square in front of the station was full of people, flags were flying, and amid this uproar, groups of young men and women, wearing brand-new uniforms, marched across the square, striking heroic poses, buoyed by a sense of the occasion. To the cheering of the masses lined up on each side, they marched into the station.

Ta-yung saw Young Swallow. Like the others, she carried a well-stuffed knapsack on her back, and she wore a large red paper flower on her chest. Her hair was cut short, and under the thick, cotton-lined military cap her face looked thinner. She pulled herself up as she paraded by Ta-yung and gave him a spring-like smile, and after passing him she did not so much as turn her head. She gradually disappeared, engulfed in a sea of green uniforms.

❖ ❖ ❖

Around the time of the lunar New Year, the square in front of the station was jammed with lines of people returning home. The express train for Ulan Bator was not scheduled to leave until 5:30 P.M., but passengers had been lining up early to get seats for the overnight journey. To save money, Ta-yung had not reserved a sleeping bunk, but asked the purchasing agent at the school to buy him a round-trip bench-seat ticket to Erh-lien. At the urging of the agent, he arrived early at the railway station, not dreaming that so many would arrive ahead of him.

Ta-yung and Young Tiger found the line for the train to Ulan Bator. Feeling tired, Ta-yung took the bedding from his shoulder, removed his cotton cap, and wiped the sweat from off his brow. Along with his kerchief, a yellow armband dropped from his pocket. On the kerchief were printed these four words: "The Peking People's Militia." Ta-yung picked it up and folded it carefully. He inserted it into the upper left-hand pocket of his uniform, and buttoned up the pocket flap.

Young Tiger looked around. He enjoyed the bustle, and he wished he were one of the travelers going to distant places.

"It would be great if I could go with you to Erh-lien to see my sister."

"Yes, it would," Ta-yung answered absent-mindedly. "Let's see next year. If she still cannot come back then we will both go up to see her."

These words, once said, gave him a foreboding. Why did Young Swallow, for the last three years, seem to hesitate about coming back to Peking? Even at the lunar New Year, she did not come back to see her mother. Was she really that busy? Or was there another reason?

❖ ❖ ❖

Ta-yung was from Hunan, his home town in a valley basin formed by the river cutting through the surrounding mountains. It was not far from Ch'ang-sha, the provincial capital, in an area that was extremely fertile and rich in agriculture and fishing.

In traditional times fertile areas had often been the seats of enormous feudal power. Since the Autumn Harvest Uprising in 1927, many of the peasants were plunged into the revolution. Ta-yung's father and his uncle had joined the movement. In 1949, after the liberation of the country, something extraordinary had occurred in the region. People who had not been seen or heard from for years suddenly reappeared, bearing the scars of struggle and wearing medals of military honor. They returned home in glory. When military honors were conferred in Ta-yung's village, populated by no more than one hundred families, no less than seventeen families produced generals, and this little town had come to be known as "the village of generals."

Ta-yung's father had been commander of the Engineering Corps, holding the rank of major general. After a two-week stay at home, he was sent to Tibet with his troops. Ta-yung was born months later, but before he was a year old, his mother, who had been head of the District Women's Association, was murdered by some thugs on the way home from a meeting. The forces of revolution and counterrevolution had engaged in a violent struggle during the big land reform confrontations of that time. Countless lives were lost and blood had stained the landscape.

His grandmother, though very old, was as sturdy as an old pine, and she nursed Ta-yung through his infancy. Fortunately, the village Party members tilled her land for her, and together with the monthly remittance sent by his father, she and her small charge were able to survive.

When Ta-yung was five, the People's Commune was established and a teacher was dispatched from the county seat to open up a Commune school, where Ta-yung learned how to read and write.

Ta-yung had grown up during a period of natural disasters and national catastrophes. His father had tried to send for him several times, but his grandmother could not bear to part with this grandson whom she had nourished and cherished from birth. Moreover, she had heard that Ta-yung's father, who was over fifty, had married a girl of twenty who was a member of the Cultural Propaganda Team. How could Ta-yung possibly get along with her?

Old trees may be sturdy, but they are vulnerable to a violent wind. In 1965, the grandmother had died suddenly at a "struggle meeting" against the man who had killed Ta-yung's mother.

The twelve-year-old Ta-yung had glared at the murderer kneeling on the platform before the eyes of the village. He was a rich peasant who had not only killed his mother but was indirectly responsible for the death of his grandmother. Ta-yung had stared at him as the Security Police took the murderer to the execution grounds.

That year, Ta-yung's father was heading an engineering team sent to help in the people's struggle in one of the fraternity of Socialist countries in Southeast Asia. Ta-yung's livelihood and education were entrusted to his father's brother Hsiao Lien-min, who lived in Peking and who was Political Commissar of the Peking Military Command.

Hsiao Lien-min's only daughter, Mei-lien, was much older than Ta-yung. She was married and taught at the August 1st Elementary School. When she saw her cousin fresh from the provinces, she could not bear to enroll him at the same school where she taught. She let Old P'eng, the house manager, take

Ta-yung to the Educational Bureau in the western sector of the city. He was placed in the first-year class of a high school not far from home.

Ta-yung felt instinctively that his cousin, who seemed strange to his way of thinking, both in manner and dress, did not like him. His uncle and aunt were always busy; they did not come home sometimes for a month at a time. Mei-lien's husband, Chia Hsiang-tung, was also preoccupied with his duties, and came home once a month for a few days. The people living in the large residential compound, three four-sided buildings, one inside the other, included a cook, a nurse, a chauffeur, and four house guards, all under the thumb of his formidable cousin.

Mei-lien and her husband lived, along with their child and their nursemaid, in the innermost building; in the middle building lived Ta-yung's uncle and aunt. All the functionaries lived in the outermost building. When Ta-yung arrived, there was a question as to where to house him. The unoccupied east wing of the innermost building served as Mei-lien's study and music room and a large grand piano dominated the middle room of the wing. Of course, nobody had ever heard her play the piano, but she was, after all, a graduate of the Conservatory of Music. *Not* to have a piano would be unthinkable. Ta-yung could not be put in the next building, either. True, his uncle and aunt often lived away in the Military Command post, but there were many confidential documents in these rooms, and not just anybody could be allowed to live there.

Luckily, Old P'eng solved the problem. He called Ta-yung to his own tiny room and said, "Although this is not much more than a place to lie down in, it will have to do."

Old P'eng's small room had scarcely one foot of clearance after two wooden beds had been moved in. Close to the kitchen, it was formerly used as a woodshed, but it was given to Old P'eng, who fixed it up nicely and lived there himself. When Ta-yung moved in with his belongings, he was to stay for five years.

Old P'eng, already nearly sixty years old, was the major-domo of the household staff. To his mind, loyalty to the Party meant three things. First, it meant to love the Chairman. In the Yenan period, he once had shaken hands with Chairman Mao, and it was the greatest thrill of his life. Ta-yung would hear him describe that encounter a hundred times over during the next five years. Each time P'eng recounted it, the words he attributed to the Chairman were different. The dialogue changed as the political situation changed, and each version happened to bring out the fact that Old P'eng was the most faithful and obedient of the Chairman's followers.

The second absolute loyalty was to the company commander. When Old P'eng served Commissar Hsiao as orderly and personal guard, Commissar Hsiao was then company commander in the army. Now, even after the commissar had attained his new high rank, Old P'eng still addressed him as "Company Commander" to show how venerable their relationship was.

The third loyalty he did not have to explain, it was obvious to everyone; it was to Mei-lien. According to Old P'eng, it was he who had raised her. When the Communist contingent was playing hide-and-seek, trying to elude the Nationalist general Hu Tsung-nan, it was Old P'eng who had carried the two-year-old Mei-lien on his back for hundreds of miles. It was Old P'eng who had adamantly refused when the company commander insisted, on three occasions, that Mei-lien be entrusted to the care of the local villagers. Later on, he learned that Hu Tsung-nan had caught up with the children who had been left behind and had killed them all. Old P'eng could truly be said to have saved Mei-lien. Mei-lien treated him no differently, for all this, but scolded and abused him along with everyone else.

The first day of high school, Ta-yung wore a red scarf and it was Old P'eng who took him to school. When Mei-lien hastily had filled out the forms indicating his family background, she wrote "Revolutionary soldier" under the entry identifying his father's profession. Because of this, the school officials thought that Old P'eng, an orderly in the revolutionary army, was Ta-yung's father. They did not know that Ta-yung's real father was a full-fledged general, and Ta-yung never said anything about it. When his classmates visited him, they saw that Ta-yung lived in the same small and dingy room as Old P'eng, a room in the residential compound with no space for a small table. His classmates were very much at ease with him. He was so different from the offspring of high-ranking officers whom they regarded, at a respectful distance, with contempt and fear.

In less than a year, the Cultural Revolution was under way. Ta-yung did not join any movement or organization unless Old P'eng had investigated it beforehand. Several organizations in the school exerted pressure on Ta-yung to join, but Old P'eng brought the other guards, in civilian clothes, to stand at the gate of the school so that there would be no physical intimidation from any of the revolutionary leaders.

Gradually, Ta-yung became the leader of a group of students who did not join any organization. When the Workers Propaganda Unit came to the school, they discovered Ta-yung's actual background. They were surprised that a son of a general should be pursuing his studies at such an ordinary school, and that he should behave with such modesty and simplicity. Because of this, they gave him a key role to play.

Those Red Guards who had caused the trouble were branded as "May 16th"* types or were "transferred downward" to the countryside or ordered to "relocate their residences." The students who were allowed to stay in school were

---

* Chairman Mao, on May 16, 1966, gave instructions from Hangchou to commence the so-called Cultural Revolution. A splinter group from the Central Committee of the Communist Party, headed up by Madame Mao and Ch'en Po-ta, caused various excesses of the Red Guard, including, in 1967, the vilification of Premier Chou En-lai, an intolerable affront to the conservative ruling elite. Consequently, the Central Committee ordered that such excesses be discontinued. Madame Mao, to save her neck, disavowed herself of the extremists of the splinter group. This disavowed group became known as the "May 16th" group, becoming synonymous with excessive left-wing zealotry— TRANSLATOR.

mainly those who had followed Ta-yung. Of these, Young Swallow was one.

As to Ta-yung's work assignment upon graduating, it was Old P'eng who had managed it behind the scenes. He had analyzed in detail the assignment of each of the previous graduating classes, and he had weighed the pros and cons of each. Taking advantage of a visit home by Commissar Hsiao, he had reported the situation to him. Commissar Hsiao had picked up the phone and spoken briefly with the head of the Central Supply Section, and it was all arranged.

Old P'eng kept it a secret, and waited for Ta-yung's reaction to the news. He was greeted only by Ta-yung's disappointment, shame, and anger. Ta-yung did not eat when he came home, but went straight to bed, leaving Old P'eng and the other servants to finish the delicacies that had been specially prepared for him.

◇ ◇ ◇

After six months at the Technical School, Ta-yung was assigned to work at a newly constructed, up-to-date defense plant, located near the Five Pines suburb west of Peking.

Because he had studied welding, he was assigned now to a military company of repair mechanics, divided into three platoons, each with twenty-six or twenty-seven men. The leader of Ta-yung's platoon was an old worker who had joined the Party more than thirty years ago. He was addressed by everyone respectfully as "Master Lu." One week after Ta-yung started work, Master Lu spotted him and took him under his wing to teach him the tricks of the trade. Ta-yung came to work early and left late, and he learned the ropes bit by bit by conscientiously picking all the heavy and complicated jobs for himself. His behavior was in marked contrast to that of young men who knew only how to pour tea, light cigarettes, and buy treats to ingratiate themselves with Master Lu, but who adopted the style of "avoiding the hard and taking on the easy" in their work. In less than a year, Ta-yung became Master Lu's right-hand man; in emergency repair situations, he was always ahead of the others, never gave up before the job was done, never complained about fatigue or difficulty. He had so pleased Master Lu that the old worker would break into a smile at the mention of Ta-yung's name. Everyone teased Master Lu and said that he should not have married off every one of his four daughters: he should have kept one back so that he could arrange for Ta-yung to become his son-in-law.

At the end of one full year, the performances of the workers were graded. Ta-yung jumped immediately from a novice-level worker to the third level, something which had never happened before. When the head of the Factory Party Committee came personally to investigate, he had to agree with the recommendation of Master Lu, whose opinion was seconded by six other veteran workers.

Ta-yung's wages were raised from 18 to 34 *yüan*† a month. With bonuses and allowances, he could earn as much as 40 *yüan* some months, minus 12 *yüan* for food and the American equivalent of 70 cents for lodging. He would save the balance. In addition, he saved the supplemental living allowance his father sent him, and soon had a bank account of over 500 *yüan*. Several female staff members of the People's Bank were alarmed enough to alert the Security Department of the factory to the unaccountable prosperity of this young worker.

Ta-yung had long since moved out of his uncle's house, and now lived in the communal dormitories in the residential quarter of the factory district. Six people shared a single room measuring four by three meters, with three double-decker beds, a footlocker underneath, and two desks back-to-back in front of the sunny, iron-latticed window. In the area there was a restaurant, an athletic field, and a recreation room. Every Tuesday and Thursday, night classes were held at which veteran workers from the Military Technical School and the facto-

† A unit of "people's currency" (*Jen-min-pi*); one *yüan* is roughly U.S. $.55 —TRANSLATOR.

ries took turns giving lessons and lectures, either demonstrating their skills in a particular art or discussing theoretical questions in a subject of their choosing. Ta-yung was tired after work, but he attended these classes. A year later, he was also to distinguish himself in these studies. And he joined the Party.

It was at this time that his uncle was attacked, removed from his job, and sent to participate in study groups for ideological self-rectification. His aunt was also vilified in several hundred *Ta-tzu-pao* ("big-character posters"), and she stayed at home in the city. Whenever Ta-yung was on vacation to see Old P'eng, he always saw him disconsolate. Everyone else looked somber, and a knock at the door would make them tense. Only Chia Hsiang-tung, who seldom came home these days, was in good humor. To congratulate Ta-yung for his promotion, Chia had given Ta-yung a wristwatch which, though old, was an impressive calendar watch, waterproof and self-winding, with three hands. Young Tiger said this watch would fetch 500 *yüan* on the market. Ta-yung thought it too heavy and did not wear it when he was working, but he never thought of selling it.

Ta-yung thought constantly about Young Swallow. His love for her persisted, and he wrote ardent letters, describing his progress at every stage, but her replies were always curt. She was busy with her work, her job was very time-consuming and complicated, and there was no point in writing. She visited Peking once, two years after she had left, looking thinner, her face weather-beaten. She seemed still to feel something for Ta-yung, and they went to a revolutionary opera together, walked about in the Wang-fu Ching ("The Well of the Prince's Mansion") Shopping Center, but she never let their relationship progress beyond that of classmates. "Perhaps she is shy," Ta-yung thought.

Every month Ta-yung visited Mother Ch'i, so that he heard news of Young Swallow. But Young Swallow seldom wrote home, and Mother Ch'i found this unsettling.

63

One day, the head of the Factory Party Committee informed Ta-yung that he had been proposed for admission to Tsing-hua University, and that he should begin preparations for the entrance examinations.

With only two months to study, Ta-yung reviewed mathematics, physics, chemistry, and foreign languages, all subjects he had not touched for a long time. Although his performance on the examination was none too impressive, he was admitted and assigned to the Mechanical Engineering Department, specializing in tractor machinery. He was launched on a new struggle.

There was no problem about his livelihood. He was promoted once more before he left the factory, to fourth-level status with a monthly wage of 45 *yüan*. After he entered the university, he was provided with a monthly income, so that he had no worry about finances.

Keeping up with his studies was his biggest problem. Some of his classmates looked as if they had never done manual labor, in agriculture or in industry, after their graduation from high school. It seemed they did nothing but stay at home reviewing their lessons. In their eyes, the rate of progress in class was too slow, and the level of performance too low. These classmates were all from the families of high-ranking cadres.

Particularly effective when discussing Marxism and Leninism, they were also well-versed in foreign languages, as if ready to go abroad at a moment's notice. But those who, like Ta-yung, came from the countryside and the villages were bewildered by much that went on in the classroom.

Ta-yung gritted his teeth and studied diligently. When the lights were turned out in the study room, he would go out to the corridor; when the lights in the corridor were shut off, he went into the lavatory with a candle to continue studying. After two years of this regimen, he was thin and weakened. What was to become of him?

Old P'eng's words rang in his ears:

"How wonderful it will be! Our 'village of generals' is producing an eminent engineer. Ta-yung, you must work hard! You must vindicate your mother."

Nor could he forget the parting words of Master Lu:

"Ta-yung, this is the proletariat developing its own home-grown intellectuals! Do not waver in your determination. And when you know how to run, do not forget the mother who taught you how to walk."

"Run! Why, I can barely crawl," Ta-yung thought. How was he to manage it?

Ta-yung joined the Urban Workers Militia branch right after he enrolled in the university, but because of his heavy curriculum, he could find little time to participate in the training and the discussion sessions. He thought that to fulfill his mission as a student was to fulfill his duty as a Party member, so he pushed everything else to the back of his mind.

Then Chairman Mao offered up for public discussion and debate the letter sent by the Party representative at the university to the Party Central Committee, and Ta-yung and other students from worker and peasant families, under the meticulous explanation of the Party representative of the Militia, realized the following: that the "capitalist-roaders" were trying once more to restore the predominance of the old academic subjects as well as to reinstitute the old academic procedures. On the surface the academic level of the students was being elevated so they would be prepared to meet the demand for technical expertise on a par with international standards, but actually it was more of an attempt to block access to the technical professions for young people from worker backgrounds, and to continue the capitalist-revisionist direction of the university, which had been established, after all, by imperialist interests. This was a real class struggle, and not merely a matter of academic subjects and procedures. Ta-yung believed that a pointless curriculum, with not the slightest practical application, could produce only bookworms who had nothing to offer the people.

It was then that Ta-yung began to devote all his energy to

65

organizing discussion meetings, pasting up sheets of the big-character posters, and co-ordinating the people who came from the various provinces. Under the instructions of Party Emissary Hsieh of the Peking Urban Workers Militia Command, he and his fellow students fired the first shot against Chou Jung-hsin, Minister of Higher Education. Then they raised their sights and went after the leader of the capitalist-roaders, Vice-Premier Teng Hsiao-p'ing.

Ta-yung's organizational skills now had a chance to develop. He became the leader of the People's Militia Section of Tsing-hua University, and participated in the activity of the High Command of the Peking People's Militia. Amid the tumult of this new struggle, a new leader had been born.

After the T'ien-an Men Incident, the chief of the capitalist-roaders fell, but his cohorts continued to stir up trouble throughout the provinces. Although it appeared to abate, the conflict continued to develop into a struggle to the death.

Though Ta-yung would soon be faced with another work assignment, he did not much care where he was sent, for he had thrown himself body and soul into this struggle.

Just before the lunar New Year, he learned from Mother Ch'i that Young Swallow had decided not to come home for the holidays. Ta-yung wanted to settle matters once and for all with Young Swallow so he asked for a two-week leave from the Militia Command to visit Young Swallow and tell her what was in his heart.

❖ ❖ ❖

Young Tiger called out suddenly: "They are letting them in. The line is moving." Indeed, the line was inching forward. People were shouting and pressing toward the gate. Ta-yung lifted his bedding and followed the crowd pushing ahead. Young Tiger stepped back to one side, waved at Ta-yung, and turned around to leave.

There were fourteen cars on the International Express to

Ulan Bator. Aside from the dining car and six sleeping cars (two with soft mattress beds, four with hard wooden "beds"), the other seven cars had hard benches with open seating. After their tickets had been checked and they had squeezed through the milling crowd at the gate, the travelers ran frantically down the platform to scramble for a seat in the hard-bench cars.

Ta-yung squeezed onto the platform and started to run. Then he saw an old man in peasant clothing holding two big bundles, straining to move forward, his face paling at the effort. Ta-yung could stand the sight no longer. He tightened his knapsack on his back and said, "Old man, let me carry this for you. Follow me!" He lifted the two bundles and began walking past the sleeping cars and hard-bench cars, looking for a seat for the old man. Ta-yung gritted his teeth and carried the bundles to the door of a compartment; the old man followed, short of breath. Ta-yung looked quickly through the doorway and his heart sank. All the seats were taken, even the aisles were filled with women and children. He noticed that those sitting down were healthy, wholesome, rosy-cheeked soldiers, horsing around with each other and making jokes. These sounds, mixed with the wails of the babies in the aisles, made a lamentable chorus. It suddenly dawned on Ta-yung that this favoritism for soldiers was typical in China. All military men were allowed to board trains thirty minutes before anyone else so that they could be guaranteed a place to sit down and rest in order to remain forever ready and fit to protect the people.

Ta-yung put the old man's bundles into the washroom (situated across the aisle from the toilet) in the adjacent car with the hard wooden "beds." He asked the old man to sit down, and he could only stand himself by the doorway. In less than five minutes, the doorway was jammed with people so that even Ta-yung was pushed into the washroom.

Gradually those inside began to settle down, and people started to arrange their luggage and find corners in which to squat down. Suddenly someone called out: "Coming through . . . coming through! Why, you can't even get through to the toilet."

The voice was familiar, but Ta-yung could not identify it. He craned his head for a look, and found himself face to face with his cousin's husband, Chia Hsiang-tung. The two of them looked at each other in astonishment.

▨ FOUR

Sunday, February 10   3 p.m.

     The majestic and peaceful T'ien-an Men Square bisects Ch'ang-an Avenue into east and west sections. This spacious and direct thoroughfare, fifty kilometers long, runs right through the heart of the city. Toward the west, it goes through the spot where the old Restoration Gate (Fu-hsing Men) once stood, and passes by the beautiful setting of the Pond of the Jade Depths (Yü-yüan T'an). Farther on, it runs past the awesome complex of military buildings along the Grave of the Princess (Kung-chu Fen), Five Pines (Wu-k'o Sung), and the Street of the Jade Springs (Yü-ch'üan Lu), then comes upon the mysterious and imposing Mountain of the Eight Treasures (Pa-pao Shan). Finally it winds up in the heavily industrialized area of the Mountain of Rocky Vistas (Shih-ching Shan), where the clusters of chimneys look like a forest grove.

East of T'ien-an Men Square, the road runs by the internationally famous Peking Hotel and the Well of the Prince's Mansion (Wang-fu Ching); it goes past the gateway to the capital, the Peking Railway Station, as well as the old site of Establishing-the-Nation Gate (Chien-kuo Men), whereupon it enters the newly constructed compound of high-rise residences. Going farther east, it reaches the Garden of the Lang House (Lang-chia Yüan), the center of machine and chemical factories as well as other kinds of light industry.

This thoroughfare, which symbolizes the prosperity and well-being of the people of the new China, was completed in 1959. At the time the street was being completed, the workers, the cadres, the soldiers, and the students of the capital were also struggling to complete nine other projects, working day and night. These included T'ien-an Men Square, the Great Hall of the People, the Historical Museum, the Telegraph Building, the Military Museum, and the Palace of the Minority Peoples. These extraordinary constructions manifested the achievement and the remarkable spirit of the Chinese people in the ten years after the Liberation.

After taking Ta-yung to the station, Young Tiger walked out of the station alone, hands in his pocket, his head lowered, and, looking around, he turned into East Ch'ang-an Avenue.

◇ ◇ ◇

Two years ago, when Young Tiger had graduated from high school with an impressive record, he naturally hoped the authorities would accommodate his wishes and assign him to work in an electrical factory. The authorities, however, after reviewing the situation in the city, decided to assign him for relocation to a commune in the mountainous region of Yin-ch'eng county, in Shansi Province.

With tears in his eyes, his jaw set, he took leave of his mother, his brother, his brother's wife, and with his bedding on his back and a big red paper flower on his chest, he boarded the train. One year later, he came home with empty hands. He could not stand the ordeal, so in the company of a few like-minded "buddies" among his classmates, he had walked back to Peking, hiking at night, taking cover and resting during the day.

When his brother, Ch'i Yi-lung ("Dragon-like" Ch'i), heard about this, he rode his bicycle home all night from Shih-ching Shan and, without a word when they met, slapped him hard on the face.

Ch'i Yi-lung was worried about the financial and other problems which would be caused by Young Tiger's action. To be sure, he was a technician and a university graduate, with a monthly income of more than 70 *yüan*, but he was married, with two children. His wife also worked, but ever since her father had died she had sent most of her monthly wage to Shanghai, for the support of her mother and a younger sister attending high school. Ch'i Yi-lung gave his own mother 20 *yüan*, so his budget was tight. How could he possibly manage the support of an unemployed younger brother on top of all that? Even more serious, how would he explain his own actions, in political terms, to the authorities?

In the technical section where Ch'i Yi-lung worked, there was an engineer whose son had sneaked back from a village in Heilungkiang (Amur). This man was severely criticized for not having persuaded his son to return to the commune. It was insisted that he should have used every means to convince him to continue his participation in the glorious work of agricultural production. The engineer not only failed to achieve these objectives, but he also told other stories about the cadres in the village communes, undermining the solidarity of workers and peasants. The Party cadres amassed the evidence against him, convened a "struggle meeting," and immediately transferred him downward to work in the most arduous compound in the iron mines.

These thoughts had disturbed Ch'i Yi-lung, and it was in this impulsive state that he had slapped Young Tiger.

Young Tiger fell back into a corner of the room, one half of his face swollen red. Stunned, he stared at his brother.

Young Tiger's father had died when he was very young; his

brother and his sister, Young Swallow, were both much older than he, so he was used to obeying his brother and treating him with respect. But in this instance, he had to put forth his own views. He could no longer follow anything or anyone blindly, not any more. This was a critical decision, and he had already undergone all the hardships he could endure.

After Ch'i Yi-lung had slapped his brother, he saw how thin and frail he had grown. He fell against the edge of the bed and said to Mother Ch'i, "That does it for us! Young Tiger has ruined not only his own life, but our lives as well."

Mother Ch'i dropped her head, tears in her eyes, and said, "Yi-lung, you cannot blame all this on Young Tiger. He is a victim of circumstance."

"But how can you defend him? What am I to say to the authorities?" Ch'i Yi-lung was in a rage. Mother Ch'i turned her face and fell silent. The room felt as if with the slightest spark it could ignite and explode.

Some moments of silence followed. Young Tiger mustered up his courage, stood up in the corner of the room, and replied with anguish and anger in his voice:

"Older brother, when I was first assigned, though I was really dead set against going, did I not go all the same? At the time, we talked, and neither of us thought that relocation to a rural area would be such a dead end. So long as a person worked hard, we thought, he could grow and develop anywhere. So I made up my mind to work hard and to improve in my ideological thinking. I tried my best to be a progressive intellectual youth, I tried to enter the Party, hoping that in three to five years I could be transferred back to a factory or university. For that, I would have gladly suffered any kind of hardship.

"I had not thought that as soon as we arrived at the commune, the cadres would interrogate each one of us. They were bent on finding out my allowance each month. I said that I had only one elder brother who worked, who did not make much money, and who had many demands on his resources.

They began to lose interest in me right away. They dispatched a bunch of us, all from families who could not send them much money, to production teams deep in the mountain ranges, which were among the most barren and impoverished places. The children of high-ranking cadres, who could get thirty to fifty *yüan* from home, all stayed in the production teams and the commune headquarters in the river valleys. They served as storage superintendents, accountants, cultural instructors, all so that they would not have to work the land.

"Those of us who went to the mountains, on the other hand, lived in mud caves, swinging a pick at a rock pile, uprooting trees, digging ditches, constructing stone walls. Every month, each one of us received thirty pounds of coarse-grain gruel; there was no sauce, no meat, no vegetables. As the provisions were inadequate, we had to dig out wild plants and vegetables from the rocky crevices and our hands and feet swelled up when we ate them. We figured our wages at the end of the month, and they were not even enough to pay for the gruel we had eaten.

"I worked for one year and still I owed the production team forty-three *yüan* or more. The commune cadres forced us to demand money from our families, and I knew that my family had no way to make up the debt. In the dead of winter, we, supposedly young intellectuals, had no cotton jackets, no heavy quilts to cover ourselves with, and nothing to barter. Everything we had was already traded away for food with the local commune members. No one bothered about us and we were not permitted to come out of the mountains.

"Those who were sent to visit from the higher echelons would see only the intellectual youth in the posh river valleys and in the commune headquarters. How could they know that we were living a life not fit for human beings? One year later, those whose families could round up one or two thousand *yüan* for the basic fund of the commune would be issued a letter-certificate and be allowed to work in the Peking factories. Some children of high-ranking officials spent less than a year before they were transferred back to the universities as 'model' workers.

"For those of us with no connections or no money, the debts mounted. If we worked until the day we died, we still would not be able to work our way out of them. There was simply no way for us to live. We decided we would rather break out and come to Peking to find some way of surviving here. Big brother! Everything I have said is true. If you want me to live, do not put me in a bind, give me a way out! If you think I have added to your troubles, just say it, and I will leave Peking on the spot, and try my fortune elsewhere. Whether I live or die is up to you."

Inside the room it was quiet. Ch'i Yi-lung, agitated, smoked one cigarette after another, pondering the situation. He saw the look on his brother's face; he also saw, in his mind's eye, the bloodless, humorless, "progressive" elements of the technical section where he worked. He longed to tell Young Tiger, "Young Tiger, I know that everything you've said is true, but for the sake of my peace of mind and the well-being of our family and the future of my children, you had better go back." He raised his head to look at Young Tiger, but he could not say it. This was his blood brother, whom he had brought up since he was a baby. He could not send him back to hell.

He put on his cloth cap and pushed open the door. He took his bicycle and rode out of the courtyard, his eyes brimming with tears, and disappeared into the shadows in the alley.

❖ ❖ ❖

Someone from the Police Registry came to investigate, and Young Tiger was summoned for questioning. The cadres and activists from the Neighborhood Committees took turns talking things over with him, but he remained tight-lipped, sitting in the corner of the room like a pile of discarded clothing, and gradually everyone lost interest, particularly when they realized that the Registry Office would not pursue this case.

Young Tiger's brother came several times to visit, but he did not say anything about sending him back to the commune. He did say to Mother Ch'i, "I cannot support Young Tiger. Let him fend for himself. Whether he stays here or not does not matter; I still cannot afford to feed him."

In fact, Mother Ch'i could not afford to feed him either. Since Young Tiger was registered at the commune in Shansi, he was absolutely forbidden to re-enter Peking. Without a registered residence in Peking no one could get rations for the basic aliments, cooking oil, cotton cloth, or other provisions. Anything could be bought at the city's black markets, but where were they going to find the money?

Mother Ch'i could not bear to see Young Tiger go without food. At first he ate the solid foods while she ate gruel; but half a month later, he was sharing her pasty gruel. Luckily, Mother Ch'i got along well with the neighbors and some households, aware that she was short on food, secretly gave her ration coupons, and in this way, Mother Ch'i and Young Tiger managed to get by.

Young Tiger waited until things quieted down and then he got busy. He formed a group with a few "buddies" and together they tried to make a living.

They organized a "production commune," at first collecting used books and torn papers. Later they discovered a way of making use of the little Red Book of Chairman Mao's sayings. They took out the red plastic covers and cut them into long strips, and the girls in the gang would weave them into intricate, attractive toy animals which they put up for sale in the markets. The toys were a big hit with the shoppers. As autumn turned into winter, they found some shards of firebrick from the discarded materials in the factory, and carefully grinding them into fireproof material, they went everywhere patching up the insides of furnaces. Some of their buddies learned how to repair radios and began to fix old broken-down sets purchased at junk dealers, and after putting new wooden cabinets on them, they would sell them in the rural markets.

Gradually, Young Tiger had a monthly income of 10 to 20

yüan and he managed to bring home fifteen to twenty pounds of grain. He did not say where he got it, and Mother Ch'i could not bear to ask him.

Young Tiger's "commune" was sufficiently equipped with human and financial resources to develop a small electronics business, using their own skills. Some parts and equipment they managed to find by the "co-operative method," buying the material from cadres in the supply sections of the factories with whom they had good connections. For these cadres this was not, strictly speaking, a violation of the law, because Young Tiger's "commune" was a bona fide business registered at the Neighborhood Residence Committee. The name of the enterprise was "The Young People's Industrial Co-operative of Ch'ien-liang Street in the Eastern District." They made a big round seal as an insignia for their commune and were able to write to various factories for spare parts. But they had to establish secret personal contacts with cadres by giving them cigarettes, bolts of cloth, imported powdered cocoa. These "gifts" were, naturally, sent to the families of the cadres.

Some of the spare parts were openly available for sale at the market. So long as they kept their ears to the ground, were quick on their feet, and got there early enough, certain parts could be bought.

The parts most difficult to come by were voltage transformers and miniature speakers, and these had to be bought from the special "communes" who produced them.

Young Tiger was the co-ordinator of supplies. He had to keep in his head a large file of who could get what, who lived where, who belonged to which commune, who had connections with people in Tientsin and Shihchiachuang, who did business in Shanghai, T'aiyuan, Shenyang, and other cities, who went specially to the villages in Hopei, Liaoning, and Shansi, and who were active in the urban-rural exchange. All this he had to retain in his memory.

What he admired most were the fearless and imperturbable gangs that hung out on Mei-shih ("Coal Market") Street outside the Ch'ien-men ("Front Gate"). If you wanted ideas, they would give you ideas; if you wanted something done, whatever the job, they would do it with dispatch and ruthless efficiency. To their fellow outlaws, they observed a code of justice, but they would draw a knife on anyone else who crossed them. Thankfully, there was someone dubbed "Chuko Liang,"* who, though short and scrawny, could stay the hands of "Big Gun" Hsü and "Tall Man" Li with a blink of an eye and a few soft-spoken words. The word was out that they would not have survived down to the present without the canny leadership of this Chuko Liang. Without him, these outlaws would have been destroyed long ago, either killed in armed struggle, stranded in the countryside, or starved out in the city.

Young Tiger established contact with them when he was seeking to traffic in goods. In the beginning, they did not think much of him and skeptically checked the first radio he presented to them, a radio that had taken two months of painstaking work to produce. They carped at this and carped at that, claiming that if they sold this, their reputation would be damaged. No, they could not handle the merchandise.

Young Tiger saw that no one wanted the things he and his friends labored so hard to produce. If their means of making a living were cut off, how could they survive? He could not hold back his tears.

How could he have guessed that these people were vulnerable to the "soft" approach where they might have resisted the "hard"? When they saw Young Tiger crying, surprisingly they gave him some helpful suggestions, and agreed to keep the radio. The standard procedure of the gang was first to give an estimate, which, if accepted, meant that they would keep the merchandise. Half the price would be paid, the other half only after the merchandise was sold. Should anything happen to the

---

* Chuko Liang was Prime Minister during the famous but short-lived Epoch of the Three Kingdoms, A.D. 220 to A.D. 260. The history of that epoch is familiar through *The Romance of the Three Kingdoms,* known to every Chinese schoolchild. Chuko Liang was reputed to be extremely clever and wise, a wily strategist and a loyal minister—TRANSLATOR.

goods, then the second half would not be paid. Everything was based on trust; no receipts were exchanged and no accounts recorded.

In time, the merchandise produced by Young Tiger's band got better in quality and in attractiveness, so it was accepted for sale without difficulty and sold at a good price. The gang treated Young Tiger with a little more respect. When they got to know each other, they became friends, but not yet "brothers." Once, Young Tiger entered the gang's headquarters, but finding no one there, and hearing a voice from the back room, he peered in for a look. He saw a platform in the center of the room overflowing with items, from sewing machines to bicycles. A large wooden chest, opened, was full of clothes and fabrics. On the table there was a hand-operated mimeograph machine, with piles of white paper beside it, as if someone were just reproducing a document. Tall Man Li, his back turned toward Young Tiger, was squatting on the floor, stirring the ink in the can. When Young Tiger made a noise, Tall Man Li bolted upright, and with one push forced Young Tiger out the door. It was clear that he did not altogether trust him.

You really could not blame him. Young Tiger was a late "recruit" and had not seen much action. In the words of Big Gun Hsü: "One who has not shed his own blood in the river of warm blood, how could he be a brother?"

Young Tiger came in time to know each of the various contact men. He was especially friendly with one of them named Hsia Yu-min, who was called "Paleface Scholar."

Paleface Scholar did not often come to the headquarters, but when he did, he always had his head buried in a book. What he read were all bizarre medical texts in foreign languages; nobody knew where in the world he found them.

He could read English, Russian, and German, and according to some, he could also manage Latin. At the time of the Cultural Revolution, he had been a fourth-year student at the Peking Medical College. Athough he was from Peking, his mother was from Canton, so he could speak Cantonese. When the Peking Medical College wanted to establish "revolutionary links" with Canton during the Revolution, he was sent there to participate. Some said that before he went there, he was totally indifferent to politics, and had been a cloistered bookworm. His only ambition was to become a surgeon. He had a girl friend, a classmate, who was just the opposite; she had been very active at every gathering or meeting, never failing to speak out. Her words could rile the crowd and stir their passions. Everyone thought it remarkable that these two people, so unlike, could be as close as honey and wax.

Ch'u Feng-chün, Hsia Yu-min's girl friend, was appointed Assistant Group Leader, and with Group Leader Liang Ch'ang, Instructor of Political Ideology at the Peking Medical College, she headed a team of twenty-six of the rank and file that went into Canton to give support to the struggling factions of Red Guards at the Sun Yat-sen Medical College.

By that time, the situation in Canton was already well defined, and clear lines of opposition were drawn. Several hundred revolutionary groups, each with a different banner and a different slogan, had been contending. In time, they polarized around two groups, the "Red Flag" group and the "Consolidated Action" group.

The Consolidated Action group included a high proportion of the children of top cadre members; they had the backing of the military, they had more than enough economic leverage, and they were fully equipped with arms. One only had to look at them, with their standard crew cuts, their spanking-new uniforms, riding their new bicycles, all forty or fifty of them, slashing through Hai-chu ("Sea Pearl") Square like a gust of wind, to see that they were the high and mighty. By contrast, the Red Flag group wore shabby clothes and marched barefoot, rubbing their bloodshot eyes still smarting from the fumes of the homemade smoke bombs of insect spray burned upwind by the Consolidated Action group. Despite all this, they defended their positions.

It was during these circumstances that the reinforcements from the Peking Medical College arrived in Canton.

The Red Guard organization "East Is Red" of the Sun Yat-sen Medical College joined the Red Flag group and established the first-aid center for the wounded campaigners of that group. Hsia Yu-min was not terribly good at mobilizing people or at physical combat, so he performed the role of major surgeon. It would be easy to look down on his genteel airs, but he operated on his feet for twenty consecutive hours without a rest, and his hands were quick and sure. Even the experienced head nurse admired his work.

Ch'u Feng-chün came from Hunan, and since there were many Hunanese in the rival Consolidated Action group, she took the loudspeaker for more than ten hours at a time to harangue them in a Hunan accent. With her eloquence, one would have thought she could convert some of the enemy. Although no one changed sides, some of the Consolidated group sent a bus full of provisions to the hospital, which relieved a severe food shortage that had lasted two days. When Consolidated Action showed that they were about to attack, Ch'u Feng-chün vilified them mercilessly, undermining their resolve and dampening their spirit. Of all their rivals, the Consolidated Action group hated her the most. They set up loudspeakers in the hopes of besting her in argument, but one after another, they retired in defeat. This made the Red Flag take heart. They claimed that she alone was a match for an entire division.

Because the repeated attacks failed to breach the Medical College, the Consolidated Action strategy changed its target to the Chu-chiang ("Pearl River") Film Studio, creating panic there.

Group Leader Liang Ch'ang was busy day and night on the phone with Peking, but as Peking's instructions to stop the fighting were somehow misdirected, no orders moved out of the Canton Military Command.

Finally, Ch'u Feng-chün could bear it no longer. In the dark of night, she took forty or more people and stormed out in a bus, hoping to lend support to their besieged comrades defending the film studio.

As dawn broke, the defenders at the Medical College discovered several bodies across the street. They were what was left of the rescue patrol that had gone out during the night. The Consolidated Action group had cut them down, and had brought them back before the defenders to intimidate them.

Among the injured and dying was Ch'u Feng-chün. When they stretched her out on the operating table, they tried to hold back Hsia Yu-min, to spare him the sight of her wounds. But he lunged forward to see. She said only one thing, "Carry on the Revolution!", and stopped breathing.

The other survivors of the night mission told it like this; nearly five hundred people surrounded their bus, broke open the windows, threw torches into the bus, and forced those inside to come out. Then, as they emerged from the bus, each one was set upon. Someone recognized Ch'u Feng-chün. They hit her with the butts of their rifles, and then, using their daggers, they stabbed her repeatedly until, finally, unconscious, she was left for dead.

Hsia Yu-min returned to Peking, and not long after, all those who had participated were stigmatized as: "May 16th anti-revolutionary, extreme leftist rabble-rousers." In a fierce "struggle meeting," Hsia Yu-min was sent to the New Birth Agricultural Camp in Ch'ing-hai (Kokonor), for five years of hard labor. He was released on account of his good behavior, and in view of the fact that he had performed only medical services at the uprisings.

Though they let him go, he was not allowed to re-enroll in the Peking Medical School, he was not issued a residence permit for Peking, nor was there any job open to him. Since he had studied medicine, the authorities sent him to a county in the outlying hilly suburbs to instruct fledgling "barefoot doctors." When he arrived there he was turned away as soon as they learned of his involvement in the May 16th affair. No one wanted him, and there was nowhere to find work, to earn a living, or to secure food rations. He had become one of the superfluous men in China.

Big Gun Hsü heard about his situation and told him: "You

should write a letter to the State Council, and to Premier Chou." But Chuko Liang shook his head and said, "Any more trouble from you, and you will be sent back to Ch'ing-hai. You had better join us!"

Hsia Yu-min was of medium height, thin and pale, cool and collected in crises, and to look at him, one would say he had a certain style. With these traits, he was much in demand as a spokesman and liaison man.

There was one incident, a story still recounted, which everybody laughed about when they heard it.

Half a year ago, Hsia Yu-min and Tall Man Li had delivered a big bundle of goods to Tan-tung City in Liaoning Province. In the package there were fabrics of silk and some bronze bowls, items much in demand among the people of that area. After they got off the train, they discovered that the railway security guards at the exit were diligently checking the luggage of each passenger. Both were wearing a "money" belt in which they carried watches and rings of pure gold. If caught, not only would both of them be sent away for ten years, but their entire band of cohorts would be ruined.

Hsia Yu-min had on a dark blue woolen Mao jacket and carried a black leather briefcase. Tall Man Li wore a blue cloth Mao jacket and although he was holding a bundle, he still looked neat and presentable. At the critical moment, Hsia Yu-min did not get in line but walked coolly to the side of the exit where the inspector in chief stood, and pointing to Tall Man Li, he said, "He is my guard. Do we have to be inspected too?"

The inspector stood at attention and gave them a military salute. He opened a small side gate, and let them walk out.

After this incident, Tall Man Li really thought that he had become Hsia Yu-min's guard, but if anyone else said so, he would be in for a fight.

Tall Man Li also admired Chuko Liang. In the days after Premier Chou En-lai's death, he had been stricken and saddened. At the Ch'ing-ming Festival, he had taken a large flower wreath of paper, asked Hsia Yu-min to write a poem in commemoration, and had placed it himself at the Memorial Plaque for the People's Heroes in T'ien-an Men Square. He insisted that his wreath be placed highest of all, but the self-appointed group that kept order thought this would spoil the over-all aesthetic effect, and an argument ensued. His height, as well as the dagger he took out, made it hard for anyone to back down. Luckily, Chuko Liang spoke a few words of counsel at his side, and managed to calm him down.

Afterward, Chuko Liang sent out an emergency notice, instructing his comrades-in-arms to observe the following orders: "First, in the next few days, no one is allowed to go to T'ien-an Men Square; second, everyone is to stay at home for the next few days and make frequent appearances at the local police station, just to show your face."

Indeed, the morning of the second day after Chuko Liang's emergency notice, an incident occurred in front of T'ien-an Men Square. In every building and in every street, the police conducted a thorough search, requiring everyone to explain where they had been on April 5, and to produce an alibi. Thanks to the foresight of Chuko Liang, none of the members of the gang had anything to worry about, including Tall Man Li, who even received the praise of the Police Records officer. "On this occasion, you have certainly maintained the right position. Very good."

Soon after this, General Chu Teh passed away, and the Chairman became indisposed and could not receive any foreign visitors. This prompted another warning from Chuko Liang:

"Exercise the utmost caution. Should the sun leave to join the Almighty, it would be the most trying and the most vulnerable moment for us, and this moment is fast upon us. In order to avoid complications, parcel out the accumulated merchandise to different storage sites in secure locations; those who do not have residence permits must keep a low profile. Do not show your face outside."

83

What Chuko Liang anticipated occurred, and almost at once.

That afternoon, Young Tiger was holding buckets at the water pump at the end of the street. This was one of the household chores he performed every day. He managed his buckets in such a way that, no sooner had one iron-rimmed bucket been filled than another took its place, and with such deftness that not a drop of water was spilled. Young Tiger enjoyed these feats of dexterity and smiled to himself. His eyes met Old Man Chou, who was in charge of the water pump on this day, and he noticed he was tense and panicky.

Old Man Chou stood at the wall two meters away from the water pump; he was listening to the radio from a small window on the wall above.

"Is this another earthquake?"

The bucket filled with water, and Young Tiger lifted it up. An old woman, who had been standing behind him, moved up to take his place.

"Old Man Chou, what have you heard?"

"It was an announcement from the highest echelons, but I cannot make it out. Sounds like someone passed away."

Many aging leaders in China had died recently, and Young Tiger did not pay much attention to Old Man Chou. He lifted the buckets and headed for home. As he poured the water into the large storage jar, he heard a commotion in the courtyard. Mother Ch'i, who was putting a fresh piece of coal into the fire and poking around in the ashes, stood up, aghast.

❖ ❖ ❖

There had been that one night in the summer of 1976, when it had been pouring outside. Suddenly, the house had shaken violently, the paper on the ceiling had torn into hundreds of pieces, and the thick brown earth covering the roof had come crashing down like rain. Young Tiger had wakened in the darkness. The shelves had fallen down, and the bottles and cans in the cabinet had rattled about. He had covered his head with a thin blanket and had sat up. What was going on? Was it raining that hard? Perhaps three days and three nights of incessant rain had soaked through the underpinnings of the house, and it was about to fall. Mother Ch'i had run to his bedside and the two of them had held each other tightly through the tremors. There seemed no end to it. The ground had trembled, the houses had shaken, and the beams had seemed about to break. Things had crashed down, and the world had seemed to be coming to an end. Could anyone survive?

Suddenly it was still. The trembling had stopped, the houses were left intact, the beams in their places. It had been raining and there had been the sound of water leaking. Young Tiger had groped for the electric switch; to his surprise, the light went on. It looked as though a bomb had burst.

Still in shock, they had heard screams from the courtyard, cries of terror and despair. Young Tiger was never to forget those outcries. And he would never in his life wish to hear that sound again.

◇　◇　◇

But now in the courtyard, he heard the cries once more, and the sound of wailing. Another earthquake? No, it was something else.

Young Tiger bolted out of the door. The inhabitants of the compound were crowded outside the northern and western wings. Several old women were crouched on the ground, wailing. The door to the main room in the north wing was wide open, and several men gathered there around the radio. Their faces were grave.

"The Chairman is dead!" Young Tiger realized suddenly what was happening. "The Chairman is dead!"

No one said anything. Perhaps it was grief. Or they were just numbed by the news.

Everyone had, of course, a different reason for his grief. Old Man Chou was now an activist in the neighborhood; ten or more years ago he had been a model citizen who had donated his house to the state. But at this moment, years of pain welled up in his heart. He thought of the old days, when he had been a bank manager. He had sent his two daughters abroad, and the Liberation came just as he retired. He had lived through thick and thin and had survived everything, up to now. War lords, the Japanese occupation, recovery and victory, Liberation and Revolution, he had seen them all. Now that the Chairman was dead, what other changes were in store, and would he be able to live through them?

He had once coveted material things. A house, some furniture, all the things that meant comfort for him and raised his status in the eyes of others. But in recent years, after the Red Guards had ransacked each house and confiscated all the valuables, he felt differently about material goods. Then there was the big earthquake, when people had been ordered outdoors and not permitted to go back home. He took out only a small chair, opened an umbrella, and sat in the street for fifteen days and nights. Suddenly, he came to a realization. He did not need anything, not one thing, except to survive.

The great benefactor, Chairman Mao, had succeeded in converting Old Man Chou from a bank manager into someone who cared only for survival, but now the Chairman had himself failed to survive. Old Man Chou was uneasy, for he feared that the demise of the Chairman forfeited his own chances for survival.

But the others who gathered around the radio did not think this way. They belonged to levels of society that had had no place before the Liberation. What should they do, now that the Chairman was dead? The sun may stop shining, but the Chairman should not die, for who was to lead them now? The Chairman was omniscient; he had never made a mistake. If, in recent years, one could no longer say this, it was because the Chairman himself was modest. Everyone knew in his heart that the Chairman was a genius, not to be found again in ten thousand years. He was the helmsman of the Chinese people, their teacher, and their commander. No praise could express the respect and awe in which they held him. The Chairman was dead. Who was there to put the finger on such villains as Liu Shao-ch'i, Lin Piao, Teng Hsiao-p'ing? What would they do when other villains appeared on the scene?

◈ ◈ ◈

Young Tiger raced ahead for the Tung-tan Station, just managing to catch the Number 20 bus. He looked out the window, his throat and eyes constricted. Everything was unsettling.

The traffic policemen were already wearing black armbands. Those from the People's Militia who had stood with such pomp on the street corners the night before were now solemnly lined up by the walls, wearing black armbands and looking deflated.

The bus passed by Nan Ch'ih-tzu ("The Southern Pond"), turned left along the edge of T'ien-an Men Square, and headed for Ch'ien-men ("Front Gate"). There was not a soul on the Square. All around it, the Militia were standing guard, and they let no one in.

When the bus reached Ta Tsa-lan ("The Big Fence"), Young Tiger got off and walked through the familiar byways.

◈ ◈ ◈

Ta Tsa-lan used to be the most prosperous area in the Outer City of Peking. It was also the only part of the city in which the streets did not run in a north-south, east-west direction. In this commercial area, there were large buildings several hundred years old, as well as sizable high-rise commercial buildings constructed fifty years ago. But the majority of the houses were small, two- or three-story structures built out of wood and brick. During the "Dig Deep the Tunnels" movement, an intricate network of underground passages had been dug out underneath these streets and these buildings. It became a model for the whole country, and received the praise of visiting representatives from every province.

Unfortunately, Heaven did not smile on this enterprise.

Something unheard of happened. The big earthquake had erupted in North China, and it had not only destroyed these underground streets which had taken tens of thousands of people one year to build, but it had also damaged the streets and buildings on the surface, killing or injuring a great many people in their sleep. Streets above the underground tunnels had collapsed and buildings had been left in shambles. Secretary Hu of the Peking Revolutionary Committee had visited the sites with his aides in sedan cars, and had made a speech to residents who had been living in the open for a week or more, saying repeatedly that this was *only* a natural disaster; whoever suggested that this might be a human disaster would be spreading propaganda against the Chairman and the Revolution. He went on to say that natural disasters could be easily overcome, since man could conquer the elements, and so on.

After the bodies had been extricated from the ruins, the people were allowed to return to see what was left of their homes. The underground network was no longer of value as a showpiece, and it had been abandoned. There were so many government buildings and high-rise residences for foreign visitors that needed repair, that the houses of the common people had to wait. Some suggested that a new Ta Tsa-lan be constructed, the old houses demolished, and a brand-new, well-planned commercial area put in their place. This meant that all the repair work would have to be deferred.

Secretary Hu, who had been in charge of construction for the underground system, had become known throughout the country for his achievement. He had caught the eye of the Central Committee, which considered him a model for carrying out the theories of Chairman Mao. In the past few years he had been promoted a number of times, and he was about to be appointed Chairman of the Standing Committee of the People's Congress. Now, he was very busy. How would he have time to supervise more? So the residents in the area were pawned off on district revolutionary committees, and they had suffered from the "three negligences." The area was not governed by neighborhood organizations, nor regulated by the Police Registry, nor controlled by Militia. An old rope cordoned off the area, and wooden placards were set up, with writing one could barely see. On closer inspection, they read: "No entry!"

◈ ◈ ◈

Young Tiger squirreled his way through this area, familiar grounds to him, through the door of a roofless house, then out the back door, emerging into an opening of broken walls and rubble. He zigzagged on, leaping over and crawling under, finally reaching what had once been a three-story building. Amid piles of broken brick, he proceeded down some steps, pushed open a door, and entered the gang's headquarters.

Young Tiger took for granted that those inside had not heard the shocking news. There were only two people in the front room. Tall Man Li sat beside the small charcoal burner, eating some potatoes he had just baked, and Hsia Yu-min leaned against a seat under the skylight, absorbed in his book. Hsia's lips moved silently, and without a glance at Young Tiger, he kept reading.

"Have you heard the news?" Young Tiger said.

There was no reaction, so now he played his trump card to attract their attention: "The Chairman is dead!"

Tall Man Li wrapped up his leftover potato skins and flung them through the broken glass of the skylight. Carelessly he said, "We heard the news."

"If you throw your garbage out like that," Hsia Yu-min said, without raising his head, "people will know where we are."

Young Tiger stood there, crushed. These creatures had no feelings, even at the death of the Chairman.

Young Tiger wanted to puncture them a bit. He did not dare try anything with Tall Man because he would have simply lifted Young Tiger up and thrown him out. Hsia Yu-min was too refined, and he would not have lifted a finger. Lately he had been working very hard on his Japanese, not only listening to short-wave broadcasts, but reading used copies of Japanese books. Young Tiger knew why he was studying Japanese, because Big Gun Hsü had inadvertently let something slip out. Hsia Yu-min often went to Chilin (Kirin) on assignment, and since he had good rapport with the underground organization there, he had got wind of a way to get out of the country.

Since the re-establishment of diplomatic relations between China and Japan, many Japanese women who had stayed in China had applied to return home and were permitted to repatriate with their immediate families, including husband and children. The "organization" in Chilin exploited this channel. They inserted the names of revolutionary youths into the lists of the immediate families of the applicants, and they managed to switch identities. The heads of the households would swear that these youths were their own children, who had been raised by others in times of economic difficulty. In this way, they contrived to leave the country and flee safely to Japan. When they arrived there, they organized new People's Revolutionary Groups, and with refugees in Hong Kong, as well as with revolutionary youths who were recent émigrés to Canada, they promoted propaganda campaigns abroad calling for a new revolution.

Hsia Yu-min had already checked out the escape route for himself and was waiting for the right moment. In the meantime, he was studying diligently.

Young Tiger found a place to sit down and said coldly, "You don't want to be Chinese, do you? Of course you would not be upset by the news of the Chairman's death!"

Hsia Yu-min blinked his eyes, shifted his gaze from the book to Young Tiger, then turned back to the book. He remained silent so long that Young Tiger did not think he was going to answer, but then he said, calmly, his eyes never leaving the book:

"To wail and moan in order to show my concern and to prove that I am Chinese through and through. Is that what you want?"

"How can you be so cynical? He was at least the leader of the Chinese people!"

"Ah! Do you think he was an effective leader?"

"Without him, would there be a Party, a Liberation Army, a new China?"

"Poor Young Tiger, your thinking is tainted by the poison of Lin Piao and Ch'en Po-ta. It is not really your fault. That is all you could know from what you were taught growing up."

"But in any event, he was certainly a great leader."

"There are two parts to that claim: one, that he was a 'leader'; and two, that he was 'great.'

"To judge a person, one should judge his final achievement. It is true that until the last minute of his life, he was still the leader, but what kind of leader was he? Do eight hundred million Chinese love him in their hearts? No, the majority of them only pretend to in order to survive! As the Party leader, why is it that several of his personally designated heirs later turned against him? Why is it that central authority is splintered just now into different factions? Why cannot the various central and local authorities co-operate with each other? Why is it that the powers that be in the Party are all members of his family? This is the People's Republic of China, but he has transformed a country of the people's democratic hegemony into a family-ruled, Socialist-fascist dictatorship. Is that what you call being a good leader?"

Hsia Yu-min sat upright, and closed the book.

"Secondly, do you think he was great? In his drive to regain power, he launched the Cultural Revolution, and exploited the youth in order to destroy for him the various vestigial power bases in the Party, the government, and the military. But once he had acquired power, he retracted the right to rebel and used military troops to suppress the young revolutionaries. In less than two years, he took the power of the army and crushed Lin Piao, who had once served him as its head. Then, for fear that the rest of the army would not obey him, he reinstalled Teng Hsiao-p'ing. First he made Teng Vice-Chairman of the Military Affairs Committee, then he used him to shake up the commanders of the ten military regions, to weaken their hold on the provinces and to prevent them from becoming local hegemons. When this strategy was accomplished, he took Teng Hsiao-p'ing down. Someone like this, how can you claim he was great?"

Young Tiger knew what he said could be true, so he had no choice but to lower his head and listen.

"Young Tiger, think about it. Why are we sitting here? Why are we jobless? Why are we trafficking in illegal goods in the black market? Do we really want to do this?

"The people who used to live right here, did they really want to dig in the ground below to build air-raid shelters? Did they really want to see their families crushed to death under the debris of their own crumbling houses? Do they really want to be packed up and shipped out by train to the villages of Shansi Province as part of the 'residential relocation' program?

"You tell me, Young Tiger, how many people in China would say what is in their hearts? Can you share what you think in your heart with your father, your mother, your brothers and sisters? Can you confide in your classmates, in your friends?"

"Isn't my situation different?" Young Tiger asked, his face flushed in confusion.

"You are not the only one. How many unregistered families are there in Peking? At least two hundred thousand. And what about those who are registered? Do they have nothing to complain about? How many of them are there?"

"The way you see it, is there going to be another big revolution in China?"

"It is not impossible. Now, revolutions come and go, but people are still people, and leaders always ride on the backs of the people."

"What point is there, then, to revolution?" Having heard what Hsia Yu-min said, Young Tiger lost heart.

"In order to raise the cultural standards of the people in general, the more people who are educated, the greater the power of democracy. After a certain stage, the policy of deceiving the people will not work. Only at that moment will there be a meaningful liberation."

"What you say may take many years."

"The day when the 'Four Modernizations'† are achieved is the day when the true turnaround, the true revolution of the people, takes place. It is not far off."

"The 'Four Modernizations'? Will I live to see the day? At the moment, I cannot even manage to put clothes on my back." Young Tiger looked through the opening in the skylight.

"Tall Man Li, find him something to wear."

Tall Man Li stood up, then bent down to enter an inside room. He lifted up a big wooden board, to reveal a room below. Young Tiger went down after him, stepping gingerly. The stairs were steep, and it was pitch dark. A dank, clammy wind whistled by. Tall Man Li turned on the switch. Originally this had been part of the underground street that the local residents had dug out, which had been blocked up in the earthquake and not used since. This was the perfect place for the secret storage room in the new headquarters.

From one of the wooden chests piled up on the side, Tall Man Li took out a military uniform made of cotton. Young Tiger said, "But it is still autumn, and cotton clothing . . ."

"What difference does it make whether it is autumn or winter? If it covers your ass it will have to do. Do you want it?"

◇ ◇ ◇

Young Tiger now wore the cotton uniform and sauntered along Ch'ang-an Avenue. He also wore a waistbelt around his middle, a gift from Hsiao Ta-yung. The jacket was a bit large and looked incongruous on his slender frame, but he did not

† "Four Modernizations": from the January 1975 speech by Chou En-lai before the Fourth People's Congress, in which he proclaimed "modernization" in four areas: industry; agriculture; national defense; and science and technology—TRANSLATOR.

93

mind. He was wondering whether he should return to the production commune or to the headquarters beyond the Ch'ien-men.

He heard at his rear the loud scream of sirens. He turned to look. What a huge procession! One vehicle after another, type-3, deluxe "Red Flag" sedans, whipped by. He could not make out who was inside. People stood agog on the street. After the "Red Flag" sedans went by, ten "Shanghai"-model cars moved majestically down Ch'ang-an Avenue toward the west.

Ten meters behind these cars, four or five hotshots on bicycles followed in the wake of the entourage, causing the traffic policemen to yell and wave them off. The people who had a moment ago craned their necks in astonishment laughed heartily at this spectacle.

Young Tiger had never had a bike of his own. As he watched these youngsters fly by, his heart flew off with them as they pursued the fast disappearing cars.

FIVE

Sunday, February 10   3:30 p.m.

       Ch'en Yi-min closed his notebook and looked up at a big map hung on the wall. Yu, head of the section in the Department of Petrochemical Industries, was reviewing productivity in the petroleum industry last year and projecting a growth rate for the next year in the fifth Five-Year Economic Development Plan. He had put up this map to make things clearer for the audience.

  From the briefing and discussions just held, Ch'en Yi-min saw a torrent of "black gold" gushing from the derricks that dotted the basins, steppes, plains, and offshore areas, rushing through well-maintained pipelines that extended throughout the provinces, pumped through under great pressure, and distributed to the huge up-to-date refineries in every part of the land.

The meeting hall, as large as a basketball court, was located on the second floor of a building in an imposing bureaucratic complex that ran along the edge of a three-mile river in the western part of Peking. The complex housed many of the central offices of national organizations, such as the National Economic Planning Commission, the National Commission on Science and Technology, the National Commission for Major Construction, the National Bureau of Statistics, and the First, Second, and Sixth Departments of Mechanical Industries. This whole area, known as the Three Departments and the Six Commissions, had become the control center of the entire country, regulating economics, industry, and construction.

The hall was rather empty. Only about ten secretarial cadres attached to various department heads and to the Vice-Premier were still there. Their heads were bent over their desks as they sorted out the notes and documents of the meeting just concluded. The executives had all moved into an adjacent room to the right, for relaxation and informal conversation. There were long tables set up on which were scattered empty cigarette packs, teacups and teapots, pieces of crumpled paper, and ash trays piled high with butts.

Nearly four hundred people were attending this national convention, and the meeting hall had been filled to capacity. But after the meeting, people had left in droves, and there was now only the sound of a few old janitors cleaning up.

Ch'en Yi-min sat on the left of the chairman's place, staring at the map. He was thirty-six years old, but there was already some gray at his temples. His physique was spare, and his back was slightly hunched: he showed no resemblance to what he looked like sixteen years ago when he had been the outstanding athlete on the basketball team of the Manchurian Industrial College.

Since graduation, he had been assigned to the Planning Commission in Peking. He sat at his desk day and night, searching for discrepancies in the data that was piled on his desk, and checking out figures. He had not even the leisure to stretch his legs, let alone play basketball.

Taciturn, hard-working, and unassuming, Ch'en assumed the responsibilities others sloughed off with a patience and diligence that soon earned him the nickname "Camelback." He accepted it good-naturedly, for he had a generous character and was well-liked.

Camelback also had his love interest, which came as a surprise to many of his co-workers. What was more surprising was that Camelback, at 6'2", married a co-worker "Little Miss Li," who stood a mere 4'4". The discrepancy in their heights made it clear to everyone exactly why Camelback was so hunched over.

Not long after his marriage, he was transferred to the Secretariat and became Deputy Secretary. He had seniority in the Party and was one of the most loyal among the "faithful," and he was designated Executive Secretary, adding more to his heavy workload.

The nation was affected by political disturbances at the start of the seventies; and industry, mining, and transportation, as well as major construction projects, had encountered disruptions of one kind or another. The job of striking a new balance among the nation's resources, capital, and output (which had lost any semblance of co-ordination), and of implementing new economic measures throughout the country, had required maximum patience and care if anything were to be accomplished. Besides preparing statistical materials for meetings that his boss, Li Fu-ch'un, would attend, Ch'en had to stay after the meetings, which often lasted until three or four in the morning, to collate and collect the materials as well as to prepare the minutes. On these occasions he could not go back to his dormitory, but had to rig up a board in his office as a bed. He had worked for five years in this way when Vice-Premier and Chairman Li Fu-ch'un, old and suffering from a long-standing illness, had passed away. His successor, Chairman Hsü, did not change a thing, so Ch'en Yi-min had continued to serve as Executive Secretary and had maintained his eighteen-hour work schedule.

The meeting just held was for the purpose of reviewing the actual performance of national economic construction since April of the previous year, and to plan key economic measures for implementation nationwide as part of the fifth Five-Year Plan. The meeting was to set industrial production goals and major construction targets for each region and for each department, as well as agricultural production quotas for each province.

At first, everybody had been in a depressed mood. There had been drought in the north and floods in the south the year before, as well as recent abnormalities in the climate. In addition, the North China region had just sustained a series of earthquakes, and both industry and agriculture had suffered major setbacks. Even after a national meeting had been held to promote the example of "Learn from Tachai," there were still many agricultural cadres who did not understand the spirit of the Central Committee policy. On the contrary, they had adopted an extreme leftist posture of their own and absorbed into the communes the peasant-owned plots and domestic livestock. They had also reduced the work-point credits for each production team, to augment the public funds of the communes for the purchase of more agricultural machinery. They had wanted to put this short-term crash program into effect to accomplish the long-term goal of mechanizing agriculture. The idea was sound, but they went astray in carrying it out, and the results had been the exact opposite of what they had hoped for.

As a result, the peasants had lost a sense of working morale, and even young and able-bodied peasants would leave for the cities. This naturally had affected the mood of peasants in other areas, and the total volume of agricultural productivity had been reduced for the year.

Since 75 per cent of the population in China was engaged in

agricultural production, its policy was the key problem of the total economy. Therefore, this conference was being closely watched by the central authorities. It was attended not only by Chang Ch'un-ch'iao, Vice-Premier and Standing Member of the Politburo (who also delivered an address), but also by Ch'en Yung-kuei, currently Vice-Premier, who had himself come from peasant origins.

One point emerged clearly from the conference: theories that looked good on the drawing board would not work in practice. What was needed was a core of commune cadres who understood the spirit behind the guidelines, and who could adapt them to the local conditions and determine what were workable methods of implementation. Commune members would have to understand right from wrong, and possess the highest qualities of selfless, public-spirited devotion, and co-operate closely with their leaders. Such a commune, if developed over a period of years, fortified with national subsidies, supported with manpower from surrounding communes, could conceivably become a model for the country, but it would be difficult to achieve on a national scale. After the debacle of the plan advocated by former Premier Teng Hsiao-p'ing at the last national conference, no one dared put forth a new plan now. They could only hope that the theoreticians would recognize their own errors when current realities exposed them.

The VIPs left on the third day of the conference. Staying behind was Vice-Premier Li Hsien-nien, who had always been in charge of financial and fiscal problems. He had pared down the unrealistic demands of some departments, and he had pressured others to accept the necessary production quotas. Chairman Hsü, who had originally chaired the meeting, was greatly relieved to have the Vice-Premier take over. "When an old general saunters forth, he is worth ten of any other."

❖ ❖ ❖

As Ch'en Yi-min gazed at the map, Secretary Ko stuck his head in the door of the meeting hall and yelled out, "Secretary

Ch'en. Telephone call." Ch'en Yi-min picked up his notebook and ran out the door. Secretary Ko was still standing in the corridor by the door, and with a meaningful look, he said: "It's on line number three."

There were three telephones on Chairman Hsü's desk. The first was used for internal communications by the Planning Commission, and did not connect with the outside. The second was specifically for outside calls. When these two phones rang, the extension also rang in the secretaries' office, and could be answered by any one of four secretaries. But the third line was special—it did not ring, but flashed a red light. The switchboard for this line was not located in the central telephone office, but in a heavily guarded building on the Yü-ch'üan ("Jade Springs") Road in the western suburb. Maintenance and repair at this station were handled by the military. This line was used exclusively as a tie-line linking up the offices and residences of key people, members of the Politburo, members of the Military Affairs Committee, standing members of the People's Congress, commanders of the various armed services, as well as the Peking lodgings of the regional military commanders, the Premier and the Vice-Premiers of the State Council, department heads, and heads of various commissions. It was a top-secret line; in the Planning Commission, aside from Chairman Hsü, only Ch'en Yi-min was permitted to answer it.

Ch'en Yi-min rushed into the chairman's office. The red light was flashing insistently; he picked up the receiver and spoke in a mechanical tone.

"This is Ch'en Yi-min of the Planning Commission. Chairman Hsü is attending a meeting. May I ask who is speaking, please?"

"Is Vice-Premier Li there?"

"Yes, but he is also at the meeting."

"Please ask him to come to the telephone. It is an emergency. Hurry."

Ch'en Yi-min knew that it was Deputy Secretary Ho Yi-ming of the Secretariat Office of the Party Central Committee. He had developed a knack for recognizing voices when answering calls from high officials unwilling or disinclined to identify themselves.

Ch'en Yi-min opened the thick wooden door that connected the chairman's office and the lounge, and entered the smoke-filled room.

The lounge was for use by officials and cadres at the level of vice-department chief or higher who had come to attend the meetings. On the side facing the street were high arched windows, four by three meters, and outside a long balcony extended to both ends of the building. The stone balustrades were still covered with snow.

Twenty plush sofas were arranged in an ellipse, and on the tables beside them were porcelain teacups and ash trays of fine ceramic.

Vice-Premier Li Hsien-nien sat with his back toward the center window, engaged in discussion with the Deputy Chief of the Department of Foreign Trade about the question of gasoline and its future fluctuations on the international market. Ch'en Yi-min walked to the back of the seat, bent down, and whispered something. Vice-Premier Li raised his eyebrows and smiled.

"Ah! The telephone catches up with me even here." He walked to the adjacent office, asking as he went, "Where is the telephone? Would you show me?"

Ch'en Yi-min ran ahead into the room and handed the receiver to the Vice-Premier. He then backed up and stood near the door.

"Yes. It is I! What? . . . You cannot come here? . . . What has happened? . . . Is that true? . . . Why are you not calling a meeting? . . . Ah! I understand. Right . . . Thank you."

The Vice-Premier's voice had become hollow and limp. He gently hung up the phone and gripped the table with both hands. He looked as if he were going to faint.

Ch'en Yi-min rushed over and held up the old man, now past seventy, who was customarily so robust.

Vice-Premier Li brushed aside his helping hand, and

straightened up. Signs of fatigue and dejection showed on a face usually proud and implacable. He turned, opened the white satin drapes, and with some strain pushed open the high windows, which had not been opened for a long time. The wind ruffled his full head of white hair, but he strode out onto the balcony, and stared toward the northwest.

Ch'en Yi-min went to the adjoining room to find Chairman Hsü.

"Sir, could you come to your office for a moment? Vice-Premier Li is waiting."

Chairman Hsü was startled to find Vice-Premier Li on the balcony without an overcoat. He asked Ch'en Yi-min to fetch an overcoat, and told him to bring in Li's secretary, Old Wang.

Ch'en Yi-min rushed out and grabbed his own overcoat as well as Secretary Ko's heavy cotton parka. When he re-entered the office, Chairman Hsü was standing at the Vice-Premier's side.

After handing the overcoats to Chairman Hsü, Ch'en Yi-min went to look for Secretary Wang in the general lounge. He was there, watching color television, along with other secretaries of department heads. Ch'en Yi-min moved up to his side and pulled at his sleeve. The savvy Secretary Wang understood immediately and followed him out.

In the office, they saw Chairman Hsü still standing on the balcony, along with Vice-Premier Li. Both of them had coats wrapped around their shoulders and were gazing out toward the northwest.

Facing the west of the building was the Yü-yüan T'an ("Pond of the Jade Depths") Park. The park site was originally a patch of marshland where wild birds gathered in virgin woods. After the Liberation, the people had enlarged the basin bottom, expanded the pond into two star-shaped lakes, one large and one small, and planted fruit trees and flowers. Every summer and autumn, it makes for a beautiful scene.

But now that it was winter, the water was frozen, and the trees bare. Ch'en Yi-min and Secretary Wang stood behind the window to block out the cold wind. They looked through the glass at the two men, who seemed unapproachable in their solemn discourse.

Were they looking off at the foreign visitors' quarters? Yes, that was it toward the northwest, an extensive area formerly known as the "Fishing Pier" (Tiao-yü T'ai). In 1958, that barren land had been transformed into an exquisite park, interspersed with magnificent two-story dwellings, each built in the style of a country house.

Every building was a triumph of craftsmanship. Each was designed by an architect from a different country, reflecting the style of that country. The appointments inside were handcrafted by Chinese workmen to duplicate the national styles. No expense or labor was spared to achieve comfort and beauty. Unfortunately, these residences were seldom occupied. Groundskeepers and custodians had dutifully cleaned these buildings inside and out for eighteen years, even though they were usually empty. The Russian-style building had once been occupied by Khrushchev, but it had stood empty ever since. The Indonesian residence housed Sukarno on one visit. And Nehru's daughter, would she come back? Who was to tell? When Nixon came some years ago, one more construction was undertaken. When Tanaka visited Peking, it was suggested that a golf course be added. Some thirty families living behind the guesthouse had to be moved away, and the flat spots were graded to form hills and traps. Suddenly, construction stopped and the plans were abandoned.

Is it possible that unexpected guests had arrived? Is that what caused these two top officials to pay such particular attention? If so, why the long faces?

As Ch'en Yi-min tried to figure it out, Hsü muttered to Li: "Our comrades are waiting for the summation of the meeting. We had better go back in."

Vice-Premier Li did not hear. He had transcended any interest in the present. Staring at the distance, where the mist rose from the mountains, he saw forty thousand tired troops and countless families following in the Long March of some forty years earlier. They had been fighting for over a month, walking a route stained by their own blood, and they had arrived within sight of the Yellow River at Chin-yüan county in Kansu Province. In front of them was the river. Following fast on their heels were the two cavalry detachments of the war lords Ma Pu-fang and Ma Pu-ch'ing, who had earned their reputation as cutthroats. The two detachments pressed close on three sides, and cannon smoke rose in the distance. At that time, he had stood on top of a hill, wondering what to do next.

He had been thirty-one years old. Crossing the Yellow River then was to step into the present now. Yet the river of destiny before him today had its own treacherous currents: on it were rafts of "shrimp-boat" soldiers and "crab-shelled" generals thrashing about while many veteran campaigners had drowned in the waters. How ironic that Madame Mao's adopted name should be Chiang Ch'ing; ironic that her name should mean "Blue River." How many more times must comrades struggle through the poisonous currents of Chiang Ch'ing's river of turbulence? He was now past seventy; could he fight to cross such a heavy toll-taking river once again?

No, it would not do to retreat. He would not betray the achievements of the Revolution, bought with the lives of so many. Now it was no longer a problem of forty thousand or fifty thousand crossing the river. It was a matter of eight hundred million people struggling on the road to well-being.

As soon as Li came into the room Ch'en pulled down the window and drew the satin drapes. He heard Vice-Premier Li on the telephone: he was using line number three.

He was summoning people together. He called the Department of Foreign Affairs, the Military Affairs Committee, the Department of Public Security, the Peking Military Command, as well as many department heads not represented at today's meeting. It looked as if he were setting up an emergency meeting.

Vice-Premier Li turned to the three people who had been standing beside him:

"You had better go to the conference room and stay there for a while. Do not let anyone leave. No matter how important their other appointments, make them stay. Tell them I said so. And you, Secretary Wang, prepare some hot tea for everyone. Also, tell the people outside to stick around. Ch'en Yi-min, you watch and do not let anyone interrupt our meeting. Now go."

There was the sound of a car halting at the gate. A gust of cold wind carried in the sound of voices and the clatter of footsteps. Six people walked in: the one in front Ch'en Yi-min recognized as Ch'iao Kuan-hua, the Minister of Foreign Affairs.

When the newly arrived dignitaries were seated in the lounge, Vice-Premier Li began to speak.

"Thirty minutes ago, I was called to the telephone. Let's not worry about who it was; take my word for it, it was someone reliable. He told me that information has been leaked to him that several military commands and several departments in the central government have banded together and are plotting a coup. Now, I have gathered all of you here to determine if there is any truth to these accounts."

All the people in the room froze. Ch'en Yi-min was concerned that plans for national economic construction, lately agreed upon, would be disrupted by still another nationwide cataclysm. What was going to happen now?

Foreign Minister Ch'iao broke the silence:

"Which section is responsible for getting this intelligence?"

"Division 8341."

"Is there anyone or anything to corroborate this?"

"Not that we know of."

"The bosses of the Cultural Revolution faction—what are they planning to do?"

"The People's Militia will take over the various departments of the central government, and they will be totally responsible for maintaining law and order in the country."

Silence again.

Ch'en Yi-min recalled the big upheaval in February 1967. Red Guards with armbands, led by a few building janitors, mail clerks, and some office personnel, had taken over the important offices, had absconded with the official seals, and had established the so-called "Revolutionary Committees." Disregarding previously promulgated directives, they had signed orders in the name of the National Planning Commission, seemingly at will, requisitioning goods and materials from national storehouses, and creating havoc in production and construction.

The most regrettable act of that mindless bunch of self-styled revolutionaries was that they had arrested the various heads of departments in the Planning Commission, and had applied tortures to extract confessions that admitted to links with the Liu and Teng anti-revolutionary clique. The majority of those arrested denied any connection, and every day in the courtyard of the Planning Commission offices, "struggle meetings" had been held. Some cadres in responsible positions had one hand tied to one foot, with the end of the rope fastened to a pole four meters long, which was raised by five or six people so that the victims were suspended in mid-air and spun around, the person bound looking like a dragonfly that children would tie to a chopstick, spinning around and flying about. This form of punishment was invented by the Red Guards in the early stages of the Cultural Revolution, and had remained a favorite form of entertainment. As the victim was spun around, his limbs would thrash about and after several turns, his body would be stretched taut. Someone came up with a very appropriate name for this, and called it "Flying an Airplane." Anyone who had experienced this routine would suffer irregularities in blood pressure or malfunctions of the heart. But in time, they would recuperate.

Political Commissar Sha, of the Peking Military Command, spoke up.

"On this matter, let me say a few words. Three weeks ago,

the Military Command received a strange printed document, which opposed the decision of the Politburo meeting held before the Chairman's death and after the T'ien-an Men Incident. This decision was made according to the document made when the Politburo members were intimidated by the presence in Peking of five hundred thousand of the People's Militia. The document demanded that Party organizations in each region agitate for new elections of representatives to the National Party Congress; they would in turn convene another meeting, at which a democratic vote would elect new Politburo members as well as new leaders of the Party and of the government. The document, after the political section of our Military Command had studied it initially, was sent to Commander Ch'en for his scrutiny. Along with the Department of Public Security, we have tried to uncover the source of this document, but because it was sent through internal communications, and because it was printed, that has proved extremely difficult. Deputy Chief Hsieh of Public Security and I have analyzed this question more than once. He asked me to keep this matter confidential, and so I did not divulge this information to any of the other departments. Whether any of this has anything to do with what is happening today, I leave for you all to determine."

All at once, several asked for permission to speak. The Finance Minister was first.

"We also received this document in our department, and we studied it discreetly in our own Party group, and later transmitted it to the Department of Public Security for further investigation. We know nothing else beyond this. And the Department of Public Security has not told us anything of what they might have found out."

"In our department," the head of the Railway Department said, "we received not only this document but also another letter, with the same printing, which we could not trace." He crushed out his cigarette in the ash tray, and continued in a low voice: "This letter demanded that we should not disrupt railway traffic when the revolutionaries rose up, nor should we refuse to let anyone without tickets board the trains."

"Was this letter given to Public Security for analysis?" Vice-Premier Li asked.

"Yes, of course, we sent it to them. All the offices in our department received a copy. Interesting that they should know exactly the structure of our department. Public Security sent some investigators over, collected forty-seven copies of the letter, and arrested two cadres."

"What for?"

"Because they posted this letter on the wall."

What the others said did not differ very much from what had been said. What surprised Ch'en Yi-min was that the Planning Commission did not receive these documents. And there was something else. It was absurd that the various departments of the government and of the military had come upon the same letter and that each had remained quiet about it until now. The document had had a wide circulation and had made a big impact.

Vice-Premier Li stood up, and looked around.

"With the Cultural Revolution, our thinking underwent yet one more great transformation, and we were made aware once more of our duties and responsibilities as Party members. Since the death of the Chairman, our responsibility is even greater. On the one hand, we must maintain the normal functions of our national institutions; and on the other, we must also nurture a new generation of successors who will adroitly direct the ship of state. This is where the future of China lies.

"In our country, the major task for the present is to recover from our recent calamities. The damages suffered in the earthquake have not yet been entirely repaired. When you add to that the death of the Chairman, it is no wonder that the people are disoriented. In this period, we should restrain ourselves from taking bold initiatives. The situation both at home and abroad requires that there be a stable center of political gravity in our country, as well as a period of peace. We definitely should not allow any coup at this time.

"Has anyone present participated in this movement? Step forward and explain your reasons. If the reasons are cogent, I too will join; everyone will join. If the reasons are fallacious, then the movement must stop. I personally guarantee that what transpires today will be held in the strictest confidence: do not worry, you will expose yourselves to no danger whatsoever."

The persuasiveness and the magnanimity of these words moved everyone. But no one said a word.

"I can confidently predict that among those here, there is no one capable of participating in this so-called coup d'état." Ch'iao Kuan-hua said this with a thoughtful air, his chin resting on his hand.

"A coup d'état normally means that the top leadership cannot resolve their contradictions, thus giving rise to political cataclysms. Most coups are resolved by military force. From the documents which we have just discussed, it is clear that the plotters will not be found among those present. The plotters are persons of reckless ambition and come from the masses. Their objective is clear. They hope to split the Party leadership, so that the two factions will be at odds with each other. They also want to see the military intercede in the conflict, causing a general anarchy which they can exploit.

"Why am I putting it this way? Because I have discovered their Achilles' heel. Where do they get the power to create chaos? It is not from the various departments of the central government, nor from the troops of the various military regions, but ultimately from the youth 'transferred downward' to every part of the country.

"They have betrayed their intentions in the letters to the Railway Department. They wanted the railway to guarantee free access to railroad transportation, so as to facilitate the influx of self-deluded youth into the city where they can incite insurrection."

Vice-Premier Li hit his fist against his palm but then he said in a low voice:

"I was told by the one who called me that Madame Chairman and her Cultural Revolution group are going to beat them to the punch and arrest some people."

"Which ones?" people asked in unison.

"Cadres who were attacked during the Cultural Revolution and the capitalist-roaders who have been attacked recently in the big-character posters."

"Looks like I'll be 'flying a plane' again!" Chairman Hsü said with a bitter smile.

"This is ridiculous. Vice-Premier Li, sir, my house has been ransacked once already. They did not leave me so much as a pair of pants. My old wife committed suicide. Is this all to happen again?" Secretary Hu lowered his head, tears streaming down his face.

"This matter should be reported at once to Ying Lao* and Commander Ch'en. They should show themselves and put a stop to all this. Sir, perhaps you should go to talk with them too." Everyone's eyes were on Li, as if he were their salvation.

"How am I to talk to them? Madame Chairman's group happens to think I am the leader of the coup, and I will be the first one they will arrest."

Everyone stood up, stunned, as if there were someone at the door to apprehend them. Some hastily picked up their pens and notebooks and made ready to leave.

"Quiet down. Don't panic. I will talk to them. Don't fall into the trap of the plotters, who want to sow dissension and distrust. This evening Premier Hua is scheduled to receive some Japanese friends at the Great Hall of the People. At that time, we can talk things over with him. Whoever wants to join us should meet us at nine-thirty in the Sinkiang Hall." It was Ch'iao Kuan-hua who spoke.

The meeting broke up.

Vice-Premier Li did not leave. He decided to stay and wait for the upshot of Ch'iao's conversation with Premier Hua. If he

* General Yien Chien-ying, Vice-Chairman of the Military Affairs Committee, affectionately known as "Ying Lao"—TRANSLATOR.

was to be arrested, let it be here. His wife would not survive another shock.

Ch'en Yi-min saw the officials out. When he returned, the door to the chairman's office was locked from the inside, but Chairman Hsü was not inside. He had been dragged off by Commissar Sha to see Commander Ch'en, to explain the situation.

The sound of an old man sobbing came from inside the office. This outburst mourned a lifetime of devotion to the Revolution, spanning fifty years, and now it had come to this. He was to be abandoned, mistrusted, and calumniated.

▧ SIX

Sunday, February 10   4:30 p.m.

The procession of cars sped along Tung-huan-pei Lu ("Ringing East Road, North Section") past the towering, handsome Agricultural Exhibition Hall and slow, donkey-drawn wagons in the streets. In the first "Red Flag" sedan sat Mr. Inada, the head of the Japanese economic delegation.

Mr. Inada was chairman of the Japanese Iron and Steel Association, a post he had held for many years, and he had visited Peking several times to participate in economic negotiations. On some of the previous occasions, he had been received by Premier Chou. In their candid talks, they had established a friendship based on mutual trust, understanding, and respect. But the Premier had now died, and Inada's visit was touched with a trace of nostalgia for former times.

There had been a send-off party and elaborate rituals and

ceremonies at his departure from the Tokyo Airport. Obayashi, the deputy head of the delegation, had politely but tenaciously discussed key points of the negotiation with him in the plane. Actually, these problems had already been decided two weeks ago at the meeting of the Economic Consortium, but judging from Obayashi's attitude, it appeared he wanted some revisions. Still, he had never said so openly, and Inada could not dismiss the policy without further consideration. All he could do was answer politely, and with no rest during the three hours on the plane, he felt especially tired.

Fortunately, there were no appointments scheduled until 7 P.M., when the welcoming dinner and reception were to be held. He could have a good rest and prepare himself for the first round of negotiations, to be held at two o'clock the next afternoon.

He closed his eyes, rested his head against the velvet seat back, and took a catnap.

◈ ◈ ◈

Sitting in the second "Red Flag" sedan was the deputy head of the delegation, Mr. Obayashi, president of the Bushito Association.

Although this was his second visit to Peking, Obayashi looked about excitedly. He customarily sat on the right-hand side of the back seat. Both side windows were covered with purple silk curtains, but because here in China people drove on the right side of the street, Obayashi had a clear view directly ahead.

The sharp-eyed Obayashi had observed that the traffic signals were still managed by manual control; they had not yet installed either a system of signal switches or a system of staggered lights. Probably, since there was not much traffic in Peking, and very few accidents, modernized traffic regulation systems were not thought necessary.

The cars turned right and entered the thoroughfare by the Chien-kuo Men ("Establishing-the-Nation Gate"), which was the eastward continuation of Ch'ang-an Avenue. Traffic suddenly increased in the well-proportioned, eight-lane thoroughfare. There were long buses painted red, trackless trolleys, trucks full of goods, and swarms of bicycles moving slowly ahead against a buffeting wind.

The procession of cars plunged into the crowd like a tiger into a sheepfold. The vehicles along the way moved over to the side, leaving the center lane free for the delegation's cars. Across the thoroughfare, Obayashi could see the T'ien-an Men tower, with its yellow tiles reflecting the rays of the setting sun.

Obayashi had noticed that in other countries the cities straightened out crooked roads and widened the avenues, but the buildings were of various heights and sizes, and showed a variety of styles and structures. They were neither uniform nor compatible; still, they stood as unmistakable symbols of individual freedom, the proliferation of competitive interests, and the acquisition of wealth. Always noteworthy were the eye-catching advertisements, signs that stimulated acquisitive instincts, venality, and a sense of personal self-aggrandizement.

But in the cityscape before him now, there was uniformity, flatness, and monotony. A sense of the self was overwhelmed in monolithic monochromes. Obayashi was secretly worried about his current mission.

◇ ◇ ◇

The last few sedans of the procession were the "compact" models of the "Shanghai" type. There were sounds of merriment and mischief in one of them, much to the annoyance of the Chinese driver.

Sitting at the driver's side was special correspondent Okamura of the Tokyo Economic News Agency. He was describing in detail the episode in which Watanabe, the solemn-faced reporter of the *Maiasa Shimbun*, had his tape recorder damaged.

Also in the back seat, between Watanabe and the youthful

Nakada, was a woman reporter, Kobako Nagashima, representing a well-known women's periodical in Japan. The purpose of her visit to Peking was to interview foreign women living in China. She had managed to promote this trip to her management only through her own persistence and perseverance. It was a surprise to her when she stepped from the airplane to find herself collared by reporter Okamura, an old acquaintance. He put her into a small car reserved for reporters, where she found herself surrounded by three senior Peking hands on their way to the Peking Hotel.

Kobako Nagashima was single and twenty-five years old. She had joined the staff of the magazine upon graduation from college, and was now assigned to writing about active women figures in social and diplomatic circles. Naturally, she paid attention to her clothing and make-up. Even though many knowledgeable people had admonished her before her departure for China to be simple in her dress, she thought she should keep her own style and not pretend to a simplicity she did not feel. The object of her mission was to interview the wives of the foreign diplomats from Europe, Asia, and Africa who lived in Peking. So her normal dress, she thought, would do nicely.

When reporter Nagashima, who thought of herself as very ordinary, appeared at the airport, the veteran reporters at the Peking airport took one look, and started vying with each other for the attention of this beautiful newcomer by offering her advice on how she could proceed with her assignment.

"That evening," Okamura resumed his story, "there was a cocktail party at the Embassy, where we expected the top-echelon Chinese to give speeches, so we arranged to meet in the afternoon at the International Club and go to the party together."

"The weather was somewhat hot, so we sat by the new swimming pool, sipping beer."

"That is enough," Okamura protested. "No need to make up

any more. Miss Nagashima, do you know how dull life is here? There are no night clubs, no Japanese restaurants, no bars, no golf courses. In addition to our work, aside from watching a movie that is changed only once a year, we can return to our rooms where we turn up our tape recorder and play mahjong on the sly. For unmarried men, it is like entering a monastery."

"But you have been married for some time," Nagashima said pointedly. "Aren't your wife and family living here?"

"I am, of course, the exception. I am referring to people like Watanabe and Nakada here, as well as the Peking representatives of many commercial firms."

"Mr. Okamura has a beautiful wife," Watanabe interjected, "but with no Japanese restaurants and no bars, even he feels at loose ends."

"Don't interfere with my story. Don't you want to hear about Watanabe's adventure at the International Club?" Okamura was bent on continuing his recital. "Well, Mr. Watanabe arrived at the pool entrance and we called him over to where we were sitting. At the time, there were very few people in the pool, only a few East European and Russian women who were not afraid of the cold. There was that Soviet girl, Miss Alyoshenko, who really turns all the heads in the International Club. She was wearing a bikini, and she flapped about in the pool, smiling and waving to Watanabe. Now, Watanabe was fully dressed, with tape recorder and camera strapped across his shoulder, and he walked blindly *right* into the swimming pool."

"Did he really fall in?" Nagashima asked innocently.

"Of course! His tape recorder hit his face, which broke not only the recorder and the camera, but also his glasses."

Nagashima looked at Watanabe in disbelief. There was a wrinkle at the corner of his eye. It *could* have happened.

Nakada and Okamura were laughing, and Nagashima realized she was the victim of a gag. She smiled, too.

Watanabe was not peeved, but he did not smile. He was

quietly recalling the actual circumstances in which his tape recorder was damaged.

◇ ◇ ◇

It happened at the time of the Ch'ing-ming Festival. For several days, people had been coming from all parts of the country to T'ien-an Men Square to place flower wreaths in front of the Memorial Plaque for the People's Heroes, constructed in memory of the martyrs who dedicated their lives to the anti-imperialist, anti-feudal cause of the people's liberation. The outpouring that took place was unprecedented. Foreign newspapermen who lived in Peking all agreed they had never seen anything like this, and they went every day to collect on-the-spot material, including interviews and photographs.

At that time Premier Chou En-lai, who had been loved and admired by the Chinese people, had been dead for nearly three months. The majority of the population was still overwhelmed with a sense of loss, but there were some who were plotting even then. The plotters were trying to contain the demonstrations for Chou En-lai, while at the same time launching campaigns, with great fanfare, against the "capitalist" faction. They pointed an accusing finger at Teng Hsiao-p'ing, who had assumed the responsibility of carrying out Chou En-lai's policies in the Party, the government, and the military. They stirred in the people a gnawing malaise, a presentiment of a "gathering storm."

Was one to promote the line of national reconstruction through the "Four Modernizations," as advocated by Chou En-lai, or was one to support the line of "continuous revolution"? The population of Peking and its surrounding regions chose to indicate their preference by commemorating Chou En-lai at the Ch'ing-ming Festival. This was the first time that the Chinese populace had freely expressed its wishes by the use of a new method, that of "casting a ballot."

From April 1 to 3, every day, students from the middle and primary schools, workers, cadres, and soldiers passed by in procession, holding flower wreaths and memorial couplets on white banners, their numbers increasing from ten thousand or more to a hundred thousand, until on the day of the Ch'ingming Festival, they reached one million. They filled every inch of T'ien-an Men Square. The people were very orderly, standing quietly, staring at the majestic Memorial Plaque, their faces showing their grief. This white monument had become the embodiment of the spirit of Premier Chou, a symbol of the aspirations of the people for a life of peace and happiness, and the signpost pointing the way to national wealth and power.

The flowers were made of white paper. How many hundreds of hands, restraining tears, had wrought the delicate blossoms that went into those wreaths, some as big as ten feet across? How much devotion was represented by this display? Tens of thousands of wreaths of all sizes were offered on the first two sets of steps leading up to and surrounding the Memorial Plaque. The wreaths were offered to Chou En-lai, who had given his whole life to the cause of the Chinese Revolution, to the Party of the proletariat, and whose love for his country and for its people was boundless.

But at two o'clock at night, trucks pulled up at the deserted Square, disgorging soldiers wearing the armband of the Urban Workers Militia. They worked for four hours and removed the flower wreaths and the memorial couplets from the Plaque. Then they washed down the steps. The next day, students, workers, and cadres passing by the Square on their way to work were astounded at the sight of the immaculate Plaque, now stripped bare of ornament. They wondered why the wreaths and flowers, made with their own hands, had disappeared overnight.

Those who wanted to look at the Memorial Plaque were discouraged by the Urban Militia now posted around it. These Militiamen were contingents of students organized from Tsinghua and Peking universities, students who had been specially selected from the villages and the factories. It was these two universities, of course, which were the source of the political blitz campaign against Teng Hsiao-p'ing. If one connected these two observations, it became immediately clear that the policies of Chou En-lai would be undermined and his memory defamed.

The indignant crowds that went to the Square grew in size. Before 10 A.M., nearly a hundred thousand people had gathered. The Militiamen were shoved aside by the crush. Some of them, under duress, admitted their complicity.

New wreaths were placed at the Plaque. High up on the monument hung an oversize portrait of Chou En-lai. Memorial couplets were once again draped over the banisters on the steps. These couplets were no longer laments; now they took the form of angry outbursts:

"Grief-stricken among baying demons,
 I cried and the jackals roared.
 Blood sacrifice mourns the heroes,
 I raise my head, and draw my sword!"

* * *

"China is no longer the China of the past."
"People are no longer contemptible dupes."
"The feudal society of Emperor Ch'in is gone forever."
"The despotic reign of Empress Lü must not be seen again!"
"We believe in Marxism-Leninism!"
"Let those effete ideologues who castrate Marx and Lenin go to hell!"
"What we want is true Marxism and Leninism!"
"We are not afraid to spill our blood for true Marxism-Leninism!"
"When the monument of the 'Four Modernizations' is finished, we will toast its architect!"

Then, someone had written in huge characters:

"The bow is bent, and arrows cut the champion down:
 Whither the Revolution? On this day, we shall see.

From time immemorial, royalty is forever debauched,
They toy with evil, slay the good—the clowns of history!"

On a strip of white cloth was written in blood:

"Defend the cause of Chou En-lai to the death!"

People yelled out slogans, and some used bullhorns and called to the crowd. There were people clustered in circles; in some areas they were holding mass meetings, in others they were scuffling. Tens of thousands roared out, "The Great Hall of the People belongs to the people! Now, when the people want to hold a meeting, why is it shut?"

The soldiers tried to fend off the mob, but the masses yelled out to them, "Soldiers of the people! Stand with us!" The political theories the soldiers had been taught were scarcely applicable in this crisis. Even if out of control, these people were not the enemy, and the soldiers could not fire on them.

Amid the uproar, the three Japanese reporters, Watanabe, Nakada, and Okamura, in the company of interpreters and drivers, had arrived on the scene.

The interpreters saw the situation, and demanded that they leave. Otherwise, they said, they could not guarantee their safety.

But the reporters' job was, after all, to get the news. They had to be oblivious to danger, especially before this kind of outpouring in the sacred precincts of T'ien-an Men Square, at the very heart of the capital. This news would leave its mark on history. For reporters who had studied China over the years, this was the chance of a lifetime. There was no way they would leave the scene.

The outraged crowd grew. They looked for the missing wreaths, and demanded that those who had removed them admit their guilt. Speeches blared out over the loudspeakers. Watanabe heard attacks on the disregard of the wishes of the people by those in power, on the decision to cremate Chou En-lai and to disperse his ashes, and on the attempts to erase every vestige of Chou En-lai's influence, to divert the plans for the "Four Modernizations" which had already been promulgated by the People's Congress.

These outcries expressed the deepest sentiments of the people. For Watanabe it was the first time in his two years in China that he heard such comments. Those speaking were entirely different from the people he had normally encountered; some had always looked nervously toward the interpreter, or others had recited line after line from the *People's Daily*, or had spoken only about the good, not recognizing the bad. He turned on his tape recorder to capture this testimony.

Watanabe would never forget the incident. In an instant, his tape recorder and camera were smashed to bits, and he sustained a nasty cut near the corner of his eye. All foreign reporters were then ordered to leave the scene immediately.

Back in his apartment and as soon as his wound was bandaged, Watanabe told Okamura and Nakada that he knew if they could get to the Peking Hotel they could get a good view of T'ien-an Men Square from the sixth-floor window in the room occupied by Anfuji, a member of the Japanese Diet. Excitedly, the three each secured a pair of binoculars and left on the run for the Peking Hotel.

It was almost 6 P.M. Ordinarily there would be a crush on the sidewalk of people returning from work, and the street would be crammed with bicycles like fish in a barrel. But now, the street was as deserted as if it were five o'clock in the morning. Quickly locating their car and driver, they started out, passing first by the Workers' Gymnasium, where the reporters noticed hundreds of "Liberation"-model trucks parked around the tall circular building. Young people, wearing the armbands of the Militia and carrying clubs, were flocking around the entrance of the Gymnasium. Their driver suddenly speeded up.

It was empty all along the wide thoroughfare from Ta-ch'iao Lu ("Big Bridge Road"), and as they turned into the big street running by the Chien-kuo Men, which linked up with Ch'ang-an Avenue. Only a few half-empty buses now and then passed by. No other vehicles or pedestrians were to be seen. Squadrons of armed Public Security guards were patrolling the city, and martial law had been declared.

On the sixth floor of the Peking Hotel, they found Diet Member Anfuji and his secretary looking through their binoculars at the demonstrations in the Square and in the surrounding areas. When he saw the three reporters approaching, Anfuji was annoyed at the interruption, but granted their request.

From above, amid the groves of greening trees, the rooftops looked especially bright. The sun was slanting toward the west, and the street lights had been turned on. On the west side of the T'ien-an Men Square, surrounded by red walls and yellow tiles, a stream of white smoke was curling upward. Around the white Memorial Plaque there was a sea of people. In the distance a deep voice could be heard blaring out over the large loudspeakers on top of troop-carrying trucks in front of the Square. Public Security guards were deployed everywhere along Ch'ang-an Avenue. Those who separated from the crowd and crossed the streets looked like rats as they formed single lines and sneaked away along the walls, their heads lowered, scurrying to avoid the rough attentions of the Public Security guards.

At 9 P.M., truckloads filled with Urban Workers Militiamen entered Ch'ang-an Avenue. As the Militiamen disembarked, they advanced from all four sides of the Square. Viewed from above, it was a spectacle like that of African aborigines closing in on monkeys. As the circle tightened, the dark patch of people at the center converged toward the white Memorial Plaque. For a moment, it looked as if the two forces would hold each other off, but then the crowded center broke open in all directions. The entire scene suddenly became a slaughterhouse where thousands of people fought for their lives. Watanabe thought he could hear the death screams of men and women. His hands no longer had the strength to hold the binoculars and he turned and walked away from the window, to collapse into a chair.

◇ ◇ ◇

If Okamura had not mentioned the incident of the tape recorder, that episode would not have been brought back so vividly to Watanabe's memory. What point was there in bringing it all back? How much of the shocking truth would ever be revealed? Watanabe looked out the car window at the pedestrians on the sidewalk, staring woodenly as the procession passed before them, betraying their awe and misgiving.

▧ SEVEN

Sunday, February 10   7 p.m.

        The dinner for the Japanese economic delegation, organized by the Foreign Trade Liaison Office of the State Council, began at seven o'clock, as scheduled.

    In the dining hall of the new annex of the Peking Hotel, above the speaker's platform, was hung a horizontal banner with yellow characters against a red background: "A Cordial Welcome to the Japanese Economic Delegation." There was no one on the platform, but two microphones stood ready for use.

    The large room could accommodate twenty-four tables, but there were only seven on this occasion. A round table in the center, near the platform, had been reserved for the heads of the guest and host delegations, and on either side of the center table, there were three tables reserved for general cadres, with hierarchies carefully established by the seating order.

Eight were to be seated at each table, and attendants stood with hands at their sides, waiting by the red columns at both sides of the hall. The Chinese were represented by the leadership of ten cadres. Each was accompanied by an interpreter, making twenty in all who stood in receiving lines on both sides of the entrance to welcome the Japanese delegation as they entered the hall.

The Japanese delegation consisted of seven members in addition to the head and the deputy head, ten aides, and four reporters, including the beautiful Nagashima, twenty-three in all.

The head and the deputy head of the delegation met first with the others in the lounge of the old building. Following Section Head Yüan, who was in charge of Chinese liaison, they entered the lobby of the new building. It was exactly seven by the giant clock above the door as the delegation filed in, by rank, in two columns.

All the reporters were seated in the back of the room with the four attached to the delegation being placed at the far left and far right tables.

At the loudspeakers Mr. Yüan made a short welcoming speech. The head of the Japanese delegation followed with thanks for the warm reception. Reporter Nagashima, who could understand little Chinese and had no interest in politics, was bored. She glanced at the place card at the empty seat beside her. Reporter Nakada had not shown up and she wondered idly what had happened to him.

◇ ◇ ◇

Reporter Nakada was madly dancing to a Sammy Davis recording with a French blonde, amid a crush of people.

Since arrival in Peking, he had not attended a party that was so much fun, and he was trying to make up for a whole year of loneliness and monotony in a single evening.

When Nagashima had been deposited earlier at the Peking Hotel, and members of the delegation had gone to their rooms,

Nakada, Watanabe, and Okamura had returned to their apartment.

When Nakada had entered his room his telephone rang. His friend Bill, who was press and public relations officer of the American Liaison Office, was on the line.

"We're having a press conference here tonight and want to invite you and your journalist friends to come."

Nakada had politely explained that because of the arrival of the Japanese economic delegation in Peking everyone was busy, and he was afraid they could not make it.

"But after the conference, we're having a big party to celebrate Mrs. Robertson's birthday. Liquor will flow like water, the music fresh from Las Vegas, all the international beauties in Peking, and that new movie, *Fringe Benefits in Washington*, from which nothing is cut."

This was altogether too much for Nakada. At least he had to look in.

"When will the press conference begin?" he wavered.

"In an hour. But you're welcome any time. Tell your friends. Don't miss this one. I'll be looking for you."

Nakada consulted Watanabe and Okamura, and they decided that work came first. They agreed that Nakada should go to the press conference, but he was to come back afterward to the Peking Hotel to report. If the party at the American Liaison Office looked good, they would bring Nagashima along after the reception ended.

Nakada went, listened to the boring press announcement, and had two drinks. After dancing with the green-eyed personal secretary of the French Ambassador, he had no wish to go to the Peking Hotel for the dinner. The news dispatches he must send off he could write with his eyes closed. It would be just as easy to wait until the reception dinner was over and call in with his news of the party.

The music had a convulsive beat, and the rooms were crammed with guests. In the corridor, empty champagne bottles were stacked atop a long table and on the floor underneath. Whiskey and vintage V.S.O.P. cognac were flowing freely. The hollow pretentiousness of the usual diplomatic party had disappeared. It was like being at the home of a wealthy and magnanimous host where one could enjoy himself without restraint. The birthday hostess flaunted her new gown through the crowd, but no one paid her any attention. It had been a long time since anyone had seen a party like this in Peking.

Nakada looked for his glass. There were no Chinese attendants left; they had all departed after their shift of duty. "Can't find my glass . . . I'd better get another one . . . It's free, at any rate."

He wiggled his way through the dancing mob and out of the room, picked up some snacks at the table in the corridor, and poured himself a refill. It had been a busy afternoon, and he was hungry.

Through the open front door, he could see a big sedan pulling up in front of the house. A few late-arriving guests emerged from the car, and it took only one glance for him to spot Miss Alyoshenko.

Her hair was piled high to show her glittering earrings. Wearing a long white fur coat, she walked gracefully into the entranceway, her head tilted up. Following were her tall, thin escort and a fat, balding man with a box in his hands, presumably a present.

As they were about to enter, two big American types in dark suits jumped out to block their way.

A young American officer, responsible for the food and drink, and posted behind the long table, hurried to the noisy reception hall and came out with the host and hostess, as if to receive the newcomers.

But they were not *receiving* the guests. Instead, Nakada saw them escort the Russians back to their sedan. Miss Alyoshenko looked furious, and taking the box from the bald man, she flung it to the ground before getting into the car.

The car gunned down the road. The host and hostess came

back into the house as if nothing had happened. The box, brought as a present, now crushed, was removed by one of the big fellows at the door.

Nakada felt sorry for the beautiful Miss Alyoshenko.

Glass in hand, he walked back to the reception hall and saw that the French girl was dancing with a West German journalist, so he turned around and entered the study. It was called a study, and books lined the walls, but actually it was a large living room, now filled with guests sitting on all the many sofas and couches. In front of the fireplace, seated on the floor, was Ali Singh, the new correspondent from India, already drunk, and arguing in a loud voice.

Nakada scouted the scene and saw that he was the only Japanese at the party. Feeling suddenly isolated and uneasy, he remembered that he had forgotten to call Watanabe and Okamura. It was almost nine o'clock!

He quickly found a phone and called the Peking Hotel, but it took him awhile to get through to a hotel staff member who spoke Japanese. He found out that the Japanese economic delegation, and all the Japanese newspapermen, had already left.

"Where did they go?" Nakada asked.

"Tonight the Chinese leaders are receiving many Japanese friends and guests, including the Japanese economic delegation. They have gone to the Great Hall of the People."

Nakada hung up, dumbfounded. He picked up his glass and downed a shot of whiskey. "Damn! Tomorrow I'll have to borrow Watanabe's notes and photographs. Watanabe always takes more pictures than he can use."

◈ ◈ ◈

On the west side of Peking, close to Ch'ang-an Avenue, there is an area once occupied by American troops at the time of the imperialist invasion of the Manchu empire. After the Liberation, this place was converted into offices for the Department of Public Security, which has charge of public security throughout the country, responsible in particular for the suppression of the "Five Black Elements": landlords, rich peasants, anti-revolutionaries, evildoers, and rightists. The Department's mission is to safeguard domestic security, and it symbolizes the strength of the proletariat.

The Peking Public Security Bureau is directly under the authority of the Public Security Department, and is responsible for maintaining law and order, registering the inhabitants of the city, and directing traffic. However, the tasks of protecting the agencies of the government, safeguarding important buildings, and providing security for foreign legations in the capital are the responsibility of the Public Security Department. The soldiers in that Department wear khaki-colored uniforms, and have a different organizational structure than the policemen of the Peking Public Security Bureau, who wear white and blue uniforms.

In the spacious compound of the Public Security Department in a newly constructed three-story office building, Section Head Li, wearing his khaki uniform, had just hung up the receiver, and immediately asked to be connected with the Ministry of Foreign Affairs.

Section Head Chu, who was on duty at the Foreign Ministry, was surprised at a call from the Public Security Department.

"What has happened?"

"It may be nothing. But there is something developing I think you should know. What was the scheduled function at the American Liaison Office?"

"Ah! . . . Let me check . . . Yes, a birthday party, in honor of the first secretary's wife. Is anything wrong?"

"Something curious. There has been a huge commotion over there, with a lot of noise, and who knows what kind of strange music. The guards at the gate report that, from the windows, the men and women inside look as if they are shaking with palsy. Are they on drugs, by any chance?"

"Who is at the party?" Chu felt anxious at the mention of drugs.

Chu wrote down the names, and realized that there was something strange about the invitations. After listening to the list read over the telephone, his suspicions were confirmed.

"Something else was interesting," Li went on to say, and recounted the incident of how three people from the Soviet Embassy were turned back at the party and how they had flung a package on the ground and left.

Section Head Chu thought a while and said solemnly to Li, "We had better keep a close surveillance. Something is not right. At the moment, we do not know who attended the party from the American side, but the male guests are all reporters from capitalist countries. Aside from the Japanese reporters, they are all there.

"Obviously they are not entertaining reporters from the Soviet Union or the East European bloc of countries; only those from Yugoslavia are included. What is behind all this activity? Personally, I think something big is brewing between the Soviet Union and the United States."

"Right. My feeling exactly. Conflict is inevitable between the two superpowers, but we must find out why."

"Let me communicate immediately with the American Liaison Office, but you must redouble the watch at your end. If anything new comes up, keep in touch."

And so the Public Security Department and the Foreign Affairs Ministry were thrown into frantic activity, as they searched for the cause of the new hostility between the Soviets and the Americans.

◈ ◈ ◈

The majestic building situated on the west side of T'ien-an Men Square was completed in 1959; it occupies 171,800 square meters, is 600 meters long, and 45 meters high. This is the Great Hall of the People, the pride of the whole country. When construction began in the spring of 1958, every region contributed to the historic undertaking. Eighteen provinces and cities, from as far away as mountainous Tibet and the

South Sea Islands, sent their most skilled artisans and workmen. People considered that to help fill the quota of necessary materials for this building was their most glorious opportunity to contribute to their country, and they more than met the demands in a spirit of magnanimity, dedication, and pride.

During the construction of the Great Hall of the People, which is a stellar addition to the Square, there were some twenty thousand construction workers, as well as students, laborers, and cadres of the city of Peking, involved; even soldiers volunteered their services. Every day, tens of thousands of people carried bricks, moved earth, brought in tile, and excavated the ground. During the summer sun and the icy wind of winter, many hands were worked to the bone, many shoulders were swollen from the strain, yet people gritted their teeth and toiled on, to build a place where the representatives elected by the people themselves could convene. This blessed country, with its glorious future still ahead of it, was to belong to each person who labored in it.

The Great Hall of the People is composed of three parts. The center facing the Square is a hallway in the ancient Roman style, consisting of twelve columns, each two meters in diameter and forty meters high, with support beams nine meters thick and thirty-two meters long. Behind the spacious entryway is a four-tiered auditorium with a seating capacity of ten thousand; even the stage can accommodate spectaculars involving a thousand performers at once. This is an edifice that will live in history.

The southern part of the building is the office of the Standing Committee of the People's Congress. In addition to a sumptuous meeting hall seating three hundred, there are some thirty spacious conference rooms on the second and third floors. Each conference room is named after a province, a major city, or an autonomous region and each was designed and constructed by architects and workmen from the area, in a style befitting that locale. All this manifests the strength of the various peoples that make up China.

131

At the north end of this immense building, the end that faces the Chung-shan Kung-yüan ("Sun Yat-sen Park"), is an enormous dining hall. The kitchen takes up the entire basement below the dining hall. In the dining hall, the ceiling is three stories high. There are beautiful crystal chandeliers, and four rows of marble columns run along both sides. One hundred tables can be set up in the hall, seating a thousand people.

When this great monument to the people was finished, the people of Peking looked at it with pride and self-gratification. "Ah! I put up this brick or that tile!" When they saw foreigners taking photographs, they thought, "Take a picture! This is the fruit of our labor; it is the triumph of the people!"

They came from all parts of the country, one after another, to look at it, and were astounded by the enormous interior. They exclaimed: "From now on, the representatives of the people will have a proper place to meet, and they will be able to bring this country along the road to its glorious future."

But reality is ruthless. The dreams of the people were soon shattered. The year was scarcely over before the "natural disasters," actually human miscalculations, had brought misfortune. The daily needs of the populace suffered from extended shortages following the Great Leap Forward. By November, fruits, vegetables, and eggs had become treasured items. As for meat, each person was rationed 250 grams a month (one half pound), which was reduced two months later to 100 grams. There was nothing in the way of cakes and sweets. A panic for food took over.

It continued into the winter of 1960. People became sick in all the urban areas as a result of chronic malnutrition. In Peking alone, those who were suffering from hepatitis and from dropsy constituted 70 per cent of the population. It became common practice to work only half a day. Reports were heard that whole families had committed suicide because their ration coupons had been stolen. Incidents of looting provisions in villages everywhere were reported by rural refugees who flocked into the cities. The people were starving and desperate. Food was never far from their thoughts or their conversations. The more they talked about food, the hungrier they became, and the hungrier they became, the more they talked about it.

It was just about this time that a small dinner was being held every third day in the Great Hall of the People. A big feast was held every fifth day. The chandeliers were lit brilliantly, and distinguished guests filled the halls. Plates and tables were stacked high with food. Those high-ranking cadres from the Party, the government, and the military, who had the privilege of attending these dinners, were bored by them, first, because they had to attend so many, and secondly, because they already received ample rations of chicken, duck, fish, meat, and cartons of vegetables and fruits, delivered to their homes by the truckload. They wanted for nothing in the way of food or drink. There were many occasions for these banquets, the most frequent being the receptions for representatives of friendly foreign powers. Of the usual one thousand participants at such a banquet, there were often more than nine hundred fifty hosts and but a score or so of guests to wine and dine. There was a lot of food left over, which benefited the help in the dining room and the kitchen. They did not eat these leftovers, since they could eat all they wanted on the job. Instead, they took these scraps, even the burnt crusts in the rice pots, and made them into "nutrition supplements," paying the American equivalent of 20 cents for each five hundred grams and taking them home. Some they gave away to friends as presents; others they sold at the price of an American equivalent of 50 cents per five hundred grams to their neighbors and acquaintances. Truly it was:

Rotten scraps from the board of the rich and overfed—
Food fit to fight over for the poor and the starving.

The Chinese people had to revise their image of their leaders of the past ten years. They had seen them as unassuming, approachable figures, willing to share the travail of the people. But now, they viewed them as hypocrites whose outward actions never corresponded with their inner motives, as aloof and arrogant bureaucrats who enjoyed their special privileges with no sense of embarrassment. A great split took place among the Chinese people. In the "classless" society, two groups emerged. One was the "impoverished" proletariat who could not see beyond their next meal; the other, lording it over the less fortunate, reaping the fruits of the people's labor, was the "aristocratic" proletariat.

During this three-year period of hardship when the economy sputtered and then went out of control, when shortages of food were commonplace, when commodities were virtually unattainable, it was precisely the group branded as "Red capitalists" by the extreme leftists in the last stages of the Cultural Revolution that alienated themselves more and more from the people.

Administrative cadres above the rank of bureau chiefs, and military cadres above the rank of colonel, not only had special provisions, but also special purchasing certificates that they could use to buy commodities at low prices in shops (forbidden to the people) on the fifth floor of a skyscraper in Wang-fu Ching. One could claim that they were the leaders of the country and needed special accommodations, and one could have tolerated the situation. They could not be expected to climb trees to pick the barely edible leaves on the topmost branches; nor could they go into the outskirts to pick wild berries and plants to stave off hunger.

Deluxe restaurants had become their regular eating haunts. To celebrate a birthday, they thought nothing of chartering a plane to Canton to enjoy a banquet with their drinking buddies. Their sons and daughters entered elite elementary and middle schools, and admission to a university was as easy as picking up a phone. Whole families would go to such summer resorts as Pei-tai River and Lu Mountain, and to such winter resorts as Canton and Kweilin. One could find the country houses of these people everywhere. They had many low-ranking cadres in their personal employ. Under the slogans "For the Leaders" and "Vital to the Leaders," functionaries of all ranks basked in reflected glory, exploiting the situation, and sharing in the spoils.

Those responsible for creating this special privileged class in China were not, therefore, the only ones who reaped the benefits; another group derived certain advantages by leeching on the first. It became most dangerous when this category of "leeches" worked their way up to the privileged classes and became power-mongers.

In the beginning of the Cultural Revolution, quite a few of these power-mongers fanned the embers of long-standing dissatisfaction among the youth and incited them to attack the privileged class in order to rid the country of them. These youths had illusions of a democracy modeled after the Paris Commune, of a society that was totally egalitarian. They attacked the various governmental organizations and party organs; they even besieged the Great Hall of the People, and proceeded to attack Premier Chou En-lai, whom they wrongly took to be the representative of the "Red capitalists." But these young people, who had been exploited, then betrayed, were eventually shipped out to the countryside, where they became the serfs of the 1970s, with no hold on life, and no release through death.

Special privileges still existed, and these were rationalized by the Socialist theory of "to each according to his worth." And so, the soil was fertile for corruption, favoritism, and bribery. The formula that circulated in Peking about these people was entirely apt: "In speech, a Marxist-Leninist; in life-style, a bourgeois capitalist; in motives, an imperialist; in thought, a feudalist."

Where was the democracy symbolizing the new vigor of the early period of the People's Republic? The representatives were no longer elected by the people, but were appointed by the highest authorities. Even the constitution promulgated by these appointed representatives was now only a piece of paper.

There was no longer a Chairman of the Republic, though there was a Party Chairman. Now, even the occupant of this highest post had passed away. What did it mean, then, to have a National People's Congress? Should one retain the Great Hall of the People as a historical monument, commemorating the loss of the people's democracy? Definitely not! The people built it, and the people would resurrect it.

❖ ❖ ❖

Premier Hua received the Japanese guests in the Sinkiang Hall. The original purpose for the occasion was to receive the delegation of the incumbent party in the Japanese Diet, headed by Fujisugi. The Japanese economic delegation was invited merely as secondary guests.

Diet Member Fujisugi had once been Japan's Foreign Minister. In recent years, he had become the main advocate for the People's Republic in the Diet, where he had just won re-election to his seat. The Diet was now in recess, and he had taken the opportunity to visit China along with other members of the Diet. They had been warmly received as guests of honor and had held discussions with various department heads. In addition they had been taken on an excursion to Hangchow, accompanied by Vice-Premier Chang Ch'un-ch'iao himself. Since they were leaving for Japan the next afternoon, Premier Hua was compelled on this evening to receive them, no matter how pressed he was for time.

Premier Hua looked tired, his eyes were bloodshot, and he drank cup after cup of tea. He asked the delegation few questions, though Ch'iao Kuan-hua made up for it by asking about a number of matters. Foreign Minister Ch'iao wished to conclude the Sino-Japanese Friendship Treaty as quickly as possible and he had high hopes that the new Japanese cabinet would accomplish this.

Reporter Nagashima, unlike the other Japanese reporters, who were diligently taking notes of the various speeches or seizing on the right moment to take photograph after photo-

graph, paid attention to only one person, the female interpreter, the only other woman in this vast room crowded with
people.

She carefully observed the interpreter's speech, movements,
and manner of dress. She knew that she was born in Japan,
was married, had children, and was now a representative of
the People's Congress. She wondered where the interpreter
would go after the meeting was over. How would she manage
her home life? How would she resolve the difference in status
between herself and her husband? This was someone totally
different from her in outlook and in her philosophy of life. It
would be marvelous if she could talk with her.

Nagashima was taken off guard when the meeting ended
suddenly. Premier Hua stood up, and everyone rose with him.
The Premier and a few Chinese leaders were at the door to say
goodbye and to shake hands with each of the guests. Nagashima seized the chance to give her name card to the female
interpreter.

"I would love to get together with you for a little chat.
There is so much I would like to know about you. If you have
the time, please call me, will you?"

"Of course, with pleasure. I will call you tomorrow." The interpreter flashed her a smile, shook hands, and left.

By this time almost all the foreign guests except Nagashima
had left the room. She noticed Foreign Minister Ch'iao speaking to the Premier and saw the Premier's surprised look as he
went back to where he had been sitting earlier.

Nagashima walked through the large, ornately tooled
wooden doors and at the end of the corridor she saw Watanabe
and Okamura by a window, waiting for her.

Suddenly, from the opposite end of the corridor, she heard
running footsteps. A dozen people rushed toward her, their
faces solemn. Obviously something had happened. Nagashima
stood there until the group had passed by her into Sinkiang
Hall.

EIGHT

Sunday, February 10   9:30 p.m.

After the Russians had been turned away from the
American Liaison Office, Shlovsky sat silently in his car. The
chauffeur, a lieutenant in Soviet Security, asked, "Comrade
Colonel, where to now?"

Shlovsky was at a loss for an answer. He had been too sure
of his own judgment, and had failed completely.

That afternoon, at 5:25 P.M., he had received his instructions
from Moscow, and had hastily put a plan into operation. All
leaves of the Embassy personnel were canceled and they were
instructed to stand by for further word.

Later, as instructed, a group of laughing, boisterous Soviet
diplomats and their wives left the Embassy for dinner at the
International Club. Among them was Vishinsky.

Vishinsky had been told to invite the reporters of the capitalist countries to join the group for drinks. When enough people had been gathered together, he was to phone Shlovsky. Shlovsky and Natasha would arrive, and announce the shocking news. "What a stir it would make!" Shlovsky had imagined.

While Shlovsky waited for the call, he had tried to memorize the data in his files on the capitalist journalists. What especially concerned him were their habits, hobbies, weaknesses, and financial status. He looked at his watch; it was already seven-thirty.

"Why didn't Vishinsky call? Son of a bitch! Once he hits the bottle, he forgets what he has to do."

Another twenty minutes went by. The telephone finally rang.

"You must really have been hitting the booze," Shlovsky said coldly.

"Not very much. Just a tiny little sip." Vishinsky was flustered and his words were incoherent. "Up to now, none of our guests have shown up."

"What!" Shlovsky was completely taken aback, for it was totally contrary to previous custom. Every Sunday evening, the journalists gathered at the club to drink heavily. Had the Chinese lured them away so that they would be out of the way just before the big event?

"Where are they? Are they still in Peking?"

"Yes, but I'm told they have all gone to attend a birthday party for Mrs. Robertson of the American Liaison Office."

"All of them?"

"Looks as if they were all invited."

"Break off the drinking," Shlovsky roared. "Not a single drop more, do you understand? And get your ass back here!"

Shlovsky had a serious problem on his hands. Moscow would certainly wonder about his abilities if he could not plant his story with the foreign press. For his own future, he had to work it out.

He dug out the data file on Robertson. Shlovsky had met Robertson a couple of times over the past two years, and had also met Robertson's wife, sporting the latest Paris fashions.

It was a birthday party, after all. Even though he had not been invited, if he brought a gift, surely he would not be turned away. Even a cold shoulder from the Americans would not matter, as long as he could meet the reporters. Hell! Once the news was leaked, it would probably stop the show. Even Robertson would not be able to get to a phone fast enough.

The women in the kitchen had been called together. Quickly, they changed the icing on a cake they had already baked. In less than a half hour, using powdered sugar and fresh fruits, they had created a cartoon of a meeting in space of Soviet and American satellites, and added the words: "Happy Birthday!" The big cake was put in a cardboard box, wrapped in colored paper, and tied with a ribbon.

That the gift would end up crushed on the pavement was not Shlovsky's plan.

Suddenly it dawned on Shlovsky that perhaps the respectable Mr. Robertson was not a career diplomat, after all, but in the same line of work as he. Perhaps he was a "plant," nothing more than a ruthless operative.

Obviously, the party had been given with a purpose in mind. All the journalists from the capitalist countries had been invited to it. That was really something! Three points were immediately clear to him: one, the United States knew about the intended coup; two, it did not want the news to leak out; three, it knew about Moscow's instructions to him. That was why they had pre-empted the journalists with this birthday party ruse.

If he was to complete his mission, he would have to avoid the Chinese security agents on the one hand, and engage American Intelligence in open combat on the other. He mustered up courage. "We'll see who will come out ahead in the end!"

"To the International Club!" Shlovsky commanded, and the chauffeur took off.

❖ ❖ ❖

The dining room on the first floor of the International Club was not crowded as Watanabe, Okamura, and Miss Nagashima entered. Nagashima chose a table away from the window, and sat with her back toward it. Watanabe sat on her right, affording him a view of both Nagashima and Miss Alyoshenko, whom he had just spotted.

Nagashima appreciated the peaceful atmosphere, but thought the decor of the restaurant was too distinctly West European. One could not believe one was in Peking, the capital of China—that is, until a solemn-faced attendant wearing a white uniform approached the table.

They placed their orders, and the attendant said politely in Japanese, "Mr. Okamura, a Mr. Nakada has called three times for you. He wants you to call him at the American Liaison Office."

Okamura rose and walked to the telephone in the corridor. He had a hard time reaching Nakada, but finally got through. Nakada was obviously drunk, and his speech was garbled.

"You . . . better come . . . quickly. The movie's about . . . to . . . begin. Really good." In the background Okamura heard the din of music and voices.

"Maybe we will come over in the next half hour. But you had better cut out the booze. I am not going to carry you to the third floor!"

As he hung up the telephone, a bald, middle-aged Russian came over to make a call. Politely, speaking impeccable Japanese, he said to Okamura, *"Konbanwa"* ("Good evening"). Okamura returned the greeting, and went back to the restaurant.

As the reporters joked about Nakada, the same bald Russian came up to their table and said, "My name is Vishinsky. I once studied at Kyoto University. It was quite some time ago, and nowadays I do not have much of an opportunity to speak Japanese, so I have all but forgotten it." He pulled up a chair. "Can I chat with you a bit? I cannot tell you how much I miss Kyoto."

Watanabe and Okamura were annoyed. They had seen Vishinsky in the club frequently on diplomatic occasions, but they had never heard him speak Japanese. Although they were not happy at being disturbed, there seemed no way to get rid of him without being rude.

They stood from habit, and introduced Vishinsky to Miss Nagashima. "She just arrived a few hours ago in Peking."

"So you had lunch in Tokyo. My! My! What is the news from Tokyo?" Vishinsky asked eagerly.

"Does this lady come from Tokyo?" A couple sitting at the bar came over to the table. "My name is Seaman, but my friends all call me Bill. This is my friend, Alice. Both of us lived in Kyoto for a while and miss it very much. Could we join you?"

Okamura looked up at the speaker. He was a young man, tall and robust, not over thirty. His sport jacket and close-cropped hair marked him instantly as an American.

Alice shook hands with Nagashima and chatted with her in Japanese.

As Watanabe pulled a chair over from the next table, he saw Miss Alyoshenko, in the company of a tall, slender man, coming toward him from her table near the window. The man was a well-known Soviet Intelligence officer. Watanabe had learned about him from his predecessors. Normally, Watanabe avoided this kind of meeting. What would the Chinese make of it, if they saw him in such company?

Perhaps it was because it was Sunday evening, and the dining room was not busy, that everyone felt a little lonely and in need of company.

After introductions, the attendants put three tables together and, when they were all seated, Shlovsky ordered an expensive bottle of scotch. Speaking in halting but passable Japanese, he said, "Tonight, it is on me. Let's drink a toast to welcome Miss Nagashima to Peking. Bottoms up."

"Miss Nagashima, what is your assignment in Peking? Is there anything we can do to be of help?" Bill Seaman asked amiably.

The conversation turned to the experiences of European and American women in Peking. Natasha had much to say on the subject, and Vishinsky translated from Russian into Japanese. Nagashima listened with interest as she studied this woman from the capital of a Socialist country.

Alyoshenko spoke with passion, complaining about the material and spiritual poverty in China. She found nothing acceptable.

The American woman, Alice, smiled disarmingly and spoke very little. As Alyoshenko rattled on, Shlovsky was not interested in the conversation, and tried to change the subject.

"I hear that Premier Hua has just been receiving some Japanese guests. You must have been there." He spoke to Okamura, having discovered early on that Watanabe was not the most convivial of conversationalists.

"Yes, we were there," Okamura admitted.

"Did Premier Hua seem very tired to you?"

"Why? Should he look tired?" Okamura perked up, stirred by professional instinct, but feigning indifference.

"He has not slept for two days and two nights."

Watanabe started to listen. Now that he thought about it, there had been something funny about Hua at the party. He drank a lot of tea, he spoke little, and the reception was unusually brief. He had seen the high Chinese officials enter the dining hall after the reception. None of this would have bothered him had the Soviet agent not pressed the point. Was China going through another major political upheaval?

"It's probably another one of those silly rumors about internal changes within the Chinese hierarchy," said Bill with a smile. "Hong Kong has reports like this several times a year."

Bill now faced Watanabe. Obviously he had been listening to both Natasha's tirades and the other conversation.

"That goddamn son of a bitch is from the CIA!" Shlovsky cursed to himself. He reached for the bottle, took the glass that Bill extended to him, and filled it to the brim. "If we were in the Middle East or in South America, we would have had him dumped in the waters for shark bait. Now he's drinking my scotch and wrecking my show."

"Oh! I'm getting drunk." Bill coyly addressed his glass, speaking in English.

"Drink up . . . Drink up . . ." Shlovsky quipped. "When you drink enough, you will not talk nonsense." Then he added, "Of course, the news that comes out of Hong Kong is made up by your people, but what I am talking about is genuine news."

Watanabe and Okamura looked at each other. They could not understand exactly what was happening, but news was their business. If Shlovsky had any important news, it was their job to get it out of him.

"Are you sure that Premier Hua has been occupied two days and two nights at a stretch?" Watanabe picked up the previous point.

"Of course I am sure. There is no doubt about it. You saw him for yourself tonight. Think about it."

"Why has he been so busy?" Watanabe asked again.

"He is trying to find the source of these stupid political developments that have been circulating in Hong Kong and Moscow," Bill said sarcastically.

"In the past few days, there has not been much news from either Hong Kong or Moscow about China." Shlovsky spoke seriously. "But the CIA headquarters in Virginia has special secret intelligence from a Chinese official that there is about to be a large-scale coup in China, and that a counterattack has been launched. There will be many key officials arrested in the next two days.

"How did you manage to capture all the foreign journalists in Peking at your Liaison Office party? Was it to get all the foreign correspondents drunk for the next three days? Was it to hold up the news about what was happening in Peking and prevent it from leaking to the outside? Your Congress, the day after tomorrow, will be debating an important bill concerning diplomatic relations with the People's Republic of China. The news in Peking would be a little unsettling."

"On the other hand," Vishinsky turned to the Japanese, "no political decision regarding China is imminent in Japan, is that right? So, ladies and gentlemen, my case is closed. You will have to make up your own mind as to whether or not you want to get out a dispatch."

Even the attendants were listening in stunned silence. Shlovsky stood up, bowed slightly, and left. Natasha and Vishinsky followed without saying goodbye.

Bill Seaman, relaxing against the back of his chair, looked at the glass he held and said, as if to himself, "If I were a reporter, I would not spread this news unless I first got verification and clearance from the Chinese authorities. Otherwise you are not only putting your reputation in jeopardy but your job and your residence permit."

He gulped down his scotch and said, "It's been a pleasure meeting you, especially the lovely Miss Nagashima. Alice, let's go home. This has been quite a Sunday!"

After this departure, the three reporters were alone in the large dining room. Even the attendants had left.

Okamura felt intuitively that this was urgent news that would make the headlines for a number of days. But how should he handle it?

Watanabe was also deep in thought. He was determined to send the information off to Tokyo, but how could he explain the source of the information? No one would swallow news coming from a Soviet Intelligence officer.

Nagashima was no political reporter, but she fully appreciated the gravity of the news. She found most surprising the face-to-face combat between the American and the Soviet Intelligence officers. At least they were not using guns or bombs, as in the movies. But the two female agents, Natasha and Alice, had given her enough material for a story she could entitle: "Miss America meets Mother Russia: the CIA versus the KGB."

The lights in the restaurant suddenly dimmed. Watanabe looked at his watch. It was eleven o'clock sharp. Closing time at the club. As he stood up to go, an attendant suddenly handed him the bill. My God! He would have to pay for that damn bottle of scotch!

Forgoing the party at the American Liaison Office, the two men dropped Miss Nagashima off at the hotel, then went home. Neither said a word in the car.

Watanabe and Okamura both lived in a seven-story apartment building, constructed especially for long-term foreign residents of Peking. Okamura did not want to return immediately to his apartment because his wife and children were no doubt in bed asleep. He followed Watanabe to his fifth-floor apartment, and once there, fixed himself a cup of tea.

"What shall we do?" Okamura asked.

"Nakada has not come back yet."

"He said there was a movie. He probably won't be back for another two hours."

"The press statement issued at the American Liaison Office tonight will certainly not appear in tomorrow morning's paper."

Okamura looked at his watch. There was only half an hour before his deadline for tomorrow's edition.

"What shall we do with the information from the Russian?"

"Yes. I have been thinking the same thing. It is a problem."

"Let's talk about it tomorrow." Okamura finished his tea and left for his own apartment.

There was much for Watanabe to think about. The report was probably true. That an important Soviet operative had offered the information must mean something major was brewing. Was there Soviet involvement in the Chinese coup? Why did the Soviets want the Japanese reporters to announce the news? Why didn't Tass broadcast the news itself?

Watanabe wondered if the United States really knew what was happening. If not, why would they hold a birthday party, and why would they have sent two agents to the club to interfere with the Soviet scheme?

Since the death of Chairman Mao, the Soviet Union had adopted a soft, conciliatory attitude toward China, in an attempt to improve Sino-Soviet relations. The Russians were trying to appeal to the capitalist-roaders in the Party, the government, and the military for support. They certainly did not want to see the collapse of the capitalist wing in China. It was likely that Moscow had received intelligence on the situation, and they wanted to communicate it immediately to the capitalist clique. They did not dare compromise their position by direct contact, which was why they wanted the news agencies of other countries to spread the word.

Watanabe remembered the accusation the Russian had made to the young American. He got up and looked into his files. Sure enough, he discovered that the American Congress would be convening the very next evening to vote on an important question concerning foreign relations with China. It was obvious that the American government wished that no disruptions occur in China before the congressional vote. But since the United States could not prevent developments within the Chinese power structure, they could only try to temporarily suspend the process of news gathering and dissemination.

He had figured out the situation, but what to do now?

He had been with the newspaper for more than ten years, and had become something of an expert on Chinese affairs. He was recognized as an authority both inside and outside the newspaper field. It had taken many years before he had sufficiently impressed the Chinese for them to accept him as the special correspondent to Peking. His assignment was now approaching its end, and he wanted to leave Peking without a fuss, retaining his good image so that he could come back for future visits. Should he play it safe and maintain his position with his newspaper and with the Chinese government, or should he take a big gamble and report this news?

The information was not really acceptable by his own standards of accountability. Perhaps when he returned to Tokyo, he would become the laughingstock of his colleagues. Watanabe made his decision. He would not send out the story. Having decided that, he finished his cup of tea, and went to bed.

◇ ◇ ◇

Okamura was bent over his desk, writing a letter. This news was too sensitive to transmit over the telephone, so he would give his letter to one of the diplomatic couriers going to Tokyo tomorrow, and in that way get the news to his editor in chief.

◇ ◇ ◇

Miss Nagashima had taken her bath. Looking in her mirror, she massaged the corners of her eyes, where the wrinkles were most likely to show. Why, she mused, didn't Nakada notice her at all today?

Her thoughts turned to another Japanese reporter who was knowledgeable about China. Unfortunately, his newspaper and the Chinese authorities did not see eye to eye, and for him to come to China was out of the question. Before she left Tokyo, Nagashima had seen him, and he had said to her, "Give me a call when you get to Peking, and let me have an idea of your impressions of the place." Why not call him and tell him about what she had just heard? She found his telephone number in her notebook, and picked up the phone by her bedside.

◇ ◇ ◇

Section Head Li of the Public Security Department had just finished listening to another report from his agent at the International Club. The situation was not a simple matter of a few people getting drunk and having an argument. It was now a political incident affecting internal and external affairs of state.

He picked up the red telephone that connected with internal communications, which in turn ran directly into the residence of Deputy Head Chao of the Public Security Department. A familiar voice answered the ringing. "What is it?"

"Shlovsky, head of the Soviet special agents, has just spread some false rumors detrimental to our country at the International Club."

"What did he say?"

"He said that there will be a coup in our country, and claims that in the next few days, many department heads will be arrested."

"That shithead! Who was he with?"

"Three Japanese reporters, and two staff members of the American Liaison Office."

"Was he drunk?"

"No, he was very sober. The American from the Liaison Office tried very hard to cut him off; they even came close to making a scene."

"You mean the American was trying to keep him from blabbing it out?"

"Yes. But Shlovsky was intent on having the Japanese spread the news right away."

"Who were the Japanese reporters?"

"Watanabe of *Maiasa Shimbun*, Okamura of the Tokyo Economic News Agency, and Miss Nagashima, who arrived this afternoon."

"Call a meeting of the emergency task force right away. We must take immediate action. Inform the Foreign Ministry to send someone. We will meet in ten minutes in the main office building."

Deputy Head Chao hung up the phone in his bedroom, put on some clothes, and gave orders to his secretary and chauffeur to get ready to leave.

The telephone rang again. It was Section Head Li calling again to report that the Japanese woman reporter had already transmitted the news to Tokyo. Should they take any action against her?

"That fast? It is too late to cut if off! Did you tape her conversation?"

"As prescribed by procedure, the conversation was taped from the very beginning."

"Translate the content of the telephone conversation and bring it to the meeting. We will discuss it there." Chao felt that the situation was becoming grave. There were many international ramifications, and a high-ranking cadre from the Foreign Ministry had to be invited to the meeting.

He picked up the private line connecting him with the central government, and demanded to be put through immediately to the home of Ch'iao Kuan-hua.

It was near midnight, but Ch'iao was not asleep. He lifted the receiver as soon as it rang.

Chao explained the situation succinctly, and was surprised to have his news taken so calmly.

The Foreign Minister agreed to attend the meeting in person, something that Chao had also not expected. Chao felt the matter now important enough to notify Premier Hua. But for two days no one had seen the Premier at the Public Security Department. Where would he be now?

Chao directed the supervisor on duty at the switchboard to find Premier Hua, and to connect him with the Public Security Department.

It was almost midnight. Chao prepared to leave his bedroom, but had a sudden sense of foreboding. From his drawer he took a pocket revolver, checked it, and left the room with it in hand.

His residence was within the compound of the Public Security Department, itself surrounded by high walls and sentry posts, and heavily guarded. From his house to the main office was only a four-hundred-meter walk. One would think that a safe distance, but a few years ago the previous head of the Public Security Department had disappeared as he was on his way from the residence that Chao now occupied. The next day, after a thorough search, the body had been discovered in the conduit leading down to the sewer. The central authorities tried to find the murderer. The deputy head at that time, a man named Yü, could not take the pressure exerted on him and had shot himself. The case was still unsolved, and Chao was on his guard.

His secretary and six guards were already waiting for him. Outside, they got into a bulletproof car and drove the four hundred meters to the main building. In the meeting room were twenty section heads waiting for the emergency meeting to start.

Shortly after Deputy Chief Chao arrived, Foreign Minister Ch'iao and several section heads arrived and began to compare notes on the situation. The attendants at the International Club and the chauffeur who had driven the Japanese reporters had also been brought in. Gradually, they reconstructed the sequence of events, and traced it back to the party at the American Liaison Office.

According to passport records, Mrs. Robertson's birthday was September 19. Why then was the celebration ahead of time, on February 10? And why were diplomats of other countries not invited? Aside from a few female staff members, the invitations had been issued to men, all of them reporters. Why were reporters invited to the party, when Robertson was not the Press Secretary? The more they explored the problem, the more complicated it became, and the more questions were raised.

Section Head Li, who had been interviewing the attendants from the International Club in the adjoining room, entered with a sheaf of notes. He was on to something, and he whispered to Chao: "This is a complete transcript of the speech by Shlovsky as reconstructed by our comrades. The last section is particularly significant."

Foreign Minister Ch'iao took the notes from him. He read that the Soviet agent had identified the American as an agent,

151

and that a Chinese official had today leaked the intelligence to the CIA. What was not clear was how the information had been transmitted.

"The Russians assume that both China and the United States know. Chao, do you know anything about this?" Foreign Minister Ch'iao's gaze cut like a dagger.

"This is entirely a fabrication of the Soviet agents," Chao answered indignantly. "There is no problem with the solidarity of our Party."

One of the section heads had been called away from the desk to take a telephone call. He returned, his face anxious.

Chao knew that something was wrong.

"This morning, at nine twenty-five and at ten forty-seven, two phone calls reached the Soviet Embassy. One came from the Hsi-chiao Airport, the other from the Electronics Materials Storeroom of Central Supplies."

"What did they talk about?"

"It was all in code. We have a transcription, but we cannot make it out."

"Who made the calls?"

"In both cases, it was the same person who made the calls, and the same person who took the calls. We have just identified the caller as Chia Hsiang-tung, head of the Telecommunications Section of the Central Committee Special Headquarters."

"Where is he now?"

"We have no lead on him. He should have returned to the Special Headquarters, but he did not. Even his wife does not know his whereabouts."

"He must be a special agent planted by the Soviets. We must put out an all-points bulletin for this man, especially at the airports, harbors, and railway stations. Under no circumstances must he be allowed to slip through our fingers and leave the country. Notify also the frontier defenses at the Soviet-Mongolian border and tell them to redouble the watches."

"Has the Special Headquarters been notified?" Foreign Minister Ch'iao asked.

"We have contacted Assistant Superintendent Hsü of the Secretariat."

"Why did you not contact Superintendent Wang directly?"

"We could not find him, so we had to tell Assistant Superintendent Hsü."

Foreign Minister Ch'iao tugged Chao's sleeve and the two of them walked into a small empty lounge next to the meeting room. Ch'iao whispered, "Something big has happened in the Central Committee Special Headquarters, but exactly what is up at the moment, we do not know. I heard about this four hours ago, so I asked Premier Hua but he said nothing. All he said was to maintain Party discipline. But now the situation has become serious. The agent has leaked information to the Soviet revisionists and to the American imperialists. The Japanese reporter has notified Tokyo and tomorrow the whole world will know. Ask yourself, how are we going to handle this?"

"That Soviet agent is usually very cautious in what he says. Why was he so deliberately expansive tonight? He would not do this if there were not something at stake."

"No matter what, he should not be allowed to operate so highhandedly in our country. First thing tomorrow, we will notify his Embassy that he must leave the country."

"What about the Japanese reporters?"

"They had nothing to do with it. No need to bother about them."

"According to the reports of the guards, the behavior of the guests at the American party was really out of line. The music they played could be heard two blocks away."

"I will mention that to the Americans the next time I see them. Don't worry about the rest. Old Chao, in a few days, you will understand completely. Have you found Premier Hua?"

"Not yet."

"He must be very busy in the underground area of the Special Headquarters. In any event,. I am tired, and I will leave now, before you do. If anything comes up, check with Section Head Li."

He left through the side door and the sound of his heavy steps faded into the distance.

Chao sat alone on the sofa and lit a cigarette. Premier Hua's words ran through his mind: "We must maintain Party discipline!" But just how are we to do that?

❧ NINE

Sunday, February 10
Midnight

Chia Hsiang-tung was alert to every sound around him on the train. Whenever footsteps passed his bunk, he blinked open his eyes, gripped the pistol he held under the blanket, and tightened his index finger on the trigger.

He still had his shoes and his clothes on as he lay on the hard lower bunk bed; his cotton overcoat hung by the window. If anything were to happen, he could open the window, wrap his coat around his head, and jump from the moving train.

The hard-bunk sleepers were all full, and he was lucky to have found a place. He thought that perhaps the forged letter certifying his work detail had something to do with it.

After he had made the second phone call to the Russians, he knew he had been found out. He did not know whether to run or to wait around to be arrested. He imagined the handcuffs on his wrists, the accusing gaze of his old boss, Wang, the slow, painful months and years, spending the rest of his life in the labor camps. No amount of favoritism, no measure of sympathy would be of any help to him. There was no other way but to escape, and at once!

According to the original plan set up with Natasha, he had waited by the trackless trolley station in front of the Agricultural Exhibition Hall. A "Volga"-model sedan had pulled up and screeched to a halt. Chia saw that the driver was bald, and Russian. He had never seen him before, but he had to take his chances. He got into the car.

The sedan picked up speed, and the Russian spoke in Chinese, "Quick. Get down! Lie on the floor. Cover yourself with the blanket on the seat."

Chia Hsiang-tung did as he was told. He wrapped himself up and lay down. The buffeting of the car, plus the strong sheep smell of the blanket, made him want to throw up.

"Now listen to my instructions. I'll say it only once, so listen carefully. And remember everything I say.

"In the center, underneath the back seat, there is a little ring-pull. Pull it to the left, and you will find a hidden compartment. Inside there is a satchel. Please take it out."

Chia Hsiang-tung groped, and found the compartment and the satchel.

"Do not open it now. There are identity papers, cash, and food coupons inside. Somehow, you must get on the International Express for Ulan Bator this afternoon at five-thirty. Buy a ticket to Erh-lien-hao-t'e, but you must get off at the village of Sai-han-t'a-la. On no account go all the way to Erh-lien. Note that carefully. After you get off, take a local to Hsi-li. When you arrive, find a way to stay there. Every morning between nine and ten-thirty, you are to wait in the restaurant opposite the train station. Eventually someone will get in touch with you and take you across the border. You must pay special attention to the following points.

"One, from now on, you are no longer Chia Hsiang-tung, but the person indicated in your papers.

"Two, from now on, you are not to contact any friends or relatives, and you are not to go back home.

"Three, your itinerary must be in strict accordance with instructions.

"Four, your contact will recognize you by the satchel. Whatever you do, do not lose it. He can identify you only by the satchel; he does not know you. You must not forget this.

"Five, your contact may not show up for a couple of days, so you must wait at the prescribed time every day. Be patient.

"Six, you are to follow exactly the orders your contact gives you. Is that clear?"

"Yes, that is all clear."

"Oh, by the way, Natasha sends her best. She is waiting for you on the other side of the Mongolian People's Republic."

"Please tell her that when we meet again, nothing will ever separate us."

Vishinsky nodded, but he thought to himself, "This man is dreaming."

The car stopped in a deserted spot. Chia got out, and Vishinsky drove away. In an instant, there was no trace of him.

Chia Hsiang-tung held onto the satchel and stood, bewildered, at the roadside. On both sides of the road were empty fields with snow in spots. The bare trees bent with the wind. He touched the pocket revolver that he had tucked under his belt, and felt reassured. There was a small mud hut in one of the fields. Going around to the back of the hut, so that he could not be seen from the road, Chia examined the old satchel to see what distinguished it from any other.

He found nothing unusual about it. He wondered why he should be told that the contact would recognize the satchel and not him. How could the satchel be spotted?

Chia opened it. Inside there was an ordinary portfolio made of black leather. He unzipped it and found some identification papers, a few letters, and two envelopes.

There was a military identity card, on which his photograph was pasted. The name underneath was Ho Ko-meng. He was listed as Head of Personnel Security with the 8341 Division.

He took out his own identity card and compared it with the forged one. They were identical. The documentation papers and letters of introduction looked totally authentic. His new name and position were clearly marked on the work detail certificate. There were no addresses on the letters of recommendation. Another letter was addressed to the political commissar in the Ha-sha-t'e region of Inner Mongolia, asking him to assist Ho Ko-meng's investigation into the family background of La-erh-chen, a Mongolian soldier of the 8341 Division who was applying for membership in the Party.

In the small envelopes were 500 *yüan* in used currency, and twenty national food coupons, each one good for one pound of rations.

From his experiences traveling to various work assignments, Chia Hsiang-tung could see that these documents were in impeccable order, a tribute to the outstanding work of Soviet Intelligence. Suddenly he took out a handkerchief, wrapped up all his original documents and identity papers, along with a fountain pen inscribed with his name, and tucked them into a crevice in the brick wall, which he covered with mud.

Later, Chia made his way back into the city and had lunch at the crowded and colorful East Wind Market, and bought some toiletries. Luckily, he still carried some coupons for cloth and merchandise, and with these he could buy toothpaste, a toothbrush, and a face towel. Then he rushed to the Peking Railway Station and strode into the room where tickets were issued to the military.

He did not stand in the line for ordinary soldiers, but pushed open a wooden door and entered an office. He walked over to the desk of the supervisor, who was on the phone, and sat down in front of him.

"I'm from Division 8341, Personnel Security Section." Chia Hsiang-tung took out his military identity card and waved it in front of him. "I must rush to Erh-lien-hao-t'e. Get me a place in the bunk bed section."

The supervisor hung up the phone.

"Ah! The places on this train have all been taken for a week." He looked at Chia apologetically.

Chia was well aware of the "pecking order" and political significance of cigarettes in China, *especially* the three top brands. He knew, for example, that the Panda brand was authorized only to the ranks of Chairman Mao and his confederates. Similarly, the China brand was available only to departmental chiefs and, in the military, to officer ratings above the rank of major. Lastly, factory chiefs, junior military officers, and senior technicians could purchase Great Wall cigarettes. Lower than those top three strictly controlled distribution brands, the masses could purchase a myriad of coarser, cheaper so-called cigarettes. Chia offered the supervisor a cigarette from a pack of China cigarettes. The supervisor, conscious of the implication, accepted. Chia then placed the pack of China cigarettes on the supervisor's desk.

"You had better look at my work assignment papers!" Chia put them on the desk.

"Now, now, there's no need of that! How can anyone have any suspicions of comrades from your division? Let me find a way." The supervisor hadn't paid much attention before, but he noticed then that this was the crack 8341 Division. He stood up quickly and walked hurriedly to the room outside. Chia Hsiang-tung was a little nervous. Was he going outside to inform Special Headquarters? Involuntarily, he felt for his revolver.

Ten minutes later, the supervisor came back, his face all smiles.

"I got one from the Foreign Ministry, a lower bunk."

As he watched Chia Hsiang-tung leave the office, the supervisor sighed with relief and took out a China cigarette. Before he was able to light it, the telephone rang again.

◈ ◈ ◈

The voices in the compartment had petered out, and the lights went dim.

Hsiao Ta-yung sat on his backpack, leaning against the door of the washroom. He tried to doze off.

"Ta-yung! Ta-yung!" A soft voice woke him up. Chia Hsiang-tung was calling across the passengers around the door. He beckoned Ta-yung over.

Ta-yung stood up with much effort. His feet felt numb. He could not squeeze his way through the crush of people to Chia.

"In a little while," Chia whispered to him, "we will pull into Chang-chia-k'ou, and the people around me will get off there. I have already told the conductor to reserve a bunk bed for you. Once we get to Chang-chia-k'ou, you can come over."

Chia did not wait for a response, and he turned away.

Ta-yung had been exhausted these last few days. He had thought that there would be no problem getting some rest during the night, but he did not dream that he would be jammed in the train, with no room to stretch his legs, and not even a place to sit. He could bear the strain himself, but felt sorry for the old folk, the women, and the children crowded in with him.

Ta-yung had lost his sleepiness. The murmur of conversations reached his ears.

"Nothing can be done for this child's father. Less than two years after the communes were established, he escaped to the Northeast.* He finally managed to become a woodsman in the Forestry Service. Last year, we got the papers to go to the Northeast, but now the government has moved against the capitalist-roaders, so they hauled us back to the commune, and we can't even spend the New Year together." A woman was speaking, between sobs.

"Isn't it a little better in the commune these days?" someone asked.

"Are you kidding? Last month we bumped into seven or

* The Northeast is known in the Western world as "Manchuria"—a name detested by the Chinese.

160

eight peasant workers from the same commune. They had all worked out the year and when all the work points had been totaled up, they could not buy enough gruel to eat for the next year. So, what the hell, they might as well take their chances in the mountains of the Northeast cutting wood and picking up odd jobs.

"In our village, people talk about mechanization day in and day out, but all they do is make machines out of people. We work the whole day, and every day, for less and less food. Our own 'private plot' is commandeered by the commune, and eating so much as a piece of mugwort will cost us a work point. At the end of the year, they figure out our earnings and our expenses, and we find that we owe our ass to them. How the hell can we live like that?"

Ta-yung figured that the speaker probably was once a rich reactionary peasant. Why should she be allowed to besmirch national agricultural policy! He felt the need to fight against the reactionary elements who were talking this anti-revolutionary ideology. He could not let her get away with this nonsense.

He stood up and was about to say something, but he stopped short.

In the corridor were peasants wearing ragged cotton jackets, the dirty lining showing through the holes, and pants that had been patched time and again. A middle-aged woman held a baby in her arms, and a skinny child leaned against her, asleep. She munched a piece of cold cornbread, which she warmed in her mouth before feeding it to the baby. Her hair was in limp disarray, and she looked as if she wanted to cry, but could not.

The train was slowing, rocking from side to side as it pulled into the station. "Chang-chia-k'ou!" the conductor yelled out.

Everyone woke up, and the people in the corridor prepared to leave. Chia Hsiang-tung squeezed his way over, picked up Ta-yung's bedding, and barged his way back to his bunk bed.

Ta-yung had mixed feelings. He felt guilty about his earlier indignation. He could neither help the woman nor prevent her from speaking as she did, and had decided to leave well enough alone.

The three people in Chia's compartment left the train. Immediately their places were taken. Aside from Ta-yung, there was a middle-aged man and a younger man, both of whom looked like soldiers.

They had just boarded the train, and there was still some snow on their collars. After taking off their coats, they opened the window to receive cartons which people outside were passing in. The area in front of the window was soon piled high with them.

Those passengers still trying to sleep yelled out: "Who opened the window? Close it, damn it! If you're not afraid of the cold, then get the hell outside!"

The young man answered the complainers, "We're bringing our stuff on, there's no other way to do it."

This only inflamed one of the men who was complaining. He got down from his bunk for a closer look.

"What is this, a passenger train or a freight car? Are you doing this on your own, or do you have official authorization? I can't believe this!"

The young man was about to explode, but the older one restrained him.

"I say, don't talk like that. Is it wrong to open a window?"

They continued to move things in, stacking one carton on top of another, until there was a pile three feet high.

When they were finished, the older man wiped off his sweat, and explained to the bewildered onlookers.

"Comrades. We are from National Farm Unit Number 74. The items sent to all of us on the farm for the New Year have been held in Chang-chia-k'ou for a month, and we have been able to clear the shipment only this evening. We would have sent them by freight, but then we would not have had them for the New Year. There was no choice, and we got the permission of the Political Commissar of the Railway Station to ship them on this express train to Erh-lien. We apologize to one and all for disturbing your night's sleep."

Someone muttered something about how difficult it was to ship anything by freight. Another said, "First they meet, then they discuss, then they check their instructions, then they adopt a policy, and in the end, the job simply does not get done."

Something was gnawing at Ta-yung. National Farm Unit Number 74, was that the unit where Young Swallow worked?

In November 1974, the Production Corps across the country were changed to National Farms. Unit Number 74 of the Production Corps in Inner Mongolia, to which Young Swallow belonged, was now National Farm Unit Number 74. And she was now an "agricultural worker" instead of a "soldier on the farm."

Watching the men stacking the cartons in their shirt sleeves, Ta-yung had taken off his jacket and given them a hand. Chia, however, had not lifted a finger. Leaning back, he smoked a cigarette, and a wry smile played on his face.

◈ ◈ ◈

The train was now some distance from Peking. Chia could relax a bit, and let Ta-yung look after things should there be an official check-up. But he kept an eye on the two men who had just boarded the train; they might be Public Security agents. He would have to make sure they really were from National Farm Unit Number 74.

Chia knew something of the history of National Farm Unit Number 74 from the records he had studied. When he thought about that lecherous unit commander and his foolish wife, he smiled to himself.

The "records" he had seen were not newspapers or magazines on sale to the general public, nor were they reference pamphlets for general cadres or for those above the rank of section head. He had come upon them in a small publication issued in Moscow and edited by the Special Central Committee of the Chinese Communist Party (Russian wing), headed by Wang Ming.

Chia had found these publications in the home of Natasha's girl friend. Supposedly, they were published for Mongolians who were studying China. At first, Chia Hsiang-tung would merely glance at them and throw them aside indifferently.

Occasionally he would flip through them while Natasha was asleep. There was some unusual information in them which he had never heard about anywhere else, and he started to become interested in the Wang Ming way of thinking.

Chia was himself a Party member, a cadre with the rank of Section Head. His position may not have been very high, but through his father's and his father-in-law's connections, he had been able to enjoy all the special privileges and benefits of higher-ranking cadres. These he did not consider "special privileges" but justified them with the rationalization that "From each according to his abilities, to each according to his achievements." He had contributed to the work of the Revolution, why should he not have more of the benefits?

To get along in society, to have friends, to help one another, what was wrong with that? What was all this about "getting in by the back door"? Nothing but envious tripe from the incompetent and from those with no influence.

Chia hated the effete theorizers, sycophants, and "young Turks." It was these people who had stirred up the so-called "revolution" in the sixties and made a mess of China. They had pitted themselves against the Soviet Union and the United States, intimidating the ignorant masses into mobilizing for defense, but, in fact, they had just dug a few holes in the ground, flaunted a few useless .38-caliber guns, and to what purpose? Should there be a real war, Moscow could push a button and reduce China to another Hiroshima, and then the revolutionary spirit would not be worth a crap.

The transformation of Chia's thinking had been engineered by Shlovsky. Half a year ago, Chia had signed an oath of allegiance to the Special Party Organization of the Chinese Communist Party, and thus became a member of the Peking branch of an active organization established by the late Wang Ming.

Chia looked forward to a big change in China! In the midst of cataclysm, the Special Russian Wing of the Central Committee would return to Peking and become the wielders of power. On that day, Chia would be recognized as a distinguished revolutionary pioneer. When that time came, what position would he want? Something in the military? No. Life there was too dull. The diplomatic service? Ambassador to Russia would not be bad, he and Natasha would be together . . .

As he daydreamed, the two men loading the cartons returned to their bunk beds, along with Ta-yung.

"Thank you so much for your help," the older man said to Ta-yung. From his old cloth bag, he pulled out something wrapped in oil paper and opened it. Inside there was a whole roast chicken and several white dough balls. "We didn't have our lunch. The comrade at the reception office pressed this food on us. There is plenty for all. Come, have some!"

Ta-yung had eaten the bread biscuit that he had brought along on the trip, so he was not hungry and declined their offer.

The older man then offered Chia some food. Chia was feeling hungry, and he pulled off a chicken leg and nibbled on it.

He did not want to eat the food without offering something in return, so he took a bottle of wine from his satchel, and the four of them drank contentedly from teacups.

"Are you a student from Tsing-hua University?" The young man made out the characters on the T-shirt under Ta-yung's sweat-soaked shirt.

"Yes. I was assigned there three years ago by my factory," Ta-yung said, revealing his working-class background.

"We are both agricultural workers from National Farm Unit Number 74. All three of us are from the working class." The older man laughed heartily, and turning to Chia said, "You must be from the military. What is your assignment?"

"I am with Division 8341 in Peking. My name is Ho Ko-meng, and I am on my way to Erh-lien." Chia eyed Ta-yung as he mentioned his false name.

Ta-yung was taken by surprise. Why was his cousin's husband using a different name? Perhaps he had a secret mission. Better be careful not to call him by his real name. To show that he understood Chia's ruse, he picked up the conversation.

"Comrade Ho. How long will you stay in Erh-lien?"

"I am afraid I will not be able to make it back to Peking in time for the New Year. Nothing I can do about it. Those are the breaks when you are in the military."

"I retired from military service in 1974 to work on the farm," the older man said. "Now I figure that it is simpler to work in the military, where there is only one line of command. Not like all this shifting about in my present job. You apply for something here and there, and when you come up against indifference, there is nothing you can do." He drank almost half his wine.

Chia refilled his cup and asked Ta-Yung, "Where are you going?" Ta-yung's face turned red, and he said in a shy voice, pointing to the two men, "I am going where they are going."

The older man looked at him with interest.

"You are coming to our place? Are you assigned to work there?"

"No, I am going to visit a classmate."

The young man asked excitedly, "Who? There is no one on that farm I do not know."

"Her name is Young Swallow. She was sent out from Peking in 1971."

The man tried to remember a young person named Young Swallow, but the young man blurted out, "But your name is Hsiao, is it not? The son of some general or other, right?"

Ta-yung was dumbfounded by this recognition. Even Chia seemed surprised.

"How did you know?"

"What don't I know! We have heard of your rise through the

ranks. Now you are a battalion head in the Militia, and a member of the Peking Urban Workers Militia Command. Isn't that right? At the T'ien-an Men Incident, you were cited, weren't you? In a few years, you will no doubt enter the Party's Central Committee, maybe even become Vice-Chairman? Anything is possible!"

"You are drunk, Comrade Li P'ei-yi." The older man was upset. "When you are finished eating, get in the upper bunk and take a rest. We have a busy day ahead of us tomorrow."

Then he smiled at Chia and Ta-yung.

"Young people like this one here have not received a proper ideological training. It is our fault. They have been living in the steppes and in the desert for so many years, their manners have become coarse. Please forgive him if he speaks out of turn."

Li P'ei-ya continued eating, and looked at Ta-yung. His expression turned sly and sarcastic, and Ta-yung began to fidget. He did not understand why Young Swallow should want to tell everything about him. In every letter he had written her, he had described his achievements, his honors, and his citations. His original intention had been to respond to her challenge when they parted, "Let us each in our assignments compete to see who can achieve more." Since it was a competition, he had to let her know his achievements. Probably he had overdone it in his letters. Maybe she thought he was nothing but a power-monger with no interest but to advance himself and to climb up the ladder of success.

But she really does not understand, Ta-yung thought. I am not the kind of person she thinks I am. I have never exploited my father's influence. Everything I have achieved, I have managed as a result of loyalty to the Party and as a result of my own hard work.

The four men sat facing each other, ill at ease. The two other passengers on the upper deck were sound asleep.

Chia Hsiang-tung decided to turn the tables and go on the offensive by asking about National Farm Unit Number 74.

"I hear that in Unit Number 74, affairs between men and women have gotten a little messy."

The young Li P'ei-yi exploded, "Where did you pick up such nonsense?"

"It is all in some records I have seen. Am I not right?"

"You must be talking about the Lao Kan-ch'en business," the older man said cautiously. "He was executed by a firing squad in 1972. That is all over." He looked Chia straight in the eye.

"What happened to the ten or more female intellectuals he violated?" Chia pressed.

Ta-yung thought, "That happened after Young Swallow was assigned there. I wonder if she was a victim?" He felt as if a knife had been thrust into his heart. "Why has she not said anything about this business? Was it because . . . ?"

The older man smiled and said matter-of-factly, "They were forced. What could they do? They have now become good soldiers on the battleground for the motherland. Why should anyone bring this up?"

"There is something I do not understand. How can fifteen or sixteen girls be 'forced,' when they service this fifty-year-old guy willingly, one by one, day after day, for a year or more? Had it not been for the numerous requests by unmarried girls for abortions, which naturally made the hospital personnel suspicious, no one would have found out. I think there must have been some willing partners."

"Chief Liu," Li P'ei-yi said, "people from different classes view things from a different perspective." Then, turning to Chia and Ta-yung, he said, "Looking at things from the standpoint of a privileged person, the violated, the exploited, and the ravaged are always willing victims. Isn't that right?"

Chia was calm; he lit another cigarette, and slowly exhaled.

But Ta-yung was becoming nervous. This kind of talk was precisely what he had heard some of the young people blare over the loudspeakers to the crowds in those few fateful days in T'ien-an Men Square. At that time, he had listened with revulsion. The masses had pressed in to listen. There had been soldiers, veterans, students, cadres, and workers in the Square, but no one had put a stop to the reactionary declamations. On the contrary, they had listened eagerly.

❖ ❖ ❖

Early on the morning of April 5, the anti-revolutionary elements had shown their hand. In the Command Headquarters Ta-yung listened to the non-stop telephone dispatches that were coming in from various vantage points. It was time to move, to crush the mob.

The masses were setting a torch to everything, burning the watchtowers of the Militia.

Various Militia groups from educational institutions in western Peking had all gathered together. The vehicles from the Central Armory in the Peking Military Command were not dispatched, but were held back, which had the effect of undermining the Militia. The Urban Workers Militia in the eastern part of the city had also gathered in a stadium. While they had brought their factory trucks with them, there were not enough of them. If sent out, they would not stand a chance, since the mob had now grown to over one hundred thousand people. The Peking Military Command wanted no part of the affair, claiming that tanks could not enter the city, and that, without a direct personal authorization from the Chairman himself, they could not take any such action.

At this critical juncture, Commissar Hsieh had taken over. She phoned Tientsin, and called out three thousand Militiamen. Obviously, she had the proper influence, because the personnel carriers set off immediately from the Central Armory to fetch the Militiamen in the western sector. She took several staff members, including Ta-yung, with her to the Peking Revolutionary Committee meeting. One could see in action the cool and collected Hua Kuo-feng, then head of the Public Security Department, and the unruffled Wu Teh, Vice-Chairman of the Peking Revolutionary Committee. Ta-yung learned a lesson on that occasion on how to approach a crisis with composure. He also learned how to seize the vital pressure points of one's opponent and how to gain the upper hand with the enemy.

Members of the Military Affairs Committee favored immediate suppression, but they were overruled by these two men. Department Head Hua looked at the outraged and overwrought group and said, "Please think, every one of you. How many real troublemakers are there? I calculate that there are no more than a thousand. You are shaking your heads. All right, then, let us put the figure at three thousand. What is our strength? There are twenty thousand Militiamen in Peking, but only two thousand are at our disposal to march on the Square. The PLA cannot intervene; this is an internal affair. We can only use Militiamen, and the Public Security forces can only conduct a rear-guard action. Peking is an international city. We cannot use troops to crush the common people; there would be worldwide ramifications. Besides, as easy as it is to call in troops, it is not so easy to get rid of them. Who would assume the responsibility if something like the Lin Piao affair were to occur?"

"It is easy to call for immediate suppression," Vice-Chairman Wu smiled ironically, "but think it over. If we should not move against them now, we would be transforming all one hundred thousand into troublemakers. Then not even three hundred thousand troops would be enough to cope. So my strategy is to 'divide and conquer.' I will say a few words which will be recorded and broadcast to the demonstrators, persuading them to return to their homes, and, at the same time, accede to some of their demands. We will return the wreaths, for example, to the Memorial Plaque. At night, when it is dark, most of the crowd will lose steam after demonstrating all day, they will be hungry, and many will go home. When only the key diehards are left, we will surround them, and not a single one of them will escape. Now, tell me if you do not think this strategy will work."

"Let me add something to what Vice-Chairman Wu has just said," Department Head Hua continued. "The Public Security forces will keep a low profile. But from now on, every street in Peking will be under close surveillance. The investigations of the 'Five Black Elements,' as well as of the capitalist-roaders, have already begun in every part of the city. All governmental institutions, factories, schools, and neighborhood organizations have begun checking their rosters. Those who are not found at home will all be identified and listed. Not a single person will slip through our hands. Tonight, we can probably assemble ten thousand Militiamen, but they can only carry clubs, and are not permitted arms. Each platoon of Militiamen will be assigned an officer from the Public Security Department. Only he will be allowed to carry a gun. And, if anything extraordinary should crop up, only he will be authorized to use his weapon. This is an order."

❖ ❖ ❖

Thinking back to that fateful time, Ta-yung remembered how tense and upset he had been. Now, listening to Li P'ei-yi's reactionary talk, he had almost the same feeling.

"What you say is vicious calumny to our great Party and to our proletarian system," Ta-yung growled. "It is reactionary poison."

"This is not Peking," Li P'ei-yi reminded him. "Your posturings will not impress anyone. Look at the facts. I was also sent out of Peking in 1971, and, like your classmate, I studied for a month at the Production Division in Mongolia, and was then assigned to my unit.

"Chief Liu, you had not yet come. At that time, things were not at all what they are like now! The Unit was a little over fifty miles north of the Division headquarters; there were about ten wooden shacks on the high flatland, the work of the people who were there the previous year. We were divided into four teams, and those of us from Peking formed one team with the girl students from other cities. In the beginning, we thought we were being singled out for favored treatment, but then we realized that all this was a vicious plot on the part of Lao Kan-ch'en, the Unit head.

"In a few months, summer came to the steppes. The farming area of our team was in low-lying land, and the grasslands were still marshy, the mud reaching to our waists. Lao Kan-ch'en ordered us to dig out water ditches. Our legs became swollen after several days standing knee-deep in water and mud. At this point, Lao Kan-ch'en came to the commune, not to inspect our work, but to 'examine' the women in our team. He said he had had some medical experience in the army.

"Everyone believed him at first, until some of the women ran from his examination room. They said they preferred to work in the mud, even with swollen feet. Those who stayed in the room were transferred to work in Unit headquarters, where they ate well and lived comfortably. Young Swallow was examined, but when she saw that Lao Kan-ch'en was the only person in the room and that he was asking her to take off her clothes, she refused. She guessed his intention, although she never spoke out. Three other girls who were your classmates committed suicide shortly after they were 'examined.'

"We believed Lao Kan-ch'en's explanation that these girls had not been able to withstand the hardship of labor, that they could not overcome the bourgeois style of urban women, so they had resorted to suicide to escape the demands of the Revolution. Why did we trust Lao Kan-ch'en, you may ask? Because he was a veteran revolutionary, an old soldier, who could deceive us young people with one clever rationalization after another. Even when he was exposed, we did not believe what he had done was possible! We thought it was a rumor spread by the anti-revolutionary elements to undermine the prestige of our leadership. Or a dirty trick perpetrated by 'May 16th' *agents provocateurs*.

"When the facts were exposed in 1972, the Regional Military Command only stripped Lao Kan-ch'en of his position and sentenced him to five years of labor reform. But his accomplices were afraid that they would be implicated, so those sons of bitches, those running dogs, branded all of us in Team Number 2, who had been persecuted and abused, as 'May 16th'-type outlaws.

"At the same time, they sent the wife of Lao Kan-ch'en to Peking to appeal his case, not thinking that this would be brought to the attention of Yeh Chien-ying, head of the Military Affairs Committee. Yeh personally sent an investigator, who eventually changed the original five-year sentence to execution forthwith by firing squad. Lao Kan-ch'en's accomplices were all stripped of their rank and indicted, giving us some measure of justice. The action was applauded, and productivity improved in our farm unit. It had always been a unit 'on the dole,' getting our money and our provisions from above, but last fall we sent up some forty thousand pounds of produce. Now all the staff members and workers have been moved into real houses. And this year we are planning to reclaim some twenty thousand *mou* (three thousand acres) of barren land. During the last two years, everyone has been motivated to work to the utmost of his ability, and no one even thinks of going home for the holidays . . . Now, where was I?" There were tears in Li P'ei-yi's eyes, and Ta-yung was also crying.

"We must try to understand each other better," Ta-yung said, extending his hand in a gesture of conciliation. "I am not the kind of person you and Young Swallow imagine. We can become comrades." But Li P'ei-yi turned aloof and cool.

"Without going through actual experiences together, I cannot be sure whether we are really comrades or enemies who will face each other on the battlefront. One day, we might shake hands."

Li P'ei-yi stood up, gripping the edge of the upper bunk. With one pull, he did a reverse somersault into the upper bunk, as agile and as strong as a gymnast on the horizontal bar.

◊ ◊ ◊

Monday, February 11   4 a.m.

It was already four o'clock in the morning. Peking was quiet. The amber street lamps let off an eerie nighttime glow. The Imperial Palace perched like a giant sleeping lion. The white tower on the Ch'iung-hua Tao ("Island of Resplendent Flowers") in Pei-hai Kung-yüan ("Northern Lake Park") loomed majestically in the half-light, an immense apparition.

On the east bank of the lake in Chung-nan-hai stood an exquisite two-story building in the European style. Although the lights were out, one person was not yet asleep in a room on the west wing of the second floor. With his hands folded behind him, he stood in front of the closed window gazing out onto the frozen lake.

There was an equanimity in his face that reminded one of the smooth surface of the lake, but like the currents under the ice, his heart was troubled. How could he rest, when so many urgent burdens weighed heavily on him?

On which side did truth lie? Which side really represented the will of the people? Which side embodied true Marxism-Leninism? Which way should he turn on the road to happiness for the people of China?

He recalled the face of current Party theoretician Yao Wen-yüan:

"We can no longer afford to walk along the road of compromise. This is a moment of decision. We must make public Chairman Mao's last will and testament. In it he clearly stated: 'The whole Party must rally around my wife, Madame Mao, and the power of the Party, the government, and the military must be put in her hands. Only in this way can we resist Soviet revisionist Socialist imperialism abroad, and suppress the capitalistic, anti-revolutionary activity at home.' You are the Head of the Public Security Department. These developments are your responsibilities . . ."

"Your responsibilities . . . your responsibilities . . ."

What did these responsibilities entail?

When he had come to work in Peking eight years ago, it was on a cold winter night like this that Premier Chou had received him.

"I hear that the Chairman has put you in charge of the committee investigating the Lin Piao case. I strongly endorse his choice. There are many problems in this task, many obstacles, but I know you can negotiate them successfully. Our Party has been led off into the wrong direction many times, mostly toward the right. The case of Lin Piao looks as if it is leftist in bent, but actually it is also rightist. It happens to look like an extreme leftist posture and that deceives many people. Now it is important to expose that episode as a historical lesson for our Party, as well as for the people of China. I hope you will work hard to accomplish this."

Premier Chou's expression, his face and voice, were impressed indelibly on his memory. Yes, the situation now at hand must become a historical lesson for the Chinese people, but how should one present that lesson?

He pulled close the thick curtains, turned on the lights, and went to an old steel cabinet behind the desk. He unlocked it and took out a batch of documents tied with a black ribbon.

On the cover sheet of these documents was clearly marked: "Materials Relating to the Connection Between the Lin Piao Bloc and Madame Mao."† On the cover, slightly faded with time, were stamped the words: "Top Secret."

◇ ◇ ◇

Monday, February 11   6 a.m.

The violent rocking of the train compartment awakened Chia. Outside the window, one could see the beginning of a sunny day. He looked at his wristwatch. It was already six o'clock, not his usual time to wake up. What had happened yesterday felt like a dream today. A short while ago, he could not have imagined that he would be on this train, about to leave behind his home, his job, his old haunts. How could he have guessed that he would be leaving his motherland for a country he had visited before, but which still remained alien and forbidding.

† Materials concerning the Lin Piao affair form the basis of the author's new novel, *Flying Toward the Rainbow* (*Fei-hsiang ts'ai-hung*), now being serialized in a Japanese periodical—TRANSLATOR.

The train stopped suddenly at a small station, where the express trains did not normally stop. Chia was immediately on guard. He put on his jacket, took his belongings, and went to the washroom at the end of the compartment to prepare himself for a quick getaway, should the Security agents board the train for a search.

While he washed up he kept an eye on the situation outside the train. There was no need for apprehension. There was no one boarding the train; it appeared to have stopped for another reason.

Another train, heavily loaded, flashed by from the opposite direction. It was a military train. Scores of flatcars were piled high with bulky forms. Their tarpaulin covers were outlined by protruding muzzles, which betrayed the presence of tanks underneath. Chia could see at a glance that these were heavy tanks of the "T'a-shan" ("Pagoda Mountain") model, designed in 1965 and subsequently mass-produced.

The cars of the convoy train rushed toward Peking, and Chia confirmed the accuracy of his guess, that these reinforcements were in response to the secret telegram that he had sent for his division commander.

The train waited for what seemed a long time. Chia, meanwhile, was deep in thought. So many tanks were being shipped away from the Inner Mongolia frontier that it must have created a gap in the nation's defenses. The Military Affairs Committee would certainly know about this, since the Railway Department would report the switch in traffic patterns.

These troops were going to Peking. What changes, he wondered, were to befall that city?

There was a sudden jolt, and the train started up again. Chia looked out the window and saw a precipitous mountain range and an ash-gray line winding its way along the valleys and peaks. It was the Great Wall of China! In the early morning light, it reflected the rays of the golden sun. Ah! To leave the Central Plain, and to go into the steppes beyond the Wall. But the day would come, he thought, when he would return.

▨ TEN

Monday, February 11
Noon, Peking Standard Time
Lunar Calendar: 12th month, 27th day

"Don't you think the duties of the Urban Workers Militia are too broad?" Chief Liu asked skeptically.

"Why do you say 'broad'?" Ta-yung asked. "These units go wherever and do whatever the Central Committee commands."

"When you talked about your experiences in Shanghai, you said the Workers Militia performed 'three routine tasks': maintaining law and order, maintaining civil defense, and firefighting. But law and order should be the responsibility of the Public Security Department of the city. If the Militia troops have guard duty on the streets, and in addition have to protect the granaries, the oil repositories, the coal houses, the railways, and the bridges, how can they accomplish their own production quotas?"

"In general, they perform these duties after work."

"But after work, they should rest and sleep. If they continue this double duty, it will affect their work adversely."

"We do not see it that way. The complexity of class struggle and the needs of the Party's Central Committee require us to do without much rest or relaxation."

"But I am not clear about the need for military training in the People's Militia."

"Chief Liu, do you not think that the People's Militia has to develop military skills?"

"But the question is, which skills?"

"Urban defense skills."

"In our country, we have more than four million regular troops. In addition, there are another four million veterans who have undergone military training, some who have had more than enough experience in active combat. If our motherland were to be attacked by foreign invaders, these fully trained land and naval forces are capable of fending them off. The Militia constitutes a support arm of the regular army. Isn't that right?"

"Absolutely correct."

"But the tendency is now totally different. From the organization and training methods of the Urban Workers Militias in Shanghai, Peking, and other cities, it is entirely clear that you are not preparing to fight off invading imperialists; you have in mind a different kind of enemy."

"What kind of enemy?"

"The masses and the People's Liberation Army."

"What you have just said is the worst kind of heresy," Ta-yung said, becoming upset once again.

"Let us look at the facts. No need to become so disturbed. The Urban Workers Militia of Shanghai has organized eight hundred thousand people, but the real core is no more than sixty thousand."

Ta-yung was shocked that this closely guarded figure should be known by a farm unit chief from a border area.

Liu said, "But what weapons are these sixty thousand armed with?"

"I have no idea."

"All you have is anti-aircraft artillery!"

"But we have to defend the skies!"

"Are you simple-minded? Do you think that when the imperalist countries attack, they will be so considerate as to use World War II bombers and fly so slowly and at such a low altitude that you can shoot them down?"

"If the anti-aircraft artillery is not for airplanes, what is it for?"

"What is it for? Aim low and it can shoot at tanks and at houses; the tanks of the People's Liberation Army, the houses that shelter the masses."

"What proof do you have?"

"There is plenty of proof. From my own experience in the last stages of the Cultural Revolution, I can personally testify to the effect of these weapons when used in this way. For that reason, the Military Commands in the country will not issue these weapons to the Militia. You know that."

◈ ◈ ◈

Ta-yung remembered the events of two years ago. He had gone with Commissar Hsieh to the Military Command to requisition armaments. The commander had turned them away, passing the requisition on to a staff member who had processed the order in the most perfunctory way. A month later, the weapons were sent to the headquarters of the Militia. They had sent weapons, all right, but the weapons were broken-down guns, World War II issue, that had been abandoned almost a generation ago by the forces led by Chiang Kai-shek and the Americans. There were heavy machine guns that could not fire a bullet and mortars with vital parts missing.

These shortcomings had not daunted the young students and workers. In less than two months, they not only had repaired these weapons, but they had begun to construct new weapons, a light rocket launcher with a range finder at short distances, for instance. This was a weapon used to good effect by the Egyptians against the Israeli tanks during the Fourth Middle Eastern War (October 6, 1973). Two months ago the weapon was successfully test-fired, and now they were being mass-produced at Tsing-hua University.

Ta-yung had also participated in the design and production of weapons, but at the time the only targets he had in mind were the tanks of the Soviet revisionists. He never imagined that they would be used to fire upon his own people, the People's Liberation Army. Now that Chief Liu mentioned this, it all came back to him. The design and production of this new weapon were certainly guarded with the utmost secrecy. When people wanted to approach the Defense Ministry for information on the thickness of the armor on Soviet tanks, as well as related subjects, Commissar Hsieh strictly advised against further inquiries. After the successful test-firing, the radical group gave copies of the design specifications to (former) Vice-Chairman Wang Hung-wen, who was attending a meeting in Peking. He had taken them to Shanghai, and no doubt they now had this weapon there.

◇ ◇ ◇

"Do you know what kind of weapon the Shanghai Militia is currently constructing?" Chief Liu gazed out the window. Snow covered the steppes and pure white stretched as far as the eye could see. The clear blue sky joined the dazzling white that mantled the earth.

Ta-yung had no answer, and Chief Liu continued what had turned out to be a monologue.

"They are building a double-barrel, rapid-fire anti-aircraft gun, 35 mm., which can penetrate three or four layers of brick wall in one shot. During the fifteen days and nights of the bloody battle in 1967 in Wuchou of Kwangsi Province, there were two Red Guard groups, the 'April 22nd' Revolutionary

Army of Insurrection (the 'April 22nd' Red Guards) and the United Command of the Proletarian Revolutionary Insurrectionists of the Kwangsi region (the United Command). It was this gun that leveled ten blocks, reducing half the city to rubble. At that time, the United Command insurrectionist group had only six of these weapons."

The chief looked as if he were back at the scene. His face was deadly serious.

"Now Shanghai has organized two hundred and five anti-aircraft artillery companies, and if we estimate three guns for each company, then we have more than six hundred guns. Who are they going to be used against? Against the imperialists? No. Against the people.

"In the end, who do you mean by 'the people'?" Chief Liu continued. "What are their aspirations? You should think a little bit about that. All too frequently, there are those who speak of 'the people' in the abstract, but without any thought as to who 'the people' really are. On the contrary, they look at the people in real life as the mob, or as anti-revolutionary, or as 'backward' elements retarded in their ideological thinking. Actually, these individuals are themselves isolated from the people; they are the new class who, having reached the top, have alienated themselves from the people. Even if they blind themselves with brilliant theories, ignore the reality around them, and refuse to recognize the real contradictions that cannot be explained away, in the end, inevitably, they will be overwhelmed by a sea of humanity, by the sheer numbers of 'the people.' History gives sufficient evidence of this."

The train was approaching a settlement. Outside the window, more and more buildings came into view. One could see fur-clad figures riding horse-drawn sleighs, gliding by quickly on the snow.

Chief Liu got up and roused Li P'ei-yi, who had been sleeping soundly in the upper bunk. When the train reached Ta-t'ung, most of the peasant passengers got off, and the commotion in the train disappeared. When they reached Chi-ning, most of the cadres and military men bound for Huhehot, the capital of Inner Mongolia, got off to change trains. Those left in the compartment felt a sense of isolation. The monotonous snowscape provided little to see and gave them a chance to meditate and think.

Before the train reached Sai-han-t'a-la, Chia and Li P'ei-yi went to the dining car for lunch. Li P'ei-yi ate and then came back, but Chia stayed, drinking beer. Three hours passed and he had still not come back.

Ta-yung went to the dining car to look for him. It had been closed for some time. Where could Chia have gone? There was no sign of his overcoat or his luggage. Ta-yung was puzzled.

The train pulled slowly into the Erh-lien Railway Station. Li P'ei-yi opened the window and stuck his head out. Five youngsters came running and yelling alongside the train window, as if they wanted to pull Li P'ei-yi right out.

The young people were all wearing sheepskin overalls, lined with fur. They had on mittens, and long snow boots. Only their reddish faces were visible, but as they all looked alike, one could not distinguish boy from girl.

The train stopped and the hurried job of moving the freight began. Ta-yung helped to carry out the cartons, while Li P'ei-yi yelled to the people outside, "Watch out. Handle that one with care. This is honey in glass containers. That one is grape wine . . . Don't put that carton on the bottom; it's got rice noodles and might get crushed . . . This is peanut crunch . . ."

The people outside were yelling back in excitement, busy moving the cartons. As the last carton was passed through the window, Ta-yung breathed a sigh of relief. Chief Liu wiped the sweat off his face with a towel, and said to Ta-yung, "We are happy to welcome you to our farm as a guest. Let us see the New Year in together."

Ta-yung smiled. As he prepared to leave the train, the conductor hurried over from the far end of the compartment with the railway security guard and four or five Public Security agents in tow.

"The military type in the lower bunk, where did he go?"

Chief Liu was stunned for a moment before answering, "We do not know him. We have not seen him for three hours. What has happened?"

"Which unit do you come from?" asked the man in a blue uniform.

Chief Liu turned the tables: "Which unit do *you* come from?"

The fellow in the blue uniform looked down at him and smiled condescendingly. The railway security guard interrupted, "He has been sent out specially by the Peking Public Security Department."

"Oh! from Peking, eh? This fellow and I are agricultural workers of the National Farm. These are my work papers."

"Ah! You are the supervisor on the farm. A cadre of the country! You should not be so unco-operative." The agent coldly returned the papers to Chief Liu, then turned to Ta-yung: "Are you also an agricultural worker?"

Ta-yung thought the cadre was impudent, but he gave him a civil answer: "I am a student from Tsing-hua University in Peking."

"A student, eh? Do you have any identification? Why do you come to a town at the border?"

Ta-yung quickly took his student identity card from his jacket pocket, and with it his Militia armband.

"You are a Militiaman!"

"Not only that," Li P'ei-yi interjected. "He is a battalion leader."

As the man in the blue uniform carefully scrutinized Ta-yung's identity card, he became a bit warmer toward him.

"What responsibilities do you have in the Militia organization?"

"I am a member of the Peking Militia Command, as well as aide-de-camp in the Combat Section."

"Are you here on assignment?"

"No, I have come here to visit a classmate of mine. I am headed for National Farm Unit Number 74."

"Did you know the fellow sleeping in bunk seventeen?"

"Yes, he is Chia Hsiang-tung, my cousin's husband. He works at the Peking Central Garrison Division as Section Head."

"You are related then!" The man in the blue uniform perked up.

"We are, but we rarely see each other. We met only after we had both boarded the train. He found a vacant bed for me when the train reached Chang-chia-k'ou, and called me over."

The conductor confirmed the truth of Ta-yung's statement.

"What is wrong with that fellow?" Chief Liu asked.

"He is a spy of the Soviet revisionists who has committed an offense against the state. Now the whole country is looking for him."

Everyone tensed. Ta-yung collapsed into a nearby bed like a deflated balloon. The faces of Commissar Hsieh and the others floated up before his eyes. Chia was a traitor to the motherland, an enemy of the people.

Chief Liu described in detail Chia Hsiang-tung's clothing, the items he was carrying, and when he had last seen him.

"He was carrying a lot of cash. When he paid his bill in the dining car, I saw a wad of bills this thick." Li P'ei-yi described how large it was with his hands. "They looked like bills in large denominations."

"Were they new bills or used?"

"All used."

"When you had finished eating, was he still eating?"

"He was. I left as soon as I was finished. He said he wanted to drink a little more beer."

"Who saw him after that?"

The three of them all shook their heads.

"That means he got off at Sai-han-t'a-la. Smart!"

The man in blue folded up the notebook in which he had been writing, and said to the three of them, "He will not get away from the dragnet of the people's law. Thank you for your help." He got off the train with his entourage, leaving Chief Liu and the others staring silently at each other.

"What happened just now?" a boisterous youth was yelling at the entrance to the train. "You did not get off the train, and you are blocking my way."

Ta-yung picked up his pack and followed Li P'ei-yi off the train. Chief Liu was already surrounded by a group of people shouting and yelling. The cartons were stacked in neat piles on a truck not far from the station platform.

Chief Liu told the crowd to quiet down, and said, "Young Swallow, your visitor has arrived. Why don't you come out to receive him?"

Ta-yung, who was standing by the train, saw a woman turn around. That was her! Young Swallow!

Her dark face was shadowed by the furry hood of her overcoat, but it betrayed a mixture of shock, anger, and coldness; Ta-yung sensed it.

"Last week, I wrote you a letter." Ta-yung mustered up his courage and spoke to Young Swallow as she approached. "I told you that I would arrive today."

"I did not receive it. When the snow closes us in, the mail comes only once a week. Your letter is probably still in the mailbag in the truck."

"If you do not find it convenient for me to stay here, and since we have seen each other, I can just give you the things your mother asked me to bring, and I will go back to Peking."

"No, that is not necessary," Young Swallow cut him off. "It is just that you caught me by surprise, so I am a little at a loss."

"Young Swallow!" The people were already on the truck, and they yelled out, "Get on!"

Chief Liu patted Ta-yung on the shoulder, and said with a smile, "You had better get into the truck. You are lucky. Otherwise, on the snow sled it would take you a whole day to get there."

"Since you have come all this way, come see our farm," said

Young Swallow. "Chief Liu, we can put a guest up for a while, can't we?"

"Of course. Hop on!"

Ta-yung was pulled into the rear of the truck along with Chief Liu and Young Swallow. With a yell to the driver, the truck started. The wheels had chains, and they crunched against the thick crust of ice as the truck drove off.

It was an ordinary "Liberation"-model truck, produced at the first truck factory at Ch'ang-ch'un in Manchuria. This particular factory had been designed and equipped by the Soviet Union during China's first Five-Year Plan, and after ten years of improvements and expansion, the factory had not only surpassed its annual production quota of twenty thousand vehicles several times over, but it had also completely revamped its quality control. The truck weighed five tons, and it could not only drive over the steep and icy mountains of Tibet, but it could also negotiate the scorching Gobi Desert, bearing up, just like the Chinese people, under extremes.

The canvas top was pulled halfway down. The young people were unafraid of the cold and did not relish the idea of sitting in the dark beneath it, rocking up and down with the jolting of the truck. Instead they stood against the wind, looking ahead, grasping the frame of the truck. Ta-yung stood with them. He looked at the unfamiliar scenery around him, and at the same time stole glances at Young Swallow, who was staring silently into the distance.

"Why don't they drive straight ahead?" Ta-yung asked Young Swallow. "Why must they make such circles?" He asked as much to break the awkward silence as to find out.

"See how flat it looks everywhere. But over there is a big basin area over which the wind has blown the snow. In some places the snow will be ten meters deep. If the truck were to drive over there, they would not find us until next summer."

"Is it dangerous to walk over those spots?" Ta-yung asked.

"You have to wear snowshoes. Otherwise, you will sink out of sight, too."

"Then you should be careful!"

"Me? I know every river and every valley in this area as well as I know the streets and byways of Peking. Do not worry about me. It is you who must be careful."

Ta-yung changed the subject. "Your mother misses you!"

"When does a day go by that I do not miss her too? It is easy to talk about going back to spend the holiday. But in one trip, two years of accumulated savings will be spent. At home, the problem would not go away, no matter how many tears were shed. And, after the visit, I would still have to come back, feeling worse than before. One visit home would take me months to get over."

The wind blew off her hood. Young Swallow did not draw it back, but let her hair blow loose in the wind.

"Thank you for helping to look after my mother. But Young Tiger is now back in Peking, so there is someone else to lend a hand. You are busy with your studies and your work; do not feel that you have to visit her so often."

"You do not want me to visit your mother?"

"No, I do not. And furthermore, I do not want you to give her money every month. What do you think you are doing? Are you trying to buy my affection?"

Ta-yung felt wronged and misunderstood, and sensed that their relationship was now beyond repair. How many years had he loved her, how long had he given her his deepest devotion? He felt numb. Reason and feeling were at odds. His hands gripped the frame of the truck.

"Why did you make my letters common knowledge?"

"Aren't we classmates?"

"Ah, yes . . . just classmates." Ta-yung could not answer in any other way.

"There are more than ten classmates of ours here now. Of course they have a right to look."

"But I was writing only to you. Others would misconstrue what I wrote and misjudge me."

"Misjudge you? Not at all. From the day we were assigned

to our posts, everyone understood you all too clearly. What is there to misjudge?"

"In the train, Comrade Li P'ei-yi explained the problem to me. For a long time, you thought that I was nothing more than an offspring of a high-ranking cadre, receiving special privileges. Is that not right?"

"Well, doesn't that fit the facts? Do you want to be a version of Chung Chih-min? He capitalized on the 'Against the Current' movement, and criticized his father, who was a high-ranking military officer. His father had brought him from the village to the military, and had then stuck him in the university. Ultimately, Chung Chih-min was praised in the newspaper. Unfortunately, he was not as lucky as Chang T'ieh-sheng, who was admitted to the university despite the fact that he had turned in a blank entrance examination, and later became a representative of the People's Congress. The irony of it is that Chung Chih-min was 'transferred downward' to the village and 'relocated,' just as he had wished. Do you want to know what has become of him, now?"

"I have been helped by no one," Ta-yung said in a low, pained voice, ignoring the last question. "My mother died when I was a child, my father remarried, and they had very little to do with me for a long time. I lived in my uncle's house, and my life there was no different from that of an orderly in the army. If I had had family connections, I would not have attended an ordinary middle school. My admission to a technical school was determined by the authorities. My chance of going to the university from the factory was decided by the old hands at the factory. Everything I have achieved has been the result of my own efforts; there has been no family support in my advancement." He spoke without fear of being overheard.

Chief Liu sat on the cartons, and he heard every word. He also realized that the relationship between these two young people looked simple, but he knew it was actually very complicated. In his other capacity as deputy secretary of the local

Party, he normally supervised the work assignments and the political education of his farm unit, and he occasionally took an interest in the welfare of the young people under him. But he had never really thought much about their love life; these adolescent Red Guards were all too young. But they were now over twenty. When he was their age, although he had moved around as a guerrilla fighter in the T'ai-hang Mountains, he had fallen hopelessly in love with a female soldier who was now his wife, and was waiting for him back at the farm.

◈ ◈ ◈

Same Day   5 p.m.

The truck continued toward the west, and the sun hastened to its resting place. The wind had changed into a bone-chilling gale and everyone had taken cover behind the canvas top except Ta-yung, who still stood, his face numb and his hands grasping the truck frame. But his heart was not dulled by the cold. Had he not restrained himself, he would have long ago jumped from the truck and walked back to the station, hopping on the earliest train for Peking. Perhaps by working as hard as he could at the university factory, and at the Militia Command headquarters, he could drown out the pain of this meeting with Young Swallow.

The snow thinned out, the steppes showed patches of yellow, and as the truck wound around the hills, the road became bumpy, and those who had been sitting now rose. The sun had dropped below the horizon.

"We are back at the farm!" a voice yelled out loudly.

There were houses in the distance, and one could see people waving cloth pennants.

"Funny! Why don't they turn on the lights?" Li P'ei-yi asked.

"There is no storm, so the power lines could not have been blown down!"

"Maybe they are economizing."

Two shadows detached themselves from the houses, and came toward the truck on the main road. Under the fiery red sky, one could make out two riders on horseback, galloping closer and closer.

In breathless admiration, Ta-yung watched these young people riding toward him. One of the riders deftly turned his horse around, followed the moving truck a few paces, and with one hand grabbing onto the side, pulled himself into the back. He blurted out: "Is Chief Liu here?"

"What has happened?" Chief Liu stood up.

"Huang Yu-te of Team Number 7 has discovered something amiss at the border. Two hours ago, this was reported to headquarters. We telephoned the Erh-lien Railway Station, and they told us you were on your way, so we have been waiting for you."

"Why should you wait for me? Where is the Party secretary?"

"Secretary Ch'iao has taken charge, and he has sent out two teams to reconnoiter. The troops at the border defenses have been notified. Commander Shen said that he would send troops immediately to Hill 767."

"What was it that Huang Yu-te found?"

"The border markers have been pulled out for a distance of three kilometers. On the ground there are traces of tank treads. We guess that the Soviets and Mongolians sent across some four vehicles."

"Outrageous!" the young people exclaimed.

"Huang Yu-te's team had just come down from Hill 744, when they were fired upon by the enemy from behind Hill 767."

"You mean, the enemy actually started firing?" Chief Liu asked in disbelief.

"They fired over our heads."

"Did you return the fire?"

"We fired three rounds as warning shots."

"What tricks are the Soviet and Mongolian revisionists up to? Tell Old Ho to drive faster."

"Have we no electrical power? Why didn't you turn on the lights?"

"We were afraid of exposing ourselves as targets in the dark, so we went into combat alert."

"All right. But let's not panic. They seem to be offering a few firecrackers for the New Year festivities, but they won't find us an easy mark."

Coming upon the farm unit in the midst of this incident, Ta-yung saw at firsthand the value and importance of frontier outposts, and he began to understand the complexities of international relations.

Chief Liu spoke to the young man who had vaulted onto the truck. Now he nimbly jumped back onto his horse and joined the other rider. The two of them galloped back to the farm.

Halfway up the south face of the slope stood several houses surrounded by a high earthen wall forming the rural settlement. In front of the rock entrance with its wooden gate, a high-spirited crowd was already forming. The truck drove right into the courtyard, and the crowd immediately surrounded it. Ta-yung saw that everyone had a gun strapped on his back.

Chief Liu jumped off the truck and barked a few orders to Young Swallow, who was still in the truck. "You take charge of putting these holiday items in storage. Li P'ei-yi, you follow me. Comrade Hsiao, come along with us to the meeting."

Ta-yung picked up his pack and followed Li P'ei-yi into a mud-walled, thatched-roof house situated in the northern end of the compound. Inside, two ping-pong tables had been put together to form one large conference table. Chief Liu began conferring at the table with a short man, roughly forty years old. On the table was laid out a big map of the region.

"Come over, let me introduce you," Chief Liu beckoned to Ta-yung. "This is the Party secretary of our farm, Comrade

Ch'iao Chien. This is our guest, Comrade Hsiao, a member of the Peking Militia Command."

"My name is Hsiao Ta-yung. I am a student of Tsing-hua University in Peking and I have many classmates here." Ta-yung looked around, and indeed recognized a number of faces.

"Those imperialist gangsters," Secretary Ch'iao said, "took out the border markers along this basin area, for five kilometers, from Hill 714 to Hill 917." He pointed to the map.

National Farm Unit Number 74 was about a hundred kilometers from Erh-lien, northwest of Ai-erh-ko-yin-su-mu, midway to the Ulanbatorhot settlement of the Mongolian People's Republic. The border line was clearly marked. There was a T-shaped basin which was crossed at the middle by the border.

"This basin is rich grazing land, where the cattle of the farm unit feed in the summer. It should not be allowed to fall into the hands of the Soviet revisionists."

Outside, in the courtyard, the two horsemen rode in and burst through the door.

"Sir! Hill 767 has been occupied by the regular troops of Soviet Mongolia; we have no idea as to how many. From the sound of the motors, it would appear that there are a number of armored vehicles gathering."

"What areas do you still hold?" Chief Liu asked anxiously. The man pointed to the map. Hsiao Ta-yung recognized an old classmate.

"We sent out two patrols. Now, one is on Hill 744, and the other is east on Hill 658."

"Where does the sound of motors come from?"

"It is coming directly from the north, behind the basin area."

Secretary Ch'iao analyzed the situation: "Yesterday, Company Two of the Fourth Brigade sent people to the North Sea basin to arrange for the storage of fodder, and saw nothing out of order there. Yesterday afternoon, we saw our own border patrol passing through the basin along the markers, so we know that the markers were still there as late as yesterday afternoon."

"Were they taken out by the Mongolian cowherds or by Soviet troops? This is a crucial point that needs to be clarified."

"Judging from the present evidence at hand, it was done by Soviet troops."

"That's right," Ch'iao said. "Look here. In 1961, Ulanhot became the base for the Soviet revisionists. In the beginning, they had only a company stationed there. In '63, they augmented their forces with a regiment, equipped with several armored vehicles. By '68, it had increased to a full division. In '70, it expanded to two divisions, and they began to dig in. Since year before last, the Mongolian herdsmen who traveled freely in these parts and who were friendly toward us have all disappeared. Some very strange-looking 'herdsmen' have taken their place, herdsmen bent on making trouble. According to intelligence reports, the Soviet revisionists have constructed a guided missile base on this site. Its target, some six hundred kilometers away, is the heart of our country, Peking.

"In addition to all this, in 1976, an armored division was added, with an estimated strength of four hundred tanks. What, one asks, was their mission?

"Simple. This build-up of an armored division does not indicate defensive action, but is poised for a Hitler-type blitzkrieg. Once they are loosed, they could quickly overrun Hill 767, storm through our settlement here, and hit Sai-han-t'a-la to the south. Following the railway line, they would attack Chi-ning. Then, after they have joined forces with a second force on the western front that will have already attacked Pai-yün-o-po, Pao-t'ou, and Huhehot, they will attack Ta-t'ung and T'ai-yüan, besieging northern China from the rear, thus cutting off communications between the Central Plain and the northwest.

"Therefore, our mission is to guard Hill 744, recapture Hill 767, and control this corridor. This fits in with the original design of the Military Affairs Committee when it first decided to establish production divisions here. Let us keep in touch with each other by phone."

Communication lines to the other brigades were set up by

means of loudspeakers and telephones hastily arranged on the ping-pong tables. Chief Liu now assumed the role of military commander, and his gaze slashed like sharp steel.

"The lines are open with Brigades One, Three, and Four."

"Hello? This is Chief Liu. From now on, I declare the entire farm in a state of combat alert."

Ta-yung looked at his wristwatch. It was 7:10 P.M., Peking time. He listened apprehensively to Chief Liu's orders.

"All brigades will regroup into military lines of organization. Check your weapons, and make sure everything is in order. Move all foodstuffs, provisions, daily necessities, and production tools into the underground tunnels. Organize yourselves into work teams to set up defenses and redouble sentry watches. No one is allowed off the compound without orders.

"The Fourth Brigade will dispatch two teams to relieve the teams on Hill 744 and Hill 658. Take three days of rations with you. We will dispatch two units to set up lines of communication with your command posts on the hills, so that we can keep in constant touch on the situation.

"I would guess that the Soviets will not launch a large-scale attack just now. They are probably massing invasion troops at the moment. No sense alarming them unduly. Do not break cover but keep a close watch, and do not shoot unless it is absolutely necessary."

Chief Liu looked at Secretary Ch'iao, and handed the receiver to him.

"Comrade farm laborers," Ch'iao said. "When the motherland needs us, we become soldiers guarding her frontiers. We will never allow our sacred homeland to be encroached upon by the enemy. However, you must maintain poise and discipline. You must definitely not fire the first shot. Do not give them any cause, or any basis of truth for their foul slanders and their vile propaganda. Orders must be obeyed to the letter!"

The people in the room put down their guns. Smiling, Chief Liu said, "Members of Brigade Two, do not be so impatient.

You have other missions to perform. There may be more than enough combat missions tomorrow."

Everyone heard the roars outside: "Second Brigade! Fall in! Second Brigade! Fall in!"

Everyone stormed out of the barracks, and stood in formation in the courtyard.

Young Swallow did not join the formation, which was some four hundred strong. Wearing a belt of bullets across her chest, with a short-barrel gun on her shoulder, a first-aid pack on her back, she stood facing the troops. She appeared to be a commanding officer.

Li P'ei-yi stepped forward one pace and barked: "Company One is responsible tonight for guard duty and for reconnaissance. Company Two will be in charge of transferring all foodstuffs and provisions into the tunnels. Company Three will inspect all defense installations, and will be in charge of ammunition supplies. Dis-missed!"

They scattered like ants from an anthill that has been disturbed. Li P'ei-yi entered the room, saluted Chief Liu, and gave his report.

"Sir, the two communications units are set to go!"

"Take off now. And be careful."

Ta-yung spoke up, "Can I go too?"

"You want a taste of combat action, eh?" Chief Liu smiled. "How about tomorrow? You are still completely new to these parts. You had better stay inside."

Ta-yung stood at the gate looking at Li P'ei-yi leading a dozen men carrying telephone wire out of the courtyard. They disappeared into the darkness.

▧ ELEVEN

Monday, February 11   10 a.m.

Since early in the morning, the offices of the Ministry of Foreign Affairs had been a beehive of activity. At nine o'clock, the head of the Russian and East European Section in the Ministry summoned the Soviet Ambassador to Peking by telephone, and told him to appear at the Ministry offices.

At ten o'clock sharp, the Soviet Ambassador arrived. In the reception hall, the dour head of the Ministry's Russian and East European Section appeared in person to lodge an official protest against the improper actions of Shlovsky, the attaché at the Soviet Legation; he also informed the Ambassador that Shlovsky was henceforth persona non grata and demanded his departure from the country within forty-eight hours.

He did not expect a protest, but the Soviet Ambassador insisted on clarification of the specific actions deemed objectionable.

"On matters such as these, our government is not obliged to explain."

"Then, on behalf of my government," the Ambassador continued, "I must express with deep regret that I protest most vehemently the ill-advised action of your government."

"It is now February 11, 10:05 A.M., Peking Standard Time," the section head retorted. "I repeat, Shlovsky must leave this country forty-eight hours from now. Please attend to it."

Without waiting for the Soviet Ambassador's response, the section head and his interpreter both left the reception hall. This hard-line posture was unprecedented, and the Ambassador and Vishinsky, who had been temporarily pressed into service as an interpreter, were both breathless with outrage and indignation.

As they left, the Russians bumped into a group of foreign reporters exiting from the press reception room, used exclusively by the Foreign Ministry Press Bureau. From the transparent expressions of dismay on the Russians' faces, the outcome of their visit was obvious.

While Vishinsky felt defeated by the treatment they had received, he was somewhat elated by dreams of glory. With Shlovsky expelled by the Chinese government, his career would be finished. Back in Moscow, he would be relegated to pushing papers until he was retired. But for himself, he should be sitting in the number-one chair in Peking, free to work out his own particular ambitions. The beautiful Natasha would stay, her Chinese lover gone, and he would be the boss!

In the midst of this enchanting picture, Vishinsky looked up to see the newly appointed correspondent of the national television network in India, Ali Singh, and the Yugoslavian reporter, Mihute, walking toward him, talking in hushed voices. Vishinsky nodded his head in greeting.

"Aren't we all busy this morning!" he said, affecting ingenuousness.

"There was some earth-shaking news this morning," Ali Singh said. "It is rumored that a 'pillar' in the Soviet Embassy has just been toppled. Can you confirm it?"

"Don't worry about it. We will have it all taken care of shortly. But look at that notebook of yours, it looks empty. Won't your boss deduct from your salary?"

"No problem. My boss understands my situation. His advice was, 'Go to a place with no bars and no news, and take a rest for two years.' So here I am."

"How was the party last night?" Vishinsky turned to Mihute.

"Marvelous! What a pity they would not let you in."

"What? How did you know?"

"Why would I not know?"

"Then there must be many things you don't know."

"On the contrary, there are so many things I really know, but which I have to pretend I don't know. Otherwise, I would have to pack my bags and go home."

The three laughed heartily. Although they were speaking in English, the receptionist from the Foreign Ministry escorting them out appeared upset. As he watched them getting into the car, he said to himself, "This kind of impudence must be reported to the authorities."

◇ ◇ ◇

Same Day   3 p.m.

Ch'iao Kuan-hua was not at the Foreign Ministry. He had attended the first meeting with the Japanese economic delegation at two o'clock, and had gone directly from there to the Planning Commission. On Minister Ch'iao's arrival, he had found Vice-Premier Li and Commissar Sha talking.

"Commander Ch'en thinks that, when necessary, there should be an emergency meeting of those members of the Party Central Committee resident in Peking. This recommendation has met with the approval of General Yeh Chien-ying, head of the Military Affairs Committee. As to the exact time of the meeting, we will leave it to you, Vice-Premier Li, to decide."

"If you want to dump the load on me, I'll carry it."

"It is not a question of responsibility. The military cannot take it upon themselves to inform the Committee members without risking being misunderstood."

"You have a point there," Vice-Premier Li said. Then, turning to the other member of the group, Chairman Hsü of the Secretariat, he said, "Chairman Hsü, will you find out how many members of the Central Committee are now in Peking, and give me a list?"

Chairman Hsü, who had been silent, immediately walked to the Secretariat Office. Vice-Premier Li noticed Minister Ch'iao, though he had been in the room for some time.

"My old friend Ch'iao, what is going on at your end?"

"We are very pressed. A Japanese newspaper published the story. Although it specified that the source for the news was a Soviet Intelligence officer, the impact has been tremendous. Early this morning, almost all the foreign correspondents came crowding into our Press Bureau. We had no choice but to call a press conference, and managed to get over the worst of it. Their feeling of dissatisfaction was understandable, but now that the fire has burned through the paper, we cannot use it to wrap things up."

"What is the reaction of the various legations?"

"Not a word."

"This must mean that they are taking a wait-and-see stance. The credibility of the Party for several decades cannot be ruined like this."

Vice-Premier Li showed his agitation. He stood up, put his hands behind his back, and paced back and forth in the room.

The door opened. The Deputy Chief of Staff of the PLA, Wu Wei, who had authority over the Peking garrison, stormed into the room, his face red. From years of habit developed while he was in the service of Vice-Premier Li (when Li was his superior in the army), he saluted Li as he stepped in.

"What do you have to tell us?" asked Li.

"Sir, the Peking Workers Militia has called its troops to order for an urgent campaign. They are now occupying various key locations in the traffic flow of the city. Since they did not inform the Peking Garrison Command of their action, I have come here to report the situation."

"How many of them are there?"

"According to our estimates, it is only a part of the Urban Workers Militia, or roughly one hundred thousand. None of the peasants from the outlying areas have appeared yet. Altogether, though, if they all should turn up, they could total over eight hundred thousand."

"Are they armed?"

"All fully armed. Which is why we are so concerned."

"Fully armed!" Chairman Hsü, who had returned from the Secretariat Office, spoke in alarm. "This violates our agreement. During the earthquake, the Militiamen sent out to maintain law and order were not permitted to bear arms. This—"

"We did not want any mishaps, so we have withdrawn the regular PLA patrols."

"Why did you call them back?" Li asked angrily.

"Because in some areas of the city Militiamen put up barricades and did not let our soldiers pass through."

"Has it come to that?" Now Minister Ch'iao was alarmed as well.

"What is the Public Security Department doing?" Chairman Hsü asked.

"It seems they are co-operating. They are in the streets in civilian clothes."

"So, the big troubles, the wholesale arrests of 1966, are to be re-enacted all over again."

Commissar Sha stood up and addressed Li. "Vice-Premier. It is the moment of decision. Are we going to convene an emergency session of the Central Committee?"

"Call a session of the Central Committee? What would be the point? When Comrade Teng Hsiao-p'ing was ousted, there was also a Central Committee meeting. Tens of thousands of so-called Militiamen were standing across the street; if we had not voted in favor of ouster, they would have marched right into the meeting room."

"Chairman Hsü, is that list ready?" Li asked. "If not, then never mind. I personally propose that all the Central Committee members as well as the department heads withdraw to Paoting."

"Withdraw to Paoting?"

"That's right. Is there anywhere in Peking that our security can be guaranteed? Can the troops of the Peking Military Command be sent into the city to protect the personal safety of government officials? Will two guards at the door be enough to fend off twenty Militiamen who come to make arrests? Hsü, you are an old hand, what do you think?"

"If the Public Security forces are washing their hands of the situation, then there is no safety for anyone," Hsü said in resignation.

"All right, Chairman Hsü, try to inform the various department heads and the Central Committee members that they must congregate in Paoting tonight for a special plenary session of the Party Central Committee.

"Transportation and safe-conduct along the way will be the responsibility of the Peking Military Command of the PLA. As for the members of the Central Committee elsewhere, we will go through the channels of the Peking Military Command and then ask General Yeh Chien-ying to contact them, particularly those commanding the large Military Regions."

"What if the Militiamen block the Central Committee members and government officials from leaving Peking?"

Minister Ch'iao, who had been sitting to one side, smiled. "In two hours, we will be seeing several members of the Japanese Diet off at the airport. We will immediately telephone everybody to come to the airport to join the farewell entourage. That would serve nicely, don't you think? Vice-Premier Li, why don't you and I take the same car to the airport? Shall we go now?"

◇ ◇ ◇

Same Day   5:30 p.m.

After the Japanese departed, the party that had gathered to see them off did not leave the building. At Vice-Premier Li's request, they congregated in the airport conference room.

Not all the members of the Central Committee had been informed, and many of those who had been notified were not present. Chairman Hsü took the list from Ch'en Yi-min which Ch'en had checked out. He gave it a glance, and handed it to Vice-Premier Li, who was listening to Commissar Sha's report.

Nearly two hundred were crammed into the conference room; many did not have seats. Most of them understood the urgency of the meeting but no one was very clear about the reasons for it.

Vice-Premier Li consulted Ying Lao (General Yeh Chienying) again, before standing up. The murmurs of the group died down.

"The reasons for this meeting are complex and urgent. Please do not take notes. This discussion is strictly confidential.

"From the day Chairman Mao passed away, our Party has been handling the various internal problems within the Party in accordance with the original principles underlying the leadership hierarchy.

"Our Party is marching resolutely forward according to the precepts of Marxism-Leninism, and following the guidance of Chairman Mao. There are many difficulties in our path. But if the rank and file in our Party stick together, there are no obstacles we cannot overcome.

"Unfortunately, there is a small contingent which does not proceed from the essential principle of Party solidarity. They connive, create factions, and exploit the actions of a few bad eggs in our society, spreading rumors of plots to trump up new political purges. They have now sent in their own camp followers and mobilized the Workers Militias in various parts of the country. They are presently in control of Peking, Tientsin, Shanghai, Wuhan, Chungking, Shenyang, Harbin, altogether more than ten cities. They have taken over the local security organizations in the cities, and are challenging the Military Commands in those regions.

"Twenty minutes ago, the Peking Militia Command Headquarters demanded that the State Council and the various government departments relinquish their administrative power to the Militia representatives who have suddenly emerged in the various departments. So, if you return to your offices and sections, you will be working under the authority of the Militia representative.

"This action is illegal. It does not conform at all to the organizational principles of our Party; it absolutely violates the articles in the Party constitution.

"Our request to convene an extraordinary Plenary Session of the Central Committee has not met with approval from all sides. Given the present situation in the capital, the fundamental conditions of democratic process within the Party no longer exist. For this reason, it is impossible to convene a full-fledged meeting of the Central Committee in Peking with members from all regions present."

Vice-Premier Li bent down to take a sip of tea. The gathering was deathly silent. Everyone tensely awaited a decision. This was a life-and-death moment for Party democracy. To announce such a decision required tremendous courage. General Chu Teh and Premier Chou En-lai had this kind of courage and daring, but they were gone, Liu Shao-ch'i was also a man of the past, and could not re-emerge at this time.* Teng Hsiao-p'ing was capable of giving orders, but he was weak and soft at

* At the time of writing (late summer, early autumn 1976), the death of Liu Shao-ch'i had not been confirmed. In spring 1977 it was revealed that Liu had died in 1971 and his manner of death was indicated; but subsequent reports contradicted this—TRANSLATOR.

the most crucial moments. Everyone looked expectantly at the only two left, Vice-Premier Li Hsien-nien and General Yeh Chien-ying.

"For the past two days, we have been waiting. We have taken a wait-and-see posture. But it seems we cannot wait any longer. If we do not act now, everything is finished.

"Ying Lao and I, along with a few others, have decided that if we were to remain in Peking under conditions that offer no guarantee of Party democracy or of personal safety, and passively wait for the convening of the Party's Central Committee or the Party Congress, this would be tantamount to presiding over the demise of the Party and of the country. This is the least desirable option.

"If we sent regular PLA troops into the capital, in order to safeguard the normal functioning of the various departments, so that we could convene a meeting of the Central Committee in accordance with prescribed Party procedures, this would inevitably lead to armed conflict between the PLA troops and the Militiamen. For us, this would reflect badly on Party prestige in the international arena. How many times have we exercised forbearance in the past? But these people cannot be given another inch. Now we can retreat no further even if we wanted to. We have no choice but to engage them in battle, although this is not a desirable option.

"We have now gathered all of you here, and according to our tabulations, half of the Central Committee members are present. Add to that the members from the other regions, and our numbers exceed two thirds. If we also include the government officials on hand, then we have more than 70 per cent of the Central Committee present. With this quorum, we can now legally convene an emergency session of the Central Government. We would like every one of you to vote.

"We propose the following motion: 'Whereas the circumstances for a special session of the Central Committee in Peking no longer obtain, be it resolved that such a meeting be convened in the city of Paoting in Hopei Province.' Those in favor, please raise your hands!"

There were only two people who did not raise their hands, Deputy Head Chao of the Public Security Department and Vice-Chairman Wu Teh of the Peking Revolutionary Committee.

Chairman Wu Teh stood up and, smiling, said, "The news of impending arrests may not be exactly accurate. Maybe we should wait until the news is confirmed before we decide."

Foreign Minister Ch'iao, who had been silent, spoke.

"How can we confirm it? I would like to know."

"Perhaps we should ask Premier Hua to come to tell us."

"But we talked with him last night. He did not admit the truth of what was happening, nor did he deny it. Over and over, he reminded us to obey Party discipline. But 'discipline' means nothing unless it applies equally to both sides. If 'discipline' applies only to us, then what we have on our hands is a hell of a farce."

"Oh! You conferred with him last night." Vice-Chairman Wu looked at the indignant and tense expressions around him, and beads of sweat began to appear on his forehead. "I obey the will of the majority," he said, "and I endorse the decision to hold the meeting at Paoting."

Deputy Head Chao stood up and checked everyone's reaction before he coolly addressed the group:

"By all reports, the security of the country is, at the moment, very precarious. If there should appear a split in the Party's Central Committee, the 'Five Black Elements' plus the misguided gangsters will certainly incite the masses with low political standards to cause havoc and destruction and the whole country could sink into anarchy. Whether the Soviet revisionists will exploit this opportunity to commit aggression, we cannot tell. I am staying in Peking because my work requires it. Whether all of you should go to Paoting or stay in Peking is for you to decide for yourselves. I do not want to interfere. But I will definitely guarantee the safety of the relatives of anyone who might go to Paoting. That is within my power to do."

Vice-Premier Li looked around, nodded, and said, "Then our

proposition is approved. Commissar Sha, are the airplanes ready?"

"Three passenger planes for a domestic flight are waiting outside ready for takeoff," Commissar Sha announced. "All ranking officials and secretaries may board the planes, but the guards will have to go later tonight by train. I have been in touch with Commander Ch'en and tonight a special military train will leave from Feng-t'ai, which will transport a troop division for guard duty at Paoting to ensure the security of the deliberations of the Central Commtitee."

◇ ◇ ◇

Foreign Minister Ch'iao watched as the third passenger plane flew into the night sky without incident, and then turned away from the window and looked at Deputy Minister Hsieh, whose head was bent low, deep in thought.

"Let's go, Old Hsieh!"

Deputy Hsieh waved his hand, and said: "You go on. I have to think a few things over."

Ch'iao left the conference room, and as he did, Vice-Premier Li's guard, Old Huang, approached him to report: "I have been appointed head of the temporary squad of guards. There are altogether one hundred and forty-three in the squad. We are now ready for departure to Feng-t'ai and to board the train, according to Commissar Sha's instructions. But we have no means of transportation from here to the station. What should we do?"

"What about the vehicles you came in?"

"They are all outside, but the driver comrades have their own ideas, and they say that they also want to go to Paoting. They won't take us to Feng-t'ai unless we take them the rest of the way to Paoting."

"Then let them come along. Incorporate them into your squadron. Put them under your command."

"Minister Ch'iao, I am clear about the situation now, but I

still have one question. Why are you, sir, staying here? This place is too dangerous."

"Old Huang, we all serve our Party, don't we? Just carry out your assignment!"

Ch'iao walked out of the door to where his chauffeur was waiting. As his personal guard opened the door of the car, three trucks of Militiamen suddenly sped down the main road into the airport. Ch'iao smiled, and said to his secretary, "They have arrived just a minute too late." And then he ordered his chauffeur: "To the Special Headquarters of the Central Committee!"

◇ ◇ ◇

The Yugoslavian reporter, Mihute, sat in front of his typewriter, nimbly banging away at the keys.

"An incomprehensible event is about to unfold in the capital of this Far Eastern country. Last night, an unprecedented gala given at the American Liaison Office attracted all the Western reporters in this usually unsocial city. Only a few Japanese reporters were absent, and they learned some top-secret news from Soviet intelligence officers. A mammoth coup is brewing in Peking and certain top-echelon leaders will soon be removed.

"Although a possible coup was denied this morning by official Chinese spokesmen, most observers on the scene feel that the news leaked out by Soviet Intelligence is probably true.

"Since 4 P.M., masses of Militiamen have made their appearance on the streets of Peking, carrying arms and setting up barricades. The streets are emptying quickly. Stores are closed. The military types normally patrolling the streets are nowhere to be seen and the city seems to be under the control of the Urban Workers Militia. What issue these developments will have, it is too early to say. But as on the eve of all big political storms, the stillness is pervasive."

As reporter Watanabe of the *Maiasa Shimbun* was hastily writing his news dispatch the doorbell rang. He put down his pen, and opening the door, saw Nakada.

"The telephone in my room is out of order. Let me use your phone, will you?"

"Who are you calling? I have to make a call soon."

"It will only take five minutes." Nakada smiled slyly as he picked up the phone.

"Eh! There's something wrong with your phone, too!"

Watanabe snatched the telephone away. The line was dead!

Okamura's loud voice came through the door. "How come the phone works when there is an earthquake, but goes on the blink the moment there's a political shakeup?"

Okamura appeared in the doorway, wearing his coat, holding several sheets of paper, and looking peeved.

"Your telephone is not working? Shall we go to the telegraph office? The phones there can't break down, can they?"

"But can we get a car?" Nakada wondered. European reporters could drive their own cars, but Japanese and East European reporters did not have this privilege and must be accompanied by a Chinese driver. Since the big earthquake, the drivers balked at anything that was not strictly ordered by their superiors.

"Ali Singh wants to go to the telegraph office too. I have asked him to let us go with him."

Although the Volkswagen was small, Ali Singh was accommodating and good-natured. Once they had driven away from the San-li-tun Building, Watanabe felt a sense of freedom, a feeling which he usually did not experience in Peking. He could talk freely, go anywhere, and . . .

It was already past nine o'clock. In the street, except for a group of people standing at the corner, there was no one about. As the car approached the distant corner of the street, several people ran to the center of the road to block their way.

The car slowed down, and approached the blockade. It was the Militiamen pointing their rifles, ready to shoot. One of them who seemed in charge came up to the window. Ali Singh rolled down the window to receive a gust of cold wind and a barrage of questions:

"Who are you? Where are you going this late at night?"

"We are foreign reporters," Ali Singh answered in English, showing his identity papers.

The Militiaman collected all their identity papers, and looked them over carefully with the aid of his flashlight, and returned them. He said in Chinese, "Does anyone here understand Chinese?"

Okamura, proud of his proficiency in Chinese, responded. The Militiaman said in a commanding tone, "Today, starting at nine o'clock, a curfew has been imposed on the capital. No one is permitted to pass without special permission. Please return to your residence."

"Why the curfew? Tell us the reason."

"That is privileged information. Please go back."

In the distance truck after truck was filling up with Militiamen, leaving the Workers' Gymnasium, and disappearing into the night. The cold was bitter. Ali Singh rolled up the window, turned a half circle, and drove the four-hundred-meter distance back to their residence.

There was no telephone communication, no way to lodge a protest with the Foreign Ministry or reach their Embassy.

◇ ◇ ◇

Same Day   10 p.m.

A battered jeep barreled along the Peking-to-Tientsin highway. The canopy was sealed tight, and no wind penetrated. As it passed the towns and villages along the way, the driver slowed down and switched to parking lights, as if he did not want to attract attention. On reaching a paved stretch where there were no vehicles, he again turned on the high beams and drove on at full throttle, to make up for lost time.

The jeep passed over the big bridge crossing the Pei-yüan River, left the highway, turned north, and in less than ten minutes arrived at a sentry post.

The jeep halted, and a middle-aged man in blue uniform stepped out. He went to the brightly lit guardhouse, showed his identity papers, and entered the reception room behind the sentry booth.

On the wall of the room, instructions had been posted under the heading: "Guidelines for Guards." At the end, six words appeared: "Issued by the Peking Military Command."

After the man in the blue uniform explained his business, the officer on duty phoned and spoke with the staff headquarters of the Military Command.

"There are three people here from the State Council. They want to see Commander Ch'en . . . They have important messages to deliver to the commander in person . . . Yes . . . All right . . . We will let them pass . . . Very good, sir."

Five minutes later, the jeep pulled up at a simple two-story office building. The man in the blue uniform again left the jeep and entered the building. Fifteen minutes later, he returned to the jeep and muttered something to the other occupants, who continued to wait quietly.

From the rear of the office building, two jeeps started up. Escorting the visitors' jeep, they drove into an area with row upon row of military barracks. On reaching a small single-story house with a tile roof, the jeeps stopped.

Four guards stepped out from the first jeep. They stood at stiff attention on each side of the entrance. The second jeep made a tight U-turn, and stopped on the other side of the street, leaving vacant a space for the visitors' jeep to pull up and disembark its passengers.

The man in the blue uniform stepped out, followed by a big

man with a muscular physique and a penetrating look, who straightened his overcoat and strode into the small house.

In the jeep across the street, a voice spoke out: "Commander Ch'en, sir . . . isn't that Premier Hua? No doubt about it, that's him."

The passengers in the jeep across the street now stepped forth. One was over seventy. He also marched into the small house, followed close behind by an aide-de-camp.

The cold night wind whistled overhead. It bent a few gnarled date trees, whose bare branches trembled.

◈ ◈ ◈

The temperature had dropped to thirty degrees below zero centigrade. The wind pressed down like waves on the grasslands and blew the snow into drift after drift. There was no sound, no movement in the thousand-mile sky. A crescent moon hung over the horizon, and constellations of stars glimmered in the deep void. From time to time, shooting stars trailed across the sky and sank below the horizon.

Li P'ei-yi lay crouching on a slope. Behind him were four other members of his patrol. Before them was Hill 658, which was now so dark one could not discern any life or movement. Li P'ei-yi could neither expose himself to the enemy nor be mistaken for the enemy by his own comrades, so he inched ahead gingerly.

Deciding to go ahead on his own, he whispered his plans to his four companions, and then picking his way, moved ahead.

Suddenly, on Hill 767, no more than two thousand meters away, more than ten bright searchlights flashed on, lighting up the entire area. Even the exposed withered grass on the ground turned silver-white.

There was a deafening roar behind the hill. Li P'ei-yi was startled by what sounded like hundreds and hundreds of tanks! How did they manage such a massive military force?

After ten minutes of the deafening roar, the searchlights were extinguished, and the steppes returned to their previous silence. Li P'ei-yi felt blinded, and could see only blurred dots of light.

As soon as he was able to focus his vision again, he jumped up and rushed across the open ground, toward Hill 658.

Halfway up, he heard an urgent voice calling out, "Who's there?"

"Li P'ei-yi, of Farm Unit Number 74, Team Number 2."

"We are Team Number 4, just arrived to relieve our outposts. My name is Chan Cheng."

"Stay here and cover us," Li P'ei-yi said. "I'll go to draw up the telephone lines."

Li P'ei-yi turned and ran down the hill. In no time, he was back with his companions, pulling the telephone lines with him, and met up again with Chan Cheng. Together they climbed to the top of Hill 658, hooked up the telephone wires with the receiver, and connected the line.

"Calling farm headquarters! Li P'ei-yi here."

"Where did you connect the telephone?" Chief Liu's anxious voice was on the line.

"Hill 658."

"We just saw bright lights on Hill 767. What's happening there?"

Li P'ei-yi reported briefly what he had just seen and heard. As he was speaking, there was another flash of light, and the roar of heavy armor could be heard again.

"One hour between flashes, on the button," Chief Liu said. "The border defenses have arrived at the farm. We are sending a small squadron to your position. When they arrive, bring the communications unit back with you. Now, don't hang up. Keep the line open."

Li P'ei-yi handed the telephone to one of his men, and relayed to Chan Cheng the instructions received from headquarters. In the glare of searchlights, the tense and angry expressions of each person could be seen. Li P'ei-yi, although not in charge of Team Number 4, checked over each person's gear, ammunition, and supplies, helped to set up effective barricades, and gave tips on how to ward off the cold.

Little Tung had been sent down the slope to escort the defense troops, and now returned, breathless, bringing with him some ten or more soldiers from the border defense. Li P'ei-yi explained the situation again, then led the communications unit back down the hill. As they proceeded toward the rear lines, columns of light flashed once more in the sky. Little Tung said with a smile, "Thanks to the Soviet revisionists, the street lighting here on the steppes is pretty good."

▧ TWELVE

Tuesday, February 12
5:30 a.m. Peking Standard Time
Lunar Calendar: 12th month, 28th day

The shaking of his bed woke Ta-yung from a sound sleep. He opened his eyes, and in the dim light saw the thumb-thick brown branches tightly lashed together with straw that made up the roof. On top of the branches was laid golden-colored thatch, which still gave off a grassy fragrance.

Suddenly Ta-yung was wide awake. What happened at the border last night? He sat up abruptly. People around him were just rising; he had not overslept.

In the communal dormitory for men, there were twenty or more double-decker wooden bunks on either side. At the end of the passage were two big stoves, on which kettles had been set to boil water. Ta-yung borrowed a washbasin, hastily washed his face and brushed his teeth, and followed everyone to the mess hall.

Young Swallow had already prepared breakfast for Ta-yung, but seemed impatient at having to wait for him. As soon as she put the food in front of him she left in a hurry, without so much as a word.

Ta-yung gulped down the *kao-liang* gruel in two or three big mouthfuls; he did not want the corn biscuit, so he put it in his coat pocket, and walked out of the mess hall in search of the building where the meeting had been held the previous night.

He had not realized how big the courtyard was. The earthen wall surrounding it was two meters high, one meter thick, and sat on a stone base. Inside, neatly lined up, were row upon row of buildings, including dormitories, a mess hall, repair shops, a storage shed, a recreation room, a broadcasting station, an infirmary, and other installations: a complete, self-contained community.

Ta-yung, searching for the meeting room, came upon a memorial plaque.

In the center of what appeared to be a garden, there was a flat foundation stone, on which an upright stone memorial had been set. On the front of the memorial stone red Chinese characters were engraved, carved deep into the stone, as if intended to last for thousands of years:

"The power of the people is forever."

Underneath was the following: "In memory of our fallen comrades Yu Ming-ya, Chu Li-ta, Wang Hsiao-lan."

Behind the memorial stone were three mounds. Ta-yung poignantly remembered the faces of the girls he had known in school. What evil force drove them to their deaths? What was the real explanation? Why had they not resisted actively rather than passively commit suicide?

Ta-yung took off his hat and bowed before the memorial. With a grieved heart, he left the garden and found the assembly ground. He was not aware of a swarthy young man who was following him at a distance.

Many people had congregated at the northern end of the assembly grounds; people were jammed in the meeting room, some hanging out the windows. A meeting was taking place. Ta-yung felt out of place and waited at one side, curious about the situation at the border.

As he stood in the cold his feet became numb. He stomped on the ground to improve the circulation in his feet, and heard a call:

"Hey! You Militia head from Peking!"

Ta-yung turned toward the speaker, and saw a sturdy young man grinning at him.

"I'll lend you a pair of boots. Otherwise you will have to be carried back to Peking."

Ta-yung smiled in gratitude, and followed him back to the dormitory.

"My name is Ta-yung. You can forget that cute title."

"My name is T'ang. But everyone calls me 'Big Bugle.'"

Big Bugle found a pair of used sheepskin boots; the fit was fine. Big Bugle also found under his bedding a pair of woolen socks, which he gave to Ta-yung.

"Look, you do not even have gloves; you are suffering from chilblains on the back of your hands."

Ta-yung's hands had felt itchy, and he saw that they were already swollen.

"I have a pair of cotton gloves I will lend you, but you must return them to me when you leave, as my mother made them."

From his pillowcase, he took out a pair of new gloves. It looked as though he had been reluctant to use them, and slept every night with the gloves under his pillow. It touched Ta-yung to see how precious the gloves were to the young man. The sound of a whistle was heard outside. Big Bugle picked up a rifle leaning against the side of the bed and rushed out, yelling, "Fall in!"

Ta-yung followed Big Bugle to the courtyard and lined up behind him. When all the people in the courtyard were lined up, they marched out in neat formation behind Li P'ei-yi.

In the steppes early in the morning, wisps of thin, milky-white mist had collected in the lowlands. There was scarcely any wind. Granite hills were everywhere; on the side away from the sun, snow not blown away by the wind flecked the slopes. The romantic image that Ta-yung had of the steppes was somewhat shaken:

"Raising the whip, driving the horse, startle a flock of swallows: Blowing the grass low, the wind looks in on cattle and sheep."

Perhaps summer was the season when the steppeland was beautiful, he mused to himself, as he followed the troops down the slope.

In the east a blood-red glow appeared on the horizon, gradually paling into yellow. At the horizon, the sun appeared, sending out shafts of white light, a light that basked the steppe country in golden radiance. All creation looked vital and magnificent and in the clusters of withered grass one could see new grass sprouts. The earth was getting ready to burst forth again with exuberant life.

Li P'ei-yi led the troops into a gully, and after a few hundred meters, they turned into a big cave. Inside was the supply depot for Team Number 2: food, farm implements, seed, medicine were piled up in the deep recesses of the cave on both sides. The troops started to move out mortars, heavy machine guns, bullets, bombs.

Ta-yung picked up four heavy dynamite bombs, and together with Big Bugle, who was carrying a mortar launcher, he followed the troops up along a steep path. Li P'ei-yi was waiting at the opening of the tunnel and took the four bombs from Ta-yung. With a sudden laugh he said, "You are not armed. Why don't you take two of these? Do you think you can handle them?"

Ta-yung reached out to take the bombs and said without hesitation, "For the defense of the motherland, I have the courage for anything."

Li P'ei-yi stopped smiling, and glared at Ta-yung.

"That's right. For the defense of the motherland, we have the courage for anything."

Li P'ei-yi turned and entered a tunnel on the right. Ta-yung and Big Bugle moved forward, and emerging from the tunnel, arrived at a deep trench.

Proceeding along the trench for a few hundred meters, they came to a granite cliff rising some two hundred meters high. Nearby, to the left, there was a basin; to the right, another promontory facing it. Between the two hills was a patch of open flatland nearly three hundred meters across.

Big Bugle pointed and said, "That is Hill 658. Together with this hill, 744, the two command access into the valley behind. If we control this high ground, the enemy will not be able to break through because between Erh-lien and Ku-erh-pan-wu-lan-ching, for more than a thousand miles, the border line runs through either desert or granite hills. Only here at this mountain pass can trucks and other vehicles pass."

The other men began to climb. Ta-yung had been accustomed to climbing tall mountains since childhood and the granite cliff was a cinch. He checked the two bombs strapped on his back and unbuttoned his cotton jacket. With one hand, he held the lower edge of his jacket, and with the other, he helped Big Bugle carry the mortar launcher.

When they reached the peak, Ta-yung picked out a large rock for cover. It was strangely quiet, almost as if they were the only living creatures in the barren steppes. A third hill, slightly higher, about two hundred meters ahead, showed no trace of the enemy. Ta-yung was disappointed, but the silence sharpened his sense of vigilance.

The fourth team, which had been guarding the pass through the night, gave Young Swallow a briefing on the situation. Young Swallow picked up the telephone and made her report to headquarters in hushed tones.

"This is Young Swallow of Team Number 2. We are now taking positions on Hill 744. Everything appears normal. No developments so far."

They calmly kept watch. On the mountain path that wound around from the distant hills to the right, there was no movement. The pass was as flat as Ch'ang-an Avenue in Peking.

The wind on the steppes was dry and cold; it whistled over the withered grass beside their cheeks.

The wind brought with it sounds of clanking metal. Everyone listened intently to the sounds and signaled each other with their eyes.

Ta-yung closely watched Hill 764, which the enemy commanded. There was no one to be seen, and not a sound. The noise they had just heard must be coming from behind the hill.

Suddenly there came again a roar like the crash of a thousand thunderbolts, as if hundreds and hundreds of tanks were on the move.

"Come on," Ta-yung thought, "we are waiting for you."

◇ ◇ ◇

Young Tiger woke up before dawn. He lay on his wooden bed and stared at the ceiling pasted over with old newspapers. After the earthquake, Young Tiger had repaired the ceiling on his own. The previous evening, Young Tiger had attempted to deliver two reconditioned radios to the new outpost outside the Ch'ien-men ("Front Gate"). But there were Militiamen posted at all the street corners telling people to go home. Pedestrians were being searched and questioned. Young Tiger had immediately ducked into a small alley and had returned home as quickly as he could. After stashing the two radios away, he had ventured to the end of the alleyway to look the situation over.

In the streets, people were rushing home. Buses and trolley cars had stopped running. Cyclists could only ride slowly along the edges of the street, in order to keep the middle lanes clear. Trucks filled with Militiamen zipped down the center of the streets in reckless haste. Children hid in the corners of the alleyways, in disregard of their parents' warnings, to watch what was happening in the street.

The old men and women of the Neighborhood Committees, displaying their armbands, passed out notices issued by the police station from house to house: "Due to recent disturbances, everyone is asked to be on guard. Do not go out into the street, and do not let strangers enter your homes."

The night was now over, but had the curfew been extended? That was the question that concerned Young Tiger.

Voices could be heard coming from the east wing of the compound.

"Last night, Hsiao-wen's father stayed in the factory. We still have not had any message from him."

"Old Chang in my family will not be able to get back for another three to five days. At least we'll have some peace and quiet around here for a change."

"Are you going to work today?"

"Of course. No one's going to say that I won't work because of a little trouble."

"Are we allowed to walk the streets?"

"The buses are running. I don't see why not."

Young Tiger jumped from his bed at once. In less than ten minutes, he was out the door.

Militiamen were still on the street, but they had been changed. The day before the Militiamen were wearing new blue cotton uniforms with leather belts at their waists and thick black cotton pants. In their broad-brimmed Yenan-style hats, carrying automatic rifles, they were most impressive. But now the Militiamen on the streets carried only clubs, and wore nondescript civilian clothes. Some leaned against the wall, shielding themselves from the wind, and smoked. Others squatted in front of the closed shops to eat their rations. They paid no attention to the fearful glances of those walking by.

Young Tiger sauntered over to the Tung-tan Station and caught a bus which was almost empty. The ticket-seller sat on his seat near the door, legs folded. With an annoyed look, he took out his roll of tickets from a leather bag hung over his shoulder, and tore one off.

Around T'ien-an Men Square, Militia barricades were set up again. Since the incident at the Square, the slightest hint of trouble had been enough to close it off, repeatedly.

At the Ta Tsa-lan ("Big Fence") Station, Young Tiger left

the bus, and sneaking into the forbidden area, he saw two figures slinking under the eaves at his usual entry into the headquarters. Was this a secret post set up by the Security people? Affecting unconcern, he walked past the entry he normally used and ducked in another opening in the rubble. After worming his way through two ruined houses, he was surprised by someone suddenly grabbing him.

"Oh, it's you! What are you doing here?" Big Gun Hsü spoke in a low, gruff voice. "Thank your stars I did not smash in your head."

"There were two undercover men out there. I did not want to risk giving away our hideout."

"But they are our men."

"How did you expect me to know that?"

"At any rate, you've come at the right time. We're about to change shifts. Go get 'Old Goat.'"

Old Goat got his name from his stomach trouble. His frequent belches sounded like the bleatings of an old goat. During the Cultural Revolution he had been asked to paste up the big-character posters, which he did without even knowing what they contained. He had been picked up as an activist in the anti-Party bloc, and had been sent away to the mountains. It was there that he had contracted the ailment that led to his belching. When eventually he was given special permission to return to his original work unit in Peking to work as an assayer of precious metals, his illness had become aggravated whenever he was tense. On returning, he met up again with those who had criticized him in the "struggle meetings" that had sent him away, and he had started to belch uncontrollably. This had caused so much disruption no one could work in his presence, let alone conduct meetings. The only recourse had been to give him sick leave, but six months after he had stopped working his wages were reduced 40 per cent—hardly sufficient for the livelihood of his family. Chuko Liang was his old classmate and had given him jobs repairing old electronic parts over a year ago.

Young Tiger entered the basement, where he found Tall

Man Li cutting white paper, and Paleface Scholar hunched over a small desk, writing. Several others were eating "scallion pancakes," and the room was filled with their aroma.

Tall Man Li tossed his pocketknife into the air and caught it deftly. He fixed Young Tiger with a stare.

"Where did you crawl in from?"

"Big Gun Hsü has asked me to find Old Goat and relieve him."

"Big Gun has another two hours to go. What's his hurry?"

Young Tiger did not answer. The smell of the food made his stomach growl with hunger, but his sense of self-respect restrained him from asking for something to eat.

"Come here, give me a hand!" Tall Man Li spoke. He pointed to a pile of white paper on the floor, and set Young Tiger to cutting sheets of paper, each the size of half a newspaper page, into four parts.

Hsia Yu-min called out that he was ready and Tall Man Li went into the inner chamber to bring out a mimeograph machine.

Hsia Yu-min picked up the stencil he had just prepared, placed it on the drum, and tucked in the ends. Tall Man Li poured the ink he had made ready into the drum, put in the sheets of pre-cut white paper, and turned the lever. A sheet of mimeograph copy appeared, the characters neat and clear. The meticulous appearance of the calligraphy was a credit to Hsia Yu-min.

Tall Man Li continued operating the machine. The mimeographed sheets slid out one after another. Young Tiger had been set to collate them and he read the headline: "What the People of the Capital Think of the Current Political Crisis."

◊ ◊ ◊

In an hour, the mimeographing of the handbills was finished. Young Tiger wolfed down a cake that Hsia Yu-min had offered him. The door to the inner room opened and Chuko Liang stuck in his head to announce: "Everyone is here. It is time for the meeting."

Young Tiger helped Tall Man Li pick up the mimeographed handbills and followed Li through the other room, down to the basement.

In the basement, damaged wooden boxes were piled on both sides in a forty-meter area and forty to fifty people were sitting around on the boxes, quietly talking.

Chuko Liang now stood behind a roughly constructed wooden table at one end of the room. The yellowish light from the naked light bulbs hung from the ceiling was reflected in his eyes.

"Today, we are lucky to be able to gather here," Chuko Liang said. "Ten years ago, we gathered in Pei-hai Park. Together we revolted against the Red capitalists and showed the strength of our people.

"At that time, we were all young; we were exploited and discarded; we had no experience, and no political savvy. We were frequently broken up, disarmed, and destroyed one by one.

"You who are present have survived. Every one of you has experienced hardship and tribulation, but you have overcome. But to do this, we have had to commit acts which we clearly knew were illegal. Many of our comrades and fellow fighters are still in the labor reform camps scattered throughout the country, sentenced to hard labor, never to see the light of day. How long can we tolerate this?"

Young Tiger heard the middle-aged man sitting beside him begin to sob.

"Two days ago, one of the heads of the Consolidated Action group came to talk to me and told me about an important plan."

Everyone's attention was riveted to Chuko Liang as he continued his account.

"When Ch'in Shih-huang (first Emperor of China) went to heaven, Empress Lü could not manage to attract a leadership that would bend to her will, and that system of central dictatorship disappeared. Conflicts spread to many areas of national life, and seriously affected the livelihood of the people.

"Nothing has really changed since that early time, because

this is exactly the current political situation in our country. The ever deepening contradictions in the decision-making echelons in the Party, the government, and the military, now that they lack the divine guidance of Holy Writ, are going to crack wide open.

"The Consolidated Action group has suddenly condescended to ask for our co-operation. This does not mean that they have just opened their eyes to the truth and have given up their butcher's knives, but rather that their ambitions are greater. It also indicated that we have now reached the explosive point.

"Who is the real power behind the Consolidated Action group? You and I know all too well. Two days ago, their spokesman Yen P'eng-fei in his secret talk with me at the T'ao-jan-t'ing Kung-yüan ("The Pavilion of Blithe Spirits Park") said that in the days to come they will incite revolutionary uprisings simultaneously all over the country. They want us to join them. I did not accept his proposal. Last night, unexpectedly, he sent me a courier with an urgent message. They have decided that the nationwide uprisings are to be set off tomorrow morning at nine o'clock, and the sparking point will be at T'ien-an Men Square."

Everyone in the basement jumped to his feet. Young Tiger's heart started pounding.

"Settle down!" Chuko Liang commanded.

"The activities of the Consolidated Action group have been carefully staged. Up to now, we have received the following information:

"Yesterday, at five-thirty in the afternoon, the Militiamen were out arresting people. We have some concrete details on that. Old Kuo, why don't you fill everyone in?"

A short, fat, middle-aged man, sitting in the center, stood up and gave his account:

"In accordance with the directives of the executive group of our organization, some of our comrades infiltrated the Militia organization. I myself joined the Militia and was appointed platoon leader.

"The order to assemble reached our chemical factory at four o'clock yesterday afternoon. It was just at the time of a change of shift, so the Militiamen of both shifts were mobilized. The factory trucks were commandeered and we went to requisition arms in Pei-hai Park, and then were ordered to proceed and take over the railways.

"With the co-operation of the Militiamen among railway personnel, we were easily able to take over the central switchboard and the control room. But when we made the rounds to check on the cadres, we discovered that all the cadres at the rank of section head or higher were missing. The key figures we were going to arrest had left half an hour before we arrived. Obviously someone had tipped them off, and had organized countermeasures.

"Afterward, I returned to the Militia Command Headquarters in Pei-hai Park, where I heard from other companies that the same thing had happened to them. It seems that the leaders of the various government bodies have all fled. That concludes my report."

Young Tiger was shocked at these disclosures. To see this ordinary worker, looking like a despicable Militia platoon leader, and find out he was in actuality a fellow comrade-in-arms was almost too much to believe.

Chuko Liang turned to another man and asked him to report as well. Pulling himself together the man slowly stood up.

"From the information I get from one of our sources, nearly three hundred people left Peking last night by plane. Among the three hundred were the heads of key governmental departments, as well as some deposed in previous political campaigns. Among those on the planes were Teng Hsiao-p'ing, P'eng Chen, Sung Jen-ch'iung, Liu Lan-t'ao, T'ao Chu, and Chou Yang.*

"They are gathering in Paoting in Hopei Province, and convening the National Party Congress, to elect a new Central Committee, and to organize a new Politburo. Some Military

* All high-ranking cadres purged during the Cultural Revolution—TRANSLATOR.

Commands have lent their support; others have not indicated where they stand."

"Can representatives be elected democratically in the Party?" asked the man who had previously reported.

"Of course not," Chuko Liang answered. "The tradition of democratic process within the Party was buried by the Ninth Plenary Session (April 1969). If they convene a new Plenary Session at Paoting, the representatives who attend will represent the wielders of power in the different regions. They are not elected representatives of the Party masses."

"If this is the case," another asked, "why does Consolidated Action need to incite insurrection?"

"That's the question. I find those in power ludicrous. They have been criticizing the outmoded philosophies of Confucius and Mencius for years, yet they still cling desperately to one of the main tenets of Confucianism—monolithic orthodoxy. Those members of the Central Committee who opted to stay in Peking hold fast to the credo of orthodox traditionalism and to the divine throne of Ch'in Shih-huang. Using these two magic wands, the baton of tradition and the scepter of despotism, they try to command the country. Those who are meeting at Paoting are likewise intimidated by these magic wands. Since they believe these tenets cannot be disposed of, they want to hold on to them for their own future use.

"We have not been opposed to insurrection. In times past, we have been insurrectionists. But the insurrection this time is radically different from that of the Cultural Revolution.

"The plan expounded by Yen P'eng-fei is lethal. The plotters want to exploit once again the most idealistic of the young intellectuals, and use them for cannon fodder. Later they will pluck the scepter of power from the sea of blood shed by the people.

"Many comrades here, including myself, have been members of the Party and of the Youth League. We know the history of China, especially our record of humiliation over the past hundred years. But we also have a history of heroic struggle by revolutionaries who have passed the torch from one generation to another at the cost of thousands of lives. The lesson they have bequeathed is: China needs a center, a heart of revolutionary power for the people. We need a central collective leadership that is strong and dynamic, to lead our nation by democratic means and develop our motherland into a rich, democratic, modern country. This center of power was the Chinese Communist Party, accounting for its victory in 1949. But by 1957, the people's democratic rights were abrogated. By 1966, the democratic processes within the Party were destroyed. The center was split and after the Lin Piao incident, there were further divisions causing our people to be suspicious of the power center now that it had lost sight of its original mission.

"Since the sixties, the power that maintained this center no longer came from the spontaneous force of the people as it did in the fifties. Rather, the power became oppressive, the result of the military, the police, and bureaucratic organs fostering the fanaticism of propagating The Word. In the seventies, this deranged center of power does not even trust the military organization that it established and has created the Militia, a counterpart of Hitler's SS. This center of power is absolutely not one around which the people of our country can rally; it has become a nightmare that the people want to tear out and destroy.

"But our people lack insight, organization, and are unaware of their strength. To achieve real liberation, we will probably need another half century. The only thing we are able to do now is to support the more rational elements in the leadership."

Chuko Liang picked up the declaration that had just been mimeographed, and went on to say, "Our executive group discussed the matter all night, and we have decided to join the insurrectionists, but only under certain terms.

"The Consolidated Action group has set its strategy in motion.

"It will call upon all the youth sent to the countryside, the mountains, and the villages to return to their home cities on the lunar New Year. It will deceive the youth into thinking that by returning home before the lunar New Year, they will be reinstated and can secure work in the cities. We estimate half of the youth will fall into this trap, and will rush home in droves. There are nearly twenty million of these youths, five hundred thousand from Peking alone.

"Now, please, I want you to think this over carefully. When these young people, who have been detained for so many years in the villages and the mountains and who have practically lost all hope, return to the city, what do you think lies in store for them? Certainly not a warm welcome. Certainly not job openings. *A hail of bullets!* Bullets fired by the Militiamen ostensibly for the purpose of protecting law and order. What will happen? It might be that the Militiamen will die at the hands of the people, but how many intellectual youths who will be fighting with bare fists will die with them? One million? Five million? Who is the ultimate beneficiary of all this? I don't need to say.

"From yesterday's developments, what has happened fits the Consolidated Action scenario. Therefore, we held an emergency meeting and are now trying to inform our operatives in all the major cities in the country. We will participate in the uprisings, but our main objective will be to rescue and protect the intellectual youth who come back to the cities.

"To speak specifically about Peking, when we have helped launch the insurrection, we will quickly establish a "liberated zone," from T'ien-an Men Square stretching toward the south as far as Yung-ting Men ("The Ever Secure Gate") Railway Station. We will then be able to usher the youth who have flocked to Peking into our zone, and prevent their systematic massacre at the hands of the Militiamen.

"Strategically, we will secure our defenses around the liberated zone, relying mainly on political argument, and avoiding face-to-face confrontations with the Militiamen. We will bide our time, and wait until the new Politburo of the Chinese

Communist Party emerges. Then we will enter into negotiations.

"You are representatives from many areas. If you have questions about the strategy or about the plans that our executive group has drawn up, please raise them now."

"Will the defensive and protective action establishing the liberated zone be carried out in conjunction with the Consolidated Action group?"

"No. We will proceed independently. Their area is north of Ch'ang-an Avenue; ours will be south of Ch'ang-an Avenue. We have agreed on mutual non-intervention."

"What about our provisions, weapons, supplies?" another asked.

"After the September 5th instructions which prohibited weapons were issued in 1967, we buried some arms. Tonight we will uncover them and have them sent over from such places as Mi-yüan and Fang-shan.

"Some of our comrades working in the People's Bank today managed under various pretexts to secure currency; tomorrow, when the insurrection starts, that money will be made available for use. All the materials in the liberated zone will be dispatched and distributed by our executive group. Measures will be taken to prevent looting; we will also assume responsibility for law and order in our zone. We will mobilize the masses, and together we will perform this function and attempt to prevent the 'bad elements' from using this opportunity to kill and loot. We imagine that those elements will join the activities of the Consolidated Action group tomorrow, so security in the east and west parts of the city may be a problem."

"What if the Militiamen attack our zone?"

"We will inform them early of our position and give them our declaration. They should be so busy fighting the Consolidated Action group that they will leave us alone."

"But what if our strategy is discovered by the Consolidated Action people, won't they move against us?"

"Of course they will. So we must at the same time be on our guard against that. Now, because time is short, we must decide. Are you all in favor of or opposed to the decision of the executive group? Please indicate your vote by a show of hands. Those in favor, raise your hands."

All hands were raised. Young Tiger was not officially a representative, but he raised his hand too. Tall Man Li, who was conducting the hand count, stared disapprovingly, but Young Tiger only raised his hand higher.

❖ ❖ ❖

Same Day   9:30 a.m.

On the steep slopes of tall hills of sand, under a murderous, scorching sun, Chia Hsiang-tung sank down into the hot sand, trying with great effort to crawl up a hill; the dry wind, mixed with sand, pelted his face and lifted his satchel up in the air. "My hope for life is this satchel!" He held out his hands to grab it, but his legs sank deeper into the shifting sand; he wanted to yell out but could not. He covered his face and suddenly broke out of his dream and sat up abruptly.

The earthen *k'ang* on which he had been sleeping was unbearably hot. The moisture in his body had evaporated, his mouth was dry as dust. Chia jumped out of bed only to hear heavy footsteps outside his door. Returning to reality, he removed his handgun from the holster buried under the pillow, and bolted behind the door until the footsteps passed and proceeded to the other end of the corridor.

Last evening he had checked into a small inn in Hsi-li. With his impressive work-detail documents and his imposing outward manner, he had been given the best room in the inn.

Chia looked at his wristwatch. It was already nine-thirty, so he dressed quickly, tucked the gun under his belt, and hurried out on the street carrying his overcoat and satchel.

Hsi-li was not much of a town, just a street in front of the station and a score of small one-story wooden buildings on either side, looking like service sheds for the herdsmen. There was a general store, a grocery store, and one restaurant in front of the station. It was filled with a noisy crowd, and not a single seat was vacant. Chia stood in the restaurant for a moment, grateful for the warmth, but he could not abide the stench of sweaty sheepskin jackets, of scallions and lamb, and the smoke from long-stemmed pipes. Chia had lost his appetite, and after a brief wait to see if anyone were paying attention, he walked out and took in a deep breath of fresh air.

In the general store Chia noticed pairs of fur-lined boots hanging inside, and realized that his feet were already numb. He entered and bought some boots.

Immediately wrapping his feet in thick cloth, he put his feet into the fur-lined boots, and felt warmer. Walking through the snow, he felt reinvigorated. He had also bought a pair of leather gloves and a big sheepskin hat, which he had stuffed into his satchel.

"This pair of shoes, does it belong to you?" a middle-aged Mongolian cowherd asked, holding the pair of shoes that Chia Hsiang-tung had just taken off, as if afraid Chia might have forgotten them. Actually, Chia wanted to be rid of them, so when no one was looking, he had quietly stuffed the shoes into a snowbank in front of the general store. He had not been aware that he was being watched.

"They're worn through. I don't want them."

"But they look new. Where are they worn through? If you don't want them, I'd like to take them. Is that all right?"

The Mongolian cowherd looked at him with his head half turned away, and his smile baring his blackened teeth; his dirty face was covered with a full beard.

"If you want them, help yourself."

The cowherd laughed so hard and bent over so low that his head almost touched Chia's satchel.

Suddenly the cowherd's clumsy Mandarin turned into a pure, sonorous Peking accent, and he whispered, "You dumb shit! Follow me, will you? And keep twenty meters behind!"

Chia's mouth opened in shock. This was his contact! He followed Big Beard to the end of the street, and to the rear of a big storage shed filled with hay. A sleigh was waiting for them, its old frame and dirty sheepskin cover all of a piece with the appearance of Big Beard. The sleigh was harnessed to a sturdy gray horse, whose strong front hooves pawed at the snow, welcoming the return of its master.

Big Beard checked the sleigh out, looked around, and lashed out at Chia, "Get the hell under the sheepskin fast, you numbskull, and be quick about it!"

▨ THIRTEEN

Tuesday, February 12   10 a.m.

The roar of the motors reverberated through the cliffs and ravines, spreading out to the grasslands. Tank treads whirred and crunched. Lying on the granite hills, Ta-yung shuddered, not from fear, but from tense expectancy. It was the first time in his life he had ever been exposed to anything like this.

He held tightly to the dynamite bomb. But how to use it against a tank?

He checked the oblong-shaped cotton sack; on one side there were the two cloth straps, so that it could be carried on the back; on the other side was a small pocket with flap which he opened, and found a small steel ring inside. This had to be the firing pin.

"It explodes five seconds after you pull out the pin," Big

Bugle yelled out as he crawled over to him. Big Bugle picked up one of the bombs and tossed it around, shouting, "When you play with one of these babies, you've got to have nerve."

The two of them continued to lie on the rocky ridge, side by side, looking over the mountain pass to the next hill. In the blue sky, white clouds drifted overhead and the sun shone brightly. The expanse of land was once a part of China and had been taken from the motherland by force. When would it be returned to the bosom of the people's China?

Big Bugle suddenly gave Ta-yung a strong poke. Ta-yung followed the direction of Big Bugle's pointing finger and saw first a turret appear, and then a tank slowly and methodically crawling up the ridge. The turret turned slightly, and the hatch on top lifted up. A streamer of white cloth came out, waving back and forth.

The noise came to a halt. If it were not for the Soviet T-62 heavy tank standing there on the road in the distance, raising its gun barrel, sighting down ominously, one would think it all a dream.

A head had appeared in the turret wearing a gunner's leather helmet, and finally, it was followed by an upper torso.

A loudspeaker barked; the man in the tank spoke Russian. Ta-yung could not understand a word, until the man began to speak in Chinese.

"We are the border troops of Mongolia. Here is our ultimatum: you have encroached upon the Mongolian People's Republic, and we give you ten minutes to withdraw."

"What kind of shit is that?" Ta-yung thought to himself. "They have removed the border markers, and sent tanks over the border by two thousand meters."

Ta-yung was ready to explode with anger.

"No one is to expose his position, and no one will fire a shot." Young Swallow gave the order with finality. "The Command Headquarters calculate that they are merely trying to probe our positions; don't fall for their trap."

Then, on Hill 658, opposite, someone yelled out: "The Chinese People's Liberation Army demands that you withdraw immediately!"

The man in the tank quickly ducked his head down into the turret, like a turtle withdrawing its head under the shell. Before the hatch was even closed, the tank began its retreat and, in a wink, disappeared behind the hill.

The people on Hill 658 cheered at this turn of events, as if they had won a victory.

At a sound like mosquitoes humming, Ta-yung turned in another direction, and saw a small black dot in the distance coming closer, and soon a small helicopter drew near, flying toward them from the other side of the border.

"Take cover!" Everyone quickly flattened to the ground, seeking cover.

This dragonfly of steel hovered above them, then swooped down like a hungry eagle eager for prey.

From the other side of the granite hills, four black dots trailing white smoke burst forth and exploded in the middle of Hill 658. The shrill sound of their flight across the sky and the sound of the explosions tore at the eardrums. Loose clods of earth and shards of granite flew in all directions. Ta-yung held his breath and ducked his head lower against the rock.

When the smoke dispersed, Hill 658 still stood intact. But the rockets were fired a second time, and aimed a little too high, they landed in the steppe area behind the hill. The helicopter was still circling, two or three hundred meters above Hill 744 where Ta-yung and his comrades were. That must be the son of a bitch who was directing the fire.

A third round was fired, and this time hit its target on top of Hill 658. In the deafening sound of explosion, Ta-yung could almost hear the moaning of his comrades, and see their shattered limbs. He shouted, "Come on, avenge our comrades! Let's get those bastards!"

Two men of the heavy machine gun unit formed a brace; a

third aimed at the sky. All the others raised their gun sights, seeking out the helicopter, which arrogantly lowered its altitude and circled about at close range.

"Shoot!" Young Swallow commanded. In a flash, the heavy machine gun, the light machine guns, the carbines, all emitted angry flames of revenge in the direction of the helicopter flying insouciantly a hundred feet above.

The helicopter sputtered, suddenly jerked upward, as if trying to regain altitude. It veered toward the left, out of control, and passed Hill 714, tilting toward the left. The sputtering became louder, and then stopped as the helicopter plunged into the snow on the northeast section of the basin.

Forgetting to take cover, everyone stood up to cheer.

"Great! But we'll have to wait until next summer to pick up our souvenirs," Big Bugle said with wry regret. "The snow over there is about thirty meters deep."

The sound of rifles burst out. Rock exploded into dust as bullets pinged off and everyone ducked for cover. The enemy on Hill 767 had opened fire.

In the midst of furious return fire, Young Swallow picked up the telephone, and then announced, "We are ordered to withdraw on the double! Let's get out of here, and head for T'ung-tzu-kou. Move out!"

Ta-yung and Big Bugle formed the rear guard. When they were halfway down the slope, they heard the crashing sound of explosions, and four or five of the platoon were hit by rock shards. Their comrades shouldered them up, and helped them across the open ground into the trenches.

The shelling continued. In the intervals between explosions was heard the sound of tank engines and tank treads.

Ta-yung pulled at Big Bugle's sleeves, and they cut across the slope of the hill to the other side to see what was happening. Three tanks in a V formation were advancing, and had now reached the bottom of Hill 658.

From behind the rocks of Hill 658, a figure rushed out, carrying a bomb with his left hand, another on his back. Like a mountain goat, the soldier nimbly jumped on a tank advancing on the hill, then jumped off and stretched out on the ground.

A red flash was followed by an explosion. The tank had become a pile of scrap iron, the turret blown off.

The man jumped up, took the bomb from his back, and stalked the middle tank from the rear.

The tank on the right had stopped, and now, the turret turned, the hatch opened. A man emerged. He deftly rested a submachine gun on the turret and began to fire at the foot soldier, who was running in a low crouch.

Ta-yung saw it all instantly. It was Li P'ei-yi. How could he help him? Before he had time to move, the sound of machine-gun fire broke out, as Big Bugle opened fire on the tank. The tank gunner suddenly fell, draped over the tank, motionless.

One round and he had hit his target. Some eye, that Big Bugle! While Big Bugle's aim was accurate, it came too late. Li P'ei-yi had fallen, and was lying on the ground.

The tank in the middle swung around, making a 180-degree turn. It now faced Li P'ei-yi, stretched out on the ground no more than sixty meters away.

Li P'ei-yi, it seemed, was not done for. He turned over, crouched on top of his remaining bomb, and stood up, only to topple over amid a barrage of machine-gun bullets coming from the tank.

Li P'ei-yi sat up, and crawled along the ground. The tank started its growl and advanced directly on top of him.

Big Bugle threw away his rifle and ran out. As he ran, he took the bomb from his back. The tank on the right immediately opened fire. Ta-yung was livid, and with one vault rushed into open ground, and headed for the tank on the right.

The turret turned toward the left. With one hand, Ta-yung pulled off his bomb, with the other he jumped on top of the tank.

In this one split second, he saw Li P'ei-yi, holding his bomb, roll under the other tank; there was a flash of light, followed by a shuddering blast. "I must avenge him" was all that Ta-yung could think. He mounted the turret, which began to turn in an attempt to knock him off. But he had reached the hatch.

Where was the iron ring? Ta-yung curled his finger in the ring and pulled it with a jerk, and dropped the bomb through the open turret. Someone below tried to push the bomb back. Ta-yung pushed down, also forcing back the corpse draped over the turret. He closed the lid, and jumped off. Once on the ground, he rolled and tumbled over, then felt himself lifted up in the air by the blast.

◈ ◈ ◈

Dark blue sky, cloudless for miles. A warm and soft wind caressed Ta-yung's face, bringing the fragrance of flowers and the smell of fresh spring grass. He was riding his horse and galloping in the waist-high grassland. The horse whinnied in high spirits, as it raced to the bank of a crystal lake.

The surface of the lake wrinkled with the gusts of scudding wind; iridescent trout jumped from the water, scaring the frogs hiding in the tall grass by the water's edge.

Small yellow five-petaled flowers blossomed on the lakeside slopes, and thousands of richly colored butterflies danced and fluttered.

The horse drank contentedly at the lake's edge.

Ta-yung neared the hilltop, and as far as he could see were tilled fields covered with wheat undulating like the sea. In the distance, a threshing machine was at work, and at the other end of the boundless plain were mowing machines looking like small boats on a green sea. Young people on horseback were rounding up herds of cows and sheep. As the lowing of thousands of cows and the "baa's" of tens of thousands of sheep approached, there was a medley of noises, something like the sound of wailing. Who was crying in the midst of this idyllic scene?

The happy prospect dissolved, and Ta-yung felt pain. He opened his eyes, and in the miasma of consciousness, forms gradually took shape. The grass straw strands that hung down from the cracks of the branches in the thatch roof were swaying back and forth. Ta-yung felt drowsy again.

But what had happened to Li P'ei-yi? And Big Bugle? The frontier, was it secure?

Ta-yung tried to sit up. Dimly, he heard voices: "He's awake. Hsiao Ta-yung is awake!"

Then he really was awake. He sat up, grimacing in agony, and struggled to get out of bed.

A girl in a white uniform rushed to his side.

"Comrade, don't get out of the bed!"

"It's all right. I'm okay."

"You have been unconscious for three hours. How can you say you are all right? Lie down immediately."

"Is the frontier secure?" Ta-yung asked anxiously.

"It is secure. Don't worry."

"And Li P'ei-yi? Big Bugle?"

"Big Bugle is there next to you."

"And how about Li P'ei-yi?" Ta-yung asked, as he turned to see Big Bugle in the next cot, covered with bandages. He touched himself; his left hand was bandaged.

Why doesn't she answer? With her back toward him, the nurse was fending off tears, her shoulders shaking. Li P'ei-yi was dead.

Ta-yung got slowly out of bed, and found his clothes on a stool, and despite the pain, put on his cotton pants and jacket.

The woman continued to weep as Ta-yung slowly walked out of the infirmary.

Following the road, he walked on ahead. His mind cleared as he felt the cold wind blowing. He listened, pricking up his ears, but heard no sound of guns in the distance. What was the outcome of the battle? Suddenly he heard something; it was coming closer. He could now make it out; the sound of a helicopter! Oh, hell! The Soviets had launched a surprise air attack, and no one here was making any move.

As he stumbled into the courtyard, he heard louder and

louder the sound of a helicopter and shouted, "Helicopters coming!"

Some workers in the courtyard looked up in surprise. One of the youths grabbed him and asked, "Are you all right?"

"Quick! Sound the alarm! Soviet helicopters are coming this way!" Ta-yung shouted helplessly, his finger pointing toward the sky in a futile gesture.

"Soviet helicopters? No. They are ours. Some officers from the Regional Command have arrived. Almost everyone has gone to receive them."

"They are ours!" Ta-yung felt dizzy, and he could not stand up any more.

"Come inside and rest." The youth supported him, helping him to enter the meeting room, where he put Ta-yung in a chair.

"I'll get you a cup of tea. Take it easy."

Ta-yung was alone in the meeting room. He closed his eyes and rested. No longer disoriented, he recalled the events of the battle.

On opening his eyes, he felt better, and heard the sound of approaching footsteps. The youth had returned, holding a bowl of hot gruel.

"I guess you haven't had lunch yet, have you? Here, take this."

"Thanks." Ta-yung took the bowl, and realizing how hungry he was, gulped down the food. He noticed that the youth was wearing a black armband, probably a gesture of mourning for Li P'ei-yi.

Feeling reinvigorated, Ta-yung stood up, and handed the bowl back to the youth, with his thanks.

"You look a lot better, but I think you ought to take it easy for a while. I've got to return to work now."

In the past year or so, Ta-yung had often worked with Commissar Hsieh of the Militia Command Headquarters. To develop the organization, train low-level cadres, distribute weapons, and draw up plans for all kinds of work projects, they had frequently been together until late at night. Ta-yung admired Hsieh's strong will and fortitude, her poise and meticulous working habits, and her boundless loyalty to Madame Chairman. She would often say: "I have followed Madame Chairman for many years, and learned so much from her; she taught us to cultivate our polarities of love and hate, for only then can we understand the importance of contradiction in all things."

Did the telephone in the meeting room connect with Peking? Ta-yung wanted to call Commissar Hsieh and report the invasion. He picked up the phone, then realized that this extension probably had no security safeguards. His call could compromise the welfare of the country.

Mulling this over, Ta-yung heard voices followed by the entry of a large crowd into the meeting hall.

Chief Liu spotted Ta-yung and said loudly to several military types following him into the room: "This is Comrade Hsiao Ta-yung, who just took part in the battle. He is a student from Peking."

"Ah! It's Ta-yung! How come you are here?"

The person speaking was Commissar Hsiao, who turned to Chief Liu:

"He's my nephew. Is he the one who blew up three tanks?"

"No, that was Li P'ei-yi and Comrade T'ang [Big Bugle]. I had very little to do with it."

Chief Liu said gravely, "Comrade Hsiao, the third tank was your doing. I saw it with my own eyes."

"It was a great feat! One helicopter and three tanks. We had only one casualty. I'd say we got the better of it."

"I don't see it that way," Ta-yung interjected. "Why didn't regular army troops move up in time? Does it make sense to depend on the likes of us with no heavy armament to defend the border? Though the life of only one comrade was sacrificed, we lost one of our best."

"Comrade Hsiao," Secretary Ch'iao spoke, patting Ta-yung cordially, "you do not understand the situation. The decision of the Military Affairs Committee was to fight the war in Inner Mongolia by luring the enemy inside our borders. Then, closing the door behind them in a pincers movement, we could cut off their supply lines. The heroics that you helped perform, commendable as they were, destroyed the over-all strategy of battle. As of now, those hundred upon hundreds of tanks dare not enter; they only wait 'outside the door.' Several of our divisions poised in the steppes now wait also probably in vain. Therefore, from the narrow perspective, your action was meritorious, but the order was to retreat, not to stand and fight. Isn't that right?"

After listening to Secretary Ch'iao's explanation, Ta-yung was sobered. He lowered his head.

"You recognize the problem! Good. All the same, your heroism should be commended. Oh, I see you are wounded."

"He was unconscious for several hours," Chief Liu said. "He just came to."

"Where is the medical team that is to come with me?" Commissar Hsiao asked.

"In the infirmary. They are working on a soldier who is seriously wounded."

"Then let us proceed with our plan. Ta-yung, will you retreat with them to Farm Unit Number 73?"

"Retreat?" Ta-yung asked in amazement.

"Yes. We are setting fire to the buildings so that those mobsters may be emboldened enough to come in."

"I think I had better return to Peking. In the present state of affairs, I must be needed at my work post."

"In that case, come with us. We also have to bring back the wounded."

Commissar Hsiao shook hands with Chief Liu, Secretary Ch'iao, and the others, and gave his orders to a military figure standing at his side. "Battalion Commander Shen, send a company immediately to Farm Unit Number 73. If hostilities arise, your regular army units should assume full responsibility; the

Militia will only assist you. Understood?" Having said that, he left at the head of his entourage.

Ta-yung followed. From the infirmary, two men were carried out on stretchers. Big Bugle was still unconscious. Ta-yung held onto the stretcher as he looked at Big Bugle in silence. No one had come to say goodbye to Ta-yung, and he was heavyhearted.

The noon sun blazed brightly as they descended the slope, hearing the curious put-put, whirring sound of a helicopter. At a distance, the rotors on a large helicopter were beginning to turn.

But farther away in the steppes, on the line of the ridge, there appeared a few black dots which grew rapidly in size.

A group of riders reached the helicopter and mingled with those who were leaving. Ta-yung saw that they were all young people from the farm. Young Swallow was among them, pulling up tight on her rein; she cut a dashing and striking figure, with a rifle strung across her back, sitting ramrod-straight in the saddle. The horse was excitedly pawing its front and back hooves on the ground, moving restlessly back and forth.

When Young Swallow saw Ta-yung, she dismounted, and handing the reins to someone at the side, she removed a coat from another horse and came directly to Ta-yung.

Her eyes fastened first on Big Bugle. The coat she returned to Ta-yung, and then leaned down to arrange the woolen blanket that covered Big Bugle's body. She said, "Are you leaving?"

"Yes, I am needed in my job back in Peking. Are you retreating with the others?"

"Yes. We are withdrawing to the west."

"Do you have anything you want me to say to your mother?"

"Say whatever you feel like saying."

"When the war is over, I will come back here to see you."

"Do you have to?"

"I have decided that after I graduate I would like to come

here to work. You might have some use for a repairman for the tractors and mowers here."

"I wanted to tell you that I was in love with Li P'ei-yi."

"He died in glory."

"He will live forever in my heart."

Young Swallow took the submachine gun from her back, and handed it to Ta-yung.

"This is the trophy you won in battle. Take it."

"No. It was the bullet fired from this gun that killed Li P'ei-yi. Big Bugle destroyed the enemy holding this gun on the spot. All I did was to take it out of his hands. You had better use it to defend our motherland."

"All right. And oh . . . Thank you for coming to see me . . . and for bringing me so many things." She turned away abruptly.

"Young Swallow!" Ta-yung cried out.

Young Swallow stopped and turned. Her short hair was blown loose by the swirling wind, her dark eyebrows were raised. With large almond-shaped eyes, she stared at Ta-yung.

Ta-yung collected his courage, and walked toward her.

"After the fighting is over, I am coming back to see you, and I will not leave."

"You had better write me first." With a pained, uneasy expression, she looked into Ta-yung's face, ran off to her horse, and, after taking up the reins, bolted into the saddle, riding off into the steppeland at the vanguard of her group.

Ta-yung crawled into the helicopter, and the door closed. He sat near a round window.

Shaking and whirring, the helicopter ascended. The steppes became a patchwork of many hues and shades. Looking down, Ta-yung saw the riders, strung out in a thin line. The one at the head was probably Young Swallow.

From on high, the mountain pass that had been the site of so fierce a battle appeared as only a yellow gash, big as a finger. Later, Ta-yung had a clear view of the armada of tanks hiding on the other side of the border, rows and rows, a battalion of army ants, in lines that stretched out into the distance.

▨ FOURTEEN

Tuesday, February 12   Noon

       Hua . . . shush-shush-shush . . . hua-hua . . . shush-shush-shush . . . Crack! . . .

The sleigh stopped on the slope; Big Beard, who had been standing on the back runners, got off. He flashed his whip and urged the horse on, hailing and shouting.

The horse strained and started to whinny. The rear hooves kicked out clods of ice and snow, some falling on Chia Hsiang-tung, who was cramped inside the narrow sled, completely covered by sheepskin.

He had been hiding in the stinking sheepskin, suffering from the rocking of the sleigh for nearly four hours. Suddenly the sleigh started and the runners underneath made a soughing sound. The hoofbeats became more measured.

After riding for some time, there was another stop. The sheepskin covering Chia was pulled off.

Big Beard smiled at him: "Get out, there's nobody around."

Chia Hsiang-tung tried to get off the sleigh to stand up but his legs were totally numb and refused to move. He looked up at Big Beard.

"What's your name?"

"What my name is—family name or given name—completely escapes me at the moment. And I don't want to know yours."

Chia had not expected such a rebuff. He took a pack of cigarettes from his pocket, lit up, and offered the pack and the lighter to Big Beard.

"China brand, eh?" Without removing a cigarette, he stuck both the cigarettes and the lighter into his clothes.

Big Beard looked up at the sky, and said, "I wonder what time it is," casting a significant glance at Chia Hsiang-tung.

Chia Hsiang-tung caught on: he took off his wristwatch and threw it over.

"You take it. People in your line of work shouldn't be without one. This watch is genuine Swiss-made."

"Oh no, you shouldn't. A valuable thing like that!"

"Only a trifle. When we get to the other side, I will thank you properly."

"In that case, I will take it. Whoa! Do you carry a gun?"

"I left in a hurry, so I did not have time to pick one up. Do you have a spare one I can borrow?"

"No one is permitted to carry a weapon on this road. It would be curtains if the Chinese border patrol found one on you. That's why I asked."

"How much farther do we go on this road?"

"If nothing crops up, and if the weather stays okay, we should cross the border sometime tonight."

"And after we cross, how much farther before I reach a settlement?"

"You have to walk four hours to reach the nearest guard post; if they think you're worth it, they might send a helicopter for you. Otherwise, you will have to walk two days and two nights before you can board a train."

Chia Hsiang-tung took out the roll of bills from his pocket, and said with a grin, "There's no use for me to carry it. Why don't you keep this for the next time, when you come back." With this, he tried to stomp some circulation back into his legs.

Big Beard looked coldly at Chia, thinking to himself: "Too bad he's not going to live long!"

Big Beard had originally been a member of a farm production corps and had escaped to Russia from the Shih-ho ("Stone River") Farm in Sinkiang in 1967. In his early years, he had served in the Nationalist Army as a platoon leader with the rank of second lieutenant. In the War of Liberation in 1948, he was seized in the battle of Tientsin, and impressed into service with the People's Liberation Army, fighting in the northwest. Later, he had settled in Sinkiang as a member of the farm production corps. Even his dependents had been relocated there.

Gradually, he had become accustomed to his new way of life. But he had no idea that the Red Guards would challenge and ultimately bring down Wang Chen, the head of the Farm Reclamation Department, and Wang En-mao, Commander of the Sinkiang Military Region. Rumor had it then that whoever had been once on the Nationalist payroll would be arrested and sent back to his home town to be purged. As a result, several thousand people had rebelled and fled across the border into the Soviet Union, bringing along weapons, provisions, and dependents. They had hoped to lead a peaceful life in the Soviet Union, but they soon realized they had jumped out of the frying pan into the fire. All their weapons were confiscated and they were interned in an area surrounding a lake, no more than five miles in circumference. From Moscow came a few Chinese who called themselves members of the Special Central Committee of the Chinese Communist Party. After they had looked over the group, they had organized Party cells, and the people were left to lead their own lives.

Big Beard was originally from Dairen, where he had learned to speak Russian as a child. He was selected to join a group of special agents, and had been sent off for half a year's training. Some were dropped by parachute into Sinkiang; others had been sent to Manchuria. Big Beard had been assigned to Mongolia. After a few years, he picked up Mongolian, and had made a practice of assuming the cover of a Mongolian, operating on both sides of the border. Now he had been assigned a mission to escort a person from Hsi-li across the border and then eliminate him.

He took out his pack of rations and picked out a piece of dried beef and a piece of corn biscuit; with a knife he cut them into two portions and shared the food with Chia. He scooped up snow to slake his thirst. After eating, they continued their journey on the sleigh.

Big Beard sat in the sleigh and pulled the reins on the horse, letting Chia stand on the back runner. Chia Hsiang-tung stood as he had been instructed, and felt his face numbing with the cold. Later, his feet began to feel frozen, and he wished he had bought some thick woolen socks.

◈ ◈ ◈

Washington, D.C.
1 a.m. Eastern Standard Time

On receipt of special orders from the President, the technical force at Cape Canaveral had been mobilized. In forty-eight hours, satellite 8615 was sent into orbit. Passing over the Sino-Soviet border region, it transmitted photographs of the terrain over an area of two hundred kilometers to the relay satellite fixed in outer space directly over the center of the Pacific Ocean. The information was recorded by the receiving station in Houston, providing the most up-to-date and detailed data on the Sino-Soviet border area. The information was then transmitted by trunk line to the Pentagon for the White House.

The area southwest of Erh-lien, where the border conflict was unfolding, was seen in the photographs covering the two-hundred-square-kilometer area. The analysts noted the nearly six hundred tanks of all sizes, the automatic recoilless guns, as well as the armored trucks and transport vehicles, deployed in combat-ready positions. A large-scale offensive maneuver was indicated.

The same large-scale mobilization had been found concurrently in two other areas, in the T'ung-chiang City area in Amur Province of Manchuria and near T'a-ch'eng in Sinkiang. At the Soviet military airports not too far from these locations, full preparations were under way. Huge transport planes and large-sized helicopters to transport combat vehicles were lined up, ready for takeoff. An emergency situation existed.

As more and more intelligence was sent by the Pentagon to the White House, the President felt he must convene an emergency meeting to review the situation and determine a course of action.

Of the officials summoned to this emergency meeting, some arrived in dinner jackets, others in casual clothes, some bleary-eyed and barely awake. After they heard the report of the President's assistant, they remained silent in thought.

Smith, a member of the Foreign Relations Committee in the Senate, drew a sigh of relief; luckily it was not another Middle East crisis, so it would not affect his stocks. Better there be some small skirmishes between the Soviets and the Chinese, to relax the pernicious grip of Soviet influence in the Middle East.

Slides flashed on a giant screen as part of the briefing, along with a voice-over commentary, and everyone soon understood the current situation in the Far East. A spokesman gave an analysis:

"When the great leader of a Far Eastern country of nine hundred million people passed away, the leadership core, already splintered, became engaged in a power struggle that involved both foreign and domestic policies. The Chinese have tried hard to cover up, but anyone with any political acumen can discern their difficulties.

"Eight hours ago, something decisive and odd occurred. A part of the Chinese leadership, in order to escape arrest, left Peking and withdrew to a small city in Hopei Province, to convene a National Party Congress. Other leaders, centered around Madame Mao, have mobilized their armed forces, the Workers Militia, and occupied the major cities of China. But the PLA, the largest army in the world, with three million soldiers, waits outside the cities, and has not shown its hand.

"As reported by the American Liaison Office in Peking, the various departments in the Chinese Central Government have all virtually ceased to function. The entire state bureaucracy seems to be paralyzed, though law and order is still maintained in the cities. The exchange of goods and services is as usual. But there is widespread alarm among the people, who seem to be expecting a major shift in government.

"At this moment, the Soviet Union to the north of China is exerting pressure, pressure that could build up to an explosion.

"This pressure is exerted not only from three points in the north, but also from the south by sea.

"According to the figures from the Japanese Defense Ministry, the Soviet navy has steamed through the Tsushima Strait in the past two days with more than thirty ships, forming two fleets. These fleets are accompanied by transport ships and tankers. In addition, the Soviet aircraft carrier that entered the Indian Ocean in January and sent shock waves through the international scene passed through the Strait of Malacca yesterday, entering the South China Sea and joining another Soviet fleet returning from a friendly visit to Indonesia.

"The military activities from the south and the north exceed the normal level of war exercises. There is only one conclusion: a major military action is in preparation."

The officer in charge of the briefing signaled, and the slides were changed for another set of photographs taken by the reconnaissance satellite, which showed the situation in Manchuria, North China, and northwest China. From these slides, the only traces of combat preparations were in North China.

When the pictures were blown up and time-lapse sequences shown, one could see clearly that, of the two powerful Chinese armored divisions stationed in Inner Mongolia, one had been shifted from its defensive position and moved to Hopei Province, to a mountain location in the western suburb of Peking.

Everyone in the room seemed stunned. Even General Hermann, who prided himself on being a specialist in Chinese military strategy, could not attempt to explain these strange manuevers.

The discussion began. Congressman Field of the Armed Services Committee was the first to speak.

"In September 1976, I joined a group to visit China. At that time the Chinese were interested in showing us defense installations in Sinkiang, Inner Mongolia, and other areas. After we watched their demonstrations of mounted horsemen and their full-dress parades in the style of Napoleon, we returned to Peking, where we met with a few of the important leaders. I bluntly mentioned that their adversaries would be completely equipped with modern weapons and that the time when one could rely on manpower was over. I suggested that they should be using ICBM defense systems, as well as anti-tank weaponry. But they only smiled at these suggestions."

Congressman Field jabbed his cigar into his mouth, took a puff, and went on.

"When we returned, we realized, after some study, the purpose behind the Chinese invitation for our visit. It was not to secure modern military hardware from us. All they wanted was to turn us into a public forum to tell the world: 'Look! Socialist imperialism is about to invade us.' In the face of international opinion, they hoped to deter Soviet aggression.

"I think this is the Peking strategy, to use political machinations in dealing with military threats."

"Do you think that for the time being the Soviet Union does not have the nerve to invade China?"

"No evidence is available, but that's what I think." Somewhat irritated, Congressman Field answered the question of a young professorial type sitting on a small sofa across from him.

Tonight Field was in a particularly bad mood, and for two reasons. Last year, when he had joined the group of congressmen visiting China, he had carried thick brochures in his portfolio, with the purpose of selling the ICBM system (already out of date in the United States) to China. Some American firms who produced the system would then be able to secure a few additional orders before they had to abandon their specially constructed production equipment. Not only would he profit personally from the stocks he had in his portfolio, but he would stand a good chance of being appointed to a board of directors when he retired from politics.

On top of that, he and his beautiful private secretary had been spending the night together when he was called in. Only the two of them, he had thought, knew about the place, but when the emergency meeting was called at the White House, the secretary in charge of arranging the meeting had called his hideaway. The secretary was discreet enough over the phone, but the sirens of the police cars that came to get him caused quite a commotion in the sleepy little town. His cover had been blown for good. When the meeting finished, he would probably get a telephone call from his wife's legal counsel. This frightened him more than any war that might break out in a remote corner of the Far East. The frown on his face deepened.

The young professorial type, who was named Whitestone, had come to the meeting with the head of the CIA. He had studied China for many years in the university, and had stayed in Peking for a few years as an adviser to the head of the CIA, so he had a fresh approach to China's problems.

"I do not entirely concur with Congressman Field's analysis. Ever since Chairman Mao died, the Soviet Union has adopted a patient and watchful attitude, hoping for a chance to improve relations between the two countries. Why? Because they could see that Mao's heirs were split into two camps, very much at odds with each other. One camp has been led by Madame Mao; although she holds no position in the government, she plays a key role. Since it controls national media, Madame Mao's camp serves as the spiritual and theoretical beacon for the country. In their domestic policies, they rely on self-sufficiency in agriculture as the base; and their foreign policy is centered around an anti-Soviet posture. All their other activities proceed from these two mainsprings, and they achieve their ends by means of political intrigue.

"Although the political campaigns have been going on for more than ten years, the economic development of the country cannot match the rate of population growth. People cannot achieve basic levels of satisfaction in their life or in their work. So, another problem has been produced, the contradiction between those who have privileges and those who do not.

"The most representative instance of this contradiction is the antagonism between the Urban Workers Militia, established by Madame Mao's group, and the intellectual youth, who have been exiled to the countryside or who are unemployed in the cities.

"This contradiction developed as far back as 1960. One contingent in the leadership hierarchy wanted to resolve the contradiction by raising the living standards, by raising production, by expediting the rate of economic development to satisfy the material and occupational needs of the people. This approach, though it would have solved the problem in practical terms, would have changed the essential character of the original ideological doctrine.

"This task of upholding the ideological doctrine provided the excuse for retrieving power in the beginning of 1966, but after the death of the Chairman ten years later, it became an article of faith, an inviolable commandment. And this commandment embodies the already established anti-Soviet line.

"Chairman Mao, before he died, made an important decision. He eliminated Teng Hsiao-p'ing,* despite the fact that he had personally chosen him, a choice that Chou En-lai fully endorsed. Although there were many domestic political reasons behind this ouster, the most important can be found in one particular incident. Teng Hsiao-p'ing, in his capacity as Vice-Chairman of the Chinese Communist Party, Vice-Chairman of the Military Affairs Committee, and Vice-Premier of the State Council, gave instructions to the departments concerned to release three Soviet officers who had been arrested when their helicopters strayed across the border into Sinkiang. This action reduced tensions in Sino-Soviet relations, but it totally violated Chairman Mao's stated policy of uncompromising antagonism to the Soviet Union.

"After the Chairman's death, would the opposing camp reassume control of power? That is the question that has preoccupied the Soviets, but they must wait cautiously. Time and time again, they have offered overtures, but when they see what's happening in China today, their complacency disappears, and they are impatient to use military force. Why? Three reasons: to warn the anti-Soviet bloc in China, to intimidate the high-ranking military officers who have so far maintained neutrality, and to lend support to the other camp."

Finnegan, a member of the Foreign Relations Committee, after listening to this, asked, "Would the Chinese army engage the invading Soviet troops in battle?"

"It is hard to say. In the present state of paralysis in the Chinese Party and governmental structure, just who is going to make the big decisions no one knows."

"If we want to prevent this war, whom would we get in touch with on the Chinese end?"

"It should be Hua Kuo-feng, who is now the highest responsible official of the Party."

* Teng has now been formally reinstated as Vice-Premier, ranking third in the Politburo, as of September 1, 1977—TRANSLATOR.

254

"Could members of the American Liaison Office see him immediately?"

"They would have to be passed through by the Chinese Foreign Ministry, and that usually takes time."

"What if we were to contact the Chinese Liaison Office in New York?"

"That question could not be answered in a hurry, and the outbreak of war may be a matter of only a few hours."

"In that case, any action to prevent hostilities will be impossible to manage with the Chinese, and it would be futile even if we could manage to get through."

"Since China is the country that would be invaded, we should proceed through the Soviet end."

In a moment, all those present realized, in order to stave off this imminent war that might endanger all mankind, the only way left was to communicate directly with the Russian bear. But recently, whatever matters had been discussed with the Soviets, the Americans had been more or less taken advantage of, especially when Russia seized the initiative.

"What is the real motive behind the present Soviet action? Is there more to what they are doing than meets the eye?" The head of the Intelligence Bureau of the Defense Department analyzed the situation with icy objectivity. "Are they really going to wage war? I estimate the odds at fifty-fifty."

Everyone was immediately relieved, as if a way out of a difficult impasse had been found, and all listened attentively to the analysis.

"In the past few years, Soviet agriculture has consistently suffered shortages. Last year, under the worst climatic conditions, the Soviet Union declared a good yield in its agricultural production; it was, of course, a big lie. They had hoped by this ruse to bring down the price of grain in the international market, and then, at depressed prices, they intended to buy large quantities of grain to weather out the storm.

"In the past few months, we have come into possession of all the details of their secret grain purchases. If Congress should pass the bill forbidding export of grain in excess of the quantities agreed upon by the two countries, the Soviets will encounter great hardship.

"This bill has been in the House of Representatives since last week. From the Soviet point of view, what method should be used to prevent passage of this bill? we may ask. A question well worth considering.

"In addition, if the Soviet Union should attack China and initiate a large-scale war between the two countries, the development of its own economy would be delayed for ten years at least. I do not have the time to cite concrete figures for these points. Put in a nutshell, at the least, the loans and economic agreements that the Sovet Union worked for so many years to secure from us, the United States, as well as from Japan and West Germany and other countries, would have to be terminated. Trade would be affected. Also, please do not forget, any of you, that the Chinese submarine force now ranks third in the world.

"What I have just given is a political and economic analysis of the Soviet Union. In military terms, I think everyone understands the strategy of the two countries. This would not be a short-term war. It might very well escalate into a war involving nuclear weapons. But would the Soviet Union dare to undertake such risks? Are they that sure of themselves?"

"Then why are they setting it up this way?" the Secretary of State asked.

"This is skulduggery, with two motives: one, to intimidate China and to exert pressure against a certain political bloc in China, the anti-Soviet bloc of Madame Mao; two, to serve as a bargaining chip in negotiations, not with the Chinese, but with us."

"What if we ignore all that has happened?"

"They will carry out their invasion to a limited extent, thus creating a situation that we could not afford to ignore."

"To what extent, and how limited?" The Secretary of State was interested.

"For example, to invade only Sinkiang, and to establish an east Turkestan republic, eventually for annexation into the Soviet Union."

"If this were so, would China put up with the loss of Sinkiang?"

"If China were torn by internal disorder, and if there were mammoth military pressures in Inner Mongolia and Manchuria, China would temporarily give up Sinkiang and withdraw to the Kansu corridor, turning Sinkiang and northern Tibet into a guerrilla zone."

"Then the attack from the north and from the northeast are feints; the real attack is to come from the west."

"Yes, if we do nothing to prevent it."

"But China has probably seen through it already. According to the intelligence mentioned before, the Chinese armored division has withdrawn from the Inner Mongolian area. It appears to have been transferred to the western front." The Secretary of State looked at everyone in the room.

"Then the real war will break out in the northwestern part of China," Smith said, the strategy finally dawning on him.

"What effect will this have on the United States?" the Secretary of State asked.

"There would not be a country in the world that would dare to oppose the Soviet Union one to one, including the United States, because of a sense of defeatism in this country."

"Just a minute! I don't agree!" the Secretary of Defense objected. "With the Vietnam War, plus a lack of progress in Africa, we have developed a sense of defeatism and escapism, which has become a dominant mood in the country. If we should stand by while the Soviets carve out a part of China, there is no way we can rationalize that. The policy of détente will degenerate into an isolationist policy. In Europe and in Asia, the allied countries who have begun to reprimand our isolationist attitude will totally change their attitude toward military alliances with us."

The Secretary of State put an end to the discussion, which was obviously going nowhere. He interrupted, "From the majority opinion, it appears we must intervene to stop this war. Are there any objections?" He waited a few seconds. No one objected.

"There is no possibility of contacting China. We can only negotiate with the instigator of the war. This is an emergency situation; and since there is no time to go through regular diplomatic channels, I propose the President use the hot line."

The President, who had been mulling things over at the side, needed time to reflect on this request to use the hot line. After the election all kinds of domestic and foreign policy matters awaited consideration and disposition, and the development of diplomatic relations with China and its consequences at home and abroad were being weighed. Now there was this frontier outburst between China and the Soviet Union. This diplomatic war could turn into a military confrontation. If he did not take a hard-line stance, then in the next four or eight years, how could he withstand the aggressive demands the Soviets would make on every matter that would require negotiations between the two countries? How would he be able to win in a diplomatic showdown? Everyone discussed this question in depth and it was decided to use the grain sale as leverage to pressure the Soviet Union to call off the invasion. But would the Soviet Union make counterdemands?

So the various departments turned to preparing analyses on every aspect of the problem. Working late into the night, the computers were producing by the reams the answers to the questions put to them. The United States did not want to be caught unprepared or to be misled if the Soviet Union insisted on conditions in exchange for its agreement.

The President decided to use the hot line. The hot line control room situated in the basement of the White House was immediately activated. The Russian-language interpreter began to speak on the telephone transmitter. "The President of the United States of America wishes to speak with the Chairman of the Presidium of the Union of the Soviet Socialist Republics in one hour. Please acknowledge."

❖ ❖ ❖

Tuesday, February 12
3 p.m. Peking Standard Time

Foreign Minister Ch'iao Kuan-hua calmly sat in his chair, going over a file he had spread out. The file had been delivered to him yesterday. Since yesterday afternoon, the Workers Militia had taken over the entire Ministry of Foreign Affairs. Working in co-ordination with the Militia inside the Ministry, they had seized control of the entire office, and to all intents and purposes, everything was now at a standstill.

This had happened before. On the other occasion, the courageous Foreign Minister Ch'en Yi stood up to them. And the hero of that time, Yao Teng-shan, where was he now?

There was no one to ask for instructions, no meeting, no telephone, only the ticking of the clock on the wall in the quiet room. Outside, two Militiamen, assigned to "safeguard" him, were chatting.

❖ ❖ ❖

Last night, as Minister Ch'iao had entered the Central Committee Special Headquarters, he had taken them by surprise.

At the first inspection gate, he had to wait fifteen minutes in his car and had not been allowed to enter until Vice-Premier Chang Ch'un-ch'iao came out personally to escort him in. On a single railway track, to the left of the road, he had seen an arriving train, loaded with tanks. Out of curiosity, he had not been able to refrain from asking the reticent Vice-Premier: "Why have these troops been transferred here?"

"They were already attached to the Central Garrison Division. It was sheer coincidence that you should see them just when you came in." The Vice-Premier had been relaxed in his response, his eyes had sparkled behind the lenses of his spectacles.

"Does the Central Garrison Division need armed troops? For what purpose?"

"To protect the Party's Central Committee."

"Have you gone through the Military Affairs Committee to transfer these troops here?"

"We are carrying out the orders the Chairman himself gave some time ago."

"Where have they been transferred from?"

"I am not too sure. Probably from the Inner Mongolian Region."

Minister Ch'iao was so angry he could scarcely control himself. But remembering the object of his visit, he immediately calmed down.

When they reached the northern sector, they sat down in the meeting room of the first row of houses. Only the two of them were there. Vice-Premier Chang personally tended to him affably, lighting his cigarette and pouring his tea. Finally, Vice-Premier Chang sat down behind a table and asked:

"You have come so late. What can we do for you?"

"I want to see Madame Chairman immediately."

"Madame Chairman has retired. It may not be convenient."

"I have come on a matter of national importance. Even if she has gone to bed, I still must see her."

"Perhaps tomorrow would do just as well."

"Tomorrow? By tomorrow, many things may be impossible for us to discuss."

"If it is so urgent, it would be as well to speak to me."

"Can you speak for Madame Chairman? This is the first I have heard that."

"I can convey a message to Madame Chairman; please do not misunderstand me."

"I know that, but there have been entirely too many misunderstandings already. I am asking you once again, would you please ask Madame Chairman to come out and speak with me."

"All right, I will see. Please wait here."

Chang Ch'un-ch'iao left by the hallway, leaving Minister Ch'iao alone in the spacious room. The Foreign Minister sat down, uttering a long, agonized sigh. In the silence of this seemingly interminable waiting, the whole tangled skein of events that embroiled him in this madness muddled its way through his fatigued mind. When was it, 1965, that his beloved first wife had died? The appalling sense of loss and loneliness that had followed.

Shortly thereafter, or so he remembered, he again met the attractive and available Chang Han-chih. Attractive? Yes, in more ways than one to the then Deputy Foreign Minister! In addition to her obvious physical charms, she had been *the* English-language tutor, three times a week for well over three years, to Chairman Mao himself!

Be damned to the stupid rumors that there was more involved than mere English-language tutoring! The fact remained that the Old Man liked Chang Han-chih very much! Unfortunately, Madame Mao did not think too highly of the rumors that her husband was casting covetous eyes at Chang Han-chih.

How stupid of Madame Mao to think Deputy Foreign Minister Ch'iao so blind as to not see her obvious maneuvering when she took it upon herself to be the matchmaker between Ch'iao and Chang Han-chih! To be sure, Ch'iao welcomed the thought of becoming betrothed to the lovely Chang, but at the same time, he was filled with loathing for Madame Mao's Machiavellian attempts.

Troubled, Ch'iao had gone to Premier Chou En-lai and had reported to Chou what was afoot. It was Chou himself, damn it all, who had sanctioned the marriage, pointing out that there would be no harm in having his own Trojan horse in the enemy's camp.

Now, with Chou dead and the implication that Madame

Mao was close to Chang Han-chih, it would naturally connect Ch'iao in a guilt by association. *What* a potential for trouble in the future, should he be unable to clear his name.

He waited a half hour before Chang Ch'un-ch'iao reappeared and said, "Come in . . . come in . . ."

When Chang Ch'un-ch'iao saw Minister Ch'iao stride past him without so much as a glance, Chang berated himself for his own servility. After all, in the Party or in the State Council, Chang reflected, his own rank and position were much higher than this man's who used to be no more than a minor secretary who carried Premier Chou's briefcase. Why should he defer to Ch'iao?

Moreover, the move to arrest the capitalist-roaders, an order issued by Hsieh Ching-yi, had been initiated two hours ago. Everything had been proceeding smoothly according to plan. At this moment, when Ch'iao was falling into a net, why should Chang have to be so accommodating?

In the small living room in the second row of houses Yao Wen-yüan was sitting, looking the complete opposite of Chang Ch'un-ch'iao, grown thinner now every day. Yao, on the contrary, looked fat and prosperous.

"Where is Madame?" Minister Ch'iao asked in a loud voice.

"There is no need for her to see you. If you have anything to say, say it."

Yao Wen-yüan sat casually in his rattan lounge chair, his legs crossed. He did not even nod toward Ch'iao by way of greeting.

Minister Ch'iao calmly walked to the small table, pulled out a bamboo chair, and sat down deliberately. He cast a cold eye at these two men, and then he discovered, right next to where Chang Ch'un-ch'iao stood, a wooden door was ajar; he could see this door moving just a touch. Obviously someone was behind it listening to the conversation, and did not want to be seen.

"You two listen carefully." Minister Ch'iao restrained his anger and spoke slowly. "Our Party now needs solidarity, and cannot afford to be split up. Anything that leads to splits within the Party is in direct violation of the Chairman's directive. Our Party absolutely forbids it; and the people, furthermore, resolutely oppose it."

"Who is trying to destroy the solidarity of our Party?" Yao Wen-yüan asked defensively. "A small band of people, not us."

"How is it being destroyed?" Chang asked. "What evidence do you have?"

"I can offer both witnesses and documentation. The Secretariat of the Central Committee is in possession of both, and is now investigating the design behind these schemes."

"If that is the case, it should be handled by the Secretariat. The Party has its discipline; the nation has its laws; there is no need to bring in Militiamen to disrupt law and order in the country. If you repeat the same mistake as Lin Piao and throw the country into chaos, there will be no one to clean up the mess this time."

"We are carrying out the directives and the policies outlined in the Chairman's will; no one is going to stand in our way." Yao was defiant.

"The Chairman's will! This is the first that I have heard about it. A few days ago, there were rumors abroad about a will, but I did not expect to find that there really was one."

"What do you mean, there is no will? It was written in front of us all just before the Chairman became seriously ill."

"Who was present at the time?"

"There were four or five people, Madame Mao, Vice-Premier Chang, Vice-Premier Wang, and myself."

"You said four or *five*. Who else was there?"

"Ah . . . so much time has passed. I cannot remember exactly. I seem to recall Superintendent Wang Tung-hsing being there . . ."

"Oh! He was there. Then there should be no mistake. What was contained in the will?"

"This is not the time to make it public. Sorry, I cannot let you see it."

"Ah! We will bring this matter up later. For the moment, I want to say a few words on behalf of the majority of the Central Committee members.

"Since you choose not to follow Party procedures, and you disregard the concerns for solidarity in the Party, this afternoon you initiated a surprise campaign against the Party. You must bear full responsibility.

"Those Central Committee members and department heads who really have the guts to work for the Party and for the people, in order to escape your persecution, have now safely left Peking and arrived at a place where they will not be vulnerable to pressures from you."

Yao Wen-yüan bolted up in fury. But Chang Ch'un-ch'iao, standing at the side, found a chair and collapsed into it. There was a sudden movement at the door that had been ajar.

Yao Wen-yüan's somewhat bloated face suddenly contorted, his whole body was trembling, and in a soprano-like voice, he screeched, "This is anti-Party behavior! This is organized, premeditated anti-Party action! You will not escape the judgment of the revolutionary masses!"

"This is not the time or place to make accusations," Ch'iao Kuan-hua said. "Please keep your head. Since the death of the Chairman, there are no more than half of the incumbent Politburo left, an outrageous situation. It is time to convene a Plenary Session of the Central Committee, so we have taken this opportunity to hold a meeting at Paoting at this time three days from now. We hope you will be present."

"If you want to hold such a meeting, it should be held in Peking."

"Then it would no longer be a Central Committee meeting, but a congress of the Militia."

"The Workers Militia is a most progressive organization; it is the most loyal defender of the Chairman's line. Only those opposed to the Chairman's line are afraid of it."

"We are now talking about the problem of holding a meeting of the Central Committee of the Chinese Communist Party. We are not talking about the Militia."

"I am a regular member of the Politburo," Chang Ch'un-ch'iao, silent up to now, said, "and I object to holding such a meeting outside of Peking."

"We are Party members," Ch'iao Kuan-hua resumed. "We should obey the democratic principle of the minority following the majority within the Party. If you have not had occasion to follow this principle for some time, perhaps it is time for you to relearn it."

"Right." Chang Ch'un-ch'iao softened his tone. "We are all members of the Party. We can think it over." He realized then that they had lost the initiative.

"Well then, I shall await your decision." Minister Ch'iao stood up, and walked out of the northern sector in long strides.

The car was waiting in front of the guesthouse. His personal guards, Old Lin and Little Yang, were waiting for him. When they saw Minister Ch'iao walking out alone from the northern sector, his head bent, they sighed in relief.

Minister Ch'iao decided to get hold of Wang, and verify whether he had actually witnessed the Chairman's will.

Leaving his car in front of the Secretariat Office, Minister Ch'iao, his overcoat still on, entered the corridor, and stood in front of the Superintendent's office. He paused for a moment before knocking on the door.

A secretary cadre opened the door, and looked at Minister Ch'iao in surprise. He hurried inside to report.

Superintendent Wang Tung-hsing came out to receive his visitor. When they sat down, Minister Ch'iao immediately explained the purpose of his visit.

"I just heard from Comrade Yao that the Chairman wrote out a will before he fell seriously ill. Is that true?"

Wang thought for a while before answering.

"I have also heard mention of this, but I do not think it was a matter of a will. Rather, it was more along the lines of an ordinary directive."

"They say you were also present at the time of the signing."

"I present? No, I know nothing about it."

Minister Ch'iao switched to a different topic.

"I hear that the Secretariat here is in possession of evidence pertaining to the anti-revolutionary coup."

Wang nodded his head, got up from his small chair, walked to the desk, picked up a thick file, and came back.

"All the data have been analyzed, and the conclusion is that the various secret organizations that survived the Cultural Revolution have been reactivated recently. They are preparing to stir up the masses in the style of the T'ien-an Men Incident, on the lunar New Year. According to intelligence reports from the Department of Public Security, the main instigators are, on the surface, members of the Consolidated Action group. But in reality, there are some high-ranking military officers who are directing operations behind the scenes. Thus the situation has become extremely complicated and critical."

"Are you aware of the action of the Peking Militia this after-noon?"

"We thrashed it out this morning. And I am completely op-posed to what was decided. But they and Madame insisted on sending in the Militia. I have reported this turn of events to Premier Hua."

"What was his reaction?"

"He did not give any indication as to where he stood. He said he would confer with Commander Ch'en."

Minister Ch'iao told him about the decision to hold a meet-ing of the Central Committee in Paoting, and then watched Wang's reaction with the utmost interest.

Wang stood up and quickly paced back and forth across the room for some time, then suddenly paused.

"I agree with the decision to convene immediately, but the place should be Peking. I can absolutely guarantee everyone's safety."

"What about the Militia?"

"They will be called back, and their weapons returned to the arsenal."

"Can this be done?"

"It must be done. This is the most critical hour for the Party; we cannot be split against each other."

"How should we handle the uprisings planned by the Consolidated Action group?"

"This problem will be resolved by the Public Security Department. Premier Hua is also conferring with Commander Ch'en."

"If this can be managed, I am much relieved. I will relate your views to Vice-Premier Li."

"Has he gone to Paoting?"

"Would he be safe in Peking?" Minister Ch'iao retorted with a smile. He got up from the sofa, picked up his overcoat, and with a slightly hunched back, was about to leave.

Wang looked at this white-haired, middle-aged man. His long-standing prejudice against "white area" (*pai-ch'ü*) cadres (who formerly worked against Chiang Kai-shek in the Kuomintang areas and who did not participate in the Long March) was suddenly dispelled. In these days of crises, he had gained a better perception of what was happening. There was only one starting point, and that was loyalty to the Chairman and to the Party. But to choose the right direction from that starting point required the utmost courage, and the most clear-sighted consideration.

Minister Ch'iao was opening the door.

"Wait a moment." Superintendent Wang stopped Minister Ch'iao as he was leaving. "There is something else." Wang himself stepped outside the door and said to his personal secretary, "I have a few things to discuss with Minister Ch'iao. You keep watch outside, and do not let anyone in."

Minister Ch'iao sat down again on the sofa; his eyes were fixed on Wang. Wang returned and, after pacing back and forth again, walked over to the window and drew back the thick drapes. He pushed open the glass wooden-framed panels; the cold wind streamed in. The papers scattered on the table behind the window and the umbrella-shaped porcelain lampshade hanging from the ceiling swayed.

Minister Ch'iao sat, calmly waiting.

Outside the window it was deep night. One could see the piles of snow left on the icy surface of a small lake.

A beam of strong light flashed along the driveway. Three "Red Flag" sedans drove by. Superintendent Wang immediately closed the window and pulled the drapes together decisively. He turned around and looked at Minister Ch'iao.

"Vice-Premier Wang Hung-wen has just rushed here from Shanghai."

Minister Ch'iao said nothing.

"There are certain things which need to be discussed at a Party Congress. The main question is who will succeed to the Party Chairmanship. To drag on like this simply will not do."

"Has that question not already been decided?" Ch'iao said. "When the Chairman personally appointed Comrade Hua to be the First Vice-Chairman, we all agreed. How can we change our minds now?"

"There are some who think that the First Vice-Chairman does not automatically accede to the position of the Chairman, so there are problems."

"Who are these people?"

"Of course, the most important are the four people in the northern sector."

"Including Madame Chairman?"

"Do I have to spell it out?"

"Then what is your position?"

"I follow the position of the Politburo."

"Then, before the Politburo convenes, do you also support the illegal action the four have undertaken?"

"They notified me after the action had begun. I reported on it right away to Premier Hua."

"This action of theirs," Ch'iao said, "is an act of treason to the Party. They should be censured."

Minister Ch'iao bluntly bared the problem. Superintendent Wang fell silent. Big beads of sweat rolled down his face, along with tears.

"I have followed the Chairman all these years," Wang said. "I cannot bring myself to raise a hand against any member of his family now that he is dead."

"You are a member of the Party, a member who believes in Marxism-Leninism, a member of the proletarian class. It is not a feudal relationship between a member of the Party and the Party."

Superintendent Wang put his hand to his head and sat down in the chair behind the desk. Then, resting his head in his hands, his elbows on the desk, he sank into pained, troubled thought.

Minister Ch'iao picked up his overcoat again and opened the door. As a parting shot, he said, "I hope you will decide to carry out the provisions we just discussed. Call back the Militia, remove their weapons, and restore the conditions that will enable the Politburo of the Central Committee to convene in complete security at Peking."

◈ ◈ ◈

It was now three o'clock in the afternoon. Why had the Militia not been called back? Was it because the Superintendent had had a change of heart, or had he encountered difficulties?

As a result of last night's conversation, Minister Ch'iao had sent a report via the military network to Vice-Premier Li. There had been no response. The situation looked more optimistic, but the Militiamen were causing trouble in the Foreign Ministry Building.

A sudden commotion had occurred in the corridor. Section Head Ku, of the Ministry's Section on North and South America, appeared to be berating someone.

Minister Ch'iao opened his door to take a look; four or five Militiamen were blocking Section Head Ku, who was trying to reach him.

"Ku, what is the matter?"

"There is an emergency! But these fools will not let me report to you."

"We are the members of the Workers Militia in the capital," a tall fellow shouted back. "Who are you calling fools? You are insulting the proletarian class." He was holding Section Head Ku by the collar.

"Let go!" Minister Ch'iao commanded in a rage. Everyone shut up.

"Section Head Ku, come into my office," Ch'iao said.

"No, he cannot," the leader of the group shouted. "The authority of the Foreign Ministry is now in the hands of the Workers Militia. If you have an emergency, you should report to our representative in charge of foreign affairs."

Minister Ch'iao remembered the fellow; he had been transferred to the Security Section of the Foreign Ministry a few years ago from the Department of Public Security. On two previous occasions, he was at the fore in pasting up big-character posters, stirring up insurrectionist activity, and criticizing capitalist-roaders. An important figure in rebel groups, Ch'iao recalled, and his name was Chao.

"Comrade Chao. If you have something to say, let's have it. On the basis of what order from the Central Committee did the Workers Militia take over the Foreign Ministry?"

"The order came from the Command Headquarters of the Peking Workers Militia. You can call them to check it out."

"I do not have the time. Section Head Ku, perhaps you can make your report to me here and now."

"This is a top-secret affair of state. They . . ." Section Head Ku muttered.

"Then, Comrade Chao, you follow me in. If the secret leaks out, you alone will take full responsibility.

The three of them entered the office, and Section Head Ku gave a quick report.

"Fifteen minutes ago, there was a telephone call from the American Liaison Office, made by their chief delegate. According to the intelligence of the American reconnaissance satellite, the Soviet Union is preparing to launch armed invasions on three border positions. Now, in Inner Mongolia, skirmishes have already broken out at the border. The chief delegate wants to meet with you personally to discuss the situation in detail, and asks you to appoint the time."

Minister Ch'iao stamped his foot and turned angrily on Chao. "You have delayed us for fifteen minutes. Do you know how many border soldiers may have been killed in that time?"

Immediately, he picked up the top-security inter-office phone. It had been cut, and the line was dead. He then picked up the intercom and gave the order: "Connect me right away with Paoting and get General Yeh Chien-ying to the phone."

Unexpectedly the female operator at the switchboard said in a soft voice, "Is this Minister Ch'iao? The Workers Militia has ordered that you are not to be connected by phone to anyone."

Minister Ch'iao flew into a rage. He threw the receiver down and, pointing to Chao, he cursed at him through clenched teeth: "It is you sons of bitches who have ruined our country."

Chao now realized the gravity of the situation. He rushed to the phone and shouted, "Operator! I am Chao Yung-fu of the Security Section. Call your Militia supervisor, Chiang Yin-lan, to the phone . . . quickly. Hello? It's me. Something urgent has come up. An international crisis. Remove all restrictions for the moment on the Minister's calls. That's my order. No need for clearance, I take full responsibility. Good. Put him through right away. Of course, I will be here watching him."

Chastened, he hung up the telephone, and looked at Ch'iao staring out the window. This was the first time in many years that he had thought of Minister Ch'iao without hostility. Why? Against capitalist-roaders, should one feel anything but hate . . . hate . . . and more hate?

Chiang Yin-lan, the Militia head who took over the Communications Section of the Foreign Ministry, personally assumed charge of putting the call through. What was Chao Yung-fu doing? Was he betraying the proletarian class in this last decisive battle? Besides, why was General Yeh in Paoting? He should be in Peking under the supervision of Squad Number 17.

She was determined to listen in on the conversation. If there was anything subversive about the talk, she would cut it off immediately; that much she could do.

Through the long-distance switchboard, the line was connected to Paoting. It was explained that Minister Ch'iao of the Foreign Ministry wished to talk with General Yeh. The connections on the other end were quickly made.

Chiang Yin-lan informed Minister Ch'iao, and listened carefully to the two talking on the line.

"Is that Ying Lao?"

"Are you safe and sound? How did the discussion go?"

"Never mind that just now. I have received some news via the Americans that the Soviet Union has begun to invade our country in three locations. The Military Affairs Committee should be meeting at once. Have you had any word?"

"I have known since morning. We could not get through to you on the telephone. We conducted a conference call by phone with the three Military Regions of Shenyang, Peking, and Sinkiang. There is only one thing not clear. Division 4437 of the Inner Mongolian Command was suddenly transferred to North China yesterday. That puts a big gap in our defenses. Who gave the order? Even the local Inner Mongolian Command was not informed. The transfer was so swift that we could not even intercept them.

"This division is now located at the Special Headquarters of the Central Committee.

"In Inner Mongolia, the Soviets have opened fire, at about eight o'clock this morning. But they did not encroach into our territory. On the other two invasion points, there was no outbreak. They seemed to be waiting for further orders. Our armies in the three Military Regions have made their preparations. Would you get in touch with Commander Ch'en of the Peking Military Command? He said he tried to get in touch with you but could not. He sent someone to see you, but the courier was stopped by the Militiamen standing sentry in front of your building. He wanted to send a battalion to liberate you, but I restrained him."

"There is no problem with me personally," Ch'iao said. "It is only that in this critical moment, when the foreign enemy is invading, the government departments are totally paralyzed. Is this revolutionary action, or is it treason?"

Chiang Yin-lan had listened to this point. She shuddered. The situation was serious, and what had she done? Taking off her earphones, she stood up in a daze. Quickly, she rushed out to the switchboard, announcing to all the operators: "Restore all normal functions immediately. Remove all controls!"

Minister Ch'iao put down the telephone, reflected awhile, and instructed Section Head Ku, "You stay here and contact the chief of the American Liaison Office. In half an hour, I will receive him here." Then, turning to Chao Yung-fu, he said, "Comrade Militiaman, my good man, for the sake of the international prestige of our country, do you think you could temporarily release the Militia guard at the gate of the Foreign Ministry and the sentries at the second-floor reception room? What do you think?"

"Yes sir! Minister Ch'iao." Chao Yung-fu gave him an abrupt military salute, and marched out of the door with full martial fervor.

❧ FIFTEEN

Tuesday, February 12   5 p.m.

The fur hat covered Chia's head, showing only his face, numb from the cold. The relentless wind buffeted him, and the edges of his hat flapped around his ears.

The sleigh zipped quickly down the slope, moving faster and faster. Under the slanting sun, the brown hairs on the skin of the sturdy Mongolian horse glistened. His long tail fluttered like so many feathers in the wind, his front hooves kicked up the powdery snow in a misty froth.

◇ ◇ ◇

The present situation blurred, Chia heard in his mind's ear the crisp ringing sound of a bell, a small bronze bell fastened around the neck of the horse with a red-violet velvet halter. Fine crystals of snow drifted down from the pine needles on the evergreens, and fell on Natasha, tightly wrapped up in a long cape that showed only her apple-like cheeks. She was laughing. In the narrow confines of the sleigh, she tumbled around, making it difficult for the inexperienced Chia, who stood at the back of the sleigh to control the horse.

From a kneeling position, she looked back at him. "Genghis Khan, please do not carry me to the deserts of Asia. How can I take a bath in the desert? Do I use cow's milk or sheep's milk? Answer me, oh omnipotent Khan!"

She grabbed the reins, and the running horse suddenly pulled up short and stopped. Natasha jumped out of the sleigh and followed a small path of sleigh tracks. Running ahead, jumping and shouting, waving her cape, and reciting the lines of Eugene Onegin as he dueled with Lenski, she finally plunged into a snowbank by the pine woods.

Chia gently reined the horse in, and let the sleigh follow at a slow pace behind her. She looked up toward the blue sky and declaimed,

"Youth, youth, where hast thou gone?
Why have you gone, never to return?
Why do you go so far away, and leave me behind?"

Suddenly she disappeared, and her voice was heard no more. Where had she gone? The pine trees were soundless, still. Chia Hsiang-tung began to worry. He stopped and tied up the horse's reins, jumped off the sleigh, and ran into the snowy forest.

He found Natasha lying on the snow.

"I am Lenski. I have been shot through the heart by Onegin's bullet," she shouted, her green eyes shining.

The long furry cape was spread out around her. She was comfortably ensconced in this little nest, her passionate lips full, as she awaited her lover's kiss.

❖ ❖ ❖

The flip-flap of his hat beat faster. The sleigh flew over the frozen surface. Big Beard raised his long whip, bent on going faster and faster.

The fierce cold wind against Chia Hsiang-tung's face was too much. He could not help bending down, using the top of his head to buttress himself against the penetrating wind.

His body was cold through and through, frozen stiff. His fingers, covered by a pair of thin leather gloves, could only, by sheer will power, clutch the wooden sleigh handle in the back. He felt as if he were about to topple out of the speeding sleigh. This was a struggle for life.

The end of the snowy steppe was reached, an area of rolling hills of granite.

"Get down," Big Beard ordered, "and push from behind!" He got off the sleigh and pulled the leather halter connected to the bit, dragging the horse up the slanting slope.

When he saw the tense expression on Big Beard's face, Chia became apprehensive. Were they in the area of the border that was patrolled? It was not yet dark! Were they crossing the border now?

The sleigh had become a burdensome thing. Chia pushed with all his might; his numb limbs had recovered their feeling. Beads of sweat rolled down his cheeks, which the cold froze.

Crack! The long whip descended from the air, and echoed just by his ear. It did not hit him, but the intent was there; he had never had to take this kind of abuse.

Big Beard's droopy, downcast eyes suddenly glared out in anger. Tilting his head, he spat out: "Faster!" His whole expression showed murderous intent.

Chia held himself back, and vented his frustrations on the sleigh. With the effort of one horse and two men, the sleigh finally attained the top of the slope. Another expanse of white snow was spread out before them, seemingly to the horizon.

Going down the northern slope was easier. When the incline was no longer too steep, Big Beard got into the sleigh; Chia could only take up his former position. But from previous experience, he placed his feet on a horizontal strut to get more traction, and he could alternately put his hands in the pockets of his cotton-lined jacket to keep them warm.

When he thought of the crack of the whip a moment ago, Chia involuntarily pressed his belly against the wooden strut in front of him. Better be careful: "When a monk opens an umbrella against the elements, neither law (hair) nor justice (sky) can be found anywhere."* The setting sun descended to the horizon. In the distance the spires of trees in a grove appeared; gradually the grove thickened into forest. Chia discovered that Big Beard was casually sitting inside the sleigh, his whip tossed aside; one hand held onto the reins, and the other was fumbling for something under his overcoat.

Chia Hsiang-tung looked down over Big Beard's shoulder. Big Beard saw him, and gave a burst of laughter. He took out a flask and shook it in front of Chia. With his teeth, he pulled out the cork and took a few swigs. He seemed oblivious to Chia standing behind him.

Suddenly he pulled in the reins, and with one quick move, rolled off the sleigh as it came to a stop. He took a carbine from underneath the sleigh. Taking quick aim, he shot once. Chia Hsiang-tung quickly jumped off the runners, but before he could steady himself, Big Beard had jumped back into the sleigh and whipped the horse on. Chia was left behind, standing dumbly alone in the snowy steppe.

The sleigh went on another three hundred meters before it stopped. In the lingering dusk, Chia Hsiang-tung saw Big Beard get off the sleigh and fumble with something in the snow.

When Chia caught up with the sleigh, Big Beard had found some withered branches in the snow, and started a fire.

Lying on the ground beside him was a wild goat, with long and shiny brown hair, its legs shot in two. Its pathetic eyes looked at Chia.

Big Beard finished tending to the fire, and came over to the

---

* An aural pun: the original says that when a monk opens an umbrella, what one has is no law and no justice. The word for "law" is a homonym for the word for "hair" (*fa*), and the word for "justice" is a metonym that means "sky" (*t'ien*): thus, a monk, who must be shaven hairless (lawless), blocks out the sky (justice) with his umbrella—TRANSLATOR.

goat, holding in his mouth a sharp knife almost a foot long. With a kick, he knocked the still struggling goat unconscious. His left hand grabbed a hind leg, his right hand, holding the knife, deftly lopped off a limb. Blood spurted out, staining the white snow.

"If you're hungry, cut off a piece and roast it in the fire." Big Beard skinned the leg, cut it into slices, and using a three-pronged skewer, he put the meat on the fire to cook. Out came the flask again; a bite of meat alternated with a pull on the flask.

Chia Hsiang-tung was starved, but simply could not cut off another leg.

Starved, cold, and exhausted, Chia squatted on the ground, his hands folded, not making a sound, watching Big Beard eat and drink.

"Don't you feel like eating something?" Big Beard licked his lips. "I want to give you your last meal but you don't want it. All right, you can be a 'hungry ghost.'"

"How far are we from the border?" Chia Hsiang-tung asked.

"Border?" Big Beard burst out laughing. "We are twenty miles out of China. Otherwise, do you think I would be sitting here?"

Chia Hsiang-tung stood up in surprise, and looked around with renewed interest. A monotonous snowy landscape stretched out; a crescent moon hung above on the eastern horizon; in the blue-black sky, puffs of clouds drifted by one after another. Where was Natasha? He turned from the smoldering smoke and walking away, found a deep ditch in front of him. The goat must have been standing there when Big Beard shot and brought it down.

"Do you have family?" Big Beard, suddenly considerate, asked between bites.

"No one. Just me." Chia particularly did not want to say much. He answered guardedly as he walked along the ditch.

"Too bad! There will be no one to burn incense for you. Don't worry, a year from now, I'll light a few sticks for you."

"I have no idea what you're talking about." Chia was on guard. As he turned around, Big Beard's raised rifle as he sat beside the fire made everything perfectly clear.

"Brother, don't blame me. I'm just carrying out orders. I was told by the higher-ups to take you across the border and then get rid of you. I have no choice. When you're gone, don't come looking for me, look for your real enemies." He pulled the trigger, and Chia slumped to the ground.

Big Beard took out the flask again, gulped down a few swigs, then shouldering his rifle staggered over to Chia, muttering to himself, "This character must have something on him. It would be a shame to waste it."

Suddenly Chia turned and disappeared into the ditch. Big Beard hastily fired two shots, but he only hit the snow, missing his target.

Believing that Chia was not armed, Big Beard walked complacently to the edge of the ditch, and shouted down, "You bastard. Don't make me . . ."

He had not finished speaking before a burst flashed out of the dark ditch. Big Beard's hands, gripping the rifle, relaxed their hold; he clutched his throat; blood oozed from between his fingers, and he pitched forward into the ditch.

Chia lay in the deep snow at the bottom of the ditch, his trembling hands still grasping his handgun. Did he get him?

The dark form lying five meters away was still. He watched closely.

The numbness in the left side of his belly turned into searing pain; he had been hit by that son of a bitch, Big Beard, on the first round. Almost hysterically he pumped the dark form of Big Beard with two more shots. He loosened his overcoat, and took a look under the hazy light of the moon, shuddering at the sight of blood trickling from his cotton military jacket. Hastily, he tore open the lower edge of the jacket and pulled out the cotton lining. With another strip from the front of his jacket he bound the wound over his shirt.

Shivering with cold, he buttoned up, pressed gingerly with

one hand on the wound, and crawled laboriously over to Big Beard.

Chia fought off the impulse to throw up as he pulled aside the leather overcoat and located his watch, lighter, cigarette case, wallet, and the wine flask. He pulled out the cork of the flask and downed what was left of the wine.

Chia leaned against the wall of the ditch, suffering excruciating pain. "I've got to get a medic," he thought. Recalling his predicament, he let out a demented laugh.

But wait, Natasha must be anxiously waiting for him. She would never betray their love. He must get out of this ditch, find the sleigh, and move north.

Drawing on all his will power and using every ounce of remaining energy, he pushed up with his legs, grabbed with his fingers, and shoved himself up on his elbows.

Once out of the ditch, using all his strength, he staggered to his knees.

The embers of the fire had died out. Where were the horse and the sleigh that should be by the fire? He must find the sleigh and get to a settlement. Chia stood up and slowly started out, one step after another.

The snow whirled around him and the night wind grew fierce as he struggled toward oblivion.

◇ ◇ ◇

Thursday, February 14   1 a.m.

"Let us on board. We want to board the train!" The shouts of thousands of people were like angry waves throbbing against the glass panes. Although the windows of the train were closed, the sound stirred the hearts of every passenger on board.

On the platform of the Ta-t'ung Railway Station, a riot was shaping up; the railway security guards and the Militiamen were forming a human wall in front of the train to block the uncontrollable masses of people who had stormed past the ticket checkpoints. They carried small bags, their clothes were tattered, and their gaunt faces showed their desperation. Shouting angrily, they were trying to break open this last line of defense to get into the super express Number 379, from Pao-t'ou to Peking, already crowded to capacity.

Ta-yung was on board, having gotten on the train at Huhe-hot.

The Huhehot Railway Station had been taken over by the Military Command. Aide-de-camp T'ang, who had escorted Ta-yung under orders from Commissar Hsiao, had taken Ta-yung to a deserted platform as soon as they had left the jeep. The troop commander at Huhehot had received instructions via telephone and had given T'ang orders to buy Ta-yung a "soft bunk" ticket. He had handed Ta-yung the ticket with a sarcastic laugh. "Although I have bought you a ticket, it doesn't mean anything. Getting on the train is the real problem."

T'ang looked again at the ticket and asked a passing railway attendant, "According to this ticket, which compartment should he get into?"

The attendant pointed to a compartment not far away. "That's the one!"

T'ang walked over and stopped in front of a window in the center section of the compartment. Gesturing with his hands, he ordered those crammed in the train to lower the window. The passengers conferred and, finally, decided to open the window.

"I know none of you have any tickets," T'ang said. "It is illegal for you to board the train in such chaos. But this is a concern for the railway station, and I can't be bothered with it. I only ask you to leave some space for one person to get on. If he cannot get on this train, the train will not leave. You think it over."

After much debate, the window was cleared for entry. Ta-yung crawled through the window into the train, and entered the small compartment.

On both sides, the double bunk beds were occupied by four or five people. They looked over the newcomer with hostility. T'ang had crammed himself in, and forced a few young men to leave the compartment, to yield a place on one of the beds for Ta-yung.

"Comrades, I know your present mood. Let's not say any more about it. The comrade who has just boarded the train was wounded in defending the motherland this morning. Now he is in a hurry to get back to Peking. I hope all of you will take good care of him."

Seeing Ta-yung, bandaged on the forehead and on his left hand, the passengers began to move. A young man sitting on an upper bunk, with eager bright eyes, said in a clear voice, "We'll do what we have to do. But we will certainly take care of this comrade and give him an upper bunk. More people will have to go into the bottom bunk." After seeing Ta-yung settled on a top bunk T'ang left, satisfied.

Soon after, the locomotive blew its whistle and the train pulled slowly out of the Huhehot station.

Ta-yung lay on the upper bunk with mixed feelings in his heart. To the shaking of the train and the rhythmic sound of the wheels on the tracks, he fell asleep.

When he woke up, the familiar rocking and the sounds were gone; instead, he heard shouting outside the window. It was already dark.

Inside the compartment was strangely quiet. Under the dim ceiling light, extreme tension could be seen on every face. From the upper bunk Ta-yung could see the chaos outside the train window.

Ta-yung sat up, and in the dim light, he saw the people crowding outside who were now knocking on the window. All about twenty years old, young men and women, their expressions were wretched.

Inside, no one moved or said a word.

A young man sitting on the upper deck across from Ta-yung suddenly jumped down and boldly pulled up the window.

"We can take in five more people through this window," he yelled. "Female comrades, get in first." He held out a hand to one of the girls and hauled her up into the train.

"These are all brothers and sisters; we cannot watch them this way and not try to save them."

Those inside began to make way. Someone shouted, "We can take in another eight! Some of us can stand! Who doesn't want to go home for the New Year?"

"If you shove your luggage in further, we can cram in two more."

The shouting and the yelling outside became louder. The Militiamen had discovered the situation and had come to intervene. Fisticuffs broke out in some places. Ta-yung volunteered: "If I can sit, it'll be all right. We can still pack in a few more."

More and more Militiamen appeared, beating around with their wooden clubs, chasing anyone within reach.

Ta-yung held onto the window sill with one hand; with the other, he grasped the hand of a girl below. The young man who originally opened the window had just pulled a person into the cabin, and he hurried to grab the girl's other hand. Ta-yung and the young man pulled with all their strength, and managed to lift the girl in halfway. A Militiaman reached the window and, pulling on her clothes and her legs, yanked the girl down. She started to weep, and shouted: "Mama! Mama!"

Everyone was transfixed by this most elemental and heart-wrenching utterance. The long-suppressed humanity, the sense of human dignity that had almost been trampled into nothing flared out. The angry shouts were so devastating that the hands restraining the girl loosened. Ta-yung grabbed again for her hand and shoulders, discovering in his grasp how thin and wasted she was. The skin of her palm was leathery from hard work.

With many now trying to help, the girl was soon pulled through the window. Once safely in the train, she turned and shouted out: "Fang-ying! Fang-ying!"

But it was now quiet outside the window. The commotion had moved to the last few compartments of the train.

The girl hugged the other girls who had preceded her into the train, and together they wept.

Although Ta-yung was extremely uncomfortable, he was still better off than those below who could not even budge. He looked at the young people around him, all nice, all ordinary. Why had they been reduced to this? Their clothes were tattered, their bodies thin and undernourished.

Ta-yung was haunted by what he had seen. He was a member of the Militia. Why had he not helped the Militiamen? Why had he given his helping hand to the girl instead?

"Attention!" It was the train's loudspeaker. "Attention! All passengers. We are representatives elected by the passengers in Car Number 6 and we are negotiating with the officials of the Ta-t'ung Railway Station and the Workers Militia of Ta-t'ung City to release the train.

"Because it is so crowded, the departure should not be delayed any longer, for the sake of the health of the passengers.

"We object to any suggestions that our tickets or our passes be inspected, and we adamantly oppose any move to return this train to Pao-t'ou.

"According to the constitution of the People's Republic of China, everybody has the freedom to travel. It was a serious mistake for the station to stop selling tickets, and to forbid people to board the train. The railway station must be held responsible for the chaos that has erupted. We also reserve our right to protest the violent action of the Militia.

"Since we cannot communicate with all the compartments in the train, we are notifying you over the loudspeaker. If the passengers all agree to accept the three of us from Car Number 6 to be your representatives, to support our position, please open your windows facing the station platform and hold out your hands to indicate your approval."

In no time, all the windows were open, even the windows of those cars extending beyond the platform. People waved their hands, and cheered.

After the tumult had died down, the excitement in the train dissipated. The windows were still open, the cold wind blew in, bringing with it the sound of shouting voices in the distance, coming from someplace behind the station. This shouting of hundreds and thousands, coming from the dark recesses, was overwhelming.

▩ SIXTEEN

Wednesday, February 13
8:30 a.m. Peking Standard Time
Lunar Calendar: 12th month, 29th day

Snow had fallen during the night, barely covering the ground in the Square. The morning winds blew flurries to the southern corner of the courtyard in the area of the wreaths.

In the overcast sky, low-flying cloud formations slid quickly by. It felt as if snow were about to fall again, and it was extremely cold. The Militiamen who had come to stand guard at T'ien-an Men Square before daybreak were all freezing. They pulled their chins down into their collars, their clubs were tucked under their arms, and with hands folded, they stood watch with backs to the wind, looking at the passers-by, whose numbers grew steadily.

The five-star red flag flying at half-mast was flapping in the wind. Its fresh red color looked lusterless against the clouded sky. The Militiamen, lined up row upon row in tight formations, were protecting the totally empty Square. The crowds on the outskirts stared and commented as though the Militia were goods on display in the big department store open only to the tourists and not to the people.

The Militia platoon leader Tiao Yung-hung ("Sly Forever Red") rapped on the stone pavement incessantly with the edge of his club, as he watched closely the people passing by a few paces in front of him. Now and then their eyes met the gaze of the Militiamen, but they wore mocking and disdainful expressions, totally different from their previous attitude.

Tiao Yung-hung was angry. The night before, when orders had been given at the garage in the factory that all Militiamen were to assemble at four in the morning, the foreman in the garage had questioned him.

"The Party Committee and the Revolutionary Committee of our factory have challenged us to turn our grief into a source of strength, and to increase production in order to commemorate the Chairman. Do you know about this?"

"Of course I know." Tiao Yung-hung detested his interrogator. The last time the factory workers had elected their representatives, this man had received three times as many votes as he had.

"There are one hundred and forty-seven workers in the entire garage, each one with his own work assignment. Once the twenty-three of you who serve the Militia leave, other workers have to double their workload in order to meet production goals. One day is all right, but this is the third day in a row. The other workers have grumbled and complained to the members of the Party and the Revolutionary Committee. No one knows what the hell you are doing. I am bound to tell you that we will put up with your undisciplined and unauthorized activities for today; but if you do not show up for work tomorrow, you will be considered negligent in your work."

"We only follow the orders of the Militia Command Headquarters."

"I don't give a damn about Command *Head*quarters or Command *Hind*quarters. If you are a worker in this factory, you must follow our collective leadership."

Other workers had gathered around, and they chimed in:

"He says he's a Workers Militiaman. Actually, if you ask me, he doesn't look like a worker at all."

"If I had known about it, I would have sent in an application. It looks so terrific to hold a stick standing in the street! With no sweat at all, I can still get paid."

"Yesterday, after work, I met this apprentice worker who had just come from the villages, called 'Wing Flaps.' He told me that when they stand guard, they make time with the women in the Militia."

"The father of that Wing Flaps is one of those upstart cadres. If Wing Flaps wants to find a woman, he will find her. After all, he's got the blood of a revolutionary in him."

Tiao Yung-hung had listened and had become more and more upset. The other Militiamen in the factory were standing a good distance away, pretending to be busy at their work. Without the support of a gallery, Tiao had quickly lost his taste for the argument, so he had turned and quickly left the garage.

This morning, half an hour past the time when they had been supposed to assemble, only seventeen had turned up in his platoon; five others had been absent. *They are disobeying orders. I must discipline them in the "struggle meetings."*

Tiao Yung-hung looked at his watch. It was only eight-thirty, still an hour and a half to go before the time for a change of shifts. He wished for time to pass by quickly so that he could go to the Militia Lounge in the Cultural Center and get a hot cup of water and a few big bleached-flour *man-t'ou* to make sandwiches of roast pork, since he did not have to pay for these with his ration coupons.

The Militiaman standing beside him now spoke in a quiet voice.

"Sir!"

"Hmmm. What's the matter?"

"It seems to me that these pedestrians are up to something! Some of these people have been back and forth three times."

Tiao Yung-hung looked up and saw that it was Wing Flaps. Since his family name was Wing and he had two enormous ears that hung down, everyone called him Wing Flaps.

Tiao also felt that the passers-by in front of T'ien-an Men this morning looked a little ominous, very different from yesterday. Then the masses had walked on the pavement on the north side and had paid their respects by bowing to the huge portrait framed in black muslin hanging on the T'ien-an Men Tower. Today the masses walked on the pavement on the south side. Were they going to try to provoke an incident?

Now he raised his chin, which had been tucked down into his collar. He made a closer inspection. There were now droves of people walking back and forth around the Square.

He himself had not experienced the actual combat during the years of "trial by fire" (1966–70), and he was not there at the T'ien-an Men Incident (April 5, 1976), but in his routine training, he had heard the instructor talk about his experiences. These "May 16th" types were vicious and ruthless beyond belief. In 1969, a large cavern was discovered about fifteen miles from Peking, in which more than sixty people were found who had been buried alive, men and women, some with no ears, others with their eyes plucked out or their limbs lopped off. Such had been the atrocities of the extreme leftists.

Now these leftists are flaunting themselves in front of us. Why are there so many of them? I should double my guard. I had better report to the company commander.

Tiao Yung-hung looked around in search of the company commander and found him at the western corner. Something was happening. The pedestrians had gathered around the corner in a hurry; there was a disturbance, with people yelling and screaming.

"Why are you closing off the People's Square?"

"We have a right to walk on the Square!"

"You are an illegal organization. Which article of the constitution gives you the right?"

First people gathered in groups, then in a split second, dozens more surrounded them. The defense line on the east side was breached! People were suddenly running into the Square; and then, in no time, other breaches were made in the line of defense. The wooden club which Tiao Yung-hung had been gripping tightly was suddenly grabbed and, in one turn, twisted from his hand. Before he could see the face of his assailant, his stomach felt a vicious jab, the end of his club in his belly. In extreme pain, he bent over in a spasm of pain, hearing at the same time the cry of Wing Flaps beside him, "Spare me! Spare me!"

The line of defense was like a dike made of paper. The people broke through in waves, and there was no trace of it left. People now walked freely into the Square; others followed behind, carrying slogans, flags, and loudspeakers. Quickly, they congregated in front of the Memorial Plaque for the People's Heroes, where they held a meeting, spontaneously organized.

More and more people gathered. The Square was so crammed that no one felt the cold any more. Along the east and west sections of Ch'ang-an Avenue, crowds swarmed in the direction of the Square. Full of pent-up anger, they glared at the Militiamen cowering by the walls. Some stopped and hurled accusations. Some of the Militiamen took off their now conspicuous armbands and merged into the press of the throng.

A few long wooden poles were placed against the Memorial, then a big piece of red cloth was draped down from the middle of the Plaque. On the cloth, written in huge characters, was: "Long Live the People." Underneath was strung another horizontal piece of cloth, on which someone had inscribed: "The Mobilization Meeting of the People of the Capital." The banners whipped in the wind triumphantly.

The "International" was blaring from one of the loud-speakers and the people were singing in chorus, the sound resonating over the Square, across both segments of Ch'ang-an Avenue. From the east part of the city and the west, from the Outer City to the Forbidden City, residents emerged from the small alleys to the streets, now emptied of cars. There had been no sign of the Public Security men for several days. The Militia sentries huddled fearfully together. Word was passed among the people and crowds converged into a huge torrent, rushing toward the center of Peking, to T'ien-an Men Square.

◇ ◇ ◇

The train had been detained on the track for freight trains at the Feng-t'ai Railway Station for two hours. The freight section of the train yard was tightly sealed off by soldiers. No one was permitted to leave the train compartments.

Three trains had pulled in, and then another two, each one crammed with people. In some cars, the doors could not be closed. Many were hanging from the doors; others perched on the couplers between cars, and in this precarious position, they had come this far.

The passengers began to disregard the order prohibiting disembarkation from the trains. From the conversations going from window to window, everyone knew that the trains from Harbin, Wuhan, and Shanghai toward Peking had all been detained here at Feng-t'ai.

Unrest exploded first from the train coming from the Canton-Wuhan route. They had been waiting for five hours, and scattered groups began to jump out from the windows and doors to find rest rooms or to get a drink of water. But the majority of people had disembarked as a protest against the People's Liberation Army which now blocked their way.

Passengers from the other trains followed their example. Gradually all the packed trains emptied. After stretching their cramped bodies, the passengers had gathered together to figure out why the trains were not being allowed to proceed.

Hsiao Ta-yung did not get off the train. He did not want to join any bands of troublemakers, and chose to lie comfortably on an upper bunk for a rest.

He felt something hard in his overcoat, on which he was resting his head. It was the corn biscuit Young Swallow had given him yesterday morning. Now he discovered it was even harder than before. He put the hard biscuit in his mouth and chewed on it slowly.

What is Young Swallow doing now? So many things have happened, are happening around me. Now is not the time to talk about or dwell on love.

"Will Fang-ying be able to take the next train home?" Murmuring voices came from the lower bunk. Perhaps the girls who got on the train at Ta-t'ung were below.

"You always look after her. Why don't you start looking after yourself?" a gravel-voiced girl scolded gently.

"What if we cannot get residence permits in Peking?" another asked.

"The Commune has written letters. How can they refuse to register us?" The gravel-voiced girl spoke louder.

"The Commune letters aren't worth a fart. They just wanted to get us out of there, so that there wouldn't be so many mouths to feed in the winter. When things pick up in the summer, they will get us back there to work."

"Work . . . we've worked five years. When we left, we still ended up owing them our asses. What's the difference between the accountant at the Commune and the landlord renting out a house?"

"Sh-h-h. Don't talk so loud. There's still someone lying on top there. Lay off the subversive talk."

"Hell, I'm not scared. I'd say this to the Chairman himself."

"The Chairman is dead. What's the use of saying that?"

"So, those three 'C.C.'s' of water are going to run wild now, eh?"*

---

* A play on Chiang Ch'ing's (Mao's widow) name: in the original, the phrase is "three drops of water," referring to the three dots representing the water radical in the word *chiang*, which means "river"—TRANSLATOR.

"Don't worry, she won't last long either. The capitalist-roaders have the real power. Besides, they are protected by the men with the guns."

"It's the common people like us who are always the ones who must suffer. It's the same whoever holds power."

Ta-yung turned around in pain, and alarmed the people talking below. The conversation stopped at once.

The pain was not only in his body, but in his mind. His life experience had been too soft. From school to factory to university, he had never really come into contact with ordinary people. What he read was the standard line in the newspapers and journals, realities in the abstract, empty theories with no correspondence to actual life. But in reality, could he talk to such people while observing the high ideological standards of such as Commissar Hsieh? No, of course he could not. Only four days ago, if someone had told him about the kind of experience he had recently had, what would he have done? He would have patiently tried to explain it in the following manner: "This was an isolated phenomenon. The country is so huge and so vast. There are so many people. There are bound to be aberrations in so large a sample. There is always the objective contradiction inherent in things. Because these contradictions exist, we need to struggle on, and to struggle resolutely against the capitalist-roaders . . ."

And, afterward, he would have immediately written a report, to inform his superiors of the inquirer's political instability. This report would have been part of that person's permanent file and would have followed him to the end of his days.

Ta-yung shuddered. When he had written reports on other people for their dossiers, he had never thought twice. When points of view diverge, the judge can never imagine the feelings and the circumstances of the defendant; he only considers the letter of the law.

From the deserted corridor of the compartment, there came sounds of hurried steps. Several people had run up to the door, shouting, "He's here! He's here!"

Ta-yung sat up in surprise. The people, both inside and outside the compartment, stared at him.

"It's this way," a bright-eyed youth said, half out of breath. "Passengers from six trains are all now convened at a mass meeting. They want to elect representatives to negotiate with the Feng-t'ai Railway Station. Because there are relatively few passengers with tickets, we have nominated you."

"I don't want to be a representative."

All were silent. They dropped their heads.

"Don't you want to go back to Peking?"

"Of course I do, but we must follow the government's orders."

"This is not a question of government orders but a question of the interest of the people. With six trainloads, there are at least more than ten thousand passengers. Tomorrow is New Year's Eve. Who doesn't want to hurry back to spend the New Year with his family? Everybody is still being reasonable and we are electing representatives to negotiate; this is the civilized approach to confrontation. If there are no representatives, and armed confrontations break out, you can imagine the consequences!" His look pierced Ta-yung.

"All right, I'll go." Ta-yung immediately jumped down, with the people in the compartment cheering and applauding.

The junction platform was jammed full with thousands of train passengers. Ta-yung and nine other representatives made their way through the crowds to enter the office of the railway station together. The other passengers were blocked off by a cordon of soldiers and kept at a distance.

They were received by a member of the PLA, a fat, middle-aged military man.

He warmly welcomed the representatives into the meeting room and took them to the window to show the situation in the streets. Pointing outside he said, "Since early this morning, we have been busy trying to provide you with something to eat. Look! Hot water and *lao-ping* griddlecakes are being brought over. We are just about to distribute them to each train. You decide among yourselves how best we might distribute this food."

"The PLA is concerned with us," a middle-aged representative with glasses responded, "and we are very grateful for that, but as representatives, we would like to know when the trains will be allowed to leave. We hope that it will not be too long."

"We also hope that the trains will leave soon," the PLA representative said. "But the Railway Department has ordered that all passenger transport be stopped at Feng-t'ai, and the trains returned to their points of origin. Look, here is the order." He opened the telegram on the table for the representatives to see.

"What's the reason?"

"This you will have to ask the Peking Militia Command Headquarters. They have taken over all the government departments in the city."

Ta-yung was stunned. He had never expected this dramatic turn of events. He felt his palms start to sweat.

"This means that the order comes from the Militia."

"No, it comes from the Railway Department."

"But the Railway Department is under the control of the Militia."

"You might say that."

"What is the stand of the PLA?"

"We follow the orders of the Regional Military Command."

"What is the stand of the Regional Military Command?"

"There has been no response from the Regional Military Command up to now."

"When do you expect an answer?"

"I can't say. I'm also waiting. That's why I would like you to be a little patient." The fat man sat down, calmly lit up a cigarette, and courteously offered his pack of Big Front Gate cigarettes.

The representatives began to whisper among themselves. After some consultation, the man with the glasses spoke for them.

"We agree to wait up to a specified time. Now it's 9:45 A.M. We will come back in two hours. We hope you will have resolved this matter by that time."

"That's fine. During this time, we hope you will help our soldiers distribute the food properly. It's been prepared in a hurry, and there's not too much of it. It must be distributed fairly, and you must take the responsibility for seeing to it that there are no wrangles."

Before the representatives left, the military man spoke again.

"If there is anyone sick, they should be brought to this office. We have prepared a health unit; otherwise, no one is allowed to leave the area. Please make this clear to everybody."

The food distribution proceeded smoothly, and a score of sick people were moved to the station. Standing or squatting beside the trains, the others anxiously awaited further developments. More than an hour passed.

The loudspeaker on the roof of the station blared out, and the crowds listened nervously.

"Attention! Representatives of each train, please come to the conference room for a meeting." The same announcement was repeated three times. But by the third announcement, the representatives had all entered the door to the conference room.

Inside, four military officers in crisp uniforms and two railway station cadres were seated. Their solemn gaze was directed toward the representatives.

"Have you reached a decision?" The bespectacled representative asked first, breaking the awkward pause.

"According to the decision of the Railway Department, your trains are to turn back."

"We have wasted so long waiting, and now you tell us this. Are you kidding?" one of the representatives burst out in anger.

"What's your suggestion, then?" a slender military type asked.

"We demand that we be allowed to take the trains to Peking," answered the man with the glasses.

"What if the Peking Railway Station will not let you in?"

"I am a railway technician. I know how to switch the tracks."

"What if there are Militiamen blocking your way?"

"But there are ten thousand of us or more."

"Well, we can't be responsible for that," the military man said indifferently.

"We will assume full responsibility. You will not be involved."

The military man gave the bespectacled representative a cold look. Then, tilting his head to the railway cadres beside him, he asked, "Do you have enough people to take care of six trains back in the roundhouse?"

"There's enough for ten trains, if you want. There are many mechanics and engineers who originally came from the Machine Section of the Peking Railway Station; they've been clamoring to go back."

"Wait a minute. This afternoon, there will be trains still to come in later on." He turned around and said to the passenger representatives, "Whoever wants to go anywhere else will have to change trains at Peking. No one is allowed to get off here. You go back and let everyone know. Get on the train quickly, and all the trains will leave at once."

The representatives left the room one by one. The slender military man detained the representative with the glasses.

"Where do you work?"

"Are you talking about twelve years ago, or three days ago?"

"Both."

"Twelve years ago, I was with the Teaching and Research Section specializing in bridge-building at the T'ang-shan Railway Institute. Three days ago, I was with the Rehabilitation Mining Camp in Ch'ing-hai. Will that do?"

"You are a 'May 16th' type!"

"Yes, you might say that. But in reality, I am not too sure about anything."

"You had better take care of the trains, or they will take care of you and send you back to Ch'ing-hai."

"Don't worry, comrade soldier of the People's Liberation Army, little tin soldier of the people."

Hsiao Ta-yung observed all this closely. Leaving the station office, he boarded the train, but this time, he could not even cram himself in a compartment, and could only squeeze inside the door.

This is a plot, he thought. They intend that this disorderly, desperate mass of people, with no experience in armed confrontation, is to be sent to the Militia-controlled capital. It is a plan to cause a monstrous disaster. How can it be stopped?

Ta-yung shuddered with the tension that comes from anger. He did not want to see these sallow-faced, emaciated youths die. What could he do?

There was an abrupt jolt as the train moved, and the passengers cheered. The train slowly passed by the platform and Ta-yung saw a few military men standing there, watching the train pull by, seeing it head for the heart of the people, toward that great heroic city, the capital, Peking.

◈ ◈ ◈

Same Day   11:30 a.m.

The train arrived without incident at the Peking Railway Station. It pulled up beside another train which had just arrived several minutes before. The passengers squirmed happily out of the windows and doors. Ta-yung was swept up by the crowd. He passed through the long underground passageway, and leaving the station, came upon the square in front of the station.

The Militia troops, who had been summoned on short notice, had quickly organized a blockade at the exit leading to the street, preventing those who had left the train from passing through to the avenue beyond the Chien-kuo Gate. The milling crowds began to yell angrily, to push and shove, and their mood became ugly.

Ta-yung, standing underneath the clock tower of the station, saw what he had most dreaded.

A loud explosion burst in front of the crowd and waves of people immediately receded. The sounds of crying and moaning could be heard everywhere. Those who fell were being trampled. There was general chaos; some ran into the station building; others hid behind the buses parked on both sides of the street; still others took their chances and charged ahead.

The center of the street looked empty, but on the ground were many bodies, some were Militiamen, some were the young arrivals. A person who had lost an arm tried to stand up screaming with pain, fell, stood up again, and fell for the last time.

There was a sudden moment of quiet, a moment of shock at the sudden carnage.

Then, one truck after another, loaded with armed Militiamen, pulled up. The Militiamen no longer held wooden clubs; they were armed with "Hsiang-t'an"-model light machine guns. Ta-yung had used this type of light machine gun in training. If the lever was turned at the back of the gun, it could fire a round of thirty-six bullets in ten seconds, with an effective range of five hundred meters, and it could penetrate a wooden board three inches thick.

Ta-yung was determined to stop this slaughter. With long strides, he walked across the street, trying hard not to be distracted by the sight of the dead and the wounded. From his jacket pocket he pulled out his Militia armband, waved it, and in a few bounds crossed over. He walked directly toward the rows of light machine guns pointed at him.

"Who are you?" the Militia called out.

"I am a member of the Militia from the Command Headquarters. What company do you come from?"

"Stand still. We don't have anything like you in the Militia!"

"Get your company commander!" Ta-yung had no choice. His forehead and his hands were wrapped in bandages; his tattered clothes were filthy from the trip on the train. He bore no resemblance to the Militiamen in parade dress, wearing tight-fitting blue cotton uniforms, black boots, their cartridge belts neatly strapped around their waists.

"Oh, it's Battalion Commander Hsiao." The company commander who came over had recognized him.

"And you are Commander Yao. Send half of the Militia immediately to help the wounded. Have you called for ambulances?"

"I just arrived this minute. But look at what these reactionary anti-revolutionaries have done. Our superiors gave out strict orders that they not be allowed to enter Peking."

"Give the order to help the wounded!"

While the Militiamen tended to the wounded, Ta-yung asked, "If they are not allowed to come into Peking, where are they supposed to go?"

"They are to get on the same train they came in and go back to where they came from."

"I do not think they would agree to that."

"Our Command has said when necessary, use armed force to suppress them. Revolution always involves sacrifice."

Four days ago Hsiao Ta-yung also would have followed that line, but hearing it now, he felt nothing but revulsion.

"These people are organized," Company Commander Yao said in a sorrowful voice, "and they mean to carry out the scheme of disrupting life in the capital. Look how many of our comrades have already been sacrificed!" Company Commander Yao surveyed the wounded Militiamen now being carried off in stretchers.

"Is that why you want to slaughter even more people, to avenge them? Is that right?" Ta-yung looked at the crowds of people at the train station; more and more were crowding in. All six trains had obviously arrived.

"How many Militiamen do you have here?"

"We rushed two companies here, totaling three hundred. But there are already so many casualties!"

"Listen to me. I came on that train with all these people. There were more than ten thousand detained at Feng-t'ai who are now all about to be let loose here. Can three hundred of you take on ten thousand people?"

"For the Chairman, for the Revolution, there is nothing we cannot take on."

"We are not talking politics now; we are talking facts. With their bare hands, they will crush you down in no time. With guns, how many people can you kill?"

"'Revolution is not needlepoint.'" Company Commander Yao was accustomed to quoting from Chairman Mao.

"I am going directly to the Command Headquarters. You stay here and take charge of the Militia. Close off only the side that leads to Ch'ang-an Avenue and Nan-hsiao Street."

"But that means they will be let loose toward the east."

"That is the strategy. Carry out my orders!"

"This does not look like strategy to me," a cold voice from the side spoke up, "it looks like yielding to the enemy." Ta-yung looked up to see the commander of the Second Militia Division, Commissar Luan, sent over from Division 8341. Although he had changed his jacket for a tight-fitting blue cotton Militia uniform, he still wore his PLA pants. One look, and everyone knew he must be a high-ranking cadre.

"Company Commander Yao, clear out the area, set up blockades, bring out the mobile loudspeaker unit, and prepare a special attack squad."

He turned and looked Ta-yung up and down.

"Have you been duped by these counterrevolutionaries? Do you call this holding firm to your beliefs?"

"I have seen with my own eyes the unfolding of this plot. There are those who want to generate a clash between those people and us, and to manufacture a conflict between us and the people. I want to stop this scheme. We have fallen into the trap of the capitalist-roaders."

"I do not have the faintest idea of what you are talking about. You had better return to the command post." The division commander turned to the guard and ordered, "Escort Commander Hsiao back. I will assume charge here. You transmit my orders. Bring up five more companies. And be quick about it!"

Commissar Luan's sedan was parked beside the road, some five hundred meters away. Ta-yung followed the orderly to the parked car, where it was relatively out of harm's way. Many adventurous pedestrians and residents were crowding the streets for a look—workers, clerks, veterans, and government cadres.

At the side of the car, Ta-yung overheard their conversation.

"If these Militia bastards really have the guts to open fire, then, no doubt about it, the masses will crush them into meatballs."

"Those machine guns are only for show, to scare people; one look at the PLA soldiers, and they will wet their pants."

Hsiao Ta-yung sat in the car and the driver started the engine. Suddenly he heard gunfire, like the sound of a thousand big firecrackers at a village New Year. The people around him stormed forward, toward the rear of the Militia. There were so many of them, so many. The sound of gunfire stopped. The driver stepped on the accelerator, blew the horn, and zipped off through the crowds in the big street. Ta-yung turned around, leaning on the back seat, and looked back. A dozen big trucks were ablaze. A man wearing PLA pants was thrown up by the people into the furious flames of the burning trucks. It was Division Commander Luan.

▨ SEVENTEEN

Wednesday, February 13   11:40 a.m.

The sudden burst of explosions in front of the Peking Railway Station reverberated along the avenue. Some of the windows facing the street of the Peking Hotel, a thousand meters or so away, shattered.

Watanabe, Okamura, and Nakada had managed to walk the distance from their residences in San-li-tun to the Peking Hotel. They were negotiating with the plainclothes security guards in front when they heard the sound of the explosions.

The guards quickly returned their identification papers and ordered them into the hotel, warning them not to venture outside.

The Japanese stood in the parking area in front of the hotel, and watched the chaos and disruption in the street.

Five trucks rushed out from the Tung-hua Men ("East

China Gate"). Blaring horns, they forced their way through the dispersing crowds on East Ch'ang-an Avenue toward the station. The trucks were full of armed Militiamen in blue uniforms with firearms. Shouting at the people to step aside, some held their guns cocked, muzzles pointing to either side. With an arrogant air, the Militiamen looked down at the people, but the people were no longer obeying law and order, and seemed to be moving at their own whim.

No sooner had these five trucks passed by than another five rushed down the street in the same way. In front was a "Shanghai"-model sedan. The pedestrians standing on both sides began to boo the troops in the trucks; others took up the cry by the hundreds and thousands. Clods of earth and rocks were hurled from the crowd. Now and then, the missiles found their mark. The Militiamen ducked, trying to dodge the flying rocks, and the trucks sped up to get away.

The law and order that the Urban Workers Militia was supposed to maintain in the capital appeared a shambles to the Japanese reporters. Two days ago, the diplomats' apartment building had been taken over by the Militia. Old-time staff members in the apartment office formerly in charge of vehicles, housekeeping, and domestic duties had disappeared. On the door, a notice had been posted: "The Militia Command of the Foreign Ministry. The San-li-tun Office." Inside, a few solemn-looking young people sat in the hall, refusing to answer questions. Without vehicles, the reporters had no way of getting to the Foreign Ministry.

Luckily, the stores in the complex had remained open for business and there was no problem about food. Telephone service had been cut off at nine o'clock the evening before. The only medium of communication was the Embassy car. It took the worried Japanese residents to the Embassy compound. Many families had been living together as in the time of the big earthquake.

That morning, Watanabe had been arranging his notes for

the past two days when Nakada had suddenly burst in and shouted: "The Militiamen are all over in their trucks, and there are large crowds on the streets. Something big is happening. Okamura and I have decided to go out to have a look. Do you want to come along?"

"Do you have a car?"

"Idiot! How can you ask such a question at a time like this? Would you like the Chinese Press Bureau to arrange your daily itinerary for you?"

"Where are we going?"

"As far as our legs will carry us. We will see you in three minutes downstairs."

Okamura and Nakada waited for ten minutes before Watanabe appeared. Actually he had written a letter. Should anything happen, Watanabe had thought as he wrote the letter, this will be my last will and testament.

◊ ◊ ◊

When they entered the lounge at the Peking Hotel, no one was there. Finally an attendant wearing an armband appeared. After he grilled them intensively, he asked them to get on the elevator and go with him to the third floor.

In a small lounge on the third floor, they found the Japanese economic delegation, which had arrived in China a few days ago: they were welcomed enthusiastically. Nervously, the delegation wanted news of what was happening outside.

"There are no newspapers, no television, and we cannot understand what they say in the broadcasts. We are stuck here; we are allowed to move only on the third floor or above. Quick, tell us what has happened in the past two days." It was the woman reporter, Nagashima, firing her remarks in machine-gun succession.

"It is very simple," Nakada said with a smile. "You have here a T'ien-an Men Incident, but on a still larger scale. Maybe this will be called the Peking Incident in the days to come."

"Is it a coup?" another member asked. "How come the

previously scheduled meetings have all been postponed? Why don't they even inform us how long the delay might take?"

"China has no coup d'états; they only have 'class struggles,'" Okamura answered, pouring himself a small glass of Johnnie Walker Black Label. He did not care who had brought the bottle; after walking for two hours, he needed the drink.

"Please tell us the situation for the past two days," pleaded Deputy Delegate Obayashi.

"Last night I got through to Tokyo on the phone." Okamura took out his notebook. As he flipped through it, he watched the expressions of those in the room. "It seems that Tokyo has a better over-all understanding than we do about what is happening here. If you are interested, I will sketch the picture for you." With a smug expression, he saw that everyone had settled down to hear what he had to say.

"One, yesterday morning, military clashes between China and Soviet Mongolia broke out at the border. The Soviet Union has marshaled large forces along the Manchurian, Inner Mongolian, Sinkiang borders.

"Two, the Soviet Far Eastern Fleet has set out in full force. As of yesterday afternoon, sixteen warships had passed through Tsushima Strait and were headed for the South China Sea. This fleet included 'Kresta II'-class model cruisers newly built, carrying guided missiles. According to the estimates of the Japanese Defense Department, this fleet was heading toward the Eastern Sea area of China to pose a threat to the important Chinese coastal cities in the south.

"Three, our special correspondent in Washington has reported that the White House held an emergency meeting, and on the hot line asked the Soviet Union to refrain from initiating hostilities.

"Four, the Chinese delegate to the United Nations, Huang Chen, has already launched a protest in the Security Council. He has introduced an emergency resolution to censure the Soviet Union for its military aggression. The session is to be held tonight.

"Five, all broadcasts in every region of China, with the exception of Shenyang, Tientsin, Shanghai, and Harbin, have stopped. This indicates that violent political conflicts have erupted in many areas.

"Six, even now, the Chinese authorities have not issued any formal announcement or explanation, so we do not have the slightest idea as to exactly what has happened.

"Well, that is what I got from Tokyo yesterday. Here in Peking, although we are in the center of developments, we do not have any notion of what is going on. We are in the same boat as you are."

"Is there any way of reaching a high-ranking government official?" Obayashi asked.

"Probably not. The Militia has taken over everything for the time being. We can only wait further developments."

"We cannot just sit here and wait for a Sino-Soviet war to break out; we should leave China right away."

As Obayashi finished speaking, a succession of gunshots was heard, followed by the sound of ear-piercing cries. They rushed to the windows, where they could see that at the eastern end of Ch'ang-an Avenue flames were raging, black smoke curled up to the sky, and hordes of people were filling the wide spaces of the avenue, running, not in flight, but in a headlong charge toward the raging flames, a charge into battle.

❖ ❖ ❖

Hsiao Ta-yung held tightly onto the back of the front seat. The driver dodged left and right as he sped on, blowing his horn constantly. There was no traffic in the streets, only pedestrians. Several times the car almost hit someone.

The guard sitting beside the driver was crying, mourning the death of Division Commander Luan. He was holding a revolver firmly in his hands, the safety latch off.

Ta-yung felt a pang in his heart. Two companies in the Second Division were finished; three hundred lost instantly.

The Second Division consisted of "basic cadre" Militia, well armed and trained, but they had not expected to be attacked from the rear.

The Peking Militia claimed to number one million or more. But Ta-yung knew what the real figure was. Youth and peasants from the outskirts of the city constituted half of the total number, about 400,000, but their equipment and their training were inadequate; they were also backward in their ideological convictions. It had been difficult enough to find enough special cadres to volunteer their services to train them; and those who were sent out did not get along with the local cadres in the communes, nor did they have the support of their Party commissars. Thus, if it came to a really critical point in the class struggle, it was a big question as to which side could exploit the rural Militia. Would it be like 1967, when armed rural Militiamen together with returnees from the PLA crowded the cities to protect the clique in power and massacred tens of thousands of the rebellious Red Guards?

Of the other 400,000 in the Militia, there were only 50,000 who were enlightened ideologically, and who had been organized into Divisions One to Five, equipped with custom-designed weapons. Of the remaining 350,000, some were names in the lists only; others might turn their guns against the Revolution should the situation arise. The members were all around thirty years old, with combat experience during the Cultural Revolution. On the surface, they took the line of supporting the Revolution, but it was not truly known what they really believed. This type could only be handled as normal Militia; they were given wooden clubs and they served on guard duty, but they still required supervision. It would be entirely too risky to arm them.

Ta-yung belonged to the Fifth Division, First Battalion. The Fifth was a special division consisting of students from the higher educational institutions who were unshakable in their ideological convictions. Because their level of education was high, they were allowed to use more sophisticated heavy weapons and were equipped with totally automatic anti-aircraft artillery, anti-aircraft machine guns, rockets with built-in range finders, armored vehicles, and four heavy tanks.

Although there were only four tanks, over the past two years enough combat-ready personnel had been trained to man over three hundred tanks. When the situation arose, Madame Chairman planned to order a PLA tank division to Peking, and then to replace the PLA men with special troops from the Militia.

After Ta-yung had become a combat adjutant of the Central Militia Command Headquarters, he came to understand the instruction from the Chairman: "In times of peace, maintain order; in times of war, safeguard and defend the cities." In this mission, the most important task for the Urban Workers Militia was, "Prevent the restoration of the old order at home; resist the incursions of foreign aggressors from abroad." Moreover, at several meetings at the highest level of the Militia, he had gradually come to the conclusion that the Militia not only co-operated with the Public Security agents to root out the bad elements in the cities during times of peace; but also, in times of crises, they resolutely suppressed the insurgencies of the anti-revolutionary elements. The capitalist-roaders could be found in the leadership of the PLA, and this factor could not be overlooked.

Ta-yung realized that command over the Peking Workers Militia did not rest with the Peking Workers' Association. Although the head of the Workers' Association had nominal control of the Peking Workers Militia, power actually resided in the hands of Commissar Hsieh Ching-yi, Secretary of the Peking Revolutionary Committee. She was the most loyal follower of Madame Chairman and the chief executor of her policies. Only around thirty years old, she was cool, an incisive thinker of great analytical power, yet poised in her bearing. No matter how impetuous a person might be, he felt more relaxed in her commanding presence, content to comply with her point of view and to carry out her orders to the letter.

After the summary analysis of the T'ien-an Men Incident, Hsiao Ta-yung asked Commissar Hsieh the questions raised by some of the Militia members.

"We have in our hands very potent weapons. We do not hesitate to use them to eliminate the enemies who might invade our motherland, but when enemies of the proletariat incite the ignorant masses and become our adversaries, what do we do then?"

Commissar Hsieh lowered her long-lashed eyes and considered the question. Then, with a charming smile, she said, "This situation should not arise, should it?"

Then her expression became somber. Slowly, persuasively, word by word what she said penetrated his heart:

"After so many years of political education, the people of the entire country have some degree of political consciousness. In the great movements, their political positions would manifest themselves clearly. But at the most critical juncture, those who stand opposed to us could be disastrous for the Revolution. Because we protect the interest of the preponderant majority of the revolutionary masses, we must ruthlessly and resolutely suppress opposition. At such a time it is a matter of life and death. There is a saying: 'To be kind to your enemy is the same as being irresponsible to the people!' "

People! What was meant by "people"? It was too abstract. The youths in the train, were they not "people"? Those who, a moment ago, rushed from both sides of the car into the back of the Militia positions, were they not "people"? Ta-yung was no longer sure of the instruction he had received.

The sedan zipped by Tien-an Men. Here Militia sentry guards were posted, and the streets were deserted. Turning sharply to the left, the sedan passed by the small, narrow back entrance to Pei-hai Park, and through the wide gate in the old brick wall.

Along the road from the Ching-ch'ing Chai ("Mirror-clear Study") to the Wu-lung T'ing ("Pavilion of the Five Dragons"), the sedan passed a number of trucks belonging to the Militia's Second Division which were jammed full.

The car screeched to a stop at the dock at the edge of the lake. Ta-yung got out and quickly walked through the crowds of Militia, stepping finally into a familiar three-story office building, painted dark gray, at the northern end.

◇ ◇ ◇

This hastily built building stood between the newly repaired golden, resplendent Tower of Ten Thousand Buddhas and the ancient, elegant Yü-lan Hsüan ("Pavilion of the Orchid Baths"); it faced the graceful Wu-lung T'ing. In the middle of these charming relics of the past, this gray and characterless edifice, totally out of harmony with its surroundings, had a grotesque effect.

The pure waters of the Northern Lake (Pei-hai) originated in the Jade Spring Mountain and passed through the long Grand Canal and flowed through Shih-ch'a Lake. Then it fed into the Central Lake (Chung-hai) and the Southern Lake (Nan-hai), all the way to the T'ung-tzu River.

As early as the ninth century, this area had been used by the rulers of China as their vacation retreat. Later it was repaired several times in different dynasties, down to the middle of the Ming, when the three lakes, Central, Southern, and Northern, were included within the Forbidden City. Only emperors, imperial relations, eunuchs, and palace ladies could enjoy its beauties.

During the Ming and the Ch'ing dynasties, through the blood and sweat of countless people, these three lakes were made even more magnificent, especially the Northern Lake, which is a spot where, truly,

> No prospect is not scenic;
> Delightful fragrances everywhere.

The Northern Lake Park had become the site of the Winter Palace for the Manchu ruling family. (The Summer Palace was the I-ho Garden.)

After the Manchu emperor was dethroned and the Republic was established, a connecting road was built between the Tzu-chin Ch'eng ("City of Purple Gold") and Ching-shan ("Prospect Mountain") to expedite traffic from the east to the west, thus separating the Central Lake from the Northern Lake. The area of the Central and Southern lakes was where the seat of government during the early Republic was located. When the capital was moved away from Peking, the area was open to the public.

In 1949, China decided again to make Peking its capital, and so the Chung-nan ("Central"-"Southern") Lake area has become a special term, symbolizing the center of the Party of the government. The Politburo of the Central Committee of the Chinese Communist Party and the State Council of the People's Republic of China all have their offices in this sector. When the State Council received foreign guests, and held ceremonial state occasions, they used the Chung-hua Men ("China Gate") in the south. Ordinary people used the Hsi-chih Men ("West Gate") when they entered, and the members of the Central Committee and their staff used the Pei-hai Men ("North Gate").

In 1966 the Cultural Revolution broke out. The leadership of the Cultural Revolution, namely the Cultural Revolution Central Control Authority of the Central Committee, in order to facilitate its work, and to avoid the watchful eyes of personnel from the State Council, decided to move out of the Chung-nan-hai area, and took over Pei-hai Park ("The Northern Lake" Park). As a result, this beautiful park became the staging ground for the Red Guards.

After the Wuhan Incident (July 20, 1967),* the Red Guards

* In mid-July 1967 Chairman Mao, in celebrating the anniversary of his swim across the Yangtze River, went to Wuhan, where he was surrounded by the troops of General Ch'en Ts'ai-tao, commander of the Wuhan Military Region. Ch'en and other military commanders were apparently opposed to the Red Guard effort to seize power in local governmental and Party structures. Mao managed to escape, but some of the leading members of the Cultural Revolution leadership—including Hsieh Fu-chih and Wang Li—were arrested by General Ch'en. Lin Piao personally led the joint forces of the navy, army, and

gradually dispersed, and Pei-hai was opened only a few days in the year, during holidays. The area back of the lake was still forbidden to visitors, and was guarded by the soldiers of the Central Garrison Division. Tourists and visitors were not allowed to enter, and no one was permitted to take photographs.

After 1970, the mammoth underground project was begun. Not only were subways underground contemplated, but a huge air-raid shelter was planned for Ch'iung-hua Tao ("Island of Resplendent Flowers"). The air-raid shelter could also be used as a stronghold. This construction project took six years, but the earthquake in the T'ang-shan area occurred, and the original plans had to be suspended. The underground railway had been completed, but it was not ready to accommodate traffic. Because of the damage to the air-raid shelter, the white tower on the top of the mountain began to tilt. Every effort was made to repair it, but until the work was completed, it could not be used. Consequently, the Militia Command Headquarters could not move underground as originally planned, it could only be crammed into the three-story office building on the rear bank of the lake.

On the second floor of the building were two rooms, one a briefing room, the other a conference room, both part of the Combat Section. On the third floor were the offices of the various division commanders and commissars. In addition, there was a well-equipped radio station with a powerful transmitter.

The radio station had been constructed by the Department of Electrical Engineering of Tsing-hua University. Originally designed to broadcast propaganda and to issue orders in combat emergency situations, it had become an alternative me-

---

the air force in besieging the city. After three days of fierce fighting, this potential military coup was suppressed. After this incident, the commanders of the various Military Regions were summoned to Peking for a conference. Under the pressures of the military, Ch'en was given only a light punishment and was restored to his position a few months later. But Wang Li and others of the Cultural Revolution leadership were dismissed. The official journal *Red Flag* stopped publication for half a year. For a "fictional" account of this major upheaval, see the author's forthcoming novel, *Flying Toward the Rainbow*—TRANSLATOR (based on information supplied by the author).

dium of communication. After the Chairman died, the capitalist-roaders inside the Party were so obstructive that there were times when the ideas and opinions of the Central Committee could not be published in the *People's Daily*. So other ways of disseminating Central Committee directives had to be used, such as this radio station.

As a result, the residents of all of Hopei Province could listen to the instructions and reports broadcast from the Cultural Revolution Central Control Authority. Someone remarked that it was like a red star flashing across the night sky, and it became known as "the Red Star Broadcasting Station."

The Public Security Department knew the location of the radio station, but it could only tolerate its existence; it could not take any action against it, because the Northern Lake Park had become Madame Mao's haven for the Revolution, which no one dared to trespass.

◇ ◇ ◇

Ta-yung passed through the corridor on the first floor. In the rooms on both sides Militiamen were relaxing, some eating roast pork and *man-t'ou*† specially prepared for them, others leaning against the wall, taking a nap, their guns wrapped in their arms. With long strides, Ta-yung ran up to the second floor to the briefing room. He pushed open the door and immediately saw Commissar Hsieh beside the telegraph transmitter.

She was reading the teletype—the long strips of dispatches from the various sentry posts to the various communications operators. The operators, in various blocked-off sections of the room, were writing up the messages which were brought to Commissar Hsieh by the messengers standing behind the operators. Speedily and decisively, she would determine a course of action, and the messengers would write down her orders for the operators to send out.

Hsiao Ta-yung saw that she was busy and did not want to disturb her, so he sat down at his usual post. In front of him

† Flour dumpling, the daily bread for northern Chinese—TRANSLATOR.

was a big platform, the size of three ping-pong tables. Under the glass cover, there was a map of the city of Peking, to a 1:5,000 scale. From the model and the markers, he knew that the Militia was gathering for combat. They were presently deployed at key locations.

For the eastern part of the city, about ten thousand Militiamen of the First Division, composed of "basic cadre" Militiamen from a few key factories, had gathered in the Workers' Stadium outside the Ch'ao-yang Men ("Facing-the-Sun Gate"). The armaments stored in the Workers' Gymnasium next to the Workers' Stadium had already been distributed. The trouble was that the number of trucks that were scheduled to come out of the various factories were short by more than one half. This meant that the mobility they had counted on had been sharply reduced. The Militia were equipped with light weaponry, and could be deployed on foot, but time was important.

The men stationed at the Command Headquarters belonged to the Second Division. This division was composed of ideologically enlightened shop clerks, youths working in service occupations, and cadres in the official bureaucracies. The Second Division also had five battalions. Two battalions were now stationed in the Cultural Palace of the Laboring Masses; one was posted at the Great Hall of the People; only two remained in the Command Headquarters, altogether about four thousand Militiamen, all supplied with light weapons and truck transport.

The Third Division was composed of workers from the defense industry factories in the southern outskirts. Because the overwhelming majority were returnees from the army, their fighting capability was perhaps the strongest. Aside from light weapons, they were also equipped with heavy anti-aircraft machine guns, mortars, and bazookas. They were gathering in the Peking Gymnasium next to the Lung-t'an Hu ("Dragon Pond Lake"), but up to now for some unknown reason, only half had shown up, and only a few of them had driven the trucks out from their factories. What was behind this?

The Fourth Division was manned by the most enlightened workers from the heavy industries in the Shih-ching Shan area. They were supplied with heavy weapons, and had complete transport mobility. For the moment, all of them were gathered in the ancient city, and ready for action.

The Fifth Division, which was Ta-yung's, had been selected from the revolutionary students coming out of the various universities and colleges in the western outskirts. They carried all types of weapons and waited for orders to move out in the Peking People's Stadium next to the Tzu-chu Yüan ("Purple Bamboo Court") outside Hsi-chih Men ("West Gate").

The special combined division, regular army plus tanks, had gathered in Hsiang-shan Kung-yüan ("Fragrant Mountain Park") waiting to take over all the matériel and the equipment in the tank division recently transferred from Inner Mongolia.

This was the main force of the revolution. Two years of sweat and labor had gone into building these divisions.

As for the rural Militia in the countryside nearby, only the order to assemble for battle had been issued. Whether they would be moved into the city or not was still under careful consideration.

Ta-yung, having grasped the situation, realized that he was still wearing his overcoat, which he quickly took off. It was hot in the room, and he was perspiring. He stuck it under his desk.

"Battalion Commander Hsiao, please come to the conference room for a meeting!"

Adjutant Yao saw him first at the door and cried out, "Aiya! What have you got yourself into? You are wounded."

All those at work raised their heads to see. Ta-yung shrugged, not wanting to disrupt their work, and walked rapidly to the conference room.

The commanders of the various divisions and the commissars were all there. Commissar Hsieh, her head lowered, was scribbling something; everybody waited quietly.

"Our most critical moment has arrived. Now we need to summarize the present position." Commissar Hsieh spoke calmly, as if talking about household chores.

"At eight-thirty this morning, a group of well-organized criminals systematically broke through our defense perimeter cordoning off T'ien-an Men Square, and proceeded to conduct unlawful assemblies. As of now, a mob of nearly three hundred thousand is still camped there. At eleven-forty, six trainloads of returning Peking intellectual youth arrived in Peking Railway Station. The Feng-t'ai Railway Station had failed to carry out our orders. These youths were intercepted by two companies of the regular Militia from the Sixth Battalion of the Thirty-ninth Division, who were on guard outside the station. Unexpectedly, mixed in with these intellectual youths were some Consolidated Action elements, who attacked us with bombs. Later on, two companies from the Second Division rushed to the scene, and they were ambushed by Consolidated Action elements lurking at their rear. They suffered heavy casualties. Commander Luan of the Second Division sacrificed his life for the cause, and died a glorious death.

"These are the anti-revolutionary activities which have occurred in two areas of the city. In order to prevent their spread, we must retaliate immediately. We must completely extinguish the flame of these anti-revolutionary elements.

"Some comrades might very well ask why we do not use the method adopted last time in the T'ien-an Men Incident? That is, 'to divide and conquer,' overwhelming with superior military force. But the situation is not the same.

"First, in seventeen cities throughout the country, the same type of anti-revolutionary insurgency has broken out. Comrade Wang Hung-wen has just called from Shanghai that last night the anti-revolutionary forces made their move and now occupy two areas in the city. Armed street fighting has broken out. He is disturbed that the anti-revolutionary elements should be so well armed, and he demands that the Central Committee root out the sources of supply.

"Tientsin cannot come to our support this time. They are also under great pressure. We must not only quickly snuff out the anti-revolutionary outbreaks here in the capital, but we must also take over complete control of the various governmental agencies, so that we can assume command of the various military and civilian units in the country at large, so we can order them to support the left. This is the key to the success of the revolution. We cannot wait until this evening; we must act now.

"The following situation can only be discussed at this level and should not be filtered down to the lower echelons.

"The capitalist faction in our Party, taking advantage of our negligence, kidnapped the majority of the Central Committee members at the capital airport and flew them to Paoting. They consider themselves the majority, and connive at an unauthorized plenary session of the Politburo of the Central Committee. A few capitalist sympathizers in the military are also implicated in their plans. In order to attack them and to destroy their scheme, we must resolutely defend the capital, as well as convene our enlarged session of the Politburo of the Central Committee in Peking.

"Because of these factors and these conflicting developments, we cannot afford to wait, we cannot tolerate the spread of this anti-revolutionary insurgency; we must begin our counterattack now. Chief of Staff Tung will brief you on your assignments. That is all for now."

Chief of Staff Tung stood up, but before he could speak, Adjutant Yao from the combat-strategy room rushed into the room. He whispered something to Commissar Hsieh.

Commissar Hsieh's face reddened, her eyes twinkled with excitement and happiness. In a loud voice, she announced, "Division 8341, the division most loyal to the Chairman, has just arrived and will provide reinforcements for us. Victory is ours!"

⧉ EIGHTEEN

Wednesday, February 13   1 p.m.

A wooden pole of fir, more than ten meters long, was being lifted by many eager hands. On the tip was fastened a piece of red cloth which suddenly unfurled and flapped in the cold wind blowing in from the northern end of T'ien-an Men Square. On the cloth, five huge characters in black ink appeared, written in a strong, masculine hand: "The Eastern City People's Army." Amid the sound of cheers, it whipped in the face of the wind, beckoning heroically in the air.

On the other side of the Memorial Plaque, more cheers erupted; a second banner had been raised, and it read, "The People's Army of the West City." Other cheers broke out in successive waves, as people from the various parts of the city organized themselves and established their military formations, wearing hastily made armbands from shreds of red cloth.

Most held tightly onto clubs, some of which were earlier snatched away from the Militiamen; others were taken from the house-repair installations nearby. There were renovation and reconstruction sites all over the city, so wooden sticks and steel pipes became the first weapons used by the people from the city districts.

Young Tiger carried a long wooden stick, one that Tall Man Li had taken from the hands of a Militiaman. Tall Man Li had a steel pipe more than one meter long, so he had given the wooden stick to Young Tiger.

Now Young Tiger was standing on guard duty in front of the second tier of steps leading to the Memorial Plaque; a well-attended meeting of the People's Army Committee was taking place, to discuss problems of strategy, equipment, supplies, medical support, propaganda, and communications.

At the preparations meeting held yesterday in the rebel headquarters, two men had been elected to leadership roles: Jen Ch'ang-feng had been chosen as commander in chief and Shao Yung-ts'un was made chief of staff.

Shao Yung-ts'un's nickname was "Chuko Liang," and he had long been known to Young Tiger. As for Jen Ch'ang-feng, he knew only the name, not the person. Yesterday at the headquarters, he had listened to the introduction by Hsia Yu-min and Tall Man Li, and learned about Jen's background.

◈　◈　◈

Jen Ch'ang-feng's parents were both university professors in Peking. At the start of the Cultural Revolution, he had participated in the initial outbreaks, and had become an instant celebrity. Of the two groups of the Peking Red Guards—the "Heaven" and the "Earth" contingents—he had been a leader of the "Earth" group, commanding nearly five hundred thousand Red Guards in loyal and unswerving service to the central authority of the Cultural Revolution. When the Red Guards had failed to seize power by attacking the PLA, specifically ordered by the powers conducting the Cultural Revolution, central control had fallen to the PLA. While his comrades-in-arms were secretly arrested one by one, he had left Peking and, relying on the underground network, wandered in the general area of the Yangtze River.

After the initial period of suppression, the underground organizations in the various parts of the country were gradually consolidated. In order to survive, they had formed "black market" networks. These commercial activities had served also to recruit new members, had provided them with on-the-job training, and had secured much-needed material supplies. Silently they had waited for the right opportunity, preparing themselves to take revenge on those power-mongers who had betrayed the people's revolution ten years before.

During this long period, they had exploited the conflict between the powers behind the Cultural Revolution movement, and had instigated a number of large-scale lawful mass "struggles" in order to raise the consciousness of the people and to strengthen their organization. For example, in 1973, the workers were on strike for more than a year in the coal mines of Huai-nan, whence it spread to the entire region south of the Yangtze River, when all coal mines in the area ceased production. In order to protest the interference of the army, the railway workers also went on strike, thus paralyzing the transportation system of the lower Yangtze basin.

When this "struggle" succeeded, their target was shifted to the textile workers of Hangchow, where they agitated for augmented material benefits. The demands of the workers for higher wages were totally reasonable and lawful—a stand that the interceding troops were sympathetic toward. But if these workers in this one city were to achieve victory, the workers in Shanghai, those in the lower Yangtze area, indeed, in the whole country, would raise similar demands. All these prospects sent shivers through Peking.

Given this turn of events, the newly appointed Vice-Chairman of the Party, Wang Hung-wen, rushed to Hangchow from Peking and reverting to his tried and true method, dispatched the Shanghai Militia to help the Militia in Hangchow to exert pressure on the workers and force them to return to work. What surprised him, however, was the solidarity of the workers and the soldiers against the Militia. At this critical juncture, Jen Ch'ang-feng and several workers and regional leaders in Hangchow paid a visit to the Shanghai Militia, and drew them into heated debate. The next day, the Shanghai Militia withdrew all their forces and returned to Shanghai; the workers had achieved a glorious victory! Wang Hung-wen crawled back to Peking and Vice-Premier Teng Hsiao-p'ing was forced to make conciliations.

This approach to consolidating forces, using the "struggle" method, was obviously effective in educating the masses of people. It made them realize that, with solidarity, they had power. But there were also secret organizations diametrically opposed to this strategy. Such an organization might fly a red silk banner with these characters written in yellow: "Consolidated Action Committee of the People of the Capital."

◇ ◇ ◇

Such a banner had many followers near the Memorial Plaque, numbering in the neighborhood of five or six thousand. Their clothes were presentable, and many were veteran returnees, experienced in command. Everyone carried weapons; rifles, light machine guns, grenades (clipped to their waists), cartridge belts (across their shoulders). They wore big red armbands on their left arms. Underneath their flags, four or five large trucks were parked. Those who had just joined were immediately led to trucks. After they had been looked over and checked in, they were given guns, ammunition, rations, first-aid kits, and armbands, and at this point they joined the ranks.

Young Tiger looked over toward them enviously; he really wanted to cadge a gun for himself. But he remembered Hsia Yu-min's briefing on their background, and felt differently, almost antagonistic.

The leader of the Consolidated Action Committee was Yen P'eng-fei. Before the Cultural Revolution, he was a student at the Peking Dramatic Academy, where he was the male acrobatic lead. He was born into a family of Peking opera actors and had practiced acrobatics since childhood; his kicks, thrusts, and moves were both graceful and powerful. In hand-to-hand combat during the Cultural Revolution, he had held a wooden stick and twirled it like an electric fan. In doing so he had earned the sobriquet of "Whirlwind Man."

Whirlwind Man actually fronted for several leaders, but his leaders thought the time was not yet ripe to disclose their identities, so he had been left ostensibly in charge.

The members of the organization had come from excellent backgrounds; they were all offspring of high-ranking cadres and had attended such well-known schools as the "August 1st," the "January 1st," and the high schools affiliated with Tsing-hua, Peking, Kang-t'ieh (Metallurgical Institute), and the Teachers' College. They had formed the highest co-ordinating organ of the Internal Police Corps of the Red Guards in the Hai-ting, the western sector, and the eastern sector of the city. Under the direct command of such high officials as Vice-Premier and Chief of the Athletics Committee Ho Lung and Secretary-General of the State Council Chou Jung-hsin, they had been taken by surprise when the Central Control Authority of the Cultural Revolution had listed them as an anti-revolutionary organization. They had gone into underground activity earlier than the other Red Guards, and since their rosters had been destroyed, the Security Department had no means of searching them out. Up to the present, many important members of this organization had camouflaged their true interests and had become revolutionary leaders with important positions in factories and bureaucracies. These infiltrators had supplied important information and facilitated the activities of the Consolidated Action Committee.

Occurrences over the last few years served to illustrate their method of operation. To provoke international incidents, they had wounded the dependents of an East European diplomat, and had murdered a Japanese student. They had led the masses on Tien-an Men Square who had come to mourn Premier Chou into political demonstrations. Other incidents included the explosion of bombs in the Soviet Embassy; the use of insecticide bombs to create a riot at the Peking Railway Station during the visit of the Premier of Singapore; the holdups of banks to obtain liquid assets; and the posting of slogans all over the country to rail against the Cultural Revolution clique.

❖ ❖ ❖

It was for the sake of solidarity that Jen Ch'ang-feng had agreed to join forces with the Consolidated Action group, but the meeting the day before between the two groups had not been entirely successful. Whirlwind Man had not been willing to form a unified command. He had pointed out that, if the movement were not under the direction of the Consolidated Action Committee, the two groups could form parallel independent organizations that would seek to co-ordinate their activities, but would stop short of unification.

In this present scene of mass unrest, the two organizations had become polar opposites drawing supporters to each side. Young Tiger wondered from where the truckloads of guns and ammunition had come.

The crowd opened to let a formation of troops with Whirlwind Man at their head march over to the People's Army command. Whirlwind Man was attired in army uniform, carried a handgun in a holster at his waist, and walked with an arrogant stride, followed by more than twenty people, all of whom were carrying Hsiang-t'an light machine guns. In their hands, they were holding cartridge belts. Shouting passionately, they passed through the crowds of spectators, and stopped in front of the Memorial Plaque.

Whirlwind Man came up the stairs in a few bounds, and without even casting a glance at Young Tiger, stormed into the

324

area where members of the People's Army were meeting and roared out, "Look! I've brought you a few presents!"

The men who followed Whirlwind Man piled up the guns and cartridge belts and, with arms akimbo, stood smugly at the side.

"To rebel," Whirlwind Man said, "you need a material base. How can you overcome those Militiamen when they are armed to the teeth and all you have are a few wooden sticks? We of the Consolidated Action Committee, in order to consolidate all revolutionary forces, are sending you weapons. Do you want them?"

Jen Ch'ang-feng had already discussed with everyone the essential problem of armaments. Of the weapons previously in their possession, some were confiscated under the ruse of the September 5th resolution (requiring surrender of all arms), when they were compelled to hand over their guns to the military representatives and the Workers Propaganda Units. As for the other part of their weapon supply, although it had been buried or hidden, most had been uncovered through the searches of the Public Security agents over the past ten years as well as through the confessions of some of the members who had not been able to withstand the tortures inflicted on them. In the past two days, a check of their weapons had revealed that some had rusted, others had missing vital parts. Nothing substantial was left that could be used.

Weapons were urgently needed, but why was the Consolidated Action group being so generous? Why were they sending them over without prompting? What was their motive?

Jen Ch'ang-feng laughed. He did not respond immediately, but pulled out a pack of cigarettes, offered it to Whirlwind Man, and invited him to sit down and relax. The other Committee members stood up and each took a gun to look over, including Chuko Liang.

"It's not easy to get so many Hsiang-t'an guns used by the Militia."

"Only the Militiamen in Tientsin and Peking use this model. They designed it themselves. Look! There's still some blood on this cartridge belt . . ."

"They probably just got these from the battle in front of the Peking Railway Station."

"There were heavy casualties! How many do we have here?"

"Forty-seven, plus more than thirty cartridge belts."

Murmurs and muttering broke out. Jen Ch'ang-feng inhaled a few drags on his cigarette, then smiled and stared intensely at Whirlwind Man and said in an amiable tone, "Of course, we will accept your presents. But don't you need them for yourselves?"

"We have enough. These trophies of war can be of use to you. What do you think? Will these be enough?"

"It is a far cry from what we need. Can you get us more?"

Whirlwind Man appeared to expect this. He raised his head and let out a belly laugh. Then in a solemn voice, he said, "We can think of ways to supply you with more weapons. Why don't you dispatch four of your people who can drive a truck, and twenty or thirty men for loading, and have them follow me. I can spare more supplies for you.

"But I have a little condition that must be met in exchange for these guns. From now on, our people are to be allowed to pass freely through areas now under your control, areas blocked by your barricades, without being checked and searched. You will not interfere with our activities. What do you say?"

"What if something should happen that is not in the interests of the people?"

"That absolutely won't happen. We are conducting the revolution on behalf of the people."

"How about this? Members of each of our groups have the right to pass through the barricades in the territories guarded by the other, but no one should be allowed to undertake operations in the areas controlled by the other. When necessary, we will co-ordinate our activities. How about that?"

"Okay. Let's do that for the moment. Now, what are your plans for action? Have you decided on a plan yet?"

"What about you? We will co-ordinate with your plans."

"We intend to liberate the Great Hall of the People, and use it as a Command Headquarters. Then we will free the western sector of the city and the Hai-ting areas. I suggest that we take the Memorial Plaque as a demarcation line; we will take control of the north and west sectors; the eastern and southern areas will be your responsibility. What do you say to that?"

"Let us agree on this arrangement for now. Incidentally, may I ask, after we have liberated the city, when we establish the People's Committee of the capital, will you and your people join us?"

Whirlwind Man laughed arrogantly. "Our goal is the State Council; and that's the whole country." Abruptly, he stood up, brushed off his fine military uniform, glanced casually left and right, and waved his hand.

"Do it right now! Comrades, this is your best chance. Don't forget. Send four men who can drive trucks."

He departed with his followers, haughty and overwhelming. Jen Ch'ang-feng continued sitting, smoking pensively. The Committee members talked about ways to divide up the weapons. Chuko Liang, who had been quiet, suddenly spoke.

"These guns were obtained after the explosions and the fighting in front of the Railway Station. From such a large number of guns, we can surmise that the Militiamen suffered heavy casualties. Why does the Consolidated Action group give them all to us? Why are they not keeping a single gun? This is a way to lay the blame on us. These Militiamen are bent on revenge, and their revenge will be on those who are using these guns.

"While we want to demolish the Militia forces, we can't do it without enough weapons. If we use only wooden sticks and rocks, the Militiamen will probably not use arms against us immediately. Perhaps we can buy enough time to equip ourselves. If we use these forty-seven machine guns now, the Militia will have an excuse to train one hundred thousand machine guns on us, and we will be wiped out in no time. Then the field will be left to the Consolidated Action mob."

Chuko Liang looked at the group around him. Everyone was thoughtful. Everyone agreed with his analysis.

Jen Ch'ang-feng looked at him quietly; he was impressed by the appropriateness of the nickname of "Chuko Liang" for this wily strategist. It was time to wrap things up.

"Comrades. I agree with the views of Comrade Shao Yung-ts'un [Chuko Liang]. These guns are not to be used for the time being. They will all be stored in our headquarters. For the time being, we will assume a defensive posture; we will secure the liberated zone, and we will erect blockades in the streets, clearing the Militiamen and the Public Security agents out of the liberated zone. We want to win the People's Liberation Army over to our side. All units will proceed according to combat instructions."

❖ ❖ ❖

The People's Army from the various districts withdrew from the northern part of T'ien-an Men Square, and began to form a blockade at the Memorial Plaque, cutting off the east-west communications. Lumber, steel plates, and wooden beams at the nearby construction sites were pilfered. Shards of brick and pebbles were collected as ammunition for slingshots.

The troops of the Consolidated Action group also went on the move. They surrounded the eastern and northern gates of the Great Hall of the People and stormed up the expanse of empty stone steps to the closed tall gate of the Great Hall.

The sound of shattering glass was heard. Comrades stepped on the shoulders of comrades in order to crawl through the windows. A barrage of gunfire broke out. More people were running toward the Great Hall and rushing up the stone steps to collect around the big stone column.

Finally the tall gates were flung open. Crowds of people stormed inside like a torrent, cheering and yelling. The area north of the Memorial Plaque was now empty. The people standing behind the barricades could see the Militiamen in the distance along the Chin-shui River, others guarding the Sun Yat-sen Park, as well as the T'ien-an Men and the Cultural Palace of the Laboring Masses. They appeared to be preparing for battle.

Chuko Liang stood in front of the Memorial Plaque, and observed events through binoculars. He was gauging the possible future activities of the Militia from what was happening around the T'ien-an Men. The trucks used by the Militia stationed in the Cultural Palace had been habitually parked in the Square between the Tuan-men and Wu-men arches. He watched for any sign of their moving out.

Kuan Li-p'ei, in charge of communication and liaison, was adjusting the telegraph console. This console, as well as ten auxiliary units, had been used by the team who had tried to rescue the workers trapped in the coal mine during the earthquake at T'ang-shan. In the aftermath of the quake, the units had been unearthed from a ditch by Chuko Liang and his band, who had transported them to Peking in strictest secrecy. It had taken Kuan Li-p'ei and others nearly half a year to repair them and make them operational. Now they were being put to use.

The units of the People's Army in each region had a communications terminal, to keep in touch with the Command Headquarters. The remaining radio units were used by four groups organized by Chuko Liang into mobile teams dispatched to important locations to keep tabs on developments and to keep the Command Headquarters posted.

◈ ◈ ◈

Hsia Yu-min was put in charge of one of the mobile teams. He chose four people for his squad, including Young Tiger. Although unwilling to part with his wooden stick, he was asked to put his red armband in his pocket, which he did reluctantly as he followed behind Tall Man Li.

329

The destination of the squad was the area in front of the Peking Hotel. The Square and Ch'ang-an Avenue were off limits, and the five rerouted themselves along the west section of Anti-Imperialist Road. On the way, they encountered people carrying materials for blockades on their handcarts and bicycles. Entrances of the government offices were closed. Not a single Militiaman or Public Security agent was to be seen.

On reaching Ts'ung-wen Gate, they could see the nervous residents running along the street, carrying groceries. Blockades were being erected at the head of the alleys. Residents, men, women, the old and the young, were posted behind the blockades holding wooden sticks. Clearly they were bent on defending themselves, and they refused entry into the alleys to representatives of any faction, including agents of the Public Security Department.

The children who came out from the crowded alleys were cavorting in the empty street, as if oblivious to the chaos around them.

There were no vehicles along the road, which appeared uncannily quiet. The five passed Tung-tan Park and the spacious Ch'ang-an Avenue, and headed toward the crowded Tung-tan Vegetable Market.

The market was open for business, but was no longer selling; it was distributing vegetables to anyone who came. Outside the market building, a score of people were standing, with placards indicating crimes hanging from their necks. Young Tiger noticed a fat man over forty with an especially large placard. It was inscribed:

Position: Manager of the Tung-tan Vegetable Market; Party member, of small urban merchant bourgeois stock.

Offense: Using his privileges, he took subsidiary foodstuffs on display for foreign visitors as personal gifts "under the table." During the two years he held his post, he appropriated more than seven hundred pounds of fish and shrimp, more than three thousand pounds of meat, and more than ten thousand pounds of fruit, which seriously reduced the supply of secondary foodstuffs for the people of the Tung-tan area. A public people's "struggle meeting" will be held in the market at one o'clock in the afternoon. Everyone is urged to attend.

—The People's Revolutionary Team of Tung-tan Market

Young Tiger looked angrily at the fat man, but Hsia Yu-min walked by impassively.

The theaters and movie houses were all closed, but many people stood in the entranceways to look at the building opposite, the offices of the Foreign Trade Department.

Hsia Yu-min squeezed into the crowd along with Tall Man Li, Young Tiger, Yüeh Wei, and Ch'en Ch'ang-ch'iao to keep a watch on the Foreign Trade Building.

Abruptly, the glass windows on the second floor were shattered. Young Tiger looked intently into the windows and saw people fighting with their fists. Then as the crowd roared, from the front gates ran first ten, then twenty, then fifty men, some of them carrying wooden sticks or legs pulled off chairs. All wore Militia armbands. The crowds on the streets closed in, some throwing rocks saved for the occasion. Those chasing the Militiamen out of the building now appeared and together with the masses in the street, formed a horseshoe to close in on the Militiamen.

The Militiamen ran toward T'ien-an Men, but as they rushed up to the front of the Peking Hotel, the masses caught up with them. They turned to escape into the parking lot in front of the hotel.

The Militiamen inside the hotel rushed out to rescue their beleaguered comrades. Those who stormed out were functionaries at the hotel and they managed not only to rescue the Militiamen from the Foreign Trade Department Building, but also to turn back the crowds to a street intersection.

From the tall building of the Textile Department opposite the Peking Hotel, some three or four hundred people suddenly emerged and cut off the escape route of the Militiamen. Reinforcements from the Foreign Trade Department Building and the street forces stiffened their resistance. The intersection became a huge slaughterhouse. The clamor was deafening. The din attracted the local residents of the Tung-tan and the Wang-fu Ching area, and they joined in the melee.

Hsia Yu-min stood high on a promontory afforded by a garden and looked down. Tall Man Li clenched his fists and tensed his muscles, but did not dare join the fight. Young Tiger was stunned. With eyes bulging out, he stared at the life-and-death struggle in front of him. Finally the battle came to an end. Militiamen were lying on the streets, moaning. Young Tiger saw for the first time that some of the Militia were women.

The victors carried off their own wounded, some of the street forces helped their comrades, but there was no one to look after the wounded Militiamen.

An ambulance appeared, and several medical attendants started to administer first aid.

Angry shouts emerged from a crowd gathered close to the high vantage point where Young Tiger was standing. Young Tiger saw that in the center of the mass of people were three men wearing shirts, ties, and thick woolen overcoats—obviously foreigners.

Young Tiger, like the other common people, had learned from school the history of imperialist aggression on China and the enslavement of the Chinese people over the past hundred years. While he had been taught to make distinctions between foreigners of capitalist and Socialist countries, since the anti-Soviet, anti-revisionist movement he now knew that all foreigners were alike in their vileness. When foreigners came to China, they were treated as distinguished guests, and lived in the best lodgings, purchased the best goods, and the Chinese cadres hovered around ingratiatingly. The same cadres were callous toward their own people. Young Tiger's hatred toward those cadres had been transferred to the foreign guests, and he watched with great relish when the people scolded and jostled the foreigners.

Hsia Yu-min called to Young Tiger and the others in the squad, and Young Tiger turned to see Tall Man Li retracting the antenna of the radio receiver. Hsia Yu-min instructed the squad to put on their armbands, and with Tall Man Li leading the way, they walked into the middle of the throng.

"Please make way, please make way!" Tall Man Li's bellowing voice sounded like thunder. A way was instantly cleared to the center of the disturbance.

Hsia Yu-min looked with composure at the three foreigners, who were in rumpled disarray. He asked in a commanding voice, "Which country are you from?"

One of the foreigners, wearing dark-rimmed glasses, mumbled something incomprehensible; another, a short fellow, using imperfect Chinese, said, "We are Japanese reporters."

He took a thick wallet from his jacket pocket and, with trembling fingers, managed to remove a calling card which he handed to Hsia Yu-min.

Hsia Yu-min glanced at the card, which gave the bearer's name and profession: he was a reporter from the Tokyo Economic News Agency named Shōya Okamura.

"Under what authorization are you collecting news?"

"We have the permission of the Chinese government, from the Foreign Ministry."

"Political power has now been assumed by the People's Army Committee. Are you aware of that?"

There was no answer from any one of the three. Okamura was sweating profusely.

"Now I am going to ask you a few questions. If you do not answer truthfully, the Chinese people will find it hard to forgive you. Do you understand?"

All three nodded.

"Tell us, how many years have you been in China?" Hsia Yu-min asked.

"One year and four months," Nakada mumbled.

"More than two years."

"Not quite two years."

"Do you often report on the scene in China?" Hsia Yu-min persisted.

"We dispatch reports daily," Okamura answered.

"What do you report?"

"Everything. Mainly the achievements of the Chinese people."

"What are the sources for your reports?"

"The places we have seen and visited."

"What else do you report on?"

"Whatever news releases are issued by the Press Bureau of the Foreign Ministry."

"What else?"

None of the three said anything.

"Your reports have been, for the most part, reprinted in our *Reference Bulletin*. When the Chinese people read your stuff, they feel like throwing up. Don't you have eyes and ears? Your kind of reporting only deceives the Japanese reader and the rest of the world."

"We came to China to do our work in the spirit of the 'Three Principles.'* Watanabe spoke.

"What 'Three Principles'? We Chinese have no idea of the 'principles' you mention," Tall Man Li interjected, but was checked by a glare from Hsia Yu-min.

"We came here for the friendship between the Chinese and the Japanese people," Watanabe continued. He had regained some of his composure and his answers began to sound more authoritative.

"Do not delude yourselves and mislead others. Whom do you represent? The Japanese people?"

"Of course, we represent the Japanese people."

"No, what you represent is only the paper you work for. You write only what will benefit your paper."

Watanabe said nothing.

"Let us suppose, for the moment, that your newspaper rep-

---

* Mutual non-intervention, mutual co-existence, and mutual friendship.

334

resents a part of the Japanese population. What kind of people in China are you trying to befriend?"

"The common people."

"Wrong again. You are miles apart from the real Chinese people. Think about it! How did you report the T'ien-an Men Incident? Your views were diametrically opposed to those of the Chinese people. Or else you were completely deaf and dumb. To put it bluntly, people like you make a specialty of distorting facts and glorifying the ruling class in China. All you do is kiss ass! You should have been thrown out of China long ago. Get lost! Crawl back to your Peking Hotel!"

The crowd roared out appreciatively. The three Japanese reporters quickly disappeared, racing back to the Peking Hotel.

Hsia Yu-min, at the head of his group, walked away from the crowd, with Young Tiger following at the rear. Thrusting out his chest and sucking in his belly, Young Tiger struck a herioc pose. But he heard the mutterings of a few girls in the crowd.

"The guys walking in the front sure look the part, but the skinny one at the rear, he must be some sort of office boy that got dragged in."

"Looks like chopsticks in balloon pants."

▨ NINETEEN

Wednesday, February 13   3 p.m.

The roads around Peking's Nan-yüan Military Airport were completely blocked off by troops. The military guard directly under the authority of the Peking Military Command had set up tight security. As a clock sounded three in the afternoon, the door of the special waiting room was shoved open by Staff Member Huang of the Second Air Force Division.

Huang walked to where Commissar Chang of the air force was sitting with a group of officials and handed him a piece of paper.

"Have they arrived?" Premier Hua asked anxiously. The piece of paper was in turn handed over to Commissar Sha of the Peking Military Command. He had just returned to Peking early this morning.

"Everything went smoothly. In five more minutes they should be arriving at Nan-yüan."

"Why isn't Old Huang here yet? He said he would come over as quickly as he could."

"Should I call up and ask?" Commissar Sha said, looking at his watch with concern.

"No, that will not be necessary. It does not matter if he is a little late," Commander Ch'en said calmly. "The situation is under control, there should not be any problems."

"Is there any word from Old Huang? He went to Hsi-chiao Airport," Premier Hua asked again.

"Not yet. But he is due soon!" Commissar Sha answered. He glanced at Minister Ch'iao, who was sitting calmly beside him, and told himself, "Take it easy! Take it easy!"

The telephone on the stand next to the door rang. Staff Member Huang grabbed it, grunted into the phone, and then announced, "The first plane is already on its approach to the airport."

More than ten people inside the room stood up and proceeded through the door to the docking area, with Premier Hua at the head of the entourage.

The twin-engine Ilyushin passenger plane had already made a ninety-degree turn from the end of the runway. It was slowly pulling into the docking area. The noise reverberated throughout the empty field.

Staff Member Huang ran out of the building and handed a message he had just received over to Commissar Chang, who turned it over to Premier Hua. The report was concise: "The Militia in Peking has been totally disarmed. It has been isolated into several groups under the guard of the PLA. Law and order is being imposed by the Public Security forces. The action in the Central Committee's Special Headquarters has worked successfully, and everything has gone according to plan.—Ch'iao, Public Security Department."

Premier Hua was greatly relieved. With rapid steps, he walked toward the ramp placed against the plane, and his face radiated a triumphant smile of hospitality as he welcomed Vice-Premier Li, the first to emerge from the plane.

◈ ◈ ◈

The Command Headquarters of the Peking People's Army Committee had been withdrawn from T'ien-an Men Square to its original site inside Ta Tsa-lan, partly to facilitate the dissemination of commands, partly because they now expected a protracted struggle which would require a permanent command post.

Hsia Yu-min was now appointed Committee Member for Propaganda, with Tall Man Li and Young Tiger as staff members under him. The original underground retreat had undergone further repairs; the deteriorated parts had been shored up on both sides by wooden supports and the area had been expanded.

Hsia Yu-min was preparing a mimeograph stencil, while his staff of two waited for orders. The room was supported by thick wooden poles which, though old, looked sturdy. Tall Man Li had knocked on them and said, "Nothing to worry about. This place is completely safe."

A beam from a flashlight dropped down from above as it was getting dark. Young Tiger heard a voice calling him from the top of the stairs.

"Young Tiger! Are you sound asleep? Who else is down there?"

It was Tall Man Li. Young Tiger squeezed into the side of the stairwell, and stuck his head through to look up.

In the dim light, he could see something moving above.

"Can you see the electric wire on the pole?"

Tall Man Li was trying to hook up the electric lights. By using a long bamboo pole, he was pushing a wire down.

Hsia Yu-min came over with a flashlight to help find the wire. With the aid of the flashlight, they found the wire attached firmly to the sharp tip of the bamboo pole.

Young Tiger put out his hand to grab it, but Hsia Yu-min pushed him away. Young Tiger had not expected Hsia would ever be so brusque.

Hsia Yu-min totally ignored Young Tiger, who was now

quietly seething, and yelled up to Tall Man Li, "Any current in the wire?"

From above came the indistinct response: "Who knows? I pulled it from the lampposts in the street."

Hsia Yu-min carefully stripped the insulation from the electrical wire around the pole and gently joined the contacts; it crackled almost at once, and sparks flew. Young Tiger watched in a cold sweat. Had he grabbed it a moment ago, where would he be now? His admiration for Hsia Yu-min was fully restored.

Ten minutes later, Tall Man Li crawled through into the underground room. Apparently he had pulled down the electrical wiring for the entire lighting system in the street above, including the socket and base of the lamp.

But how was he going to hook it up? Tall Man Li was baffled for a few minutes and then ran out, only to reappear shortly, dragging behind him Kuan Li-p'ei. Kuan was in charge of communication repairs at the headquarters.

Furious, Kuan Li-p'ei sat down, still wearing his large earphones.

"Hook it up now. Hook it up," Tall Man Li urged, pointing to the lamp.

"What the fart has that to do with me? You've yanked the connections of my earphones loose."

Young Tiger looked apprehensively at Tall Man Li, afraid that Li would tear Kuan Li-p'ei limb from limb.

Hsia Yu-min stood up. "Old Kuan, lend us a hand, will you? There is current in this wire, but we don't know how to get at it. You understand these things; we need you to help us out. How about it?"

"That's more like it." Kuan Li-p'ei rubbed his pulled arm. He took out a pair of wire clippers from the leather belt around his waist and hooked up the connection.

The light flashed on, very bright, so incandescent it seemed to outshine daylight. Young Tiger could hardly keep his eyes open. It revealed Kuan Li-p'ei's face still showing traces of anger, and Tall Man Li laughing with glee. Hsia Yu-min turned off his flashlight and returned to work on his stencil. Tall Man Li and Young Tiger escorted Kuan out with many profuse expressions of gratitude, and Kuan was somewhat mollified as he ascended the steps to the headquarters.

In the adjacent meeting room, Young Tiger could see four people. Jen Ch'ang-feng was listening attentively to Chuko Liang's analysis.

Hsia Yu-min, carrying another draft, delivered it to Jen Ch'ang-feng to read over. Jen Ch'ang-feng scribbled a few corrections and said, "It still needs work, another rewrite. Your conceptual framework is very strong, but it isn't very effective: the ordinary masses will not understand it. The purpose of our struggle is not clear enough, it needs stressing.

"The purpose of our struggle is not to obtain residence permits in the city; it is not because we are afraid of going up to the mountains or down to the villages; it is certainly not to ask for entry into the factories and into the universities. Our struggle is for democracy and for law.

"Why has the Chinese Communist Party grown from a handful to thousands and finally to millions? This was made possible by the development of the Chinese social structure. China was a feudal society for several millennia without interruption. Without military pressures from abroad, it probably would have continued in that way. International developments did not allow China to remain stagnant, so she was compelled to change into a semi-feudal, semi-colonial country. Its people were even more cruelly oppressed. The downtrodden people in China as a whole feel desperately the need to wage concurrently the fight for democracy and freedom as well as the campaign for national independence and self-sufficiency.

"From 1937, the Chinese Communist Party hoisted the flag, the standard of national struggle, and launched anti-Japanese propaganda. This was to take advantge of the feelings of the Chinese people in their passion for national liberation and independence. Accordingly, enthusiastic and committed intellectual youth flocked to Yenan. The Party also secured the sympathy of intellectuals under the Chungking regime. It even obtained the support and co-operation of the leftist wing of the Kuomintang (Nationalist) Party.

"After the liberation of the whole country in 1949, the principal contradiction of national independence and self-sufficiency was resolved, but the problem of law and democracy became paramount. The achievement of democracy became a prime objective of the people. It was not long after that China sustained repercussions from the Twentieth Congress of the Soviet Communist Party and the Hungarian Revolution, in 1956. The movement of 'Let the hundred schools of thought contend, let the hundred flowers bloom' lasted just one short month in 1957, but in this one month, clarion calls went out to every region of the country promoting justice and advocating democracy. The effects were earthshaking, and one group in particular became so apprehensive that they quickly moved to suppress armed intellectuals. The struggle of the Chinese people for democracy was crushed.

"Why was it that this group felt apprehensive about democracy? What they mouthed was always Marxism-Leninism; they struck up slogans claiming that they represented the will of the people. Actually, they were Chinese-style Marxist-Leninists.

"China was forced to move from a totally feudal to a semi-feudal, semi-colonial society, and then in one bound it entered into a Chinese-style Socialism without the necessary materialistic base. We absolutely do not wish to put China on the road to capitalism. But China lacks one virtue of a capitalistic society: that it is not hospitable to democracy and freedom, to an emphasis on rule by the law of the people.

"The one who had responsibility for the Party for such a long time, did he have any thoughts of 'rule by law'? Not at all, no, not the least bit. On the contrary, he declared with smug self-congratulation that he would be like the monk holding the umbrella, defying alike law and justice. So long as it fitted in with his whims and his strategic needs, any law of the land or Party could be breached. Why? What is democracy to his way of thinking? It isn't worth a fart.

"And it's no wonder. He was never brought up in a democratic environment; his basic store of knowledge was very limited. The works he loved to read were *The Romance of the Three Kingdoms, Water Margin,* and *Journey to the West.* These books contained only emperors and kings, ministers and generals. When he read more of them, his mind was naturally filled with the thoughts of feudalistic emperors and kings. So, in government, he consolidated power at the top. Within the Party, he assumed the role of paterfamilias. In the internal organizations of the Party, the military, and the government, he quite naturally formed a clique from his hometown region. Therefore, the Chinese People's Republic was changed from a country ruled by a single party to a country ruled by a single family. If you take a look at the time of the Cultural Revolution, a single word or phrase from his lips became instantly the law of the land. Not only from him, but from his 'Dowager Empress.' Whoever dared to offend her would either be crushed to pieces or else would be spending years at hard labor in a dung heap, be he revolutionary stalwart or merely a seventy-year-old veteran.

"Whether there is democracy inside the Party or not is the Party's problem. The people need not concern themselves about that. It is only a question that reflects on the standards of the Party. But if this Party governs the whole country, then the people in the country will take arms against it if they are not granted democracy and freedom.

"The 'phantom of democracy' staged in the early years of this country, where is it now? How many times have the Political Consultative Conferences met at the national and provincial levels? These obedient representatives, what could they vote in favor of? To raise their hands in unison and pass a motion introduced by the Chinese Communist Party, does this suggest anything like real democracy?

"Who dares not to raise his hand? High status, a handsome monthly income, luxurious living quarters, special travel privileges, health service, purchasing rights, easy access to school and employment for one's children, and the distinction of being allowed to meet foreign guests face to face. When compared with these, what are 'justice' and 'the will of the people' worth?

"The glorious National People's Congress has changed its complexion with its third meeting. These so-called representatives, whom do they represent? The Chinese people do not know, and they do not even know these 'representatives.' The involvement of all strata in society, from bottom to top; just how far down does this bottom go? The bottom, to begin with, means merely the provincial and urban echelons in the Party. Thus, the 'democracy' is nothing more than a ruse between the central and the regional governments, and it has nothing to do with the people. In 1974, they clamored for a whole year to call the Fourth People's Congress. It was a pretty slogan, 'Consultation from top to bottom, from bottom to top; back and forth, time and again.' It looks democratic in the extreme, but in reality, the Central Government appointed representatives whom the local echelons did not approve of, so they argued for more than a year. Finally, after much wrangling, they staged a hurried five-day meeting in January 1975, and concluded the proceedings.

"This People's Congress, though convened for only five days, produced two reports at odds with each other, one by Chang Ch'un-ch'iao and the other by Premier Chou, and promulgated a new constitution with not a word about democracy.

"This new constitution announced from the very beginning that China had changed from a 'people's democratic country' into 'a country of the proletarian dictatorship.'

"In the skimpy thirty articles of the constitution, the democratic rights of the people count for nothing; there's no freedom to choose a profession, to select a place of residence, no equal rights to education, medical care, and recreational or cultural opportunities. There is no guarantee of personal safety, personal life and property, or security within one's domicile. The so-called freedom of speech, freedom of the press, freedom of assembly, freedom to demonstrate and strike, etc.— without a permit from the Party, these actions become anti-revolutionary crimes. What kind of freedom is this?

"Even if the Party approves, it can change its mind on a whim and assign guilt. Isn't this what happened with the cases in Canton of Li Chang-t'ien, Ch'en Yi-yang, and Wang Hsi-che, who either were arrested, committed suicide, or fled the country?

"May 4, 1919, was the first time that the Chinese people took collective action in striving for democracy and freedom. After this action was ruthlessly suppressed, the 'New Culture Movement' of China was established with much bombast and celebration; the Chinese Communist Party was born, and a new page was turned in China's long history.

"But this ideal has not been achieved down to the present day. The Chinese people could tolerate it no longer, so they launched a similar struggle on April 5, 1976, on the same site. But once again, they were mercilessly crushed by the running dogs of the ruling class.

"The stain of blood on T'ien-an Men Square was not washed clean by the running dogs for two and a half days. This horrendous bloodletting will never be erased from the memory of the people. The people will return blood for blood; they cannot escape from the people, from the long hand of revenge.

"Are there really classes in China now? It's ridiculous! They vanished from the scene long ago. Now all the people are poor in China; they all have become plebeians. The problem facing China now is not a problem of class struggle; it is a problem of the people's survival, their well-being, and their freedom; the question of improving the standard of living can be misconstrued as a question of who has special privileges and who doesn't, which produces the confrontation between the haves and the have-nots. It becomes an important factor in the third struggle for emancipation by the Chinese.

"We are now presently in the midst of this third struggle for emancipation. Our slogan is the same as the one used fifty-seven years ago, 'For democracy, freedom, and science.' In addition, after reviewing two generations of struggle, we find that we need to add another slogan, 'Against dictatorship, against special privileges, and against deceptions of the people.' These are the three 'for's' and the three 'against's' that we have raised on behalf of the common people of the entire country; these are the objectives behind our actions. That's what I had in mind to say. I've finished. Comrade Shao, what is your response? Please feel free to add to what I've said."

Chuko Liang had listened distractedly without saying a word. After a pause, he spoke in measured tones:

"Of course I agree with all that you've said, but I've had my mind on something else."

"What?"

"Do you think we can achieve our objectives in this insurrection?"

"Old Shao! You are an intelligent person. How could they possibly be achieved?"

"Why not?"

"The slogan 'Political power grows out of the barrel of a gun' still holds in this despotic country of ours. We do not hold the barrel of the gun!"

"Then why do we openly organize insurrection?"

"So that we can educate more and more people, the young people especially, so that they might know the real cause of our present difficulties, so that they might know the goal and the thrust of our struggle."

"Will this generation achieve these goals in our lifetime?"

"Definitely. The wheel of history is turning at a faster pace. It no longer requires decades or centuries to change the thinking of the people and the structure of society. The rate of quantitative change has speeded up so much that a minority is no longer able to prevent it by tyrannical force of arms. Qualitative changes will follow one after another. The power to make progress toward the 'Four Modernizations' is enormous.

The fires have already been ignited, and large-scale explosions will soon erupt."

"Right. I am convinced you are right. But if this insurrection should go awry, what shall we do then?" Chuko Liang asked stubbornly.

Jen Ch'ang-feng stood up; his emaciated face looked unusually pale, and his eyes stared into the distance.

"Extreme torture, exile, living as fugitives in constant fear of capture—we have experienced all three. What else can there be that's more frightening? At the very worst, we will be subject to all this once more."

"At this time," Chuko Liang said, "I would like to announce a secret arrangement made by the core command group. Keeping in mind that our forces, exposed in every region, will not have an escape route if they should encounter setbacks, the core command group has decided on the northwestern provinces as our ultimate refuge and base of operations. Should there be a crisis, we will all withdraw into the northwestern provinces. Our organizations in that area will give us sanctuary." He finished speaking, his piercing gaze falling on everyone in the audience, but everyone was looking down, deep in thought.

In the underground room, there was a hush, and the mood was meditative. Suddenly Old Goat rushed down the stairs,

"Aah-aah-aah . . . troops have come . . . uh-uh-uh . . . the troops have come . . . aah-aah . . . have come!"

Rushing in fast on his heels was another comrade who yelled out in a guttural voice: "The People's Liberation Army is on the move! They have blocked off the whole of Ch'ang-an Avenue."

Jen Ch'ang-feng glanced at Chuko Liang, pounded on the table with a crashing sound, and shouted, "So fast?" Then he walked resolutely out of the basement to the command post upstairs. Everybody followed.

Kuan Li-p'ei was sitting in front of the radio receiver listening attentively, while at the same time scribbling hastily in a notebook. When he saw Jen Ch'ang-feng, he tore off a page and gave it to him.

Jen Ch'ang-feng knitted his eyebrows, and read aloud:

"Fully armed—PLA troops in blue uniforms—forming three columns—blocking all of Ch'ang-an Avenue—it's Division 8341—four or five thousand strong—the Militiamen withdrawn to the Cultural Palace—the Consolidated Action group also fled the field—only ordinary people now in the Great Hall of the People."

Jen Ch'ang-feng scowled. "The situation has changed radically. Let's go out for a look."

Ch'ien-men Avenue was deserted. The windows and doors on both sides of the street were closed tight. The sky at four o'clock in the afternoon was somber. Black clouds hung low, seeming to press down. The violent north wind swept from the Ch'ien-men Tower.

Young Tiger found himself in the midst of the crowd, his mood apprehensive. He had enough courage to take on the Militia in battle, but the PLA was another matter.

Why was the PLA on the move? What was Division 8341 doing? Judging from the expressions on the faces of the others, especially the dark look on Chuko Liang, he sensed that the situation was not hopeful.

They turned into the Square. Behind the blockades of various sizes piled up in front of the Memorial Plaque, people were standing, craning their necks, looking toward the north. The whole expanse on the Square from the Plaque to Ch'ang-an Avenue was still. Not a child could be seen. At the Great Hall of the People on the left, it was also quiet, with only a few people running from the wide-open front gate, down the stone steps, and scurrying away toward the south.

There was not a trace of the pompous, boisterous, and arrogant Consolidated Action group. Even the big banners which they had hoisted on top of the roof of the Great Hall of the People were gone.

Jen Ch'ang-feng stood on the second tier of the steps in front of the Memorial Plaque and peered through his binoculars. Chuko Liang, at his side, was in communication with Kuan Li-p'ei on a walkie-talkie.

"Old Jen, do you see anything?" Chuko Liang asked.

"The 8341 troops are lined up in three columns, all carrying rifles with bayonets fixed. But the two columns to the north are standing with their backs toward us. Only the column to the south is facing us."

"There's a report from Sun Chih-hao's patrol at Pei-ch'ih-tze ['The Northern Pond']," Chuko Liang said. "Ten or more trucks carrying Militiamen have returned to Pei-hai Park. They have all been disarmed. In every truck, there are four or five armed PLA soldiers; it looks as if they have them under guard. At the Northern Pond, when a truck turned, two Militiamen jumped off and escaped. The PLA soldiers didn't go after them, but the two escapees were grabbed by the people milling around before they could get very far. Looks like the Militiamen have been totally disarmed by the PLA."

"I can't understand what's happening. Are they out to put us down too?"

"Have you noticed where the Consolidated Action people went?"

"That's right! Are they poised to attack, or have they run away?"

"I'm afraid they got word already, and have withdrawn."

"We must convene a meeting and discuss this new development."

In less than half an hour, the leaders responsible for various areas arrived at the command post, and they gave an account of the situation in their respective areas as reported by their patrols.

—"The police and the Public Security forces are active in the eastern sector of the city. They are not interfering with the masses. They are only arresting the Workers Militia and sending them to the various police stations, so they have the support of the masses. Some of the Militiamen who escaped home have also been apprehended by the masses and sent to the police stations. Street rumors are circulating all over; some say that the PLA Peking Military Command have entered the city, others say that the Cultural Revolution clique on the Central Committee has fallen. But there's nothing substantive behind any of the rumors."

—"The western sector of the city has been destroyed by looters. But after a while, they were put down by Public Security forces. PLA troops have stationed themselves around the State Council and other government offices. No one is permitted to pass through. Militiamen are all converging on Pei-hai Park, where they are declaiming their propaganda."

—"Inside and outside Pei-hai Park, soldiers of the 8341 Division are on sentry duty or out on patrol. Our patrols look from a distance at the Shih-ch'a area and we heard a few shots there. Later a truck stuffed with prisoners headed to the west. Those with sharp eyes saw that in the truck there was a woman who was still shouting and yelling and haranguing her captors. She looked like Secretary Hsieh of the Revolutionary Committee of Tsing-hua University."

From these fragmented dispatches, there was only one conclusion to be drawn: the Militia was completely crushed, disarmed by the 8341 Division, and herded together.

Law and order in the eastern and western sectors of the city was being maintained primarily by the troops of the 8341 Division. Though there was some sign of Public Security forces, their numbers were not large. Why was this division, delegated with the sole responsibility of protecting heads of state, assuming this job?

"Comrades," Jen Ch'ang-feng said coolly, "this is a totally unexpected new development. The crucial problem now is that our principal target has been removed. But, comrades, don't be taken off guard; it is at this moment that the underlying 'contradictions' will emerge as the major 'contradiction.' That is to say, what is the attitude of the PLA, now in control of Peking? This we cannot understand without the necessary negotiations and exchange of views. I propose that all of you return right away to your original posts, and explain the reasons to your men; you must not relax your guard. Only by close co-operation with each other can we be strong, and secure the personal benefits for each one of us."

Kuan Li-p'ei waved a piece of paper. Tall Man Li snatched the paper and handed it to Hsia Yu-min.

Hsia glanced at it and turned red.

"Big news! Chiang Ch'ing, Chang Ch'un-ch'iao, Yao Wen-yüan, and Wang Hung-wen have all been arrested!"

Everyone let out a spontaneous, heartfelt cheer. The hurrahs were mixed with unimaginable joy, happiness at seeing, at last, the light at the end of a long, dark tunnel, and relief at the release from at least ten years of frustration and anger. People were shouting, some pounding on the table, others rushed outside crying. Still others stood dazed, their fists clenched.

Jen Ch'ang-feng walked behind Kuan Li-p'ei to pick up another piece of paper:

"The Central Committee will be convened in Peking—all Militia organizations in the country are to cease their activities—the residents of Shanghai have besieged the Shanghai Party Committee—the Shenyang Military Command has Mao Yüan-hsin under arrest."

Jen Ch'ang-feng patted Kuan Li-p'ei on the shoulder and asked, "These dispatches, where do they come from? Are they reliable?"

"The frequency on which the dispatches were broadcast belongs to the Red Star Broadcasting Station in Pei-hai Park, which is still sending out a signal."

"Then, in that case, we cannot consider these dispatches authentic at all."

Kuan Li-p'ei raised his eyes and said confidently, "In the present situation, do you think the official stations, the Central Broadcasting Station and the Peking People's Broadcasting Station, can issue broadcasts as well?"

"What do you think, are these dispatches reliable?"

"Ninety-nine per cent reliable."

"All right. I trust your judgment."

Gunshots were heard outside. Startled outcries were followed immediately by the sounds of laughter. Some of the People's Army were setting off firecrackers. The people in the street had heard the good news.

Young Tiger bolted out to see Ch'ien-men Avenue crammed with people; even old folk were standing at the doors looking out.

Yüeh Wei and Ch'en Ch'ang-ch'iao were both holding bullhorns. Over and over they shouted, "The most despised Chiang Ch'ing, Chang Ch'un-ch'iao, Yao Wen-yüan, and Wang Hung-wen are all under arrest! The Militia has surrendered. Our revolution has triumphed!"

"Is that true? Unbelievable!"

"Madame Chairman under arrest! I don't believe it. These guys are insurrectionists; who can trust them? Daddy of Little Ch'uan, come in, won't you? You don't want to be implicated when all this blows over."

Some people on the second story of a shop along the street opened their window and set a big radio near the window, facing out, so that the broadcast could be heard in the streets.

Not far away, others had turned their radios up loud, setting them near their entrances, so that the people in the streets could listen.

The crowds now suddenly came alive. Small children were gamboling in the streets; the middle-aged were shaking their heads and sighing; the elderly held back their tears, their hands on their chests, saying to themselves: "We never expected to live long enough to see this day of reckoning!"

A middle-aged man said boldly, "Now we can all enjoy our New Year's Eve feast!"

Young Tiger was standing beside him. "Ah! tomorrow is New Year's Eve. Mother is home by herself. Now that we've won, I should go home to celebrate the New Year with her."

About to head for home, he thought that he should let Hsia

Yu-min know. He walked back into the dilapidated area of Ta Tsa-lan. Young Tiger groped his way through the entrance-way, then tripped against something soft under his feet, and fell. He heard the sound of an agonized moan. It sounded like Big Gun Hsü. But he had been sent to the Consolidated Action group to drive a truckload of weapons back!

Young Tiger extended his hand, and touching something wet and sticky, cried out. Two or three comrades ran in from the command post and turned on their flashlights. It was Big Gun Hsü, covered with blood. Quickly they carried him into the underground meeting room, and Hsia Yu-min began emergency treatment.

When Big Gun Hsü regained consciousness, he explained haltingly what had happened to him.

The four drivers and the other twenty comrades sent to help load the trucks with weapons reached Lotus Pond, where they waited for an entire afternoon before other trucks arrived.

After six o'clock, some trucks arrived loaded with Consolidated Action people. Without explanation, they got out and began pummeling Big Gun Hsü and his comrades to death. Big Gun Hsü had been beaten unconscious, but when he came to, he discovered that he, along with his comrades, had all been thrown out on the street near the Hu-fang Bridge. He had struggled to the headquarters for help.

Jen Ch'ang-feng immediately ordered a group to rescue the comrades at the Hu-fang Bridge. In addition, he asked Chuko Liang to notify all areas and to check again on their personnel and their position, so that they might have a better estimate of their fighting effectiveness.

Kuan Li-p'ei busied himself again. The first to be contacted was the group at Yung-ting Gate, where there was noisy activity. The commander of the People's Army answered the call. He reported that all trains coming to Peking were being stopped at the Yung-ting Railway Station. The young people with families in Peking had returned home; other young people in transit, numbering some four to five thousand, had congregated at Yung-ting Gate. The People's Army asked the Central Command for more food supplies.

The voice of the local commander sounded tense.

"The People's Liberation Army has withdrawn; it has been replaced by Public Security forces, along with many plainclothesmen. Residents of Peking have all returned home. No one is allowed to pass through. It appears that the Public Security forces are sealing off our liberated zone." As Chuko Liang heard this, his face fell.

The voice of the commander of the western sector sounded even more nervous. "No one is permitted to move from the Hufang Bridge on. Our thoroughfare has already been cordoned off. People trying to get home for the New Year are being turned back. They are trying to figure out ways of breaking through."

"What are the troops?"

"They're from Public Security. Not the PLA. Nor the 8341 Division. They left the scene long ago."

Chuko Liang turned and in dead earnestness announced to everyone: "Comrades, the liberated zone is being besieged."

▨ TWENTY

Wednesday, February 13
Midnight

A cold, fierce wind swirled along both sides of the Pavilion of the Ten Thousand Buddhas, around the Command Headquarters of the People's Militia. The men in the long lines shivered in silence.

Hsiao Ta-yung stood in the middle of one of the lines, which had been formed by the Second Militia Division, now disarmed, waiting for inspection. The inspection had proceeded slowly, and Ta-yung had been waiting his turn for more than three hours.

Finally, he entered the lounge on the ground floor. Inside, two ping-pong tables had been disassembled to form four desks. Ta-yung was instructed to stand in front of the first desk. Five officials sitting around the desk asked him a series of questions. After having noted his answers, a military-type inspector told him in an impersonal manner, "You are originally from the Fifth Division. Return to the Fifth Division for processing. Get on truck Number 9."

He was ushered out by a Public Security agent, and located truck Number 9.

There were more than thirty people in the truck, all key Militia members from the various universities in the western outskirts, dispatched to the various battalions and companies of the Second Militia Division to be political commissars. But now, sealed off by the waterproof tarpaulin, they sat, subdued, their heads lowered.

After five or six more people had entered the truck, the tarpaulin was lifted. There was no guard in the truck. Although nothing prevented their speaking, everyone remained silent.

The truck started. Everyone stood and grabbed the steel frame of the truck, shaking and swaying with the motion of the truck. There was no thought of resistance.

◇ ◇ ◇

Events had occurred quickly prior to this. Ta-yung had been in the Militia headquarters when officers and a company of PLA soldiers had entered the conference room, brandishing their handguns, and pointing them at the Militia cadres. One of their officers had charged them peremptorily: "Under the orders of the Party's Central Committee, we are arresting you as anti-revolutionary elements, plotting a coup!"

When Militia Chief of Staff Tung drew his pistol, he had been immediately hit in the stomach and knocked down. The Political Commissar of the Third Division had tried to wrestle with the invaders, but had been shot in the leg. In the melee, Commissar Hsieh had shouted, "Sound the emergency alarm!" Ta-yung had broken into the door of the combat-strategy room, but had seen the regular wireless operators lined up against the wall, and the PLA in their places at the communication consoles. They had been broadcasting over and over again:

"All Militia divisions should assemble on the double. All sentry posts are to be withdrawn. Await further instructions from the 8341 Division. Obey the new directives, discipline must be observed at all times."

Who had betrayed the Revolution? Who had betrayed the will of the Chairman?

◈ ◈ ◈

The truck was rocking back and forth. Ta-yung felt no fear even though he had no idea where he was being taken. Even if he were going to the execution grounds, the one thing that troubled him was the nature of his own feelings; had they been revolutionary or anti-revolutionary? He could not be at peace with himself until he found the answer.

The truck stopped. The soldiers dismounted, formed a line for roll call, and finally were marched through a host of other parked trucks. They had arrived at the parking lot in front of the newly constructed Capital Gymnasium, which was brightly lit. Inside and outside were a throng of human shadows, as if a spectacular international track meet were under way. On approaching the Gymnasium, they sensed the atmosphere, totally different from that of an athletic competition. The Gymnasium was lined with blockading PLA soldiers, their bayonets fixed, prepared to fend off any attack. The disarmed Militiamen passed through the blockade and were quietly swallowed up by the big gate.

Inside the huge Capital Gymnasium, the bright lights overhead had been turned on. The audience section was filled with the men and women of the Fifth Division.

In the top aisle ringing the Gymnasium PLA soldiers were standing, with rifles at the ready. Under the muzzles of the guns, more than ten thousand Militiamen sat in total silence. Only an occasional cough indicated the presence of so many people.

Ta-yung sat in a stupor, his eyes glazed. Hungry and fatigued, shaking as though with a chill, he felt that neither the flesh nor the spirit could sustain much more.

Had the Militiamen been wiped out completely? What was the situation of the Workers Militia Division in the Shih-ching Mountains area? What was happening in Shanghai, Shenyang, Tientsin? How quickly had the will of the Chairman been subverted!

Ta-yung felt as though he were in a nightmare. After all the training, the painstaking organization, the Militia had come to this! Without a single shot they had become abject prisoners. What had become of the leaders in the Central Committee? What had happened to Commissar Hsieh? The few comrades wounded for resisting, were they now alive or dead? And, the most important question: after this devastating rightist coup, would the general direction of the Party and of the country as prescribed by the Chairman be altered?

A line of troops had marched onto the deserted track. Strangely, they wore Militia uniforms, and were carrying "Hsiang-t'an"-model machine guns. The only difference in their uniform was the armband, made of yellow cloth with five words written in big red print: People's Militia Internal Security Guards.

These guards were now posted on all sides of the track, facing toward the Militiamen in the stands. Other groups of Internal Security Guards had brought in a microphone, which they set up in the center of the field.

"What the hell are they doing?" Ta-yung thought.

A commotion broke out in the upper stands. Everyone turned to look. "Militiamen" wearing yellow armbands were serving *man-t'ou* from large containers, distributing it row by row.

Ta-yung held a cold, hard *man-t'ou* in his hand, but he had no appetite. He recognized the man sitting beside him, who used to be the secretary of the Youth League in the Department of Hydraulic Engineering at Tsing-hua University. He was stuffing his mouth with the *man-t'ou,* and muttering, "They're giving us bleached-flour *man-t'ou* to eat. They can't mean us any harm."

A half hour passed. From a front entrance, a second group of the new "Militiamen" walked in. They wore red badges on their collars, and hanging from their shining belts were heavy, holstered automatics. They appeared to be the leading cadres of the Internal Security Guards.

A paunchy middle-aged man began to speak:

"Militiamen of the capital, you were created by the great and glorious Chairman himself. You were carefully selected from the class-conscious masses for the purpose of 'preventing the return of the old order from within,' and of 'resisting foreign aggression from without.' This effort must be sustained.

"Unfortunately, a small band of capitalists within the Party plotted to subvert the guidelines prescribed by the Chairman. They resorted to schemes and intrigues, and they conspired at revisionist face-changes in the Party, and at taking the 'red' out of 'Red China.' The main plotters were only a handful. They were Chiang Ch'ing, Chang Ch'un-ch'iao, Yao Wen-yüan, and Wang Hung-wen. These four capitalist-roaders, who have long been the cancer at the heart of our Party, were arrested today."

Ta-yung's eyes widened. How could they misrepresent Madame Mao, so loyal to the Chairman, as a capitalist-roader who had acted against the interests of the Chairman? What kind of casuistry was this?

Ta-yung's blood froze when his fellow Militiamen, who had received so much political education, who had sworn so many times to defend the Chairman's line to the death, started to applaud!

Someone took up the chant:

"Down with Chiang Ch'ing!"

"Down with the 'Gang of Four!'" The shouts were ear-splitting.

"Down with . . ." Ta-yung sat, dumbfounded and shaken to the core.

Get out of here. Get out of Peking. Go to the steppes of Inner Mongolia. Take up life as a peaceful agricultural worker. Tears streamed down his cheeks. He could not believe what he was witnessing. *I must break out of this dream. I must wake up!*

The middle-aged man in the center of the track raised his hand. It was instantly so quiet that the involuntary coughs of some of the Militiamen sounded disrespectful.

"Now the top echelons are following the instructions of our great and wise leader, to zero in on the key malefactors. We are using the technique of curing the disease in order to treat the patient. It is a matter of trying to rectify the erroneous departures in the past made by the Workers Militia of the capital. Militiamen of the Fifth Division, you are the core of the Peking Militia, you are the youth who have been selected from the universities in the capital as the most loyal to the proletarian cause and to the Chairman's revolutionary line. You should recognize clearly the way you must go and continue to be the model for the Workers Militia of the entire city, as well as for the whole country. You must make up for your past crimes with meritorious service, and contribute what you have to the Party and to the people."

Thunderous applause burst out.

"The leadership has decided that the capital Militia headquarters, which had pursued an errant course, is now to be disbanded. A new Militia leadership is to be established in the capital, which will be called the Peking Internal Security Guards. The Fifth Division's leader has already been appointed. Now we ask the Commander in Chief of the Internal Security Guards of the Fifth Division, Comrade Yen P'eng-fei, to say a few words."

The applause erupted again. Yen P'eng-fei, "Whirlwind Man," wearing a brand-new Militia uniform, strode proudly and with self-assurance to the center of the stage.

❖   ❖   ❖

—"The granaries outside the Yung-ting Gate have been confiscated by the Public Security Department, who forbid us to continue shipping grain out."

—"The number of youths in transit under our care has mounted to fifty thousand; we desperately need warm clothing and food as well as wood and charcoal."

—"The exiled youth who were on their way home to Peking could not break through the line of blockades. They are now concentrated at various street intersections, suffering from hunger and exposure. A few of them forced the local residents to take them in, but they were stopped by our People's Army. The situation is grave. How should we handle it? Please send instructions."

From various areas emergency dispatches from members of the People's Army were streaming into the command post without interruption. Kuan Li-p'ei was scribbling incessantly. The sheets of his transcribed messages were being circulated to every member of the core command group.

Chuko Liang's eyes were bloodshot from two sleepless nights. He spoke with icy composure:

"The most urgent problem facing us now is food, warm clothing, and bedding. If we cannot obtain these supplies, order cannot be maintained in the liberated zone. Once the hungry and the shivering and the homeless youth seize food and shelter from the local residents themselves, we will not only lose the support of those living in the liberated zone, it will affect the reaction of the whole country toward the integrity of our revolution. Thus, we would undermine the most important mission behind our activity, that is, to educate the people. Comrade Jen Ch'ang-feng, Comrade Ho Yung-nien, Comrade Nieh T'ieh-ying, we must retract our original injunction. We must use supplies that we have in the markets and the groceries, the co-operative shops, and the department stores; otherwise we will be facing a catastrophe."

"If we use these goods, will we incur the suspicion and the hostility of the local residents?" Ho Yung-nien asked.

"How much fear and resistance there is depends on how we proceed. According to our figures, there are in the liberated zone forty-one food stores with a storage capacity of more than sixty thousand pounds. If we take only half from each store, and give the rest to the local residents, then thirty thousand pounds of grain will be enough to support fifty thousand for one week."

"What happens after that week?" Nieh T'ieh-ying asked.

"Can we last for one week?" Chuko Liang barked back.

Jen Ch'ang-feng spoke with a sardonic smile:

"One week? I am only thinking about tonight and tomorrow. What will happen tomorrow night I cannot even guess. All right! Inform the various sectors immediately to help themselves to the food in the stores. But they are permitted only one third of the store's supply. They must proceed in an orderly way. When they take grain, they must consult with the residents, and issue receipts; warm food and clothing can also be taken out of the storage rooms in the department stores and shops. These items can be secured right away, but only cotton jackets, pants, and quilts will be allowed; other items are absolutely forbidden, and no one is to touch them."

The hotels, movie houses, theaters, schools, recreation halls, and restaurants in the various areas of the liberated zone were turned into receiving depots, under the command of the People's Army situated in each area.

Reports of new developments streamed in.

—"According to information received from comrades working in the Peking Telephone Bureau, the people's liberated zone in Tientsin has already been seized by the Tientsin Workers Militia. Heavy casualties are being reported. The hospitals are crowded with the seriously wounded. In the liberated zone the Public Security forces have already seized control."

—"Shanghai's masses have gathered in the People's Square in the center of the city, demanding that the leading cadres of the Shanghai Revolutionary Committee be put on public trial. A mammoth groundswell of insurrection is developing."

—"Members of the Party's Central Committee from the various outlying regions have gathered in Peking. It is thought that they will convene an emergency session of the Central Committee. They will probably elect a new Politburo."

—"Troop movements on the outskirts of Peking are now commonplace; railway transportation has come to a total halt; there are still seven trainloads of youths 'transferred downward' to the countryside who cannot get into Peking. These youths have disembarked from the train and are heading for Peking on foot. They are due to arrive in Peking around nine o'clock in the morning. Have plenty of hot water and food on hand for them."

Jen Ch'ang-feng looked over these dispatches one by one.

Kuan Li-p'ei suddenly gave a startled outcry as he tore off a dispatch. Chuko Liang quickly took it from him and read it aloud:

"The Fifth Militia Division has just left the Capital Gymnasium and is walking toward the Cultural Palace of the Laboring Masses shouting slogans along the way."

The Militia again! They were approaching once more.

If they were to be surrounded by the People's Liberation Army, all differences could be solved through negotiation. They would be able to express the aspirations of the people for democracy to the members of the new Politburo. Their leader would be arrested and exiled, but he would have opportunities to escape. All others would be safe, and the embers that glowed in the hearts of the people for democracy, equality, and freedom would be kept alive. One day, in the future, they would burst forth again in flame.

If they were to be taken by the Public Security forces it could be more complicated. They might not negotiate a settlement. There would be wholesale arrests, and many would be sentenced for being anti-revolutionaries. There could be bloodshed and anarchy.

The worst eventuality would occur if they were sealed off by the Public Security forces and attacked by the Militiamen. There would be no hope of negotiation. There would be no alternative to large-scale bloodshed. This possibility now seemed inevitable.

A protracted struggle was not viable; the stored grain could last only one week, and the sources of supply for vegetables and meat had been totally cut off from the liberated zone.

Without arms, they were not able to withstand the attacks of the Militia. The longer they tried to defend the liberated zone, the more vulnerable they would be. Their strength of numbers and their material resources were all insufficient.

"We have to act now," it was agreed, "when the pressure is not overwhelming."

"Tomorrow," Jen Ch'ang-feng said, "no, today, how can we assemble, when the youths arrive from Feng-t'ai at nine o'clock?"

"For the moment, we already number sixty thousand. By then there should be eighty thousand of us."

"What if we congregate eighty thousand people in T'ien-an Men Square and hold a mass rally?" Ho Yung-nien asked.

"What do we do after the meeting?"

"Disperse in all directions, and storm out of the blockades."

"That won't work. Our strength will be dissipated, and besides this will give the other side enough time to set up." Chuko Liang vetoed the idea.

"After what's happened, do we give up the liberated zone?" asked Jen Ch'ang-feng.

"We must give it up. The more we cling to it, the more dangerous it will be for us."

"I suggest we proceed in this way," said Jen Ch'ang-feng. "Early tomorrow morning, we will gather at the street opening on the Pearl Market. There we will form parade groups and we will wait for the youths from Feng-t'ai to arrive, and then, on the spot, we will launch widespread demonstrations. The roaming contingents will be divided into two groups; each will move in a different direction, thereby avoiding the positions guarded by the Militia, that is, the T'ien-an Men Square and the east and west sections of Ch'ang-an Avenue. The eastern route will proceed toward Ts'ung-wen Gate right up to Tung-tan, and disband at East Fourth Street. The western arm will pass through the vegetable market, turn at Hsüan-wu

Gate, past Hsi-tan Arch, and disband at West Fourth Street. Along the way, there will be people whose residences are nearby and they can duck into their homes and hide there. Those who have no homes in Peking will figure out some way to escape back on their own after we reach East Fourth and West Fourth. That's about all we can do. I can't think of anything else."

"What about this command post?" Nieh T'ieh-ying asked.

"Abandon it. We will evacuate our equipment." Chuko Liang answered with determination. Obviously he was in agreement with Jen Ch'ang-feng's strategy.

"Our losses will be very great!"

"For the future of our cause, we cannot count our losses."

"Does everyone agree? Are there any other suggestions?" Jen Ch'ang-feng asked.

No one replied. Chuko Liang spoke:

"We must remember to conserve our revolutionary strength, we must educate the people of Peking, and show the whole country and the entire world the profound aspirations of the people for democracy, equality, and freedom. This the only route we can travel.

"The core command group has already prepared pamphlets and manifestos to be distributed during these demonstrations. It is now two o'clock. We must move quickly."

"It is New Year's Eve!"

◈   ◈   ◈

Thursday, February 14   9 a.m.

New Year's Eve is the most important holiday of the Chinese. On the evening of this day it is the custom for the entire family to gather together, and to feast on specially prepared delicacies to welcome the new year.

The young yearned to rejoin their families! Their parents, using the meat and oil ration tickets, carefully saved, had bought the precious foodstuffs to prepare the New Year's feast.

The street-corner rumors had spread faster than radio bulletins. The youth from the countryside were on their way back to the city from all parts of the country, but the trains were stopped at the Yung-ting Gate Railway Station. Parents and relatives wondered if their own children were in the blockade area, whether they had enough clothing, enough to eat, or if they would be arrested.

Mother Ch'i listened to the voices in the street outside her courtyard; she wondered if Young Swallow had come back to Peking. And where was Young Tiger? He had not been seen for two days.

◇　◇　◇

The thoroughfare at the Pearl Market was crowded with the youths who had just arrived from other regions, with packs on their backs, or carrying small suitcases. Their faces were tanned, their clothing tattered and thin, a sharp contrast to the pale complexions of the residents of the capital who viewed them with curiosity.

In still another part of the city the People's Army was lined up in rows of ten men on each side, with women comrades in the center. The big slogans and the white banners were being raised and distributed among the various columns. The formations were set.

A temporarily installed loudspeaker blared out. People listened quietly:

"Comrades of the People's Army. The first stage of our struggle has now been concluded. Take off your armbands and give them to your platoon leaders.

"The second stage of struggle has now begun. This effort is designed to break through the blockades, and to help the youths from the various regions of our country to return home for the New Year celebrations. This stage will consist of parade demonstrations. Our slogans are: 'For Democracy, for Freedom for Science!' and 'Against Dictatorship, Against Special Privileges, Against Deceptions of the People!'

"For this purpose, the people of the capital are on the move!"

From the loudspeaker came the melodic rhythms of the national anthem, "The March of the Volunteer Army." The crowds joined in, and their singing burst forth from the depths of the heart, and a huge wave of feeling overwhelmed them.

The eastern and western sections of the parade of the people were on the march. The white cloth banner at the vanguard read, in large characters: "The Constitution Guarantees the Freedom to Demonstrate." A second banner read: "The People Demand True Democracy."

Countless other signboards and large portraits of the deceased Premier Chou were raised. The portraits had been taken from the warehouses of the Hsinhua Shu-tien ("New China Bookstore"), pulled out from under the piles of Chairman Mao portraits.

❖ ❖ ❖

Ta-yung curled up on the floor in a side room of the Cultural Palace of the Laboring Masses. The Militiamen were not permitted to leave or to talk among themselves. The Internal Security Guards were guarding the door. Outside, the sky was overcast; inside, it was like dusk. The Militiamen were lying helter-skelter on thin straw mattresses, huddling together for warmth. The cold penetrated the interior.

❖ ❖ ❖

The headquarters of the Internal Security Guards of the Militia was located in a Western-style building in Sun Yat-sen Park. It had once been a Western-style restaurant where foreign guests and dignitaries had been entertained. There was activity in the kitchen; breakfast was being prepared for the dignitaries in the main hall.

Yen P'eng-fei sat in the main front hall at the end of a long table. He smiled modestly and followed respectfully the lead of his superiors at the head of the table.

The waiters brought in the ham and eggs, toast (lightly

browned on both sides), and put it on the white porcelain trays with silver tongs.

A big hanging clock of glass, framed in redwood, ticked off the seconds and struck ten sonorous chimes. With the sound still resonating in the hall, the front gate was flung wide open, and a sixty-year-old man rushed in, yelling, "Is this your idea of waging a revolution? Get out of here!"

"Father!" a young man of thirty, pale-faced and defensive, replied. "We are just discussing how to organize our attack."

"What the shit are you talking about? The insurrections are already breaking out, and you are still dreaming."

The old man stormed out, seething with anger, leaving the door wide open. A strong gust of wind curled up the white tablecloth, and a glass of milk toppled over, spilling the milk onto the varnished wooden floor.

◈　◈　◈

The Cultural Palace shrilled with the sound of tin whistles; the Militiamen emerged from various rooms, shivering in the biting wind.

The members of the Internal Security Guards, having finished their breakfast, distributed wooden sticks to each of the Militiamen. In addition, each man was given three iron wires, as well as a steel wire one meter long. The following orders were given:

"Wind the wires around your waist. When you capture the anti-revolutionary elements, tie their hands up behind them with the wire."

Immediately, they set out. In a matter of moments the Militiamen ran out of the Cultural Palace into Ch'ang-an Avenue, carrying their sticks, prepared to wage a life-and-death struggle with the enemy.

◈　◈　◈

T'ien-an Men Square was virtually deserted, but at the Memorial Plaque in the distance, behind the blockade built by the anti-revolutionaries, a few people could be seen milling about. The Internal Security Guards commanding the various Militia platoons seemed confused, and waited further instructions from the commander in chief, Yen P'eng-fei.

Yen P'eng-fei was fuming; all the telephone lines were out of order; orders and instructions had been cut off. Yen P'eng-fei was in the dark as to what to do next, but he gave the order to attack.

◈   ◈   ◈

The march of the People's Army troops on the western route had not encountered any notable opposition. Its vanguard had entered the Hsüan-wu Gate, and was heading for the Hsi-tan Arch.

The residents were aroused by the sound of singing and cheering. They began to come out for a look, congregating at the intersections. Children started to follow the troops, picking up the handbills scattered on the ground. The residents were reading the mimeographed material, headlined: "The Draft of the People's Democratic Constitution," and stuffing them into their pockets.

As the procession reached the Hsi-tan Arch, the Militiamen arrived in trucks at the corner of Ch'ang-an Avenue, under the impression that the demonstrators were planning to enter Ch'ang-an Avenue. The trucks lined up to form a blockade, but the mistaken maneuver made it possible for the first portion of the procession to reach Hsi-tan market.

Hsia Yu-min was leading Yüeh Wei, Tall Man Li, and Young Tiger in distributing handbills, when they heard the sound of a commotion ahead. They quickly ran forward to investigate. The Militiamen had rushed out from the vegetable market into the columns of the procession and were trying to capture some of the vulnerable young women. They were wielding their big sticks in a fury. Terrified by the suddenness of the attack, the formation had split apart, but indignation and the instinct to rescue their captured comrades inspired the demonstrators, and they joined the melee.

More Militiamen arrived on the scene, and unarmed demonstrators searched for weapons, wooden pillars, door boards, rocks, whatever could be found. Some took out the defense weapons they had been carrying for years, six-inch-long knives. They regrouped, charged the Militia, and the Militia gave way.

Gunfire erupted behind the Militia ranks from those Militiamen wearing the armbands of the Internal Security Guards. The shots had been fired in the air, but forced the front lines of Militia to press forward against the demonstrators.

Hsia Yu-min took command. The female marchers rejoined their original columns.

With hands accustomed to heavy physical labor, the demonstrators defiantly maintained their position, some holding sticks, others grasping silver-glinting daggers. The attackers were only so-called students from the privileged classes, who had preyed upon the people for years. "All right, you bastards, come on! Come on—if you don't have a taste for life any more!"

The Internal Security Guards behind the Militia were now yelling, "Why don't you rush them? Where is your loyalty to the Party? Cut down the anti-revolutionaries! Move out! Charge!"

The "Hsiang-t'an"-model machine guns barked out, again into the air; the Militiamen moved forward amid the gunfire.

Hsia Yu-min detached himself from the wall of defenders and walked out alone into the open space between the attackers and the attacked.

Young Tiger, who had witnessed this, was thunderstruck. What the hell did he think he was doing? Tall Man Li's attention had also been caught.

All eyes were now focused on Hsia Yu-min, and quiet descended on the throngs.

"Comrade Militiamen! Listen to me!" Hsia Yu-min screamed out. "You are Chinese; so are we. You are the proletariat; so are we. You are the champions in the cause of Socialism; so are we. We all believe in Marxism-Leninism. We are all devoted to our Party. Why are we killing each other off?

"Now that the misguided leaders of the Party have been

arrested, the erroneous policies of the Cultural Revolution designed by them should also be rectified. We have been the victims of these policies. Don't we have a right to come home and be together with our families and our relatives for the New Year? Can't we insist on the rights of democracy for ourselves?

"Comrade Militiamen! You have been used by the power-mongers within the Party for some time. You have committed many atrocities on the people. Do not be used again in this way! Think about it!"

A volley of gunfire erupted. Hsia Yu-Min staggered. Tall Man Li rushed out to hold up Hsia Yu-min as he collapsed.

The wall of demonstrators advanced to fall upon the Militiamen, and the Militiamen tore off their armbands as they scattered in all directions. The few Internal Security Guards left were pummeled to the ground.

Hsia Yu-min's old cotton jacket was stained with blood. Tall Man Li carried him in his two arms, with Yüeh Wei and Young Tiger following in a daze. Young Tiger saw a "Hsiang-t'an"-model machine gun on the ground, and without thinking, picked it up. "I'll get even with them for Hsia Yu-min!"

Tall Man Li, carrying Hsia Yu-min in his arms, entered the Ta Tsa-lan area, and Young Tiger realized that Tall Man Li wanted to bring the critically wounded Hsia Yu-min back to headquarters. But the headquarters was locked and Young Tiger had to break open the entrance.

As he and Tall Man Li with his burden entered the meeting room, they found, moaning on the floor, comrades who had been seriously wounded. There were more than thirty seriously hurt, with a few women here and there administering first aid. In the dim light, they recognized some of their people. The cries of agony could be heard everywhere, and everywhere one could smell the sickening stench of blood.

Tall Man Li deftly carried Hsia Yu-min to a small room at the end. He took off his cotton jacket, spread it on the ground, and placed the already unconscious Hsia Yu-min on it. Then he

370

sat down beside Hsia Yu-min, with tears streaming from his eyes.

Yüeh Wei appeared carrying a bag of medical supplies. Young Tiger hooked up the electric light, and once he had made the connection, the room was lit with a blinding glare. Yüeh Wei was trying desperately to save Hsia Yu-min's life.

He disinfected the wounds, staunched the bleeding, applied ointment and a bandage, and gave Hsia Yu-min a shot of strychnine to stimulate his heart. He mixed salt water and started an intravenous injection. Young Tiger held the dispenser, and watched the liquid dripping down through the rubber tube. *If they should need my blood, they are welcome to it.*

Yüeh Wei went off to tend to the others and Tall Man Li left the small room, leaving Young Tiger, holding the dispenser bottle, alone with Hsia Yu-min.

A volley of gunfire broke out. Young Tiger turned to discover that the "Hsiang-t'an" machine gun that he had brought along had disappeared. Tall Man Li must have taken it.

Young Tiger, holding the dispenser bottle, could not move, but craned his neck to peer out. Tall Man Li was lying on the bottom step, covered with blood, his gun still clutched in his hands, its muzzle pointing toward the entryway.

Their headquarters had been betrayed by a member of the People's Army who had been arrested and tortured. Yen P'eng-fei was leading the Militiamen's attack. They had surrounded the headquarters and seeing no movement inside had advanced. From the center building, a tall figure had jumped out and shot: four Internal Security Guards fell. Yen P'eng-fei had flattened himself against the ground, his jaw hitting a pile of sharp rock. Three of his front teeth had come loose.

Ten guns had fired back. The figure had disappeared in a flash. Some combat veterans had rushed forward quickly to storm through the entrance.

Yen P'eng-fei was in a rage. He took out his pistol and rushed through the door.

The Internal Security Guards reported that there was no one in the house, but they had found a tunnel entrance; it appeared someone was below.

An aide asked, "Should we rush in?"

"No. Once you get close to the entrance, they will cut you down," said Yen P'eng-fei and walked outside.

Once they reached an area of safety, Yen P'eng-fei, speaking in a bizarre, toothless way, gave his aide an order:

"Return to the Militia Command Center, and get me two men with a bazooka, and bring along a few rockets. On the double!"

Yen P'eng-fei covered his mouth with his handkerchief, and looked angrily at the unsteady building. He calculated which parts of the building should be hit to topple the building down on the tunnel.

A jeep arrived with the two Militiamen. The aide reported that these two Militiamen knew how to handle a bazooka, but that neither had wanted to come, and had done so only at gunpoint.

The four rockets were lifted from the jeep. Yen P'eng-fei, still covering his mouth, gave directions as to where he wanted them fired. To avoid injury, he immediately entered the jeep and directed the driver to back up a hundred meters. The aide and the other Internal Security Guards trained their guns on the two Militiamen.

As the two prepared to fire from a squatting position, each of them kneeling on one leg, the shorter of the two whispered: "Ta-yung, I never thought that this weapon which we developed would be used for this."

Hsiao Ta-yung did not reply. He was weighing the situation. Why did they want to level this broken-down building? Were there people inside? If so, who were they?

"Get on with it!" Yen P'eng-fei shouted from the jeep.

Hsiao Ta-yung turned to look; the distance was about one hundred and ten meters, so he adjusted the range finder to one hundred and ten, and placed a rocket beside him.

The shorter Militiaman had already fired the first rocket, but only a piece of the wall had fallen. The building still stood.

It was Ta-yung's turn to fire. He purposely put the angle of trajectory higher, and pressed down the firing button, and adjusted the guidance mechanism. The rocket, following the guidance signals, shot up, and exploded against the top part of the building, without damage.

Around Ta-yung, shots pawed at the ground as a machine gun chattered. He heard an angry voice from the rear:

"You two punks! If that building doesn't fall, you're dead!"

The short Militiaman fired again. With the explosion, the whole building crumbled. Dust rose several stories high, accompanied by a shattering screeching sound. Ta-yung picked up the remaining rocket, turned his weapon around, and aimed at the jeep. The copper-wire disc whirred. Ta-yung watched the rocket until it reached the target, which disappeared in a ball of fire.

EPILOGUE

Young Tiger was semiconscious. It was pitch black. Recovering consciousness, he felt a heavy load pressing him to the floor. What had become of Hsia Yu-min? Young Tiger frantically groped about until his hand touched Hsia's form. He freed himself from the rubble, and bent over Hsia, trying to find a heartbeat. He was still alive!

Blindly, Young Tiger stretched out his arms. His hand fell upon a radio that had been brought for sale to the headquarters, which he impatiently threw aside.

Staggering and groping his way, he came upon a staircase and remembered that it was through this staircase that Tall Man Li had pulled the electric wire with a bamboo pole.

Moving closer, guided by the electric wire, he moved his hands along the wire until he could feel the tip of the bamboo pole. He tugged and yanked on the pole until he saw a small circle of light open above him.

Fresh air entered the basement room. "I must let Hsia Yu-min see the light!" Young Tiger traced his way back to Hsia Yu-min and held him up. Hsia's face was colorless. Young Tiger whispered to him.

"Can you see the light?"

Hsia's eyelids moved, but he no longer had the strength to open his eyes. His lips moved as if to form words. Young Tiger tried to catch the words.

"Winter . . . will . . . pass . . . Spring is bound to come . . ."

Holding tight to Hsia's body, Young Tiger, for the first time, wanted to cry but could not find the tears. Hsia was dead, his face peaceful in repose, with no trace of the suffering he had endured. Young Tiger felt a mantle of maturity being thrust upon him.

The eerie stillness was broken by the radio which Young Tiger had thrown aside. Someone was speaking at a demonstration. The voice was familiar. It was a voice unforgettable to Young Tiger, the same one he had heard repeatedly for several days around April 5 of last year. As the voice recited an account of the wounded and other casualities, the memories of the earlier events of T'ien-an Men Square flashed through his mind, and he knew he must escape and continue in the struggle to help his people.

A groan came from the conference room, and from the darkness, Yüeh Wei emerged. Some female comrades crawled out behind him. They joined Young Tiger to look up at the light above coming through the small opening, beyond which lay freedom and the future.

Sounds of groans behind them increased in volume. They must act now. Quietly they began to remove the barriers, even those who were wounded, not just for themselves, but for those who were helpless.

Military and Security Organizations
Hierarchy of the Chinese Communist Party (1976)
Cast of Characters

MILITARY AND SECURITY ORGANIZATIONS

Military (in Peking area):

1. PLA Peking Military Command (Peking Military Region: Ch'en Hsi-lien, Commander)—under Military Affairs Committee (Marshal Yeh Chien-ying, Vice-Chairman)
2. PLA Central Garrison Division (Wang Tung-hsing, Commander) —stationed at Central Committee Special Headquarters
3. PLA Division 8341—a special unit to protect the highest officials of the state and the Party, particularly Chairman Mao
4. PLA Peking Garrison Command—guards the city of Peking

Security:

1. Public Security Department (national) formerly headed by Hua Kuo-feng
2. Peking Public Security Bureau
3. Peking Urban Workers Militia

People's Militia Groups:

1. Ordinary Militia (*P'u-t'ung Min-ping*);
   males from ages 16–45; females from 16–35;
   peasants and fishermen in coastal areas;
   peasants in rural areas of city outskirts;
   workers, cadres, and students in cities; train three days a year;
   no "Five Black Elements"
2. Basic Cadre Militia (*Chi-kan Min-ping*);
   selected from ordinary Militia on the basis of background, ide-

ological outlook, and work achievements; train several months a year

3. Urban Workers Militia (*Ch'eng-shih Kung-jen Min-ping*):
the most trusted of the Militia groups; equipped with heavy arms; the "private armies" of the Gang of Four; enjoy the same privileges and perquisites as Public Security agents; after the fall of the Gang of Four, they were subsumed within the PLA, but they were not disbanded

HIERARCHY OF THE CHINESE COMMUNIST PARTY
(1976)

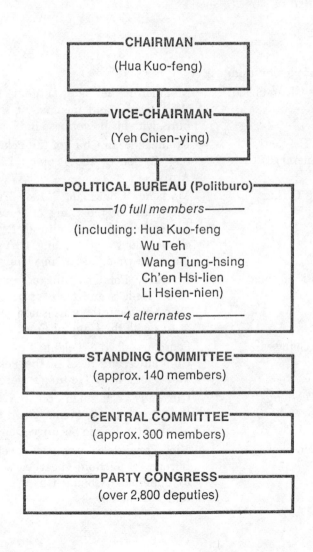

CHAIRMAN
(Hua Kuo-feng)

VICE-CHAIRMAN
(Yeh Chien-ying)

POLITICAL BUREAU (Politburo)
———10 full members———
(including: Hua Kuo-feng
Wu Teh
Wang Tung-hsing
Ch'en Hsi-lien
Li Hsien-nien)
———4 alternates———

STANDING COMMITTEE
(approx. 140 members)

CENTRAL COMMITTEE
(approx. 300 members)

PARTY CONGRESS
(over 2,800 deputies)

CAST OF CHARACTERS

Historical personages:

Chang Ch'un-ch'iao   Member of the Gang of Four, formerly Vice-Premier and member of the Politburo, with his power base in Shanghai.

Ch'en Hsi-lien (General)   Commander in Chief of the Peking Military Region of the People's Liberation Army.

Chiang Ch'ing   Madame Chairman, Mao Tse-tung's wife, head of the Gang of Four, prime mover behind the Cultural Revolution clique, along with Chang Ch'un-ch'iao, Yao Wen-yüan, and Wang Hung-wen.

Ch'iao Kuan-hua   Formerly Foreign Minister, protégé of Chou En-lai's and close associate of Li Hsien-nien's in the novel; now suspected of ties with the Gang of Four.

Hsieh Ching-yi   Secretary of the Peking Revolutionary Committee and head of the Peking Militia forces; Mao Tse-tung's niece.

Hua Kuo-feng   Currently Chairman of the Chinese Communist Party, Premier, and formerly head of the Public Security Department.

Li Hsien-nien   Vice-Premier, leader of the government's bureaucrat faction; spearheads strategy to undermine Chiang Ch'ing's coup attempt in the novel.

Ma T'ien-shui	Vice-Chairman, Shanghai Revolutionary Committee; Political Commissar, Shanghai Military Region.
Mao Yüan-hsin	Political Commissar, Shenyang Military Region; Mao Tse-tung's nephew.
Wang Tung-hsing	Commander of the Central Garrison Division, Superintendent of the Secretariat Office of the Central Committee of the Chinese Communist Party.
Wu Teh	Vice-Chairman of the Peking Revolutionary Committee.
Yao Wen-yüan	Member of the Gang of Four; formerly member of the Politburo of the Chinese Communist Party; penned the articles in Shanghai newspapers that touched off the Cultural Revolution; Mao Tse-tung's son-in-law.
Yeh Chien-ying (General)	Head of the Military Affairs Committee, member of the Politburo, associated in the novel with the bureaucrats; sometimes called "Ying Lao."

Fictional characters:

"Big Beard" (Ta hu-tzu)	Chia Hsiang-tung's "contact" at the Mongolian border; a Mongolian-type Chinese, in the service of Soviet Intelligence.
"Big Bugle" T'ang (T'ang La-pa)	Member of National Farm Unit Number 74; his given name means, literally, "Big Bugle," colloquial for a loudmouth.
"Big Gun" Hsü	Member of the underground group the People's Army.
Chia Hsiang-tung (Hsiang-ying)	An engineer, Head of the Sixth Section of the Central Garrison Division stationed at the Special Headquarters of the Central Committee of the Chinese Communist Party. Educated in Leningrad, he became a turncoat and imparted

top-secret information to the Soviet Embassy in Peking under the influence of his Russian mistress, Natasha; his given name was changed from Hsiang-ying ("Toward Heroism") to Hsiang-tung ("Toward the East"); combined with his family name, Chia, which is a homophone for "false," his change of name reflects a shift from "False Toward Heroism" to "False Toward the East." The second name may also involve an oblique reference to Mao Tse-tung, since the word for "east," *tung,* occurs in both names.

"Chuko Liang"
(Shao Yung-ts'un)

Leader and master strategist of the underground group the People's Army, whose shrewdness and wiliness earn him the sobriquet "Chuko Liang," in reference to the historical schemer, counselor, and magician who lived in the late second, early third century, and whose exploits were immortalized in popular fiction, most notably in the novel *The Romance of the Three Kingdoms.*

Hsia Yu-min
("Paleface Scholar")

Intellectual member of the underground group; a former medical student skilled in languages, who became disenchanted with Mao and his policies during the Cultural Revolution.

Hsiao Lien-min

Father of Hsiao Mei-lien and uncle of Hsiao Ta-yung; Political Commissar of the Peking Revolutionary Committee.

Hsiao Mei-lien

Chia Hsiang-tung's wife, Hsiao Ta-yung's cousin.

Hsiao Ta-yung

Son of a Chinese Communist general, but brought up in proletarian surroundings, he rises to the rank of Battalion Commander in a division of the Peking

	Urban Workers Militia; takes part in the border clashes at Farm Unit Number 74; his given name means "Great Bravery."
Jen Ch'ang-feng	Commander and leader of the underground group the People's Army.
Kuan Li-p'ei	Member of the underground group, an electronics expert and an electrician.
Li P'ei-yi	Young student worker at Farm Unit Number 74; friend of Young Swallow's.
Liu ("Chief Liu")	Head of Farm Unit Number 74 at the Sino-Mongolian border.
Mother Ch'i (Ch'i Ta-ma)	Mother of Young Swallow and Young Tiger.
Nagashima	Woman reporter for a Japanese women's magazine.
Nakada	A Japanese reporter.
Natasha Alyoshenko	Telecommunications consultant, Tass News Agency; Chia Hsiang-tung's mistress; sent by Soviet Intelligence to Peking to entrap Chia into providing classified information; works in the Soviet Embassy nominally as an engineer.
Okamura	Special correspondent for the Tokyo Economic News Agency.
"Old Goat"	Member of the underground group.
Shlovsky	Head of Soviet Intelligence at the Embassy in Peking, Vishinsky's superior, and later Natasha's lover.
"Tall Man" Li	Member of the underground group; Hsia Yu-min's friend and companion.
Vishinsky	Deputy Section Chief, Soviet Trade Commission; member of Soviet Intelligence at the Embassy in Peking.
Watanabe	A Japanese reporter, correspondent for the *Maiasa Shimbun* newspaper in Peking.

Yen P'eng-fei	Nominally head of the Consolidated Action group, rival faction of the People's Army; former Peking opera actor, known for his acrobatic skills. Dubbed "Whirlwind Man."
Young Swallow (Ch'i Yen)	Daughter of Mother Ch'i and high school classmate of Ta-yung's, a radical student leader, who volunteers for a National Farm Unit at the Sino-Mongolian border, and who leads armed skirmishes in the border conflict. (Her given name, *Yen*, refers to a swallow.)
Young Tiger (Hsiao-hu)	Son of Mother Ch'i and brother of Young Swallow; transferred to a remote commune in the northwest; he escapes and returns to Peking, where he joins Chuko Liang's underground group.

民主恨；
共產人，三民主義。

苦中國；
人民生活，

中國苦，
平等要尋；

自由可貴，

葉殷
1981年7月一日於
美國加州

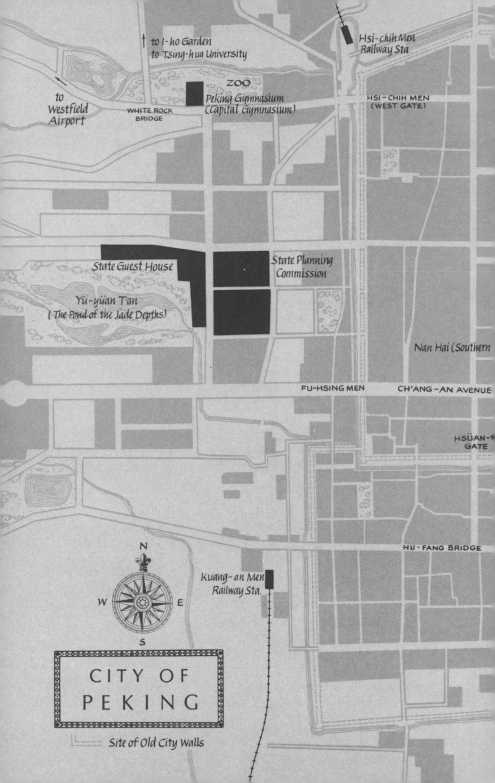